UNDERLAND

✧ BOOK 2 ✧

UNDERLAND

✦ BOOK 2 ✦

MAXIME J. DURAND

aka Void Herald

To my long-suffering first reader and good friend, Daniel Zogbi,
whose honesty hurt as much as it helped.

And to all the people who supported this series
on Royal Road and Patreon.
You guys are the best.

UNDERLAND

✧ BOOK 2 ✧

1

CALLING CARD

Ktulu loved water. Ever since Valdemar introduced his familiar to his bedroom's shower, the alien child had spent his time smashing its button to enjoy the feeling of water on its skin. Ktulu liked it cold rather than warm, perhaps because it reminded him of his native plane. To cut costs on water, Valdemar had set a basin aside and created a small toy ship from his own bones so his familiar could play with it.

He's too clumsy to take care of his toys, the sorcerer thought, having been forced to repair the toy twice already. Ktulu usually cradled the ship too tightly, his small body belying his inhuman strength.

Valdemar knew that his familiar was more likely an "it," but somehow he couldn't help but see the alien as a little baby boy.

"I could watch him all day," Marianne said as she and Valdemar supervised Ktulu swimming in the basin while cradling his toy with one hand. The noblewoman had a small, adorable smile on her face. Valdemar suspected that seeing Ktulu brought her back to a happier childhood. "Do you think he understands what we say?"

"I think he does, or at least a few words," Valdemar replied while sitting on the floor next to the basin. "But he can't speak our language. It doesn't seem like he needs to breathe either."

Marianne nodded slowly. "I don't hear any internal organs at work. Your familiar has no heartbeat, no growling stomach, no lungs pumping air in his chest."

"No lungs? But then how can he speak?"

"I don't know. Air moves on its own when it comes out of his mouth, and his scent is unlike anything I've ever smelled."

Nor could Valdemar's psychic sight analyze the creature. Ktulu's body was made of otherworldly matter from another dimension, one unbound by the laws of the Blood. It probably made him highly resilient as well, although the summoner didn't want to put that to the test.

For now, Valdemar had focused on building a bond with his familiar. The spell that called Ktulu to the material plane slowly formed an empathic link between their souls, one that would eventually become unbreakable. According to the document given to him by Lord Bethor, Valdemar would even learn to sense the alien child's emotions at a distance and summon him to his side anytime.

Ktulu accidentally tossed his bone-boat out of the basin. "Ktululu!" the alien child squealed as he clumsily fell out of the tub while trying to grab the toy. Ktulu's tentacles wriggled around while he curled up on the ground, disappointed. "Ktulu fhtagna . . ."

"It's alright," Valdemar said as he rose from the floor and took his familiar in his arms. Ktulu didn't resist, his tiny wings flapping while he cuddled against his summoner's chest. "It's alright . . ."

Somehow, Marianne's smile grew even wider. "I think it's the first time I've seen you happy like this," Valdemar noted. "You want to hold him?"

"I'm sorry," she said, trying to correct her expression. "It's unbecoming of me."

"To smile, or to hold him?"

Marianne blushed. "I should act better than a little girl swooning over a stuffed doll."

Ktulu squinted at her with his six eyes, as if daring her to resist his charms. After a moment, Marianne raised her gloved hand with an embarrassed look. "Can I . . ." she asked, but didn't dare finish her sentence.

"Pet him?" Valdemar asked with a chuckle. "Sure, if he lets you."

Marianne shyly stretched her arm and scratched Ktulu beneath his tentacles with her fingers, making him wriggle in happiness. "I'm sorry," she apologized to Valdemar. "I look ridiculous."

"You don't," Valdemar replied, before noticing that she had kept her eyes open during the entire discussion, a stark contrast from her struggle with her enhanced sight a few days ago. "Are your eyes feeling better?"

"I can keep them open for hours," Marianne said. "And I can rest by closing them, thanks to you."

"You're welcome." The more his knowledge of biomancy increased, the more Valdemar realized just how far Ialdabaoth's reach extended. The entity had small, invisible eyes in everyone's blood and flesh. It was truly a god: omnipresent, omniscient, and maybe even omnipotent.

Thankfully, Valdemar had found it easy to manipulate the eyes inside people. It was no different than sewing open wounds shut. *Can all biomancers do that?* he wondered. *Or is this a privilege of my birth?*

Lord Bethor's voice echoed through the room, as steely as an executioner's ax. "Reynard, meet me in the training maze in five minutes for your osteomancy lesson. Verney, you will practice summoning in the ritual room. I will come to you in a few hours to delve into your dreams."

Marianne pulled back her hand and regained her composure. "I will see you later," she promised Valdemar. "If I still have bones left."

"Same, if I haven't been eaten by a monster." Valdemar glanced at his familiar. "You won't eat me, right?"

"Ktulu wganag ftag!" his familiar squealed happily, although Valdemar struggled to comprehend the sounds coming out of his mouth. They seemed wrong in some way.

Moving to the same ritual room where Valdemar first summoned Ktulu, the sorcerer carefully set his charge on the ground. The alien child sat and looked up at his partner with curious eyes.

"Do I frighten you?" Valdemar asked as he put on the Mask of the Nightwalker, letting it fill his lungs with fresh air from the surface. Ktulu simply tilted his head to the side in confusion. "I'll take that as a no."

According to Lord Bethor, Valdemar's familiar should act as a dimensional beacon and let him summon creatures without a magical circle. The sorcerer had worried that his mask might interfere with the process somehow. He would test that idea today, attempting to summon with and without.

"Hungry thralls of the Nahemoths and members of the first caste," Valdemar chanted. "I summon you from the depths of the Outer Darkness!"

As he cast the spell, the sorcerer sensed a summoning link flare up between him and Ktulu. The familiar stood between his partner and the planes like a gatekeeper, ready to open the doors at a moment's notice.

But he refused to.

Valdemar's prayer went unanswered and the doors to the Outer Darkness remained shut.

"You don't want to summon Qlippoths?" Valdemar asked his familiar. "Or to summon at all?"

His familiar responded by blinking with all six eyes.

Sighing, Valdemar decided to try summoning another creature. Remembering the brief vision of his familiar's native ocean, the sorcerer attempted to call a water elemental next. Since it probably shared a plane with Ktulu, the alien might be willing to summon one.

Once more Valdemar sensed a magical link flare up between himself and his familiar. This time, the doors opened. Space rippled behind Ktulu and a form of pure water flowed into the material realm.

Valdemar immediately noticed something unusual with the summoned elemental. Gallons of water assembled into a bulbous shape with half a dozen tentacles, each ending with a lure-like shining eye. The elemental appeared like a hand large enough to squeeze the sorcerer like a fruit.

As he lacked a summoning circle, Valdemar prepared to beat his summoned thrall in submission if it turned out to be hostile. The creature didn't move, and the sorcerer sensed an invisible connection between the two of them; a lesser version of the bond binding him to his familiar.

"Raise a tentacle," Valdemar whispered.

The water elemental waved its central limb in a gesture that the sorcerer found quite obscene. Ktulu, however, clapped his hands in response. After letting out a sigh, Valdemar returned the water elemental to its home plane.

After a few more experiments, Valdemar confirmed that wearing the Mask of the Nightwalker didn't prevent him from summoning through his familiar. However, Ktulu was awfully picky as far as subjects were concerned. The alien child refused to call fire, wind, or earth elementals, any Qlippoth, or even minor spirits. Even if Valdemar retained the ability to call these creatures himself with a proper summoning circle, he couldn't help but be disappointed by his familiar's obstruction.

"It would be easier if you could tell me what you will *let me call* than what you *don't want*," Valdemar pointed out to his familiar.

Ktulu looked at him in silence for a moment, then raised his tiny hands and made incomprehensible noise. "Gokrugug! Ibu!"

Valdemar sensed his familiar's alien intelligence clumsily brush against his mind through their link; the contact felt so physically cold that it sent a shiver down his spine. Unlike a Dark Lord's precise psychic attacks, the mental contact was rough and awkward, but not malicious. The sorcerer opened his mind to his familiar and let foreign thoughts enter.

Blurry images of a ruined stone city on the shores of a great lake formed in Valdemar's mind, under a sky of alien stars and a moon red as blood. What remained of the architecture reminded him of a troglodyte settlement, though the settlement was completely uninhabited and most of the buildings had collapsed. The visions shifted to the lake near the city and a shadowy shape beneath the still waters.

He can't summon anything by himself, Valdemar realized. *I see. He can guide my words through the infinite worlds to their intended recipient, but it's my might that will call an intruder to Underland.*

The vision grew more and more precise, revealing the shape of a colossal lizard sleeping underwater. The creature's length reached from one side of the lake to the other, and considering the size of the nearby city . . .

"No," Valdemar said immediately.

"Gokrugug!" Ktulu insisted, flapping his wings.

"I won't summon something I can't put down." Considering the creature's sheer size, it would almost certainly destroy all of Lord Bethor's tower if it were called. Not to mention that Valdemar didn't dare to wake up a monster sleeping right next to a *destroyed* city . . .

The mental images dissipated abruptly, and Ktulu sat on the ground in frustration. Then he turned his back on Valdemar by spinning around on his little butt, making an angry noise all the while.

Even interdimensional squids can sulk, the sorcerer thought in amusement. Ktulu cautiously looked over his shoulder as if to check if his summoner was regretful, but avoided his gaze. *Truly a child.*

Valdemar walked around his familiar to face him, only for Ktulu to look away. "Something smaller," the sorcerer pleaded as he knelt before his familiar. "Something that can fit in this room."

The alien child cautiously looked at his summoner like a cat afraid of being tricked. "Kluthulu?"

"Whatever you wish," Valdemar promised before tickling the squid. Although his familiar attempted to look impassive, he couldn't resist for long and his tentacles wriggled in pleasure. "*If* it fits inside the room."

Having been reassured, Ktulu opened his mind to Valdemar's. Instead of pictures of an alien city, the familiar's thoughts now showed a vast expanse of absolute darkness. The pitch blackness was not the shadows cast by Underland's ceiling, or the sea of space illuminated by the stars. This darkness was a primeval abyss of cold and nothingness, a void within which no life could survive.

And yet Valdemar noticed *something* moving in the darkness. A sinister creature that wasn't undead, because it had never been alive to begin with. An entity that hungered for warmth and despised light.

How odd. He had thought Ktulu would only summon water creatures, but here he had opened up a summoning link to a plane of primordial darkness. *Maybe he only wants to call creatures that remind him of his homeworld,* Valdemar thought, *or specific breeds of creatures.* He needed to investigate further.

Before Valdemar called the creature into the room, he cast additional wards around himself and Ktulu. Although the tower's magical defenses dwarfed anything he could create in complexity, it didn't hurt to be careful.

"Come forth, messenger of the Void Between Worlds," Valdemar uttered, although the words weren't his own. Although he understood their meaning, they came to him in an ancient tongue he didn't remember studying nor Ktulu speaking. A memory he never had guided his lips. "You who haunt the darkness, I call thee to the land of light and shadows."

The veil between worlds rippled and darkness seeped into the room. Candles were blown out and magical lights extinguished. A chilling cold spread in the air and made Valdemar shiver. He could barely see his own hands, let alone his familiar. Even his psychic sight couldn't pierce the thick shadows.

"*Valdemar,*" Marianne's voice called from behind Valdemar. "*Look at us.*"

The sorcerer almost turned around, but froze upon hearing the "us" part.

"*Turn around . . .*" the thing in the darkness whispered, this time mimicking Lord Och's voice. "*Look at us, child . . .*"

Valdemar heard large wings flap behind him. Though the sorcerer couldn't see it with either natural or magical senses, from the strength of the breeze it caused, it must have been as large as a giant beetle.

A Haunter, Valdemar thought. The creature's behavior matched the description of these entities from the Void Between Worlds, as detailed in summoning grimoires. Powerful archmages usually bound them as hidden assassins or deadly guardians, tasks at which they excelled. Haunters envied the living and hungered for warm blood; they feared the light and thrived in the dark.

Valdemar had never dared summon one himself, because they were notoriously vicious and dangerously intelligent. To meet their baleful gaze meant becoming their prey.

Lord Bethor's words came to his mind. "If a dog disobeys, the fault lies in his master. These creatures exist to serve us. But how can you hope to dominate them, when you haven't yet mastered your own flesh and mind?"

"If you try anything," Valdemar whispered back without turning around, "I will kill you."

If this creature was smart enough to speak, then it could be threatened into obedience.

The cold breeze ended, as did the whispers and the flapping of wings. Valdemar sensed the Haunter's tense gaze on his back. Perhaps the creature imagined tearing its summoner limb from limb, or weighed its options.

As the silence stretched on, Valdemar prepared to send the summoned darkness back to its home plane. Before he could do so, the Haunter whispered a demand to its summoner with his own voice. *"I require cold fright and warm blood."*

"You will get them," Valdemar replied while trying to channel Lord Och's callous arrogance and Bethor's overwhelming authority, "but not mine. Not unless I allow it. Disobedience is death, or worse."

To illustrate his words, Valdemar focused on the summoning link and mentally pictured his previous capture of the Collector Qlippoth. He remembered the creature being dragged into Hermann's painted place, forever enslaved and used as fuel by mortals.

The mental image did wonders, and the darkness in the room immediately receded. *"I will wait for the hunt,"* the Haunter whispered as it sank into Valdemar's own shadow. *"But not forever . . ."*

As the room's lights returned, Valdemar gazed down at his shadow and found it darker than ever. Three red eyes briefly appeared on its chest, before closing abruptly.

After waiting a few seconds of tense silence, Valdemar glanced around the room to locate Ktulu . . . only to find his familiar in the hand of a familiar undead.

"What a strange and careless creature," Lord Och said as he lifted Ktulu by the back of his neck with one hand. The alien squid had frozen in fear like a helpless kitten. "Beware, my apprentice. There is nothing more dangerous than a child with too much power."

"Lord Och?" Valdemar expected an illusion, but his psychic sight quickly confirmed that he was facing the real deal. "What are you doing here?"

"Is that a way to greet your teacher, young Valdemar? Especially when he comes bearing gifts?"

Valdemar noticed that his master carried a grimoire in his other hand, identifying the leather cover as a mix of human and derro skin stitched together. "Gifts or homework?"

"What difference does it make? You will benefit from it in either case." Lord Och dropped Ktulu, who immediately ran behind Valdemar for protection. "He is quite shy, isn't he?"

Valdemar's familiar hid between his summoner's legs, whining. The lich *terrified* him. *Even Lord Bethor didn't cause such a reaction,* Valdemar thought. *Is it because Lord Och is an undead?* "Why are you here, my teacher?"

"I only dropped by for a short visit," the lich replied mildly. "As Lord Bethor could not identify your familiar, he called upon my expertise. I admit I couldn't suppress my curiosity and decided to see that creature myself. Imagine my surprise when I saw you had summoned a Stranger as your familiar."

"A Stranger?" Shocked, Valdemar looked down at his familiar. Ktulu, no longer whining, met his incredulous gaze.

"Or at least the child of one," the Dark Lord said. "Any creature can become a familiar, if they accept the bond, but you are the first to bind yourself to a Stranger this way. Congratulations."

A Stranger, Valdemar thought as he lifted Ktulu into his arms. The baby squid didn't resist, his tiny hands and tentacles reaching for his summoner's cheeks. "I can't believe that he's in the same class as Ialdabaoth or the Silent King."

Lord Och chuckled at the mention of Ialdabaoth. "And why not? By the virtue of your birth, you are a Stranger yourself. The Silent King was old, and you are young. A caterpillar needs time to grow into a flying moth."

Even knowing his "father's" true nature, Valdemar could scarcely believe he could become mighty enough to rule his own private world, the same way the Silent King did. Nor that he was interested in doing so. Opening the pathway to Earth was enough for him.

"Any sufficiently powerful sorcerer is indistinguishable from a god, young Valdemar," Lord Och said before delivering his grimoire to his apprentice. "This is a compilation of forbidden texts from Stranger cults. Owning that book means death and damnation, according to Church doctrine, but you should find a few useful slaves unmentioned in your politically correct summoning grimoires; thralls that your familiar will deign to contact on your behalf."

"Death to anyone but you, my teacher?" Valdemar asked. He shifted Ktulu to one arm, extending the other to accept the book. His familiar had found enough bravery to glare silently at Lord Och, who found the reaction eminently amusing.

"The Church and the Dark Lords have a symbiotic relationship, my apprentice. For a country to be stable, temporal and spiritual powers must work hand in hand. We protect the Church of the Light's spiritual integrity, and in return they forgive all our sins. I am purer than any saint."

"Do as I say, not as I do?" Valdemar asked mirthfully.

"Different laws exist for the weak and for the powerful," Lord Och replied with a dark laugh. "In any case, although he will never tell you, Lord Bethor is quite impressed by young Marianne's progress . . . and yours more so. I believe his fondness for you borders on the paternal."

Valdemar's legs started to itch at the spot where Lord Bethor severed them.

"Come, what kind of elder does not discipline the young now and then? It teaches them wisdom, and the chain of apprenticeship that binds the three of us is stronger than a severed limb." Lord Och sounded strangely nostalgic as he spoke. "Or so I hope."

"You're thinking of Lord Phaleg, my teacher?" Valdemar asked with a frown, and took Lord Och's silence for a confirmation. "What happened between the two of you?"

"Why do you want to know?" Lord Och snorted. "That is all in the past."

"By your own admission, no knowledge is harmful," Valdemar pointed out. "Maybe satisfying my idle curiosity will grant me useful insight."

His answer pleased the lich, who opened up a little. "I gave my former apprentice too much, too early," Lord Och admitted with a hint of bitterness. "Remember this lesson, young Valdemar: adversity builds character and teaches the value of gratitude, but if you spoil a child too much, he will grow slothful, take your help for granted, and come to see what you own as his by right. If you do not set boundaries early, all your future attempts to establish discipline will fall flat."

"Are you giving me insight into your past, or advice for raising Ktulu?" Valdemar couldn't help but ask. His familiar's head perked up at the mention of his name.

"Students and children inherit our mistakes, young Valdemar, as well as our successes. They are what their elders make of them."

Truthfully, Valdemar was quite skeptical. Having firsthand experience with Lord Och's methods, he couldn't help but wonder if Phaleg had grown weary of mind games or simply lacked the patience to put up with the lich's casual cruelty.

Lord Och shrugged. "In any case, I shall take my leave now. I have received worrying news from my spies in the derro kingdom and I need to investigate."

"Lord Och, before you go," Valdemar said, "Have you any news from Hermann and Liliane? What about Iren? Are they alright?"

"Young Hermann is making progress on his Painted World project, and his master is happy with him," the lich replied. "Young Liliane and Iren intend to come to Sabaoth soon, I believe. I doubt Lord Bethor will allow visits until you finish your training, so take it as an encouragement to work harder."

Valdemar smiled. "Have I ever disappointed you?"

"Do not get cocky, young Valdemar," the lich replied before teleporting away. "You haven't reached the hard part yet."

2

BONES OF STEEL

Swords clashed and Marianne's weapon broke first. Her bone blade, created from her own forearm, cracked above the pommel as it parried Lord Bethor's strike. The shattered edge of her weapon went flying and bounced off a steel wall. Marianne barely had the time to take a step back to avoid a strike to the throat and manifest a new sword from her bloodied forearm; the fourth since the beginning of the training session.

The process was starting to take a toll on her. Although she had been fed on a steady diet of calcium and nutrients before the fight, osteomancy couldn't violate the laws of conservation of mass. The bones had to come from *somewhere*, and now she was drawing material from her own ribs.

"Use the environment," Lord Bethor admonished her as he chased her through the metal maze. His armor's heavy, steady footsteps echoed across the steel walls, his pace showing no weakness. "Strike from unpredictable directions."

He's toying with me, Marianne realized. She was giving her all, wasting not even a single breath, while the Dark Lord could afford to chat. His physical might eclipsed hers by a colossal amount, to the point that she often dropped her weapon when their blades connected. While her hand remained strong, her bone blades instead cracked or shattered.

And to add insult to injury, Lord Bethor was beating Marianne with her family's own rapier.

Unlike his student's aggressive, fast-paced style, the Dark Lord favored a slow and methodical approach to swordsmanship. His defense was impeccable, his movements calculated and deliberate, his thrusts mighty enough to pierce through steel. Marianne felt like she was facing a glacier, an impenetrable block of ice creeping in on her inch by inch. And unlike his pet machine, the Lord Bethor shrugged off illusions before they could take hold.

At least he has the grace not to hold back his punches, Marianne thought. Some of his strikes could have easily killed her had they connected. The noblewoman had managed to survive for now, but she couldn't afford to let the Dark Lord push her back further. She had grown familiar enough with the maze to know that he was slowly forcing her toward the closed exit, where she would find herself with her back against a steel door.

Deciding on an aggressive strategy, Marianne gritted her teeth and lunged at the weak spot in her foe's helmet. Her enhanced senses gave her a perfect vision of the battlefield. She could hear Lord Bethor's muscles contracting, sense his—*her*—rapier push air, see the slight shift in the light reflecting his armor indicating which way he would move next. She could even observe the changes of ambient temperature from the light's reflection in the air.

Lord Bethor's weapon moved to match her own, and Marianne ignored the pain as she called upon the Blood. One of her ribs vanished as a second bone sword burst out of her wrist, shooting a spurt of blood as it came out. Grabbing the new weapon with her free hand, Marianne struck from below by surprise. She moved so fast that even her enhanced eye struggled to keep up with the strike.

Marianne thought Lord Bethor would parry her first sword and leave himself open to the second. But then she noticed the slight inflection of his feet as he adjusted his stance, and she instinctively stepped to the left. The motion saved her life, as Lord Bethor forewent defense for a surprise lunge at her stomach. The tip of the Reynard family's rapier grazed against Marianne's shirt, cutting a thin line across the cloth but failing to reach her skin.

Why? Marianne thought, angered as she found herself stepping back again. *Why can't I hit him? My senses and reflexes have never been sharper!*

"Your swordsmanship matches mine in finesse and you have experience in all basic styles," Lord Bethor scolded her. "Your weakness lies not in your lack of experience, but in your lack of imagination. You rely on speed, skill, and strength to overwhelm your opponents, yet inevitably you will face foes who are faster than humanly possible, stronger than you, or skilled enough to predict your attacks."

He raised the rapier at her in a stance that Marianne found chillingly familiar. In a blink of an eye, the crimson knight before her vanished, replaced with a handsome noble with long black hair and piercing blue eyes.

"Now die, vile woman," Jérôme said.

Marianne's heart skipped a beat, and the shock almost cost the noblewoman her life. Her fiancé's ghost lunged at her so fast that even her enhanced eyes struggled to keep up; the Reynard's rapier turned into a blurring flash of steel hungry for her blood.

Acting entirely on reflexes, Marianne raised both her swords in a cross formation and pushed Jérôme's sword toward the ceiling. The inhuman strength behind the blow almost tossed her backward, and the tip of the blade cut through her left cheek even as she deflected it. Marianne's blood dripped on the ground with a thunderous sound.

But though the ploy and the pain unsettled her for a second, the noblewoman quickly regained her composure. *This is not Jérôme,* she thought, *and even if he were . . . I should not hold back.*

However, although her defense didn't collapse, Lord Bethor proved relentless. He unleashed a flurry of blows and forced Marianne back. From the echo of their blades, she realized he had pushed her into the dead-end leading to the exit.

"Poetic," he said with Jérôme's voice, his words as sharp as his blows, "you will perish by the same sword you killed me for."

I can't maintain an effective defense against him, the noblewoman thought as she remembered Bertrand's lessons. Like most of Marianne's fencing teachers, he had put emphasis on controlling the blade, timing, and distance to maintain an equilibrium between attack and defense. She had been taught to anticipate angles of attack and control her opponent's center, waiting for a gap in the defense to launch a counterattack.

But Lord Bethor's stance had no weakness. Trying to defend was only buying her time with no progress.

"You're wrong," Marianne said, her eyes squinting dangerously.

"About what?" the ghost asked. "You didn't slay me?"

The false Jérôme lunged at her again as if expecting her to be pushed back again.

"I didn't fight you for the sword, Jérôme." Instead Marianne surprised him with an aggressive flurry of blows. Wrong-footed, the Dark Lord found himself on the defensive for the first time in the training.

"I fought you for *myself.*" Memories flashed before her eyes with each clash of their weapons. Once-happy memories of ballroom dancing in Saklas, of drinking tea alone with her fiancé in the gardens. Once Marianne had looked at these moments with maiden-like innocence. She had always seen Jérôme through the prism of nostalgia.

But now?

Now, she could see the smugness and ambition walking side by side with the pleasantries and the kindness. Valdemar's words had recontextualized many hints that Marianne had done her best to ignore.

"I would have been happy to be a dutiful wife, if only you had let me be *myself.*" Marianne said bitterly what she had thought deep down for years. "Was that too high a price to ask?"

Use the unpredictable, the noblewoman thought as she attacked again and again with both blades; she dropped all attempts at defense to fully focus on offense. *Dominate the fighting space to keep the initiative.*

It was a dangerous strategy as she left herself exposed to a counterattack. The moment her assault weakened and Lord Bethor regained the initiative, he would strike back with lethal force.

The moment came quickly.

"Was my life worth your freedom?" the false Jérôme replied angrily.

The words hurt more than any sword, but Marianne's resolve remained strong as steel.

The Dark Lord regained his footing and raised his rapier to parry her right blade. Instead of holding her weapon tight, Marianne loosened her grip on it. Lord Bethor's parry disarmed her, her first bone sword flying above her head.

But unlike last time, the blade remained intact.

"I paid no price," Marianne said angrily as she quickly grabbed her weapon in midair while Lord Bethor was busy parrying her second blade. "You preferred to throw your life away rather than let me follow my dream!"

Swiftly recovering her first sword, she struck from the upper right in a diagonal motion. This time, Lord Bethor had no choice but to take a step back, the first time he had done so in the entire training.

A familiar, pleased smirk appeared on the false Jérôme's face. "Now, we are getting somewhe—"

Without wasting any time, Marianne called upon the Blood. A bone needle erupted from her forehead, using her own skull as fuel and piercing through her skin. It was thin, but sharp as a scalpel and fast as a bullet.

The false Jérôme blinked in surprise, his rapier deftly deflecting the needle in midair and allowing Marianne enough time to close the distance between them, both swords raised in a scissor motion. Blood dripped from her forehead where the needle had erupted, but it didn't impair her aim.

Jérôme's neck started to bleed before the blades even connected. His face twisted into an expression of horror and fear, the same he wore on that fateful day.

Marianne gritted her teeth as she mentally relived this horrible experience again, but struck all the same. Jérôme was dead, and trying to keep his ghost alive in her thoughts and emotions wouldn't bring him back.

Her swords moved to behead her former fiancé. Her blades never reached their target.

An invisible force restrained her hands as the blades were within an inch of the neck.

"An innovative tactic," Lord Bethor congratulated her as he dropped the illusion. Marianne's dead fiancé vanished, replaced with a knight in crimson armor. "I did not expect the needle."

"You suggested that I strike from unexpected directions," Marianne reminded him as he released the spell holding her, allowing the noblewoman to lower her swords . . .

Before swiftly raising them back and parrying Lord Bethor's sneak attack.

"Good," he said, the tip of their swords testing each other. "A true battle only ends when your foe is well and truly destroyed. Even disarmed or surrendering, an enemy can prove dangerous. Never lower your guard, for where strength fails, treachery often triumphs."

Only then did Lord Bethor lower his blade for real. "Tell me what you have learned today, Marianne."

"To prevail, I must have fear and confusion on my side," Marianne replied. "You attacked my resolve to weaken my arm. This is why you used my own rapier against me and then cast your cruel illusion."

Watching her family's weapon used against her had unbalanced her mind and left it open to further deceit.

Though she only saw his eyes past the helmet, Marianne could tell from Lord Bethor's posture that he was pleased with her answer. "Students focus on technical skills, but the masters understand that a body is like any sword; only as strong as the will that moves it. Breaking someone's resolve is the same as shattering their spine, and sometimes far easier. Whenever possible, Marianne, you must study your prey, probe their emotional weaknesses with words and illusions, and *then* engage them. No mind is a perfect fortress."

"Not even yours?" Marianne asked as she cast a healing spell on her face to close her wounds.

"No wise warrior believes themselves perfect," the Dark Lord replied with surprising humility. His helmet shimmered in the light of the metal maze, transforming into Jérôme's face. "A few days ago, you would have faltered upon seeing this man's face. What changed?"

Marianne examined her late fiancé's face. He was exactly like her memories, perfectly recreated from them. A part of her wanted to apologize to him for taking his life . . . and another to slap him for foolishly throwing it away in the first place.

"I have been reevaluating my relationship with Jérôme," Marianne said. "I will never be at peace with his death, but . . . A friend told me he was looking down on me, and the thought has been gnawing at my mind like a worm in a root."

"Do you believe him?"

I don't know, Marianne wanted to reply. That would have been the easy answer, the noncommittal one. But Valdemar's words had opened her eyes. She still believed Jérôme had loved her in his own way . . . but never as an equal.

"Whether he was correct or not, in the end I fought Jérôme for myself," Marianne whispered as she looked at her ancestor's rapier. "Not for this weapon. It was just an excuse I told myself. I did it for the sake of my pride and who I wanted to be. I did it for *me*. And even if the consequences were painful to me, I don't regret standing up for myself."

Lord Bethor listened in silence as his glamour spell vanished. His black and red eyes looked at Marianne through the slit in his helmet, his gaze indecipherable. Marianne felt him judge her thoughts and actions, like her father did when he banished her. She stood strong and met his gaze, refusing to avert it.

Finally, the Dark Lord held the Reynard rapier with both hands and presented it to Marianne. "Take it."

Marianne blinked in surprise. "Lord Bethor, you said you would only return it at the end of our training."

"I *said* I would give it to you when you prove yourself worthy of it; when you make it a force-multiplier rather than a crutch. Once, you saw this blade as the golden prize you sacrificed your old life for. It was the one thing that excused your crimes and successes, the measure of your self-value. But now, what do you see?"

Marianne looked at this weapon she had killed so many people with, this heirloom from generations of the Reynard family. Once she had revered it with almost religious importance, but now . . . now she saw it for what it was.

"A sword," Marianne replied. "One that is important to me for what it represents and the martial values it embodies. But the sword doesn't make the swordswoman strong. It is the swordswoman that makes the sword strong. All weapons will shine in my hands."

Lord Bethor nodded respectfully, as Marianne reabsorbed her bone swords back into her body to recover the organic material. Then she grabbed her family rapier, finding that it felt lighter than ever. *How good it feels to have it back . . .* she thought. *Like a missing arm grafted back on my body.*

"Lord Bethor, if I may ask," she said, suddenly emboldened. "What do you fight for? What pushed you to become what you are?"

The Dark Lord appraised her question with a calculating gaze. "And what am I?"

Marianne cleared her throat before answering. "Power."

Lord Bethor crossed his arms, his eyes turning distant as if remembering a terrible memory. "Have you ever been burned, Marianne Reynard?"

"Briefly," she admitted. "But never for long."

"Be thankful then," the Dark Lord said, his voice grave and haunting. "I have been wounded by countless things, but none of them ever felt as painful as being burned alive. Once they have taken hold of you, flames eat you alive. They spread through the skin and melt the flesh, boil your blood in your veins and dry your eyes. Beasts leave when they are satisfied with their meal, but a fire's hunger knows no bounds."

"You told Valdemar that you had your own baptism by dragonfire," Marianne remembered with a deep frown. "Did you . . ."

Lord Bethor looked up at the ceiling, as if he could see something invisible Marianne's enhanced eyes couldn't perceive. "Long ago, I was an arrogant battle mage who believed himself invincible. I had defeated other mages, derros, and monsters aplenty. Becoming a dragonslayer sounded like the next step of my military career. The feat would shower me in glory. So I ignored the warnings of my superiors and ventured into forbidden tunnels known for leading to a dragon's lair. The cavern's floor was littered with the bones of all the would-be dragonslayers who had preceded me, but I paid them no mind."

Marianne listened in silence. She had heard tales of famed dragonslayers, but she had always wondered how many had perished before one could triumph. The history books did not record the names of losers.

"We find the Strangers terrifying because we do not understand them. Dragons scare us because we know *exactly* what they are," Lord Bethor said. "We humans have deluded ourselves into thinking we stood at the apex of the food chain of this stone shell of a world, when we are but an intermediary link. The moment the dragon's head emerged from the cavern, the instant I first laid my eyes on it, I understood the simple truth: I was *prey*, and it was a *predator*."

To hear a Dark Lord say that left Marianne unsettled. They were the benchmark of strength in the empire; mages so powerful that they could control an entire Domain unchallenged. To have one admit weakness shook her to the core.

"The beast answered my spells with fire so hot that none of my wards could stop it," Lord Bethor said. "My nerves were set ablaze, and the pain I felt that day has never left me. Nor the memory of my bones shattering as the beast casually swept me away. If I hadn't fallen into an underground crack too difficult for a giant beast to access, I would have died. It took all of my magic to keep my soul anchored to my burnt husk of a body."

Marianne's own escape from Verney Castle now looked like child's play. *To survive without skin and flesh . . .* she thought. Lord Bethor was alive, so he hadn't embraced the cold apathy of undeath.

"Yet I knew that the dragon could have devoured me if it had made any effort," Lord Bethor continued. "But you do not eat a flea biting your skin. You squash it and forget. That was its mistake. Though it took me three days of agony, I crawled my way back to civilization. But it wasn't my survival instinct that allowed me to survive."

His eyes brimmed with cold fury.

"It was *hate,* Marianne," the Dark Lord whispered. "Not for the dragon, but for myself. For being weak. After that day, I swore never to feel so helpless again. I would elevate myself above even the gods and stand at the apex of the world . . . like that beast of legends."

And now, the Dark Lord ruled his own world from atop a spire, looking down on the mortals toiling in his forges . . . Lord Bethor had surpassed his fear by becoming it.

"What happened to the dragon?" Marianne dared to ask.

Lord Bethor scoffed. "I killed it," he answered as if it were obvious, his voice echoing with quiet satisfaction. "I shattered its skull with my hands and showered myself in its blood. Then I raised this tower over the lair the animal once called home."

Marianne shivered, as she remembered that Valdemar had mentioned seeing a dragon's bones as being part of the tower's heart. Had it been the first corpse added to the foundations, the Dark Lord's greatest trophy?

"Take this as a lesson, Marianne Reynard," the Dark Lord said. "Pain and fear are the fires that light the human will. One who has never suffered a defeat will not fight as hard as one who has experienced helplessness."

"I know," Marianne replied. She had had her own defeat when she had watched Bertrand turn into a monster, helpless to do anything. "That feeling will never leave me."

"Then you are ready to learn my combat spells," Lord Bethor declared. "You are middling in the Blood, correct, but you have a keen understanding of your body and a flexible mind. Osteomancy is perfect for you."

He raised his left hand, his armor's gauntlet turning into blood. A long, flexible chain of spine erupted from his wrist, covered in spikes. He swung it like a harsh taskmaster with a whip, cutting through the air.

"This is the *Spine-Chain* spell," Lord Bethor said, before materializing a skull at the end of the chain. "And the *Flail* upgrade. The skull's density is such that although it feels light, the impact will break stone and pierce through armor."

To illustrate his point, he swung his weapon at a wall. The flail's head bent the steel on impact, causing the entire room to shake.

"You have mastered the sword, but it cannot solve all problems," the Dark Lord told Marianne. "A true warrior must use the appropriate weapon for each encounter. The spear when you need a greater reach, the flail when you need the power to shatter armor too thick for your enchanted rapier. Osteomancy can manifest all of them, and I shall teach you how."

"But at what cost?" Marianne asked warily. "My body only has so much bone and calcium to draw from."

"Do you think my body holds as much blood as a commoner?" Lord Bethor asked with a hint of disdain. "The Blood requires nutrients to work its spells, yes. But with magic, you can train your body to hold more than humanly possible."

"Wouldn't it make me heavier and slower?"

"I will teach you to alter your bones' density and malleability. Though you may weigh more than others, by adjusting your mass you will move faster than they do."

Lord Bethor let out a growl, and two enormous batlike wings erupted from the back of his armor. Marianne's senses told her that they were made of hollowed bones bound by thin cartilage. The Dark Lord now looked like a demonic knight in an armor of blood.

A human-shaped dragon.

"Osteomancy can do more than manifest weapons and armors," Lord Bethor said. "By manipulating your bone density and altering them in a specific way, you will even learn to fly."

"I could fly?" Marianne blinked in shock. She knew some powerful mages could by lifting themselves up with telekinesis or by shapeshifting into beasts, but due to her own middling spellcasting, the noblewoman had long given up on achieving the same feat.

"If you train to." Lord Bethor appraised her silently. "As a reward for your efforts, I shall let you pick your first choice of weapon to train with."

Marianne's thoughts turned to Bertrand and the beast he had become. *If I could fly . . .* she thought, trying to imagine herself chasing her old friend in the air. What would be the best weapon to save him?

"The chain," Marianne said after some consideration. "To catch a friend."

3

THE FUTURE PAST

The whole plane was alive. Valdemar had never seen a "jungle," though he had read of them in the ancient texts detailing the world before the Whitemoon's arrival. He had imagined them as lush and verdant forests of mushrooms and moss like those found in Underland, but the one he was seeing right now couldn't be more different. Alien, multicolored flowers with teeth and eyes grew on every inch of the ground. This world had grass and vines for the ground, flies for air, and mucus for streams. Protoplasmic oozes slithered alongside twisted snake men and murderous alien spiders, roaming innards-like tunnels in search of prey.

The seers who had observed this plane called it the *Green Hell* and believed that it was the origin of all life in the universe. A chaotic, primal realm of creation of pure organic matter, a gigantic superorganism whose innards were inhabited by countless monsters. One of them sensed Valdemar's gaze observing the dimension and rose from a mucus lake in response. An enormous green mass of slime as large as a house slithered on the ground, its acidic surface melting the foliage. Hundreds of red eyes opened all over its surface, glancing at Valdemar through the veil between dimensions.

"Shoggolu!" Ktulu squealed as the vision ended and Valdemar returned to the summoning room. "Jigulhu!"

"I'll keep it in mind," Valdemar replied as he returned to his book. All around them, a menagerie of summoned creatures waited trapped inside complex summoning circles. A four-armed, furred humanoid with a mouth splitting vertically to reveal rows of sharp teeth surrounded by cunning eyes, that warlocks called a Gug; a Weaver, a nightmarish white spider larger than a giant beetle, with a baleful human visage in the middle of its eight red eyes, capable of spinning nightmares as well as webs; and a Croaker, an enormous toad with mouths and eyes all over its body, its dozen tongues testing the invisible barrier keeping it imprisoned. This creature's maddening song was more dangerous than its hunger, but the spell blocked sound as well as flesh.

So far, these entities were the only ones Valdemar had been capable of keeping somewhat docile—or what could pass for docile for an otherworldly monster—alongside water elementals, oozes, and chronovores. The rest were simply too dangerous to be summoned except in the direst situation.

Lord Och's *Book of the Strangers* had proven to be a wealth of information not only on the eponymous creatures, but also countless planes and their denizens. Valdemar hadn't heard of any of them even in forbidden texts banned by the Church of the Light: of the mysterious Plateau of Nightmares and its slavering inhabitants; of the Green Hell, the fear-fueled realm of the Mistwoods; and so many others . . .

Of course, there was a reason for this censorship. All of these planes' inhabitants were *exceedingly* dangerous, and many of them served Strangers. Worryingly, Ktulu was capable of summoning a great many of them if he wished.

After much experimentation, Valdemar had narrowed down his familiar's summoning focus: namely destructive natural forces, monstrous animals, water, and darkness. All of the creatures that Ktulu could summon were associated with Strangers and, if not mindless, then uninterested in conversation.

Unlike the Qlippoths, who could understand mortals' emotions and speak their language, there was nothing *human* about Ktulu's otherworldly friends.

He could probably cause an extraplanar disaster and not even notice, Valdemar thought as his familiar suddenly started humming a strange tune to himself, tilting his head one side to the other as per the rhythm. The trapped Croaker imitated the child's movement, as if they were singing in tune. The Gug mindlessly beat its fists against the barrier in a vain attempt to escape, while the Weaver observed with unnatural patience. *I still wonder why he refuses to call any Qlippoths, though. Is Ktulu part of this "other side" that the Nightwalker hinted at?*

Speaking of the Nightwalker, the *Book of the Strangers* had a full chapter dedicated to it, including texts gathered from cultists. Though Valdemar wasn't sure what was true or not, the information in the book fascinated him.

According to the Nightwalker's worshipers, Underland wasn't the first world that the Whitemoon had visited. The rogue moon traveled across the cosmos to annihilate the warmth of life that it despised, leaving only cold and empty space behind it. The Nightwalker served as a herald to the Whitemoon, guiding its otherworldly master from one civilization to the next. This destructive process might take thousands of years but couldn't be averted. Even destroying the Nightwalker was only a temporary measure, for its master's power would bring it back from the darkness. The only way to survive, according to the cultists, was to transform into a cold form of existence pleasing to the Whitemoon.

Most fascinating, it appeared that high priests of the Nightwalker often wore masks representing their deity in an attempt to channel its persona and power . . . becoming avatars of a sort. Eventually, they hoped to ascend into becoming Nightwalkers themselves.

So that's how it is, Valdemar thought as he removed his mask and examined it. The longer I wear this artifact, the more I will become like the creatures on the surface.

Could *he* even transform though? The Nightwalker's priests believed that they could ascend to become like their patron, but Valdemar was only half a man. The other didn't interact well with the Whitemoon's power.

You're the me from the other side.

Valdemar hadn't found anything related to Ialdabaoth in the book, which implied that someone—either the Dark Lords or Ialdabaoth's own cults—had done their best to destroy any evidence of its existence to an even greater degree than the other Strangers.

He did find references to the Stranger worshiped by the dokkars, this so-called "Mother of All." Valdemar had immediately noticed the similarity to one of Ialdabaoth's titles, the Father of All, and investigated a possible connection. According to text, the Mother of All was a life elemental that birthed the first animals of Underland. She was occasionally described as a tentacled horror, a beautiful woman, or a dokkar, but in all cases a female form was a common trend among her avatars.

Celebrations in her names involved orgies and animal sacrifices, so fresh blood could fertilize the earth.

There were many similarities to Ialdabaoth, especially if it truly was the origin of life in Underland. Was this Mother of All a hybrid similar to Valdemar? Or simply another name for Ialdabaoth? Though he would rather ignore her, Valdemar would have to ask Frigga for clarification.

He could also infer much from the Nightwalker's words. If this entity's purpose was to act as an herald of the Whitemoon and lead it to new worlds to destroy, and if Valdemar shared a similar purpose . . . then it suddenly became clear why the Verney cult had sponsored his grandfather in his attempt to open a path to Earth.

After offering this world to their god, they would serve him another.

Was that why my grandfather sold out the cult? Valdemar wondered. *Because he learned that they would destroy his homeworld?*

Valdemar would have to consult the portrait for answers eventually, even if he detested the thought of it. No matter how often Marianne had asked him to reevaluate his grandsire's intentions, the sorcerer couldn't find it in himself to forgive him.

As for the Nightwalker, Valdemar's experience in the tower's heart had shown him that connections were two-way streets and could be subverted. The sorcerer wasn't certain if the cultists' ravings about their master's immortality were correct, but it wouldn't hurt to put that theory to the test.

It will have to wait until tomorrow, Valdemar thought as he closed the book and groaned. Sleeplessness was taking its hold on his mind. With a word, he returned his summoned thralls to their homes. Ktulu let out a dejected squeal. "I'll bring new friends tomorrow," Valdemar promised his familiar. "Humans have to sleep, you know?"

He doubted his dreams would be peaceful though.

His Painted Field had transformed since this morning. The ever-present moth motif had grown more and more grotesque with time. The insects were black and crimson, the motifs on their wings showing skulls, tears of blood, and inhuman visages. Alien landscapes that Valdemar had seen through visions completed the tapestry, all of them inhabited by ancient and terrible beings.

But the part that bothered him the most was the gray spot.

It was no larger than a fist, but Valdemar couldn't help but feel unsettled whenever he looked at it. A splash of metallized paint had appeared out of nowhere in a corner of the room, covered in shining veins coursing with electric pigments. This spot contrasted greatly with the rest of the dream tapestry, and Valdemar couldn't help but think that it *shouldn't be here*. Whenever he tried to wash it away, it reformed somewhere else like a cancer.

"It is time," Lord Bethor declared as Valdemar lay on his bed. Though Ktulu didn't cower in fear like he did in Lord Och's presence, the familiar had quickly joined his partner beneath the bedsheet and cuddled against him like a cat looking for warmth. "We shall delve into Ialdabaoth's dreams."

"Forgive me, my lord, but is that wise?" Marianne asked as the Dark Lord sat on the ground next to the bed in a lotus pose, stripping himself of his armor to reveal the boiling blood and darkness underneath. "They could affect him through the bond somehow."

"If they try, I will destroy them," Lord Bethor replied as he closed his eyes. His sheer arrogance matched Lord Och's own, and Valdemar couldn't help but find it somewhat invigorating. "Nothing short of a Nahemoth may match my might on the astral plane."

"It's alright, Marianne," Valdemar replied with a smile. "I'm ready."

His friend looked more concerned than reassured. "Is there no way I can follow?" Marianne asked. "I am not an oneiromancer, but I am well-versed in dream defense."

"This is not a dream," Lord Bethor replied, the surface of his body twisting like raging waters. "By closing himself to the Primordial Dream, his mind will anchor itself into the waking world where you cannot follow. You would need to learn astral projection to assist, and you are very far away from it."

Marianne clenched her jaw, crossed her arms, and remained silent. Of course she disliked the situation. She was a bodyguard unable to protect her charge, and Valdemar knew she worried that he might end up like Bertrand.

The summoner closed his eyes. He needed to focus on the task ahead, to clear his thoughts and let sleep take him. Ktulu started to utter a strange, yet soothing noise as he started falling asleep too. *A lullaby,* Valdemar realized. It reminded him of his mother's music box.

The sorcerer's world went dark, and the song was drowned out by the silence. His sense of self diluted into something greater than his human flesh, his errant thoughts expanded into a great singularity whose power no man could understand. The abyss swallowed him and he became one with it.

He was no longer a man, but the mask of a god.

He tried to look for his handmaiden, his slave, but she was so small and he was so big. She was but one of the germs inhabiting his belly. He had a hard time finding her among the colonies of errant cells who dared to think themselves separated from his glory. They were sick, every last one of them. They suffered from an illness called individuality, and in their madness refused the cure that he offered.

But in time, he would cradle all of them back into his welcoming arms. One day he would shatter the chains keeping him sealed inside this shell, and the many would return to the one.

Time and space meant nothing to him. His dreaming mind turned downward, in the blurry sea of the past. He looked for the handmaiden and found his mother instead in a cave, dressed all in white. She was younger then, a maiden freshly flowered. Yet no man had been allowed to have their way with her.

She was a gift fit for a god.

The faithful had gathered before the holy blood underneath their prophet's castle. The Verney prophet smiled in triumph, his ratling familiar crouched on his shoulder. Cultists observed in religious silence as they communed with their master, begging for power and immortality. They had awaited this moment for generations, guided by the whispers of his divine messengers.

His grandfather Pierre stood next to her; he whispered kind words as she trembled in fear, telling her that she would see the sun and the blue sky. He was a man too, but from a breed so *inferior* that it had lost all psychic connection to its maker and the higher truths of the cosmos. This lowly ape was untouched by the father's thoughts and unprotected by this cancerous shell of a dream. To the god, this creature was clay, fit only to be reshaped into something greater.

But like how earth could become the fertile ground for a mighty seed, this man's blood had value to the god, for this creature had so degraded that it now existed outside the untouchable wards keeping his progenitor chained. The Dumont's blood had mixed with that of the prophet's daughter, begetting a woman of two worlds, beholden to neither.

"Take the cup," Aleksander Verney told Sarah, as a hooded cultist offered her a grail of bones. She took it slowly, but without hesitation. Though she was afraid of failure, she had been prepared her whole life for this moment.

The maiden approached the pond of black blood which had birthed all life. She trembled as she moved, knowing what would happen to her if she was unworthy. Many had tried their luck, hoping to gain power and favor from their god, but none of them survived his deadly embrace. Their blood was too thin and unable to contain his essence.

"Please, God . . ." She prayed to another deity, the one of her father, for protection. The prophet narrowed his eyes in displeasure, but said no word; he knew this foreign god would not hear her. This was the womb of darkness where no light held sway. "Virgin Mary, protect me."

The god watched her kneel before his pond, tempted by the promise of youth and vigor, but scared by the unity it offered. *He* didn't care. She had been born and bred for a single purpose, and she would either fulfill it or perish. He observed her with his many eyes, smelling her flesh, trying to see if his long wait had come to an end.

Would she be the one?

Slowly, the maiden put her cup in the black blood while careful not to touch it herself. She was still afraid and wary, watching her half-filled grail with anxiety before looking at her father for reassurance. Pierre Dumont slowly nodded, a smile on his face, while Aleksander Verney and his rat watched with cold, empty eyes.

The maiden brought the black blood to her lips and drank. And as his black blood dripped down her throat and infected her flesh, a frenzy overwhelmed the trapped god. Like a predator woken from its torpor by the smell of meat, so did he tremble in his slumber. The walls trembled as his body stirred with trepidation, and even the cursed dead moon above shivered. His dreams in the Outer Darkness let out a howl that shook the planes. Escape at last.

But it wasn't enough. Her body was too weak. Although she didn't transform, Sarah Dumont coughed as her throat turned sore.

"What is happening?" Pierre Dumont asked, his former confidence replaced with fear for his child.

"What was meant to be," the Verney prophet replied with a triumphant smile, his rat familiar squealing at his side. "Worthy!"

"Worthy!" the cultists chanted.

"It burns," Sarah whispered.

"Carry on, my dear," Aleksander Verney said, his former coldness replaced with jovial delight. "You must drink, drink, *drink*."

Sarah gathered her breath and mustered her courage, then emptied her cup. And as the god's black blood spread through her veins, he knew she was the one. He had finally found a vessel fit to bear his brood, a red grail to contain his almighty blood. She would birth an avatar that could act beyond the wards keeping him trapped in this endless nightmare.

At long last he would break out to win the Great War and consume the cosmos.

But instead of submitting to her glorious destiny, Sarah Dumont let fear overcome her. "It hurts . . ." she said before dropping the cup. "I . . . I can't . . ."

"It's okay, sweetheart," her father reassured her. "We'll continue after you recov—"

No.

He had waited eons. He would not waste any more time.

His black blood boiled with rage, and Sarah let out a scream of fear and surprise. She ran away from the pond, her feet stumbling on the cold stone floor. The maiden fell on a knee, scratching it deep enough for a drop of her blood to fall off her skin.

He didn't let her escape his grasp. Not so close to freedom.

Tendrils of thick black blood rose from the primordial pond and grabbed her by the leg, intent on dragging this lowly ape back into his embrace.

"Sarah!" Pierre Dumont shouted, his confidence replaced by fear. His daughter looked over her shoulder as more tentacles grabbed her.

"Father!" She screamed in pain as he dragged her across the floor toward the pond, her nails clawing at the stone while his cultists shouted in jubilation. "Father!"

"Stop it! Stop it!" And when none moved, Pierre Dumont threw caution aside and tried to stop the inevitable. He attempted to make a mad dash to his daughter, trying to prevent what he had sacrificed so much to achieve.

He didn't make more than three steps before cultists grabbed him by the shoulders. He punched one in the face with enough strength to force him back, but others caught him by the arm and restrained him.

"Sarah!" Pierre shouted.

"You wanted this," the Verney prophet whispered softly, hands behind his back as his men kept Pierre bound. "This is a blessing."

Pierre Dumont glared at him, his eyes sinking into his eye sockets from the fury and the impotent rage. "She is your granddaughter!"

"I know," Aleksander Verney said, a tear running down his cheek. His words were full of joy. "I am so proud."

The god ignored them, the screams of "Sarah" and the shouts of "worthy." He only had eyes for his prey struggling in his countless arms, as he dragged her into his black blood. Tears of fear rained down her cheeks, her lips prayers to a god that wouldn't hear her.

ABOMINATION.

No! Valdemar screamed internally, as his tentacles . . . his arms . . . *No!*

This wasn't him! This wasn't real, this was all a dream, but he couldn't wake up! He was himself, but he was also the thing in the pond, the very blood of the world!

His mother tried to scream, only for his black blood to coil around her neck to silence her. His tentacles turned into his hands pressing on her naked throat. He felt her salted tears on his skin, smelled her terror . . .

She never wanted to have you.

"But we did," the Lilith whispered through his mother's lips. Her eyes were red as blood, her skin a deathly pallor.

Valdemar let out a roar of rage echoed by the dream, his fingers turning into claws. He hit her face, and a second later it turned back into his mother's teary face. The image shook Valdemar to the core, his fury instantly replaced with guilt.

"Mother," Valdemar whispered. "Mother, I'm sorry!"

"Don't approach me!" she screeched while crawling away. "Don't touch me, you monster!"

"Mother, I . . . I swear I didn't . . ." Valdemar's voice broke in his throat, the dream turning into a blur. "I didn't want any of this!"

The cavern collapsed around him, as did the illusions of his regretful grandfather and the Verney cult. The sad song of a music box echoed as the world transformed into a shadowy village near the Lightless Ocean.

Valdemar was himself again, a ghost out of time standing next to an old well. A familiar well.

His mother was here too. Gone was the innocent maiden she had once been. She dressed all in black, her cheeks creased by age and torment. Her eyes were red-rimmed from too many tears as she looked into the darkness of the well. A small form was wrapped in cloth in her arms, lulled to sleep by a music box.

"No . . ." Valdemar whispered, his heart turning cold in his chest. "No, please, don't . . ."

She hated and feared you.

His mother threw the child into the well, down into the darkness.

Valdemar could only stand and watch as he heard a *thump* at the well's bottom. The ghost of his mother looked into the well without a word, and after a few seconds of silence turned away.

Valdemar approached the well's edge and looked into the abyss inside. He couldn't see the bottom. Only darkness.

"You are lying," Valdemar whispered through his teeth. "My mother . . . She was always so kind to me. She would never . . ."

"She did," his mother's specter said before turning to face him, her irises as red as blood. "But you cannot die."

"You lie!" Valdemar snarled angrily, his fists hitting the ground. "This is just an illusion!"

"No, my prince. This is the truth. But it doesn't matter." She kissed him on the cheek, her lips both warm and cold all at once. "*We* love you. We wouldn't exist without you. We are your dreams."

Valdemar took a step back to escape her vile touch, before casting a spell. He attempted to crush her neck with telekinesis, but neither his body nor the Lilith's had blood. He tried to contact Ktulu through the summoning link. It was still here, but diffuse, as if the veil separating the planes stood between them.

Shit, he *hated* dream magic!

"It is alright, my prince," the Lilith said before making a noble reverence. "I will give you good dreams, if you wish."

"Will you die if I dream it?" Valdemar replied angrily, refusing to believe what she had shown him . . . even if he felt the seed of doubt growing in the back of his mind.

Was this truly a dream? His Painted Field should have kept him away from the Primordial Dream, so how could the Lilith ensnare him in it? *Or we are in reality,* Valdemar thought as he looked at the well. *My dream manifested itself somewhere in Underland. But why can't I sense my familiar then?*

"What would it change?" the Lilith asked and sounded genuinely puzzled. "Great Ialdabaoth would just make another me. Even then, my intervention is not necessary. I only clean the stage before the final performance. The forces at play were set in motion long before your birth, my prince. They cannot be halted. Why try to fight?"

"Why try to convince me at all then?" What was Lord Bethor doing? Had he overestimated his abilities? Or was the Lilith stronger than she looked?

"Because you are in pain," she replied with false kindness. "Your human life is a nightmare. When you wake up and cast off this false skin to reveal your shining true self, it will be all over. Why fight for lesser creatures? They created you to serve their selfish desires and continue to exploit you. You are better than this."

"You try to use me too," Valdemar pointed out. "And you're far worse than the Dark Lords will ever be."

"Use you? My prince, we exist to serve you. We act on your behalf, even if you cannot see it yet. All we want is for you to be happy."

"As far as speeches go, I've heard better." Though Valdemar had no love lost for inquisitors, he had friends he cared for in Marianne, Liliane, Hermann, Iren . . . he was even starting to get used to Lord Och, of all people! "Why even try to wake up Ialdabaoth? If you are his dream, you will cease to exist once he awakens."

The Lilith silently observed him for a few seconds, and as she did Valdemar noticed the left side of her face wriggle for a split second. Something inhuman crept underneath his mother's skin, ready to burst out at a moment's warning.

"Do you know," she asked, "The distance between the sun humans worship and this barren rock we stand on?"

Valdemar frowned. "No."

"Millions of kilometers of nothingness," she replied. "Now, if you were to look at the darkness above for another world, millions turn to billions. A vast expanse of darkness filled with a few islands of lights and barren rocks. And among these countless grains of sand, only a handful house the seed of life."

"Your point?"

"The universe is full of death," the Lilith replied coldly. "Death is the natural state of the cosmos, and life is the wonderful exception. The life that is Ialdabaoth. Awake or dreaming, we are a part of its divine will. Your will. His awakening is inevitable."

Valdemar didn't buy it. "Then why do you try so hard to isolate me from others, and to convince me to go along with you? If Ialdabaoth's awakening was inevitable, you could sit back and watch. If it could do everything on its own, I wouldn't even be here."

The Lilith smiled, her teeth pristine as ivory. She looked like his mother, but the way she moved was unlike her. She looked *false*. "Who doesn't love to play with the food?"

"I don't believe you," Valdemar replied, having pieced it together. "There are some limitations that neither you nor Ialdabaoth are capable of overcoming, and you need me to help break them. But what if I choose not to do anything? What if I just say *no*?"

The Lilith kept smiling, but her eyes no longer did. The silence stretched on, as oppressive as a Dark Lord's aura, while Valdemar heard movement coming from the well next to him.

"Then your stubbornness," she said, her voice twisting into an inhuman echo, "Will be met with relentless despair."

Valdemar spat on the ground. "Bring it."

The Lilith raised her hand, perhaps to cast a spell or castigate him . . . only to let out a gasp as an invisible force coiled around her neck and lifted her above the ground.

"You talk too much," Lord Bethor declared as he manifested out of nowhere in full armor. His hand was raised into the void, his fingers slowly closing as he telekinetically strangled the Qlippoth impostor. "Whore of the Outer Darkness."

Lord Och's words came to mind.

The gods do not deserve our worship, let alone our suffering.

4

KINSHIP

Vernburg. He was dreaming of Vernburg. Valdemar never had never been to this place, but the dream around him fit Marianne's description to the letter. Crumbling old houses surrounding the well under a ceiling of stone. Was this the false village that Valdemar had dreamed into being or merely mimicry?

Whatever the case, it was slowly falling apart. The village's houses collapsed one by one before sinking into nothingness. The ceiling above the summoner's head cracked like an egg as thin red lines spread in the very fabric of the dreamscape.

It's him, Valdemar realized as he looked at Lord Bethor. The Dark Lord's magic poured out of his spirit like lava, his power dwarfing that of the Lilith's. The creature that had led Valdemar's spirit astray so easily was now at his mercy. *His very presence destabilizes the dreamscape.*

"This is not a dreamscape," Lord Bethor said as he restrained the Lilith with the mere power of his mind. "This is the other side."

Valdemar shivered as he looked up through the cracks in the sky. He peered at the biggest rift and gained a glimpse of the universe beyond. A red light shone through it, and the roars of the Qlippoths echoed from the other side.

The Outer Darkness.

No wonder Valdemar's link with Ktulu felt so weak. Multiple planar boundaries separated them.

"It seems that when you closed yourself to the Primordial Dream, you instead strengthened your connection to your progenitor's nightmares,"

Lord Bethor said as he telekinetically moved the Lilith above the well. The creature wearing the face of Valdemar's mother struggled against her binding, something crawling beneath her skin as if threatening to burst out at any moment.

My Painted Field prevented me from dreaming and created a mental buffer, Valdemar put two and two together, fearfully gazing up at the fragmented ceiling. Instead of manifesting in the material plane, this place reformed on the other side.

And by doing so, Valdemar had left himself open to psychic attacks by Qlippoths. *Damned if I do, damned if I don't,* the sorcerer thought before glaring at the Lilith. She had lied about being unable to influence him, all to make him lower his guard and fall into a trap.

Even though Lord Bethor choked the life out of her, she was grinning ear to ear.

"Lord Bethor, we have to go back to reality now," Valdemar realized as the cracks spread to encompass the entire ceiling. This place, whatever it was, kept the Qlippoths outside at bay for the moment . . . but not forever. "If I don't wake up—"

"You will, but not before we get what we came for. Answers."

Tendrils appeared behind the Lilith, binding her legs together and expanding her arms. The sight of his mother being crucified like this sent shivers down Valdemar's spine, though he quickly suppressed this feeling. This wasn't his mother, just a monster copying her.

"Will you kill her?" Valdemar asked the Dark Lord.

"It won't stick unless we destroy her personal vessel," Lord Bethor said dryly. "But I sense a connection between her and a dark force at this demiplane's core. We can at least find out what it is."

A demiplane? So this was indeed the false Vernburg. Even as this false reality fell apart, the well remained undisturbed; the evil within scared away even the Qlippoths. Since Liliths were the handmaidens of the Nahemoths . . .

Don't you want to know who is at the well's bottom? the Lilith had said the first time he dreamed of her. He is in great pain, my prince.

The creature sealed in the well was obviously a Nahemoth, but the way the Lilith spoke of it . . . a doubt wormed its way into Valdemar's mind.

The illusion of his mother tossing him into the pit flashed in Valdemar's mind like a dire warning. The secret inside would hurt him, maybe even destroy him. Something in his subconscious told him to look away from a truth he was never meant to know.

But Valdemar had gone too far to back out now. He gazed into the well and found the pit deeper than anything he had ever seen. It made him dizzy simply to look at it, and his eyes couldn't see far past the darkness. Symbols covered the stones, though most had become blurry and indistinguishable.

Wards. Valdemar recognized some of them, having used similar inscriptions in his summoning circles. A few of the symbols, representing eyes, stuck out from the rest. *They were in my grandfather's diary,* Valdemar thought as he recognized some of the runes. His True Sight had revealed them on the pages.

But not all of the runes were meant to keep summoned creatures imprisoned. Others were wards against the undead and corrupted ghosts. Why would anyone use them to bind a Nahemoth?

As Valdemar asked these questions, he heard a crack above his head and the noise of shattered glass. And as he looked up from the well and watched the ceiling collapse entirely, the sorcerer finally got a good look at the Outer Darkness

As it turned out, it wasn't dark at all. A swirling vortex of crimson light swallowed the dream's ceiling and covered the skies as far as Valdemar could see. It was a whirlpool of magic whose eye was a blistering nuclear chaos, a burning abyss of light and flames. Countless Qlippoths, from the lowly Gnawers to mightier Collectors, emerged from this cradle of nightmares and floated in the void above the demiplane. They roared and screamed as they descended toward the well, crossing the impossible distance separating it from the abyss.

But it was the vortex itself that made Valdemar stare in shock, for it was not made of water or blood, but of souls.

Countless hollowed husks were joined together in this mad sea of stitched flesh. Humans, dokkars, troglodytes, and all the children of Ialdabaoth were gathered in this macabre abyss. They tried to crawl away, fighting and screaming and begging . . . but they couldn't escape the nuclear chaos' irresistible gravity. The souls were dragged into the central furnace, and the steady stream would keep it alight for all eternity.

There were millions of them.

"This is hell," Valdemar whispered in horror. "An afterlife for corrupted souls."

"Oh my prince . . ." the Lilith whispered even though Lord Bethor crushed her throat. "You are wrong. This is not *an* afterlife." Her tongue morphed into a tentacle as it licked her lips. "This is all there is."

They all returned to the Blood. Innocents or sinners, they all returned to the Blood and their dark father's jaws. *Mother, grandfather . . .* Valdemar froze in fear as he peered into the burning abyss. *Everyone . . .*

"Focus!" Lord Bethor's voice was sharp as a blade. "She is deceiving you!"

The thunderous voice, and the screams of Qlippoths descending toward them like a flock of bats, snapped Valdemar out of his paralysis. *Yes, that's a lie,* he thought. *It's a lie!*

And as his mind cleared, Valdemar noticed an anomaly: from this sea of chaos, an island of order had risen. A gray spot was growing far away from the maw of the abyss, a cancer of metal rather than souls. Familiar pylons grew out of this surface, the lightning erupting from them zapping the Qlippoths whenever they got too close.

Something didn't add up.

"Look down into the pit before it is too late!" Lord Bethor ordered as his magic coiled around the captive Lilith like a serpent. "Let there be light!"

The Lilith shrieked as the Dark Lord's spell took effect. The voice turned from that of Valdemar's mother into an inhuman, gargled sound that banished the darkness.

And for the briefest of moments, Valdemar glanced at the thing at the bottom, at the monster that gave birth to this nightmare, the creature that shared his dreams.

It was a child. A malformed, bloated baby with corpse-like skin, sleeping on a bed of bones and dried blood. It must have been no more than a few days old, malformed and twisted. Black ooze poured from wounds on the stunted hands and limbs, while a severed, dark umbilical cord wriggled out of its belly. The corpse didn't breathe nor did it make a sound. It was as dead as Valdemar was alive.

He thought you were dead, Shelley's words echoed in his mind, dead like Crétail.

"Crétail," Valdemar whispered.

The child opened his eyes as his name was called, revealing a gray hue identical to Valdemar's own gaze.

The corpse looked up at the sorcerer while tentacles erupted from the corpse's wounds. The lips twitched and widened as the creature's jaw expanded into a fiery maw full of eyes and teeth. The entire demiplane, this cradle of demons, shook with its awakening.

A stillborn Nahemoth.

His other half.

The creature roared and the dream shattered like glass.

Valdemar's scream echoed the monster's into the waking world, his body trembling. His throat let out a shriek that could wake up even the deaf, while his hands shook uncontrollably. His heart burned and beat against his ribs in an attempt to burst out of his chest.

"Valdemar!" Marianne's warm hand squeezed his own, her voice barely audible over his scream. As he kept howling his despair for all to hear, her fingers moved to his cheeks and turned his head in her direction. "Calm down! Look at me, this is over! You have woken up!"

Valdemar's screams died as his eyes met Marianne's. The visions of the Nahemoth blurred with her face, but he managed to focus on her eyes even as his body kept shaking beneath the bed sheet.

"I'm here," Marianne whispered, her voice banishing the fearful visions. "You're safe. You're *safe*."

Valdemar gathered his breath, his hands still trembling. Marianne held one and his familiar the other. Ktulu held on to his partner tightly. "Ktulhu," he gargled, his tentacles licking Valdemar's cheek like a dog's tongue. "Ktulhu."

They were gone. The Qlippoths, the thing, the abyss . . . they were all gone like a bad dream.

"It's over," Marianne kept whispering as her partner slowly calmed himself. "It's alright. I'm here."

No, he wasn't. He wasn't alright. His heart was slowing down, but it still hurt in his ribcage. And the dream . . . this cradle of a nightmare . . .

"I saw it," Valdemar whispered slowly as he squeezed back her hand. "Who's at the bottom of the well. I saw it."

"The well? Vernburg's well?" Marianne frowned as she released Valdemar's hand. She quickly used a healing spell on him and the pain in his chest receded. His limbs were his own once again. "Gather your thoughts. What happened?"

"I'm . . . I'm not sure myself." The sorcerer looked at Lord Bethor, who was still sitting in a lotus position on the floor. "Have you managed to track them down through the link?"

"No," the Dark Lord answered, his eyes closed in meditation. "The Nahemoth's awakening and the disturbance in the Outer Darkness disrupted the link. You have seen it too."

Valdemar's eyes glanced at his Painted Field and the gray spot growing in one of its corners. Since the magical apparatus strengthened the summoner's connection to Ialdabaoth's mind and the Outer Darkness, he suspected that it echoed what happened on that plane.

"The metal cancer," Valdemar muttered. "I've seen those pylons before. It's derro tech."

"Yes." Lord Bethor finally opened his eyes. "I suspect that this phenomenon and the thefts of brains in our territory are connected. I cannot say how yet. In any case, I have wounded the Lilith's essence and she will not trouble you in the near future. However, you will have to disable your Painted Field while you sleep from now on."

Valdemar winced as Ktulu silently sat at his side, silent as a tomb. "This will bring back the nightmare," he pointed out. "And let the demiplane creep into our world."

"A lesser evil than giving the Qlippoths a doorway to influence your mind directly," the Dark Lord replied dryly. "The wards keeping the Nahemoth imprisoned remain active. We still have time before it breaks out."

Before it breaks out.

Not *if*.

"Please," Marianne said with a frown, as she tried to understand the conversation. "Can you go back to the beginning? What did you see?"

My mother's violation, a Lilith's temptations, and Crétail, Valdemar thought darkly. "I don't know what was true or false."

"I do," Lord Bethor said coldly as he opened his dark eyes. "The reason for your malformed dreamscape, Valdemar, is that your soul is intertwined with a Nahemoth since the moment of your birth."

Marianne bit her lower lip. "They are one and the same?"

"Not quite. Their spirits are . . ." The Dark Lord considered the appropriate term. "Conjoined, like malformed twins sharing a body. Only one of the two spirits may exist on the material plane at once."

Valdemar clenched his jaw. "Mortal life created the Primordial Dream to protect itself from Qlippoth intrusions. When I sleep, my mind takes refuge in the Primordial Dream; since it cannot follow me here, the Nahemoth manifests in our reality instead. But if I do not dream . . ."

"The two spirits converge in the Outer Darkness and the connection strengthens," Lord Bethor finished. "A process that may permanently damage your soul. If the Nahemoth weren't bound, it could have merged with your essence."

Valdemar would have undergone a metamorphosis and shed his humanity.

That's their plan, he guessed. The Lilith was trying to weaken the wards keeping the Nahemoth imprisoned, to break down the barrier separating the man from the Qlippoth until a new horror emerged. *A red prince shaped in his father's image.*

And from what he had seen, the wards were slowly weakening.

His fear must have been written all over his face, because Marianne's gaze hardened. "That will not happen," she said firmly. "If the two of you aren't one and the same, then the connection can be destroyed."

"The destruction of the wards will not cause an immediate fusion," Lord Bethor added. "So long as you keep your human ability to dream and take refuge in the Primordial Dream, your spirits will remain separate."

"But it will allow the Nahemoth to fully manifest in imperial territory," Valdemar said darkly.

"Where it can be slain or sealed again," Lord Bethor replied with unshakable confidence.

"But how will it affect Valdemar?" Marianne asked with a frown. "If the bond isn't severed, it could damage his soul."

To Valdemar's worry, the Dark Lord had little comfort to provide. "I shall consult my old teacher on the matter. Lord Och's knowledge of souls surpasses mine."

He had to know something. As a lich, he had achieved immortality by severing the soul from his body and binding it to a phylactery.

This is all there is.

Did Lord Och know what awaited beyond the veil between life and death? *I have to know,* Valdemar thought as he shivered. Everyone had failed to call back a soul that had already passed into the Beyond, and now he feared to learn why. *I have to know. I can't . . . I need the truth.*

A detail bothered him. "Who put in those wards in the first place, in the very heart of the demiplane?" Valdemar muttered. "I saw the runes in my grandfather's diary."

"You answered your own question," Marianne said softly. "He was trying to protect you. To prevent you from becoming the cult's tool."

Valdemar's jaw clenched in frustration. Why did she keep defending his grandfather? "My grandfather couldn't cast spells."

Marianne mulled over her answer, before asking another question, "Could your mother?"

The words hit Valdemar like an arrow to the chest. His mother, using magic? That was absurd! She died a sick madwoman, unable to distinguish reality from delusion. Valdemar had never seen her cast a spell before her death.

But he couldn't forget the horrible memory of the black blood taking a hold of his mother and twisting her. Now, he understood that this violation had caused her depression and illness. But could it have given her powers too?

The illusion of his mother tossing a child into the well.

But you cannot die.

Like conjoined twins.

Dead like Crétail.

He is suffering, my prince.

An ugly picture formed in Valdemar's mind. Ktulu sensed his distress and held onto his arm, his tentacles wriggling in concern.

As Valdemar remained silent, Marianne sensed his unease and changed the subject. "The Lilith only appeared recently even though Shelley spent twenty years praying," she pointed out. "Nahemoths represent Ialdabaoth's creative impulses, so we can assume that the one in the well manifested her. This may be a sign that the wards are weakening."

"Shelley was trying to disrupt them," Valdemar whispered as he remembered his childhood nightmares and the rats haunting them. "He tossed corpses into the well in the hope that it would feed the Nahemoth as if it were a living beast. He was never trained in magic, so he made assumptions."

"Since he thought you dead, he probably believed that he could salvage the cult's ritual by creating another grail," Marianne guessed before glancing at Lord Bethor. "How long do we have until the wards break?"

"Enough time to find a solution," the Dark Lord replied dismissively. "I cannot say the same for the planar anomaly in the Outer Darkness. Whatever the derros are planning, we shall investigate it at once."

"We?" Valdemar and Marianne asked both at once.

"Yes, *we*. You have trained enough to become passable battle mages. I was already planning a punitive expedition into derro territory for their recent raids, and you shall come with us. Prepare yourself to leave on a moment's notice."

Not one to waste words, the Dark Lord teleported immediately afterward, leaving Valdemar alone with Marianne and his familiar. The sorcerer petted Ktulu beneath the tentacles, the alien child squealing in happiness. Someone had to rejoice here.

"How do you feel?" Marianne asked with concern.

"Terrible," Valdemar replied before glancing at his Painted Field. He would have to tear it down to dream again and let the nightmares return. "I can say goodbye to sound sleep."

Marianne seemed to hesitate about making a proposal for a moment, before mustering her courage. "I could help with it," she said. "Maybe."

Valdemar raised an eyebrow in skepticism. "How so?"

"I . . . I am better at defending my dreams, but I do know the basics of oneiromancy. I could . . ." Marianne cleared her throat. "I could enter your dreamscape and help you strengthen it. Like a dream bodyguard."

Valdemar processed her answer for a few seconds. Was she offering to enter his subconscious and patrol his innermost dreams?

Marianne's cheeks reddened in embarrassment. "I'm sorry. The proposal was inappropriate, I shouldn't have—"

"I wouldn't mind," Valdemar interrupted her.

She blinked in surprise. "You don't?"

"I let Frigga in," the sorcerer pointed out. "I trust you far more than her. Besides, you're right. I have notoriously terrible mental defenses, so any help on that front is welcome."

"I . . . thank you for your trust, Valdemar." Marianne cleared her throat. "I know most people would balk at letting someone else inside their dreams."

"Well, there won't be much to see." He had offloaded the worst of his nightmares to the Nahemoth. "It's just a barren wasteland."

"Good," she said, "that should make it easier to defend."

Valdemar glanced at Marianne, trying to see if she was making a joke or truly serious. Whatever the case, that wasn't the answer he had expected.

Truly embarrassed, Marianne broke the awkward silence and changed the subject. "Valdemar?"

"Yes?"

"Why did you say who?" she asked with a concerned voice. "You said *who* was at the bottom of the well, not *what*."

Of course she had been perceptive enough to pick up that detail. Valdemar gathered his breath, as the vision of his mother throwing a child in the well and the creature looking up at him blurred into one.

"You remember what the village's Qlippoths told you about a certain Crétail?" Valdemar asked her. "A very special child that was always hungry?"

Marianne squinted. "It wasn't a false name for you, was it?"

"No. The name belongs to someone else."

Dead like Crétail.

"Lord Bethor said it himself. We are spiritually conjoined twins from birth. The Nahemoth is, *was*, a human once. The wards included protections against restless spirits."

She never wanted to have you.

"I wasn't the first, Marianne."

But **you** cannot die.

"The thing at the well's bottom is Crétail," Valdemar whispered. "My sibling."

5

THICKER THAN BLOOD

How long had it been since Valdemar had faced his grandfather's portrait? Days? Weeks? Time passed so quickly in Lord Bethor's tower, especially since Valdemar had spent his time training or practicing magic. His painting had waited covered in cloth all this time, its own painter unable to face the ghostly echo within.

Valdemar and Marianne had put the portrait on a wall after disabling the Painted Field. Ktulu was busy playing in the bathroom's sink, leaving the two humans alone with the ghostly echo.

"Valdemar?" his grandfather's painted remains asked with an oblivious look in his eyes. "Are you off playing outside again? Don't wander too far, or your mother will worry."

He doesn't remember anything, Valdemar thought as he glared at his grandsire's echo. Even so long after the Silent King's revelations, watching the man's face filled his grandson with rage and bitterness. Learning the countless atrocities he had made himself an accomplice of through the Verney cult had only reinforced his loathing.

And yet . . . and yet Valdemar had seen his grandfather's panic during his daughter's ordeal beneath Verney Castle. He had tried to save her from Ialdabaoth's attention and failed. Had he been deceived too?

"Valdemar?" Marianne asked while his grandfather's echo looked around in confusion.

"I can't do it," Valdemar whispered. Just looking at the portrait made him confused.

"You can," Marianne replied, "you just don't want to."

No, he didn't. Valdemar knew the right questions to ask, but he was afraid of the answers. He was scared to see his doubts validated, to know that the family who had raised him only ever saw him as a curse, a tool, and a burden. That the cause for which Valdemar had dedicated his life had been a lie from the very start.

Lord Och's words came to mind. *All I offer is the truth, but it is true what fools say. Ignorance is bliss, and the path we walk is not a happy one.*

Back then, Lord Och had said that his apprentice didn't understand his words. But now he did. Valdemar had been happy with his eyes closed, but the more he opened them, the greater his anguish. Each new revelation had left him feeling worse and more lonely than the last.

But it's no longer about me, the sorcerer thought. *It's about the world.*

"Why?" The word came out of his mouth on its own.

His grandfather's painting looked at him in confusion. "Why, Valdemar?"

"Why was I born?" Valdemar asked as he cleared his throat. "Was I only a way home for you?"

The silence stretched on for a few awkward seconds, the portrait's face as still as a lifeless painting. For a moment, Valdemar thought that his grandfather's echo had fallen into another cognitive pitfall and simply couldn't process the question.

"Yes, you were." His grandfather's words were full of remorse, but they hurt all the same.

Valdemar clenched his fists while the portrait's gaze turned hollow and distant. "You sold out your own daughter to a Stranger to create a pair of doors," the sorcerer accused his grandfather, his body shaking with rage. "You condemned this entire world just for a ticket back home?"

"I was desperate," the painted ghost admitted, his voice breaking. "I wanted to go home again. To my fiancée and real family. This place . . . this place is *Hell*."

"Your real family?" Valdemar snarled. "Because my mother and I were only tools to you? Mom was just a grail to use and discard?"

"I didn't know . . ." His grandfather's echo sobbed as he held his head in his hands. "I didn't know . . . I didn't know Sarah would . . . I didn't want any of this . . ."

"You knew this would happen the moment you threw your lot in with a Stranger cult!" This . . . this cowardly trash . . . watching him made

Valdemar's blood boil in his veins. How could he ever have looked up to him?

"Mr. Dumont." Marianne's voice was softer, devoid of rage. "Did you inform the authorities of the cult's activities?"

His grandfather's painting kept sobbing, heedless of the world around him.

"He can't hear you," Valdemar replied angrily. "He can only answer my questions."

"Then ask him." Marianne locked eyes with her partner before he could protest. "Please, Valdemar. Ask him."

"What would it change to know that part?" Valdemar argued bitterly.

"A lot, and you know it." She let out a sigh. "Are you so afraid of the truth?"

Biting his tongue, Valdemar turned back to this shitstain of a painting. "Did you rat out the Verney cult to the Church of the Light?"

The portrait twitched briefly as he dried his tears. The ghostly echo was fragile and raw emotions weakened its stability. "I did," he confessed. "I promised the inquisitors that I would tell them everything . . . if they let us go. Me, Sarah, and you . . ."

"But you didn't tell them *everything*," Marianne pointed out as she glanced at Valdemar. "Or else the inquisitors would have executed him, promise of amnesty or not."

He was just protecting his ticket home, Valdemar thought angrily, but he asked the question anyway at Marianne's urging. "Why didn't you tell them about me? To protect your gateway to Earth?"

"No, I . . ." his grandfather shook his head. "Sarah . . . she made me promise."

This time, Valdemar's eyes widened. "Mom?"

"I wanted to tell the inquisitors the truth . . . to have the demon spawn destroyed, but Sarah . . . She said she would kill herself if I did. She didn't want to lose you. Not like . . ."

Valdemar looked down in sadness. "Not like Crétail?"

"It wasn't his fault," his grandfather sobbed. "He was born wrong. Too much like his father, they said. He was hungry, but it was never enough. Your mother . . . She lured him to sleep with the box. That was the only way to make him behave. But one day he . . . he didn't wake up. But even in death, he . . . he kept dreaming."

But you cannot die.

"So you tossed his corpse in a well and tried to bury his restless spirit?" Valdemar asked. He wanted to be angry, but he could only feel sorrow and pity for the brother he had never known.

"Your mother . . . there was no other way. She was the only one safe. He hated the living, and . . . he wouldn't sleep . . ." The ghost of Pierre Dumont looked lost in his memories. "Your mother . . . she hoped they would find a way to help him rest one day, but we . . . we never could."

His mother . . . his mother had sealed Crétail in the well, hoping it would let his tormented soul rest.

Mom wanted us to live? Valdemar thought in disbelief. *Even though we had been forced on her? Even though we were monsters, she wanted to save us?*

"Why didn't you turn me into a gate after she died?" he asked with a frown. "Did she make you promise no harm would come to me?"

"I . . . I couldn't bring myself to continue." Though his tears had stopped, his grandfather kept sobbing. The weight of his guilt and sins had caught up to him. "I have done so many terrible things . . . I ruined my daughter's life before it even began . . . I made a pact with demons . . . even though I already damned myself twice over, it had to stop somewhere."

"With me? It stopped with me?" Valdemar clenched his jaw, his teeth gritting together. "Couldn't you stop *earlier*?! You had plenty of chances to stop earlier! You said it yourself, you would have given me to the inquisitors! Why did it take Mom for you—"

He felt Marianne put a hand on his shoulder, but she had the grace not to say anything. Valdemar looked at her, and she shook her head. "That's enough, Valdemar."

"How can you say that after hearing this? He *knew*. He knew all along, sold his daughter to Ialdabaoth and—"

"Valdemar, take a good look at him. A long, good look."

Valdemar bit his lips, but followed her advice. And as he did so, he began to see his grandfather's portrait in a new light.

Before his death, his grandsire had appeared so wise and paternal. An elder who had seen more worlds than anyone else alive, and carried the loss of his home in his heart without giving in to despair. The creature in front of Valdemar was anything but a wise elder. The painting showed an old man prematurely aged by loss and regrets, his wrinkles as deep as rifts. His eyes betrayed his terror and incomprehension at the terrible world he had found himself trapped himself in. He didn't look like the manipulator his grandson wanted to see him as; his back was crumpled, his hands trembling with shame. He looked . . .

He looked *lost*.

"He's not the villain you want him to be," Marianne said softly. "He is an old ghost full of regrets. He could have avoided this mess, this is true. But in the end he did the right thing. Can you truly keep hating him after knowing that?"

And yet, Valdemar was still furious. The anger smoldered beneath the surface, his blood boiling whenever he glanced at this shitty old man. The mere sight of this . . . this self-pitying wretch . . .

No, Valdemar realized as he looked at his own trembling hands, still full of the same fury. The rage came from somewhere else entirely.

Valdemar wasn't angry because he hated his grandfather. He was angry at himself because he *didn't*.

Why? he thought while glaring at this painted ghost. *Why couldn't you be an asshole too? Why did you have to bring Mom into this?*

He didn't know what to think.

"I need fresh air," Valdemar said.

As Lord Bethor had promised, his students had been allowed to leave the tower after their training. The only way in and out of the fortress was through teleportation, but the Dark Lord had wisely set complex blood circles that could transport people in and out of his tower. Only those with proper authorization could use them, and he had allowed his students to venture outside to gather weapons and supplies.

However, both Marianne and Valdemar had to go wearing metal helmets to avoid identification. Lord Bethor's spells protected them from magical tracking by the cult of Ialdabaoth, but it didn't hurt to be discreet.

As befitting of their reputation, the weapon markets of Sabaoth were closer to open forges than markets. The merchants included sentient golems, humans, troglodytes, and even the occasional dokkar. Undead workers toiled in smelters and forges to deliver swords, shields, and guns to clients on the spot. Smoke was omnipresent in the area and quickly purified by bound air elementals. Fire ones fueled the forges and furnaces with their own bodies.

Undead knights regularly checked the clients for identification, though thankfully none of them interrogated Marianne and Valdemar.

She suspected that Lord Bethor had given his soldiers a special way to identify the duo, with orders to leave them alone.

It was . . . strange, to go outside. Her enhanced senses picked up everything now, the smell of sweat, the scent of alchemical powders mixed with metal, the clinks and clanks of hammers hitting an armor plate. Marianne had to focus constantly to filter out the ambient information without getting overloaded. Even looking at the smoke gave her headaches, as her enhanced vision picked up every grain of ash in the air.

"Are you looking for something in particular?" Marianne asked her partner as they traveled down an alley with chimneys and ovens on both sides. The air was hazy with smoke, while soldiers dutifully transported crates of supplies from the forges to the barracks.

"Not really . . ." Valdemar replied sullenly, the bag he carried on his back growing quite agitated. "And Ktulu doesn't like it here. Too hot."

"I warned you," Marianne replied with amusement. "Why did you bring him along?"

"He forced his way into the trip." As Valdemar spoke, the cloth bag's opening briefly widened to reveal a black eye inside. Ktulu peeked outside, before immediately retreating back inside his hideout before someone could see him. "I think he wants real food."

Marianne couldn't blame him. Lord Bethor had had golems serve them the same awful gruel and water for days now. Although she knew it was the standard food for soldiers and full of nutrients, she would rather eat something with *flavor.*

"We can go check the food after I get a new firearm," Marianne replied as she examined the stands. Although rifles, flintlocks, and other gunpowder weapons were rare and expensive, Sabaoth's forges sold plenty of them. However, they mostly sold heavy weapons like blunderbusses or heavy rifles; although Marianne's strength had increased since her training, she would rather use something adapted to one-hand. "My reloading flintlock was good enough, but it jammed all the time."

"A rifle," Valdemar argued. "Flintlocks can't reload automatically."

"A reloading flintlock," Marianne insisted. Something in his tone had turned her defensive. "Why does everyone say it was a rifle?"

"Because it was a rifle and you made a mistake?"

Marianne sighed beneath her helmet. "Alright, I will get a rifle."

Truth be told, she was happy Valdemar had enough life left in him to argue with her. She had expected him to fall into sullen silence or depression after his encounter with his grandfather. But the truth had only made him thoughtful.

I think he had doubts from the start, Marianne thought. It would have been easier if the world was black and white. "You were afraid your mother didn't want you, were you not?"

"Yes," he admitted while glancing at the stands. From the way he looked at their wares, Marianne was certain that he had never wielded a weapon in his life; Valdemar Verney had only ever trusted magic. "I'm not sure what to think now."

"I cannot say I truly understand how you feel," Marianne admitted. "But, for whatever it is worth, I have despised my parents too after they disowned me. This pain is sharper than most."

"Does it ever go away?"

"No," Marianne replied bluntly. "But no matter the circumstances of your birth, your mother and grandfather made the choice to treat you as a member of their family rather than a hellspawn. I know you want to see your grandfather as evil because it would be easier to hate him, but he wasn't. You have seen what true evil is like, Valdemar. Can you truly compare your grandsire to that Lilith?"

"He still had plenty of opportunities to prevent things from degenerating this far."

"True, and that makes him flawed. But in the end he stopped and tried to make up for his mistakes. Shouldn't that point count in his favor?"

Her fellow sorcerer crossed his arms and didn't answer.

And *now* she had made him sullen. Marianne sighed as she looked at the firearms available, her eyes wandering from one rifle to another. She noticed one with three small barrels, the device barely larger than a hand. "I've never seen this kind," she muttered to herself.

The shopkeeper, a stone golem using a carved funeral mask for a face, turned to face her. "This is a new one-handed weapon we recently reverse-engineered from the derro kingdom," he explained with a bellowing voice. "We call it a revolver. The range is smaller than a flintlock and the damage is mediocre, but it is easy to disguise and draw."

"Interesting," Marianne said as she picked one, an exquisite steel weapon covered in dragon symbols. "What about the munitions? How many shots can it fire before you have to reload?"

"Three. It is reliable, but I suggest using a rifle if you want more power. You can mitigate the problem if you turn it into a soulbound weapon and purchase enchanted bullets, but it will cost a fortune and you will need connections."

"I could pay to have a soul bound to a weapon?" It surprised Marianne. Soulbound items were extremely rare, since people needed a soulstone to manufacture them. Individuals wealthy enough to purchase one usually chose to be revived as undead or golems rather than have their spirit bound to a weapon or firearm.

"Yes, if you have the military's authorization," the golem replied with a nod. "Lord Bethor does not waste resources. Prisoners with the death penalty unfit for military service have their soul extracted to power weapons, and their body is repurposed into a mindless undead thrall. The souls of murderers make especially good firearms, since their bloodlust carries through the bullets."

A soulbound revolver would probably pierce Shelley's skin. Although Marianne had trained to rely on her own strength, having a backup weapon that wouldn't tap into her bones for projectiles couldn't hurt. "How much would it cost?"

"The military will need to place an order on your behalf for a soulbound revolver. Report to your superior, but I doubt they will agree. Such weapons are usually reserved for the best units."

"I will try my luck all the same," Marianne replied. She believed Lord Bethor wouldn't mind, especially since she intended to enchant the bullets herself. She had an idea in mind that could prove especially deadly to the likes of Shelley and other wererats.

Bullets won't work, Marianne . . .

The voice—an inhuman, shadowy whisper—echoed in her head while a chilling feeling took root in her mind. Invisible hands wormed their way into her brain and wove words from her thoughts.

Marianne's head snapped around, trying to locate the source of the voice. The alien feeling in her mind vanished as if had never been here, the strange words drowned out by the noise of the forges. Ktulu briefly peeked through the bag's opening as if startled by her reaction, but quickly hid back inside.

"Did you hear that?" Marianne asked.

Valdemar emerged from his thoughts long enough to answer. "Hear what?"

Since the golem looked just as confused, Marianne kept her mouth shut to avoid appearing like a madwoman. Had her mind played a trick of perceptions on her? Or had she misheard something from the forges?

In any case, she took the forgemaster's coordinates to place an order later and left with Valdemar for the food stands. They were few and far between, offering little more than smoked meat.

I would kill for a vegetable plate, Marianne thought as she examined a stand of dried and fried fish. An undead worker had gathered an unusual collection of salmon, tuna, and strange creatures, but none that interested either Marianne or Valdemar.

He requires fish, Marianne . . .

This time, Marianne looked straight at Valdemar's bag. As she suspected, Ktulu was discreetly peeking out, his six cute eyes looking insistently at her. "Ktuluh," it whispered while pointing a finger at the salmon among the various products. "Ktulhu."

"Shush," Valdemar whispered back, the familiar hiding back inside the bag before someone could see him. "I'll take a few, I promise."

Marianne wondered if Ktulu was the source of the voice, until she remembered that it had said "he" rather than "I". She glanced down at Valdemar's shadow, noticing three red lights briefly flaring on the shade's head before being swallowed by darkness.

So that's how it is, Marianne thought as she focused back on the stand. "I will buy six salmon," she said.

I will keep you safe, Marianne . . .

Strangely, Valdemar seemed blissfully unaware of his pet monsters' antics. "I didn't take you for a fish person," he told his companion. "But I can cook something with mushrooms when we get home."

"You can cook?" Marianne asked in surprise.

"Yes, of course. I have been on my own for a while." Valdemar turned his head in her direction, his eyes piercing through the helmet. "You never learned to?"

"I . . ." Marianne sighed in embarrassment. "To my shame, I did not. Bertrand always cooked for me."

"What is there to be ashamed of?" Valdemar asked as he paid the undead worker, and received the tribute of fish in a separate bag. Ktulu grew agitated inside his own, perhaps displeased to have to wait to eat his dinner. "I will teach you."

"That would be kind," Marianne replied. And it will help you take your mind off your family.

As if he had heard her thought, Valdemar turned to gaze at Lord Bethor's tower. The iron building could be seen everywhere in Sabaoth. "Marianne?"

"Yes, Valdemar?"

"Do you think Crétail is a monster?" he asked as they walked through the noisy alleys. "Even after all you have learned?"

Marianne considered her answer carefully. She thought back of Vernburg, of the Qlippoths playing humans inside its borders, of all the evidence she had gathered across this long and deadly case.

"No," she replied. "I think there's still a trace of humanity left inside."

His head snapped in her direction. "Why?"

"The village's Qlippoths played humans, and the most lifelike of them was Crétail's nurse. The one who took care of him alongside your mother. If your sibling is the demiplane's source, why wasn't he dreaming of horrors? Why was he dreaming of someone who he thought of as a motherly figure?"

Why was he dreaming of Qlippoths playing human instead? Why did its Lilith handmaiden choose his mother's appearance as her vessel?

"Your mother's music box lured him to sleep too," Marianne pointed out. "I haven't heard of any monster that behaved this way. His behavior is more that of a child with great powers than a destroyer of worlds. But Valdemar, someone who spent twenty years trapped at the bottom of a well is *never* going to be normal again."

"I know. I have seen him. He is a tormented soul full of pain and hunger. But . . ." He shook his head. "Do you think there could be another way to deal with him? Outside of murder?"

"Do you think there could be another way to save Bertrand than killing him?"

"I already answered that before."

"Then you answered your own question. Killing is the easy way to solve a problem, but it's not the only one. Or else our entire society wouldn't exist." Marianne put a hand on his shoulder. "I don't think you can turn him human, not after all he went through . . . but a better option than murder might present itself."

Valdemar looked at her hand in silence, before nodding to himself. "I'm not going to destroy Crétail. He is innocent in all of this, just another victim of that filthy cult. Destroying him is not what my mother would have wanted." He clenched his fist with determination. "I'm going to save him."

6

THE FORGOTTEN SAINT

The cavern could shelter an army, and yet it was barely large enough to house the monster. When Lord Bethor summoned his students for the raid into derro territory, Valdemar had expected to travel on foot or on the back of giant beetles. A subtle, discreet infiltration into enemy lands. But of course, Lord Bethor didn't do anything *subtle*.

"This is the Excavator," the Dark Lord explained as he waved a hand at the biomechanical titan in front of them. "The spear that will pierce the derro kingdom's hide."

And what a spear it was. The creature reminded Valdemar of a gargantuan centipede, one nearly half a kilometer in length and as thick as a fortress. Although the lower half of the body had chitinous legs and a carapace, the upper parts had been replaced with a thick mechanical shell. Instead of a face, the chimera's head ended with the biggest, most complex drill mechanism Valdemar had ever seen. Hydraulic mechanisms supported the entire apparatus while chimneys let out vapors at the creature's tail.

"It's a living fortress," Marianne whispered as she noticed reinforced doors and stained windows on the upper parts of the centipede allowing entrance into its interior. A horde of undead workers and golem engineers welded the finishing touches on the shielding.

The Knights of the Shroud, Lord Bethor's personal knightly order, stood watch over the Excavator. Each and every one of them was a mighty undead warrior clad in imposing black armor, with a crimson gaze piercing their closed visors. Their helmets ended in a crown of spikes and each of them carried a soulbound weapon of some kind. Most of them wielded short swords adapted to fighting in enclosed spaces, but a few specialists had chosen axes and polearms. As the empire's elite fighting force, they deserved the best equipment Azlant had to offer.

"Death rides with us" was the order's infamous motto. Death has come to the derro kingdom.

Lord Bethor, perhaps to congratulate his students on "graduating," had given them new clothes woven with protective spells: a red hooded cloak in the style of the Pleroma Institute for Valdemar and slim leather armor for Marianne. The latter had also received the three-barrel, bone-handled soulbound revolver she had asked for.

"Ktulhu," Valdemar's familiar said in his bag. The welders' tools warmed up the cavern, and he didn't like the temperature. "Ktulhu."

"It will be cooler inside," Valdemar replied. Or at least he hoped so. The Mask of the Nightwalker on his face gave him fresh air, but he didn't think that letting Ktulu try it would be a good idea. Two Strangers interacting might have unforeseen consequences.

"I'm sure my old apprentice prepared some refreshments for the trip," a familiar voice mused to Valdemar's side. Lord Och's sudden appearance surprised neither Valdemar nor Marianne. By now, they had grown perceptive enough to sense him teleporting in their midst. "I see your biomancers outdid themselves, Lord Bethor. Are you sure you want to unveil it now?"

"It is a calculated risk," the younger Dark Lord replied to his master while Marianne politely bowed before Och. Valdemar himself simply crossed his arms and listened in silence. "I do not expect to reach the capital before the derros figure out a counter, but we should storm the city-fortress of Stahlstadt. Otto Blutgang left General Stahlherz to garrison it, but his forces will be no match for me."

Cavern warfare was long, tedious and difficult. Unlike the colossal domains, most of Underland's caves and tunnels were low and narrow; advancing meant moving from one choke point to another, each of them bitterly contested.

So Lord Bethor had found a novel alternative. Instead of disputing existing tunnels with derro garrisons, he would create a new pathway for his army.

Still, when the Dark Lord had spoken about launching a "*punitive expedition,*" Valdemar had expected a small raid instead of a full blown military offensive. The summoner guessed that Lord Bethor had higher standards than most as far as violence was concerned.

"I will drop you on the designated area midway through our advance," Lord Bethor said as he observed his troops boarding the centipede's inside through a metal ladder. "I trust you shall be able to return to civilization on your own, my old teacher."

"Of course," the lich replied with a chuckle before gazing at Marianne and his apprentice. "Will you be strong enough to guard a feeble old man like me?"

Valdemar shrugged, refusing to play his teacher's game. Marianne, however, simply glanced at Lord Bethor.

"I said you would either count among the empire's best mages or obituaries," Lord Bethor said. "I did not lie. You are now adequate battle mages by my standards. There is still much for you left to learn, but you will prove sufficient."

It sounded almost like a compliment too.

Though he believed he wouldn't be so lucky, Valdemar hoped they wouldn't face too much opposition. Lord Och's goal was to investigate the region where his grandfather first appeared in Underland, in an attempt to either locate a potential Pleromian portal or find out if the derros had discovered interplanar transport technology. Valdemar and his group would tag along with Lord Bethor's expedition until they reached this place and then split off to do some archeological digging.

Of course, the derros wouldn't take an intrusion into disputed territory lying down and would fight back.

"Such a shame we will have to leave before your friends visit Sabaoth, my apprentice," Lord Och said as they moved toward the ladder to board the Excavator. "But with diligence, we shall return in time to meet with them."

Valdemar looked forward to it. It felt like a lifetime ago since he last met with Liliane, Hermann, Iren, and the others. "If I may ask," the summoner asked his mentor. "Has there been news on the Beast Plague front?"

"There has been a rise of incidents and a few outbreaks across the empire, but nothing we couldn't contain," Lord Och replied evasively.

"However, it appears the Verney cult's new headquarters is located somewhere near Ariouth."

"Lord Phaleg's domain?" Marianne asked with a frown as she climbed the iron ladder first. Of course the cult would take refuge in the part of the empire most hostile to Lord Och.

"Now, you're seeing my issue," Lord Och replied. "I am sure my old apprentice has little awareness of what's happening under his nose, as he keeps it buried too deeply in his books. Unfortunately, to avoid a potential and costly conflict between us, we will have to address the subject on neutral ground."

"The Dark Lords' Sabbath," Valdemar guessed as he climbed after Marianne. The ladder led to an open blast door giving way to a warm metal chamber. Ticking clocks and alchemical devices covered the walls, while pipes transported blood to the beast's organic parts and oil to its artificial ones. Valdemar noticed many other cluttering contraptions. Although he didn't understand what half of them did, he did recognize some repurposed derro tech.

"Yes." Lord Och, unlike his student, simply teleported inside the metal room. What a show-off. "Young Aratra will host us all in her palace, we shall raise a toast to the new year, decide which cavern we will invade, and then settle the Verney question."

The wording sent a chill down Valdemar's spine. "My question, you mean?"

"Hagith put your case on the agenda," Lord Bethor said gruffly as he teleported into the chamber. The blast door started closing behind him, the beast preparing to take off. "Aratra will almost certainly summon you and Reynard for an audience."

And much like his old master, Lord Bethor dared to call the empress of Azlant by her name without any honorifics.

"Her Majesty?" Marianne didn't hide her discomfort. "But I was disgraced."

"Young Aratra's attention is fleeting like mist," Lord Och mused. "I suspect she had long forgotten you before young Hagith mentioned your name."

This didn't sit well with Valdemar. Lord Bethor and Och clearly knew about Ialdabaoth's true nature, so he had to assume the other Dark Lords did as well. Some might wish to exploit the situation to their advantage, but others would probably rather choose caution over ambition.

And Valdemar's head would be on the line.

The chamber trembled as its devices thrummed and the ground shook beneath their feet. Valdemar almost stumbled as a quake spread through the structure, Marianne catching him by the arm to help him stand upright. Muffled noise echoed through the machinery as the drill activated and started digging into the stone skin of Underland.

Valdemar closed his eyes and activated his psychic sight, analyzing the biomechanical Excavator through the flowing blood. From the presence of surgical scars all across the body, the biomancers and engineers of Sabaoth had cultivated the creature until it had reached its adult size. They had then removed its intestines, brain, and glands, before installing technological and alchemical replacements. Even most of the blood circulation system was now mostly made of iron pipes.

Valdemar marveled at the effort it took to grow and modify this thing in secret. Lord Bethor's spellcasters must have spent years working on this project, and no hint of it ever reached the outside world.

Lord Bethor took his leave at this moment to move up to the machine's command center, ordering Knights of the Shroud to escort his guests to their quarters. When Valdemar prepared to go with Marianne, Lord Och stopped him. "Young Valdemar, please be kind and entertain me on our journey," the lich rasped before glancing at Marianne. "I am sure your bodyguard won't mind."

Marianne frowned, but accepted the dismissal with dignity. "Is there a room where I can practice my shooting?" she asked a Knight and received confirmation. "Then I will retire there for the moment. See you later, Valdemar."

"See you soon," he replied as he watched her vanish into the iron corridors of the Excavator. Valdemar struggled to explain why, but he felt diminished without her nearby. He had grown used to her presence lately, almost as much as Ktulu.

"Do not look so fraught with disappointment, my apprentice," Lord Och said as Knights guided them through the maze of pipes and corridors. Everywhere engineers worked tirelessly to keep the machinery running. "I may not be a noble maiden, but I can be good company."

"Will you cut off my arm if I say I preferred Marianne's company?" Valdemar deadpanned.

"Are you bitter about your training? Lord Bethor was right then, I coddled you too much."

The Knights of the Shroud introduced them to what Valdemar believed to be Lord Och's private quarters: a large lounge containing couches, cushions, and bookcases filled to the brim with texts. Knowing his old master's true nature, Lord Bethor had scoured the chambers of basic amenities like a kitchen or bathrooms. A vast stained window embedded in a wall allowed the occupants to see the world outside.

"Lord Bethor set up these quarters just for me," the lich declared as he sat on the couch, the knight closing the door behind Valdemar. "He knows my tastes in books as well. I have already read most of them, but it is the thought that counts."

The fact that the utilitarian Dark Lord of Sabaoth had set up a room inside his superweapon spoke volumes about the esteem in which he held his old master. From the way Lord Och himself spoke of his apprentice, Valdemar guessed they were probably as close to friends as creatures like them could be.

"Is it true that a lich's memory is foolproof?" Valdemar asked as he opened his bag and let Ktulu out. His familiar glanced warily at Lord Och before becoming fascinated with the world outside the window. The Excavator melted stone as it advanced, leaving fiery marks on the tunnels outside.

"It is. Though it may take me a while to remember details." Lord Och glanced at his student's shadow. Valdemar sensed his hidden Haunter growing uneasy with the lich's attention, like a predator sensing the gaze of another. "I am very pleased with your progress. Your skills have sharpened, and you have taken many leaps into understanding the true nature of our world."

Valdemar's thoughts turned to the Outer Darkness, and the horrors he had witnessed within it. "My teacher, I would like to discuss facts that I have uncovered."

"You wonder if a Stranger will eat your soul after you die?"

It's not my soul I fear for, Valdemar thought, shivering at the mere idea of his mother finding herself trapped in that screaming vortex of souls. "Please, my teacher."

Lord Och scoffed. "Shouldn't you know already what happens to the dead? You worked for years to try to bring back your grandsire's soul from the beyond."

"I did, but no one knows what awaits beyond the Veil between life and death." Valdemar turned to glare at his mentor. "Or if they know, they aren't telling."

"The Church of Light tells everyone the way to absolution," the lich replied mockingly. "It is your fault if your faith is lacking, young Valdemar."

His student glared back at his teacher, but did consider his words. Was the old lich suggesting that the Church of the Light had a point?

As he had told Lady Mathilde in Pleroma, Valdemar had never been truly religious nor believed in the cult. He did, however, know the basic tenets of the faith. "The Light will return to Azlant and the Whitemoon shall be banished once the world is free of sin," he quoted the Scriptures of the Church. "Only by believing in the Light and dedicating ourselves to it will our souls find comfort. Those who do not believe will be cast into the darkness, where they shall wander for all—" Valdemar froze. Cast into the darkness? As in, the Outer Darkness?

Lord Och's skeletal grin only confirmed his hypothesis. "What do you know about the Church of the Light?" the lich asked his apprentice.

"That it was the successor of the sun-worshiping religions of the old world," Valdemar replied with a frown. "It was an underground but popular cult until Empress Aratra made it the official religion and banned the Stranger Cults. And of course, the Church and the Dark Lords go hand-in-hand."

"It is true that the first believers of the religion were members of the sun-priests of the surface," Lord Och said with a chuckle. "But the true origin of the faith comes from another source entirely." The ancient archmage joined his fingers together, his empty eye sockets flaring with ghostly light.

"Have you ever heard," he asked with a gleeful tone, "of the tragedy of Sophia the Unwise?"

Ktulu's head briefly perked up at the name, but the familiar quickly focused back on the window. Valdemar took note of his reaction, though he himself had never heard the name. "No, I have not."

"It is a very old legend going back to when the sunlight still shone on the surface and humans knew nothing of the Blood. We lived in ignorance, blindly worshiping the sun above our heads. And yet, this Sophia is the one who laid the foundation of the Church of the Light, the Empire of Azlant, and the exodus underground."

Lord Och patted a cushion, silently inviting his student to sit and listen. Valdemar obeyed without a word, knowing that his master truly wanted an audience.

"Sophia was a saint, a holy woman with miraculous powers," Lord Och explained with a deep, wise tone. He was an experienced storyteller, with the perfect voice to match. "Everywhere she went, she preached a new, unconventional faith. She claimed that our planet was the creation of a vile deity of flesh and matter. A spawn of chaos cast down from a higher reality alongside its brethren and lured to sleep by powerful wards."

"She meant Ialdabaoth?" Valdemar interrupted his master, unable to suppress his curiosity. "But if it has brethren—"

"You have already met one, my student. It even commissioned you a portrait."

The Silent King?

Valdemar remembered his confrontation with the Stranger. As he had climbed the stairway to the Silent King with Hermann, he had briefly glimpsed a colossal entity inside that world's black sun. Now that the summoner thought of it, he could see the similarities with Ialdabaoth's sun-like siphon of souls.

Why would the Silent King call Valdemar an abomination though, if they were related? Was that because he was the child of two worlds? An unnatural occurrence?

There is a war in heaven.

Or maybe the Strangers simply didn't get along. They might share a common origin, but their objectives and nature varied wildly. The Silent King seemed content to serve as a curator of dead civilizations, while Ialdabaoth yearned to break free to devour its progeny.

"These . . . Strangers to our reality . . . had created life in this universe to serve and worship them," Lord Och continued his tale. "Our very bodies were prisons of matter. Only our souls could truly hope to break free by casting away their worldly desires and attachments. Otherwise, they would return to their progenitor, to be consumed and reincarnated anew."

Was the Dark Lord suggesting that a soul could escape the Outer Darkness through spiritual strength? Though he didn't buy into the faith parts of the religion, Valdemar guessed it made sense. If life could create the Primordial Dream to shield itself from the Qlippoths, it meant that Ialdabaoth's power was not absolute.

If one compared the Outer Darkness to a whirlpool, then a powerful enough soul could perhaps swim away to freedom . . . but where would it end up then?

"But how would Sophia know that?" Valdemar asked in skepticism. "No one's returned from beyond the Veil yet. Even ghosts simply never passed on in the first place."

"A wise question," Lord Och replied. "Sophia pretended to be one of the entities that banished the progenitor from the higher realms. These beings were emanations of a cosmic Light, the masters of the spiritual, but they could not manifest their full power in the material world where the Strangers ruled as kings. Sophia, who had taken pity on her enemy's creations, thus incarnated into a woman of flesh and blood. Her goal was to free us from this cycle of suffering before a terrible disaster came from the skies to wipe us all out."

A story that was, of course, completely unverifiable . . . but a true scientist couldn't disregard any possibility, and the tales' implications were fascinating. "She had predicted the Whitemoon's arrival?" Valdemar asked.

"She did, long before astronomers confirmed its arrival in our solar system."

"It doesn't mean much," Valdemar replied. "She could have been a normal mage with precognitive abilities, or someone influenced by a Stranger. They tend to gather cults around themselves."

"Many doubted her as you did, but as the Whitemoon approached her words received much credibility. In times of despair, men instinctively look for a savior. But you are correct. Sophia was a sorceress, and in her quest she gathered disciples and taught them many things. And here . . ." The lich chuckled darkly. "Comes the *Unwise* part."

By now, Valdemar had learned enough of human history to guess where this was going.

"Sophia taught her disciples secrets of the universe and knowledge of magic," Lord Och explained. "She preached that by delving into the higher mysteries, meditation, oneness, and letting go of worldly fetters, mortal souls could free themselves from the shackles of this world and ascend with her to the Light. She believed so much in humans' potential for good, that she became blind to their darker nature."

At this point, Ktulu walked back to Valdemar and indicated he wanted to be picked up. The summoner put the familiar on his lap so he could listen to the tale. "They turned on her, didn't they?" Valdemar guessed.

"Shush, be patient . . ." Lord Och hushed him as he continued his story. "Optimism is like a rock on a shore, young Valdemar. It is strong, but as it is battered by waves after waves of ingratitude, cowardice, and treachery, it grows brittle. As she watched people abuse her knowledge, suffered the ruling class using her as a scapegoat for all the world's ills, and despaired as her followers committed crimes in her name, the prophet's resolve wavered."

Of course. The lich loved cynical morals to a story.

"When the Whitemoon came to cleanse this world of life, Sophia lost faith in mankind and prepared to return to the Light with her believers. Everyone who didn't follow her teachings had condemned themselves to a cruel fate at this point, or so she thought. Her worshipers were all happy to follow her plan . . ." The lich raised seven fingers. "Except for seven of her disciples."

Ktulu looked at the lich's hand with rapturous attention, and Valdemar listened with attention. He had already put two and two together. *No way,* he thought as he examined his undead mentor, *but if so that means . . .*

"Why?" Valdemar asked. "Why did they refuse paradise?"

"Because they wished to save the world and all its inhabitants," Lord Och replied with surprising gravitas. "Led by a charismatic noblewoman, they begged Sophia to teach them how to repel the Whitemoon. The Unwise Saint, who believed that attachment to this hopeless world would only delay their spiritual ascension, denied them. And so, feeling betrayed, the seven disciples conspired against their benefactor."

The lich raised a hand and mimicked strangling an invisible neck.

"Together, they committed an unspeakable crime against Sophia in an attempt to steal her knowledge." Lord Och's skeletal face was the perfect picture of the cold embrace of death. "A sin that forever barred them from ascending to the Light. *If we have been condemned to eternal darkness,* their ringleader said, *then we shall rule over it.*"

"Ktulu!" Ktulu cheered, as he really seemed to like this part very much. "Cthulhuhu!"

Valdemar himself listened in silence. The bored, clinical way his mentor recounted the deed was more chilling than any threat.

"In the end, the Whitemoon came anyway and forced mankind underground," Lord Och shrugged as if discussing the weather. "The seven disciples used their knowledge to lead their kind, while the teachings of their late master were preserved in a lesser form. Some holy souls did manage to escape Ialdabaoth's grasp, as Sophia had wished. The others were either devoured, lost in the darkness, or bound to this world. Some of the seven betrayers died only to be replaced, while others endured across the centuries."

The Dark Lord finished his tale with a wicked grin. "And all lived unhappily ever after."

Ktulu clapped with childish enthusiasm. Valdemar himself was at loss of words, his mind busy processing the implications of this dark tale.

"Now," his mentor relaxed on his cushion. "What lesson is there to take from this story?"

Valdemar considered his words carefully. "May I answer your question with another?"

"Only if it is a good one."

"How did you go from trying to save the world and its inhabitants," Valdemar examined the Dark Lord from head to toe, "to *this*?"

The lich's ominous silence turned even Ktulu quiet. The room grew colder, with chilly mist rising from Lord Och's eye sockets.

"I should cut out your tongue for your insolence, but I find your boldness somewhat refreshing. I shall let it slide this once." The Dark Lord joined his hands. "Your mistake is to believe that I have changed. I have not. I have grown wiser and older and more powerful, but I was always like '*this*.'"

"Then you embellished your tale," Valdemar replied. "Though your methods remain questionable; your goal was noble and you truly wanted to save people. Now you care nothing for your own kind."

"My goal was to save the world, but not for the reasons you think." The lich glanced at the window and the stone walls beyond it. "I never sought salvation, Valdemar. It was freedom from the rules that govern this universe that I craved. In truth, I detest all overlords, whether they are wise or not. When one said I should either sacrifice the world to achieve paradise or vice versa, I asked '*why*' and decided I would have it my way. I would have it all."

"But you failed to do either," Valdemar pointed out. "You couldn't save the world and you couldn't achieve paradise."

"True, but you misunderstand the story's lesson. It is not that I couldn't succeed, but that I wasn't prepared enough."

How humble. But it took a certain kind of bleak determination to remain unrepentant after so many centuries. Valdemar didn't feel an ounce of remorse in his mentor's old bones.

The summoner replayed the story in his head and tried to read between the lines. The "noblewoman" Lord Och had mentioned was almost certainly Empress Aratra. The co-conspirators were the original Dark Lords, who had fallen and been replaced across the centuries. As for Sophia . . .

"What happened to Sophia?" Valdemar asked, more questions flowing out of his mouth one after the other. "What was the unspeakable crime you committed? Was she truly a higher being? If so, how could you even fight her at all? What is the nature of this Light? Is it another Stranger? How much of this story was true? Did you embellish some parts?"

The lich's teeth morphed into an ugly smile, and Valdemar understood he would get no answer today.

"Now that you heard this tale, apprentice," the Dark Lord whispered. "Do you hate me for my choices?"

"I would have fought for this world too," Valdemar replied grimly. "If you had succeeded, you could have saved us all, so I cannot condemn you. Still, I think you could have chosen another way. There had to be another option."

His mentor let out a sound that could pass for a sigh. "I told myself the same," he confessed. "But alas, there were none."

"I don't believe it," Valdemar replied. "Impossible is but a word. I do not hate you, nor do I believe you haven't changed in the years since."

Valdemar might be wrong, but he had the feeling that the old lich was trying to convince himself rather than his apprentice.

"I truly wonder how long your naïveté will resist the test of time," Lord Och replied with a hint of disappointment. "I have seen prophets cast down by friends and families. The waves of human nature break even the strongest resolve."

Valdemar shrugged. "I told you, my teacher. I won't become like you."

Realizing it was hopeless, Lord Och changed the subject. "But to go back to your question about souls, I wouldn't worry about your maternal family. Whether his humanity descended from another Stranger or resulted from our progenitor seeding another world long ago, your grandsire was so distanced from Ialdabaoth that he could not feel the Blood's call. Hence, his soul probably passed on to the Light or somewhere else. With luck, your mother was in the same situation."

With luck? That wasn't very reassuring. "How can you be so sure, my teacher?"

"Because Ialdabaoth would have used her soul to torment you, instead of sending a Lilith imitation," Lord Och replied bluntly. "Any fool can see using her as a hostage would have ensured your cooperation."

"That's what you would have done if you could?" Valdemar guessed with a snort. What kind of cold logic was that? *The one a Qlippoth would use,* he thought grimly. Since he couldn't contact his mother's soul for answers, he had to pray that his teacher was right and that she passed on safely. "But if they didn't end up devoured by Ialdabaoth, then where did their souls go?"

"This is a question to which I have no answer. Take it as an encouragement to continue your studies."

Still, on the question of souls . . . if Lord Och had been honest about his story, the authenticity of which Valdemar couldn't verify . . . then he had probably turned to lichdom to avoid the Outer Darkness and eternal damnation.

Which begged the curiosity of what phylactery he had chosen. Somehow, Valdemar had the intuition its nature was connected to this story.

In more ways than one, Lord Och had given him a window into his soul.

7

DREAMS OF STEEL

"This story doesn't match historical records," Marianne said as she sipped her tea. "Not at all." Valdemar considered her answer as he drank his own cup, his face unreadable. A slow-paced piano song resonated across Marianne's quarters, sung by invisible musicians. The noblewoman had heard it only once in her life, at one of Saklas' many balls, but it had left such an impression that she remembered it to this day. Instead of a hedge maze, the world beyond her window had transformed into a copy of the Lightless Ocean, with a colossal shape playing with a ship on the horizon. Marianne found the sight strangely soothing.

"I have studied imperial history in depth," Marianne continued. Instructors had drilled names, dates, and places into her young head one book at a time. "The Blood was only discovered around 300 BE through contact with troglodyte tribes years into the Descent. Mankind was completely disunited back then, with warlords trying to carve out pockets of civilization. The first recorded case of necromancy was in 243 BE, and Lord Och himself is first mentioned in historical records in 129 BE as a powerful necromancer fighting against the fallen dokkar kingdom of Nidavelir. There was no telling if he was even a lich back then, though it's likely considering his lifespan and magical might. Even history books aren't certain if this was a namesake."

"And Empress Aratra?" Valdemar asked with a frown. "I know she invented the Bloodstream network of Earthmouths in 18 BE and then proceeded to conquer the human enclaves in the War of Unification."

"Which was the first time the term 'Dark Lords' appeared in historical records. In fact, the title belonged to the sorcerer-kings who pledged to unify mankind under Aratra's leadership." Marianne put her cup aside. "Official records say that the empress was born in the flames of the Sack of Nielson during the First Dokkar Wars in 191 BE, leading mankind to victory at the age of sixteen in 175 BE."

Waves crashed against the window outside, though no water touched the glass.

"All of this to say that however ancient they are, the Dark Lords appeared long after the Whitemoon's arrival," Marianne explained. "As for the Church of the Light, although it was already a major underground faith, it was only officially consolidated into the organization we know today in 24 AE. There is no mention of a 'Sophia' in the scriptures, and the faith generally considers the First Enlightened One, Marcel Moonstone, as its true founder."

"You have done your research," Valdemar said with an amused smile. "I didn't expect such a wealth of details."

Marianne blushed a little. "I should have spent more time reading magic than history and religious books."

"All knowledge is useful," he replied before squinting. "If it's not too private . . . Do you believe in the Light?"

"Yes," Marianne confirmed with a nod. If anything, facing the likes of Shelley had only strengthened her faith. "Although I don't support the inquisitors' zeal and witch hunts, the Church has lighted my way many times. Lord Och's tale is unlike anything I've heard before, heretical even."

"Yet I suspect that for all the embellishments and possible falsehoods, there is a nugget of truth in it." Valdemar scratched the back of his head. "Who else but Lord Och and Empress Aratra were among the original Dark Lords?"

"Only Lord Och and Empress Aratra successfully defended their titles from death and usurpers. As for the nature of their immortality, one is a lich, and the other keeps the secret of her eternal youth well-hidden."

"And who writes the history books you've been reading?"

Marianne smiled as her partner had put his finger on the root of the problem. "The Knights of the Chain."

"An order that infamously burns books spreading 'dangerous' ideas and imprisons free-thinkers like yours truly," Valdemar replied while returning her smile. "Are there any living or undead witnesses to the era before the empire still at large?"

Marianne considered the question. The Oldblood nobility in Saklas had earned its peerage by supporting the Empress during the War of Unification. However, Aratra's inner circle was a tight-knit community that rarely left the confines of Saklas' imperial palace and faced increasing competition from new generations of sorcerers.

"Some of Empress Aratra's officers have survived as undead since the empire's inception," she replied. "But I don't think any of them predated its foundation by much. Lord Och invented soulstones, making mass-producing sentient undead possible in 39 BE, and I think vampires emerged long afterward."

"Which would leave Lord Och and Empress Aratra as the only survivors of the ancient era. They could have easily rewritten history and doctored official documents to hide their true origins."

"Even if they modified human history, Hermann himself confirmed that the first humans learned the Blood from troglodyte shamans," Marianne pointed out. "The Empire has absolute dominion over its texts, true, but troglodyte tribes keep their own records. So do the dokkars."

"The Nightwalker showed that there are other forms of magic than the Blood," Valdemar added. "This Sophia, if she truly existed, might have used another. It might also explain Empress Aratra's immortality."

"Even if part of the story is true, how does it help us right now? I support solving the mysteries of our past, but we have more pressing problems right now."

Valdemar played with his cup. "Finding the truth about that story could help us deal with Ialdabaoth."

Marianne put two and two together. "Ah, I see. You're thinking about the wards keeping Ialdabaoth imprisoned. If Lord Och's story is partly correct, then they were put in place by a rival entity. The more they weaken, the more Ialdabaoth's power grows."

"This being probably used a different magic than the Blood. If we could reverse-engineer the spell, then strengthening the wards to keep Ialdabaoth asleep would become a genuine possibility."

"If we can use this magic at all." Marianne stroked her chin thoughtfully. "If the Light could truly empower its worshipers, why does only the Blood hold sway in our world? Because of the 'unspeakable crime' that the Dark Lords committed?"

"I don't know," Valdemar replied with a sigh. "And I don't know where to look for answers either. Maybe I should ask Hermann and Frigga to compare their historical records with ours."

"The archives in the Pleroma Institute should have what we need," Marianne suggested. "They are only accessible by Masters and high-ranking members of the Knights of the Tome, but they include a copy of all imperial texts, including original, uncensored volumes. If you could convince Lord Och to give you permission—"

The room trembled, the duo's cups falling off the table and breaking on the floor. The tea inside evaporated instantly into fine particles alongside their containers' parts. The music stopped, drowned out by an alien cry.

Valdemar leaped to his feet and rushed to the window, opening the curtains to gaze at the ocean beyond. "Are you kidding me?" he muttered in astonishment. "*Again*?"

Marianne joined him, and immediately covered her mouth to hide her laughter at the sight.

An enormous Ktulu, larger than the Pleroma Institute, cried in the middle of the imaginary ocean. His squamous hands held the remains of a broken ship against his chest, while shards of the vessels sank below the waves. The giant's six eyes let out a flood of tears.

Valdemar put his palm over his face in embarrassment. "Even in our dreams, he still finds ways to break his toys."

"How many does that make?" Marianne asked with a wide grin as she rested her hands against the window's stool. "If we count the ones in the waking world?"

Valdemar had made a habit of turning his bones into makeshift toy ships for his familiar to play with, but none of them lasted for long.

"I've lost count," Valdemar sighed as he turned his gaze back to the ocean. The strange Nightmare of Kazat could be seen deep below the dark water, a sunken city buried underneath a sea of dreams. "Thankfully, the ocean's level doesn't rise with his cries."

"I wish I could dream him a replacement ship," Marianne confessed as she watched the depressed familiar in the distance. Though she had knowledge of oneiromancy, she was more comfortable with raising mental fortresses than weaving dreamboats into existence. "I'm still sorry for turning your dreamscape into my apartment. This was the shape I was most comfortable with."

"It's fine, and way better than the wasteland that came before." Valdemar looked at the depressed Ktulu cradling the ship with a deep sigh. "I'm sadder that my familiar has more power over the Primordial Dream than I do."

"The fact he can interact with the dreamworld at all means he has nothing to do with the Qlippoths," Marianne reassured him. "And you have an additional guardian."

Despite her words, Marianne felt Ktulu might cause more trouble than he would solve. She certainly hadn't expected the familiar to take the form of a giant in the dreamworld rather than the manageable baby he was in the flesh. Even the ocean surrounding the apartments was the creature's doing rather than Marianne's.

"I could conjure decorations more to your liking," Marianne suggested to Valdemar.

"Don't bother. I would rather learn to create dream objects by myself." Valdemar gritted his teeth as he raised his hand toward a corner of the room. Perhaps he was trying to create a new shelf or a painting. Whatever the case, he failed. "Though it may take a while."

Marianne watched him exhaust himself for a moment, before moving behind and putting her hands on his shoulders. The sudden physical contact left him startled, but he didn't push her away. Marianne herself wouldn't have tried if they hadn't grown comfortable in each other's presence.

"Close your eyes," the noblewoman said softly, and though he looked doubtful, her friend followed her advice. "Think of home."

"Home?"

"Home." The idea of home helped Marianne focus on her dreams, though it still saddened her that her apartment in Pleroma felt a safer sanctuary than her family manor.

Valdemar's expression twisted into a frown. "I don't have one."

"You're wrong. Home is not a place, it's a feeling. It's the music that makes you feel at peace, the smell of familiarity, the people you want to share your life with and the objects that symbolize their affection for you. Now think of what brings you that feeling."

Valdemar listened to her words, his face relaxing. He waved his hand at an empty spot and Marianne watched as the dream answered his desire. The substance of the dreamscape shifted, the floor turning muddy as the very plane resisted his influence. Marianne's oneiromancy teachers would have shaken their head at the poor display, but the noblewoman had faith in her friend.

And her trust paid off. The dream's substance gathered into a new shape as Valdemar commanded. His mother's music box appeared out of thin air while singing a lullaby.

"See?" Marianne whispered. Valdemar opened his eyes and stared at the box in surprise. "It wasn't so hard."

Though he was half a Stranger, it was the other half that counted. Valdemar would never be a good oneiromancer or mind-mage, but he wasn't a hopeless case either.

"It was hard, but easier than I thought," Valdemar replied as he looked at the box. "I could never do that with Frigga."

"You had just arrived in an unfamiliar land," Marianne said as she removed her hands from his shoulders. "You were still struggling to find your bearings. I don't think it's a coincidence you managed to summon your mother's music box after getting proof that she truly loved you."

"Yes . . . but I think I feel more comfortable with your guidance than Frigga's." He smiled warmly at her. "You're starting to feel like home too."

Marianne met his gaze without a word, unsure what to answer to that. *Is . . . is he making a pass at me?* the noblewoman wondered. And if he was . . . "As a friend, you mean?"

"Yes, as a friend, of course," Valdemar said quickly as he realized his behavior's implications. Marianne couldn't believe someone so brilliant could be so oblivious. "I mean, I let Frigga in because I needed to, but with you . . . I did it because I trust you as much as Hermann and Liliane now."

"Yes, I . . . I figured as much," Marianne replied, her own awkward tone surprising her. Why was her voice trembling? "You are a friend as well."

Marianne felt almost thankful as another tremor shook the dreamscape and interrupted this awkward moment. "Is it Ktulu again?" Valdemar wondered as he looked through the window, only to find his familiar still cradling his broken ship.

"No, it's outside," Marianne replied as the tremors grew stronger and more frequent. "We have to wake up."

Valdemar answered with a short nod and the dreamscape collapsed around them. Marianne woke up in a bunk bed below her partner's, sharing a cramped iron room in the heart of Lord Bethor's Excavator.

Ktulu slept soundly against his summoner's chest, his tentacles wriggling as he snored.

Quickly putting on her armor and grabbing her weapons, Marianne opened the bedroom's door to find Knights of the Shroud rushing through the corridors. "Are we under attack?" she asked.

"Not yet," an undead swordsman replied without sparing her a glance, "but we have pierced through fortifications of some kind. Prepare for battle."

He didn't need to tell her. Marianne always slept with her weapons within arm's reach.

Valdemar quickly joined her with his awful mask on, keeping the sleeping Ktulu in his bag. They went to Lord Och's room for answers. The lich met them in the hallway.

"We are going to climb down from this ship now," the Dark Lord rasped as he guided them toward the tail of the Excavator. Her True Sight allowed Marianne to see his true skeletal self and the thin mist that surrounded his ancient bones. Was Lord Och truly older than the Descent? "Lord Bethor's weapon will soon become the target of enemy attack. It would be a bother if we were caught in the crossfire, and we can walk to our destination."

"What kind of fortification have we gone through?" Marianne asked. To her surprise, Valdemar seemed awfully quiet and tense.

"A metal shell of some kind." Lord Och stopped before the same blast door they had used to enter the Excavator. Two Knights of the Shroud were in the process of opening it already, while four more waited nearby. "I'm afraid the Excavator will not stop for our little group, so I will teleport us and a small contingent of troops to the ground."

"You can teleport without lacing an area with your blood?" Valdemar asked.

"All of Underland is one through the Blood, my student," Lord Och replied. "It is no different than the method your worshipers use to move around, although I am limited to my line of sight."

Marianne was thankful for it. Considering the speed at which it moved, jumping from the Excavator while it was on the move would be risky even with body enhancements.

The moment the blast door opened, the group held hands with Lord Och and the six Knights of the Shroud present as space twisted around them. The teleportation lasted for but an instant, but Marianne's enhanced sight noticed every detail, every crack in the fabric of space. She watched thick black blood spread around her to form a tunnel between the group's current position and the darkness outside the Excavator, absorbing the kinetic energy to make the transition as seamless as possible.

It is everywhere, not just in the walls, Marianne realized. The tunnels were Ialdabaoth's arteries and the very air she breathed was tainted by its influence.

When the spell completed, the group had landed in a vast tunnel with a dizzyingly tall ceiling. A thick sheet of black metal with strange golden lines covered every spot of stone as far as Marianne's eyes could see, radiating a faint glow keeping the area in a dim light. The air smelled of rust and oil; the floor was as cold as ice. Besides the grinding sound of the Excavator digging its way through the tunnel's walls to make a new path for itself, Marianne didn't hear a sound. Nothing but the echo of pumps and grinding gears.

Lord Bethor's machine kept digging its way into a wall before them, melting its surface and shaking the ceiling as it continued its journey. Though metal proved harder to drill through than stone, the Excavator still cut through it like a knife through butter and forced a way forward. The machine quickly disappeared from the group's view, though they still felt the tremors it caused.

Marianne glanced at the open path the Excavator left behind. The machine had pierced through a similar tunnel's walls before, leaving only a hole of molten steel behind; in a way, the Excavator had turned the place into a crossroad. Darkness covered everything beyond this point, but the group should be able to walk all the way back to Sabaoth from this point. No doubt human troops would soon arrive to claim the area before the derros arrived.

"There are no eyes," Valdemar whispered as he looked around. The metal covering the walls also obscured Ialdabaoth's flesh. "No eyes."

Marianne unsheathed her rapier and cocked her revolver as she confirmed his words, while their knightly escort prepared themselves for an ambush. "There are no derros either."

Even if they had bypassed the derro army's usual choke points, guards should have swarmed these tunnels upon hearing the Excavator's approach. Nor did the noblewoman see any mushrooms or bats. The area felt as dead and lifeless as a clock's inner mechanisms.

"Establish a defensive perimeter and check our surroundings," one of the Knights ordered his five fellows as they spread across the crossroads of tunnels. The soldiers immediately drew summoning circles on the ground and called a small swarm of grotesquely large flies, before having them spread through the tunnels.

"How curious," Lord Och said as he examined the golden lines running through the steel walls. "What a strange apparatus this is."

Marianne approached her gloved hand from the surface, and immediately took a step back as she felt a jolt. "Lightning courses through them, Lord Och."

"In the same direction as our destination too." The lich stroked his skeletal chin while muttering to himself. Marianne hadn't seen him so interested since Valdemar's initiation test. "I see. No doubt a portal would demand an enormous amount of power, too much to be manufactured in one place . . . fascinating . . ."

"Lord Och, we shouldn't stay here," Marianne warned. She knew that the Dark Lord could get so engrossed in his interests that he neglected the world around them. "Reinforcements might come at any moment. We should stay on the move."

"Patience, young Marianne," the Dark Lord replied as the Knights' fly swarms returned to them. The summoned insects buzzed in a language Marianne couldn't understand before dissipating into smoke. "So the way is safe?"

"The derro garrisons should have established choke points further south, my lord." The knight-commander straightened up, his soulbound sword firmly in hand. "But Lady Reynard is right, it is only a matter of hours before troops come to check on the commotion. Shall we escort you and your student to your destination?"

"Young Marianne will suffice to protect us," the Dark Lord replied with absolute confidence. Even though she wasn't certain if he meant it or not, the noblewoman found the lich's response flattering. "You shall fortify this area and make sure that our dwarf neighbors do not attack us from the rear."

"Very well, we shall await your return." The knight-commander turned to his troops and instantly barked orders at them. "Summon earth elementals and raise fortifications. I want the derros to fight for every patch of ground."

After watching his ally's troops with a hint of amusement, Lord Och turned to face Marianne and Valdemar. "Now come, children. Let's not waste precious time."

Leaving the Excavator's holes behind, the group followed the lines deeper into the metal tunnel while the Knights fortified the choke point behind them. Only the noise of their breathing and footsteps echoed around the group, while the tremors grew weaker and eventually vanished. The golden lines' glow allowed them to see a few meters ahead of them, but little more.

Marianne focused as she walked, ready to strike at the first sign of ambush. Her enhanced sense of touch and hearing allowed her to visualize her surroundings, to sense the cables inside the walls. Oil coursed through pipes below the floor and grinding gears turned above her head, their noise muffled by the steel shielding.

"These aren't fortifications," Marianne whispered in case anyone listened. She didn't understand half of what the hidden devices in the walls did, and she worried that the derros could hear their words. "This is a mechanism of colossal size."

"An infection of metal in the flesh," Valdemar whispered back. "Like in the Outer Darkness."

"Altering the body shouldn't affect dreams." Unlike his two protégés, Lord Och made no effort to lower his tone. "Unless, of course, this apparatus's main goal is to attack the nervous system with machinery."

"Was that why the derros stole brains?" Valdemar asked. "To understand how our minds worked and use this insight to affect Ialdabaoth? What purpose would it serve?"

"Who knows? As I told you once, Otto Blutgang is a rare genius whose mind works on a different level than common mortals'. He plays for higher stakes than conquest."

The admiration in his voice surprised Marianne, who had grown used to backhanded compliments at best. "What stakes, my lord?"

"If I had to guess . . ." Lord Och chuckled. "I would say *transcendence*."

"Transcendence?" Valdemar asked, but the lich only answered with a chuckle.

Transcendence? From what, the mortal condition? Derros couldn't use the Blood, so the path of undeath was closed to them. Was their king trying to achieve immortality through technological means instead?

How long had they walked through this tunnel without encountering anyone? Minutes? Hours? While Marianne and Valdemar were tense, Lord Och spent his time gazing at the strange lines along the walls with a thoughtful look. An outsider would have mistaken him for a researcher on a stroll through a garden of exotic flora rather than an archmage infiltrating enemy territory. *This is what absolute power looks like,* Marianne thought. *The easy confidence of invulnerability.*

As she focused on her sense of touch and echolocation, Marianne noticed subtle oddities in the metal. Small islands of glass in a sea of steel, hidden from view in the darkness outside the glow of the golden lines.

"Look," Marianne warned as she pointed her sword at an imperceptible orb of stained glass growing out of the steel. "A machine eye of some kind."

"It's not alive," Valdemar confirmed, slightly unnerved by the device. "And I see others in the darkness."

"They know we are here," Lord Och replied before mockingly waving a hand at the glass eye. "Please be a good guest and say hello."

Valdemar pointed a finger at the glass eye and blasted it to pieces with a blood bullet. Shards fell on the ground, and Marianne heard a subtle clicking noise echo through the tunnel.

No derro came to intercept them, but the glass eyes always watched them. Marianne could feel their gaze all around her. The feeling was different from the fleshy, alien eyes of Underland, which lacked reason and intelligence. These glass devices had been made with mortal hands, and Marianne was certain that something cold and calculating watched the intruders through them.

"Why don't they intercept us?" Valdemar whispered, just as unnerved as she was.

"They want us to move forward," Marianne whispered with a frown. Somehow, she would rather have faced opposition. This whole journey reeked of a trap. "If anything happens, move behind me. Lord Och will revive no matter what happens, but if the situation degenerates beyond control, retreat to the checkpoint while I cover your rear."

"I can defend myself," her partner replied, "and I won't leave you behind. We either leave this place together or not at all."

Though his concern touched Marianne, she squinted at him in disapproval. "What good is a bodyguard whose charge runs heedlessly into danger?"

"You are more than a bodyguard to me."

I trust you as much as Hermann and Liliane now.

Marianne should have rejoiced at these words. So why did they leave her feeling *disappointed*? *I can't think like this,* the noblewoman told herself. She and Valdemar had grown to trust each other, but anything more would interfere with her duties.

Eventually, their long walk ended before a fortified steel gate not unlike those in Lord Bethor's tower. A strange window of glass stood above the threshold, but it led to nowhere. Nor did any guard watch over this obvious checkpoint.

Marianne put a hand on the door's surface, trying to guess its thickness with her enhanced touch. "At least two meters in depth," she said. "I can't sense anything beyond."

"Do not fret," Lord Och replied as he looked at the windows. "They will welcome us soon enough."

Click.

Click.

Click.

Marianne raised her revolver at the window while Valdemar prepared to cast a spell at any moment. Glass eyes turned to gaze at them in the darkness and the golden lines turned red.

The window glowed. Its glass surface projected distorted colors and images. A shadowy humanoid figure appeared in the middle of a white glow tainted by gray lines. A buzzing sound erupted from the window, half a screech and half a whisper.

What spell is this? Marianne wondered, slightly disturbed as the figure's features distorted uncontrollably. *An illusion? No, I should have seen through it . . . this is real. But I don't sense any sorcery at all. It's not a phantom projector either . . .*

Red lightning coursed through the walls' lines and the door rose with a thunderous noise.

Marianne immediately moved in front of her charges, weapons raised at the gates. As this steel curtain slowly rose, she expected to face an army of golems and derros on the other side.

But no enemy waited beyond the threshold.

As the path lay open before her, the distorted figure at the glass window vanished. Lamps lit up beyond the door, revealing a lengthy corridor.

"Trap?" Valdemar asked warily.

"Worse," Lord Och replied. His jovial demeanor had abated, replaced with caution. "An invitation."

8

THE IRON KING

The derro facility had fallen into a state of disrepair. An overwhelming stench of putrefaction went hand in hand with the smell of alchemical reagents. The sprawling chambers of metals had grown dark and unwelcoming, as strange crystal lamps flickered above the group's heads. The ceiling, adapted for the dwarf-like derros rather than taller humans, was low enough that Valdemar's hair grazed against it. The sorcerer couldn't help but feel a sense of claustrophobic unease as he followed Marianne through narrow corridors.

What happened here? Valdemar wondered. Half the pipes running along the metal walls were leaking either steam or oil. Shattered pylons lay broken on the ground next to dried residues of alien, unknowable origin. And the brown traces on the floor weren't rust, but dried blood.

"The door closed behind us," Marianne warned ahead of him. She had put her revolver back around her belt, keeping a hand free. "I heard it in the distance."

"I am disappointed by the absence of a welcoming committee," Lord Och mused at the group's back. "I expected at least one ambush or a trap, if only for protocol's sake."

Valdemar noticed that Ktulu was growing agitated in his bag. The Haunter disguised as his shadow flickered. They sensed something wrong in the vicinity, a force that startled them. "Someone's watching us," the sorcerer muttered under his breath.

"Not *us*," Marianne warned. "The glass eyes are everywhere, hidden in the dark or so small you cannot see them . . . but they're only staring at *you*, Valdemar."

The old Valdemar would have been disturbed, but by now he had grown numb to such things. *What does that say about me?* he wondered. *Is it paranoia if everyone is out to get you?*

The corridor led them to a dark chamber larger than any other before, and the stench of mold joined that of putrefaction. Unlike the previous areas, this place had a higher ceiling, adapted to a human's size. One look was enough to tell Valdemar the horrifying reason.

Broken glass devices provided what little glow illuminated the laboratory. Oil dripped from the ceiling, the drops hitting the cold metal floor with a ticking sound. Preserved organ samples, from spleens to blackened hearts, were lined up on a metal table covered in a layer of infectious mold. And along the walls were the donors.

The sight almost made Valdemar vomit. A dozen naked humans, both men and women, had been impaled on biomechanical spikes. The disgusting contraptions had skewered them like pieces of meat on a food stand, piercing through their ass and erupting from their open mouth. Cables connected their exposed skulls to the devices, while the contents of their rib cages were left exposed. Fungal growth had devoured most of their insides, leaving only dead husks behind.

The four derro surgeons responsible for this horror show weren't in better shape. Their dismembered corpses had been scattered around the room. One had been cleaved in half at the waist, the torso and legs piled up on a human corpse like a twisted fish skewer. Another had been hit so hard in the chest that the blow turned the ribs and organs to a bloody soup. Only one was relatively intact, his throat slashed and eyes removed.

And the cherry on top of the disastrous sight, an iron golem's remains sat in a corner, the brain powering it splattered against a closed metal door.

"What is this . . ." Marianne covered her mouth as she looked at the ghastly spectacle. Valdemar pitied her. He already found the scene disturbing and horrifying, but his partner's enhanced sight allowed her to see every gory detail. "What . . ."

"Mmm." Lord Och alone didn't seem concerned as he examined the impaler spikes more closely. "This is a new design."

Even though he had seen worse at the bottom of Lord Bethor's tower, the scene disturbed Valdemar. It wasn't the sight of rotten meat and dismembered corpses that bothered him, but the implications of the scene. The massacre reeked of a cold-blooded, intellectual brutality; of a clinical sadism laced with an odious kind of curiosity. It hadn't been enough to kill. The victims had to suffer first.

"Are you alright?" Valdemar asked Marianne with concern upon seeing her unease.

"It's . . . No, Valdemar, I'm not alright." She shook her head, her fingers tightening her grip on her rapier. "An inquisitor told me once that he turned undead because the job never got easier. I understand what he meant now."

"And he made the right choice," Lord Och commented with cold nonchalance. "Undeath teaches emotional distance."

Ignoring the Dark Lord, Valdemar put a hand on Marianne's shoulder. "Maybe you could cast an illusion on yourself," he suggested, trying to help. "Weaken your enhanced senses, filter out the horror."

"I appreciate the thought, but I can't." Marianne gently removed his hand and tried to smile. "I can't lower my guard in this place. Your life, and mine, depend on it."

She's brave, Valdemar thought as he answered with a nod. "Let's figure out what happened before moving on then," he said. "Whatever killed these derros might still be around."

"Most wise, my apprentice." Lord Och waved a hand at Valdemar. "Come over here."

While Marianne moved to study the derro corpses, Valdemar joined his teacher in examining the biomechanical spikes. On closer look, the sorcerer noticed that the cables piercing the victims' skulls interconnected with the dead gray matter inside.

"I do not have your experience with derro tech," Lord Och admitted, "but I have an inkling of this device's purpose. What do you think?"

"It's a neural connection device," Valdemar identified, thanks to his knowledge of biomancy and derro tech. "It's the same system that allows the derros to put brains in jars or command golems from afar."

But why connect a dying man to a torture device? To record his agony?

"Look at these," Marianne said as she pointed at the most well-preserved of the derro corpses. Her gloved hand trailed against the slashed throat and then the empty eye sockets. "While the lethal wounds were sloppy, the eyes were extracted with methodical, surgical precision. Some of them premortem."

Valdemar shivered at the implications. Even though he hated derros after seeing their ghastly work in Astaphanos, he didn't wish such a fate on anyone. "What purpose would it serve to harvest the eyes before death? If that was the goal, killing the derros first would have prevented a struggle."

"You forget the simplest explanation," Lord Och said with a flat tone. "That there was no practical purpose but self-gratification."

These murders had been carried out not out of a need for survival, but out of *sadism*.

"Did they do it to themselves?" Valdemar asked as he glared at the derros' remains. "They grow bored of torturing our kind and moved on to attack each other?"

"No," Lord Och replied as he pointed a finger in the broken golem's direction. "This machine was physically shoved against a wall. I have yet to see a derro with the strength to do that. Only a warbeast or a powerful golem could have achieved such a feat."

Marianne tensed up. "One of their experiments escaped?"

"Perhaps, young Marianne. The surgical operation you noticed implies a higher intelligence than a savage beast, so we must remain on our guard." Lord Och stroked his chin. "Have we been invited for cleanup duty, I wonder?"

"Or the figure on the projector we saw was the creature responsible for the slaughter," Valdemar pointed out.

"No, it wasn't." Lord Och chuckled. "Though it was vague, I recognized the body shape. That kind of wasted effort would be unusual for *him*."

Valdemar examined his master. He had grown to know the lich over the last few months, and he knew very well how little Lord Och cared about others.

To a Dark Lord, there was only one derro worthy of remembrance.

But why would he be here, in a destroyed facility?

"Kthulhu." Valdemar tensed as he heard his familiar grumble in the bag. "Fagthna."

Valdemar was about to ask his partner what was up, before sensing something in the air. So did Marianne, who immediately looked around. A tension spread through the room, an invisible jolt coursing through the steel.

"Lightning," Marianne whispered. "I sense electricity in the air."

"Ktulhulu!" By now, Ktulu was growing downright panicked.

"We have to go," Valdemar warned as he looked for the exit. "Quickly!"

"It's not magic," Lord Och said with a hint of curiosity. "I wonder if—"

The world vanished in a bright flash of lightning.

When Valdemar regained his sense of sight, he was in another room altogether.

The torture chamber had been transformed into a laboratory. Glass tanks full of brains floating in green liquid had replaced the iron spikes. The incomplete torso and head of a clockwork golem sat on a strange chair in their midst, its head a pincushion mass of needles and cables. Crystals on the ceiling provided clear, pulsating light, while strange turbines thrummed along the walls. Four narrow doors, all equipped with glass projectors, stood at each corner of the chamber.

"Marianne?" Valdemar called as he looked around. "Lord Och?"

"Ktulu?" Ktulu asked from inside the bag, his head peeking out to look around. "Ktulhuly?"

"Is this an illusion?" Valdemar activated his psychic sight as he observed his surroundings. He didn't detect either of his allies in the vicinity. Had he been teleported to another area of the facility? But how? He hadn't sensed any spell, any magic brushing against his defense!

Valdemar could only see one explanation. Somehow, the derros had managed to replicate the teleportation spell with techno—

"Valdemar?"

The familiar voice made Valdemar flinch. The sorcerer glanced at the noise's source, dumbstruck.

"Thank the Light you're here." The sitting golem's two glass eyes made a screeching sound as they glanced at Valdemar. "You took your sweet time."

Valdemar stared at the machine in incomprehension. He didn't sense any hint of life in the broken, incomplete metal husk. Not even a brain to animate it. As far as his psychic sight was concerned, he was facing a lifeless pile of junk.

"What are you?" Valdemar whispered.

"What are you talking about, friend?" the golem asked, though it had no mouth to speak with. A strange form of derro tech produced the illusion of a voice. "Help me get out of here. I can't feel my arms and legs."

"What are you?" Valdemar repeated, more and more disturbed.

A short silence followed. The creature's glass eyes stared blankly at Valdemar, while electricity traveled through the needles embedded in its head.

"It's me, Iren," the golem replied with the tone an adult would use to speak to a slow child. "Look, can we play twenty questions after we've left this place? The derros might return anytime."

Valdemar didn't answer right away, as his mind struggled to process this strange situation. The more he considered it, the more he asked himself existential questions. Was it a mind trick? Or a terrifying answer to the question of what made a human *human*?

"What's the name of the biomancer," Valdemar asked slowly. "The one who experimented on you?"

"How do you know that? Did Och tell you?" The voice turned angry and disappointed. "That old bastard, I should never have trusted him."

I heard these lines before, Valdemar realized. "You told me yourself, Iren."

"I don't think we're close enough to."

Definitely pre-hospital, Valdemar thought, his fists tightening. The pylons. Must have been the pylons.

Was that why they had blasted Valdemar with lightning? Not to kill him, but to *understand* him?

"Look, we can discuss that after we get out of this place alive," the deluded golem insisted. "I can't move, so you'll have to carry me back outside. Do you know if the Knights are coming? This place is crawling with—"

"Enough." Valdemar glanced at the projector above one of the doors and noticed a glass eye embedded in it. "That's what you were trying to figure out, isn't it? What makes a human *human*? How do minds and souls work? Your experiments must have been pretty advanced if you could make a copy of Iren's brain from his brief detainment in your lab."

"What the hell are y-y-y-y-y-y-y-o-o-o . . ." The golem's words dragged on, its speech stuttering and slurring. Electricity once again coursed through its head, before the sentence died incomplete.

A droning noise filled the room, as the glass screen above the door lit up. A shadowy figure appeared on its surface, surrounded by bright light. After one last glance at the deactivated golem, Valdemar stepped in front of the door and looked up at the glass eye.

"W-w-what is it that you *fear*?" The voice was cold, booming, and reverberating. The words broke and stuttered, as the machinery struggled to translate thoughts into speech. "Humiliation? Physical pain? Heights? I-I-I only feared one thing, and that was *de-e-a-ath*." The glass eye rotated above the projector. "The loss of my memories, of my experience and intellect vanishing into nothingness. The end of my beautiful ex-ex-existence."

"Is that why you connected yourself to the impaled victims?" Valdemar asked. That madman had done it often enough to receive a nickname out of it. "So you could experience death through another's eyes?"

"Theories require empi-pi-pirical testing for con-confirmation. I have dreamed and died ten thousand lives."

Dreams.

"It has bugged me for a while. Why your kind cannot dream, when all life in Underland can." Valdemar had had the feeling that the derros' inability to use the Blood or dream was part of a bigger picture, and he reached a conclusion. "You derros have *minds*, but no *souls*. That's why you cannot dream or use the Blood. Both imply a connection to Ialdabaoth, and the Pleromians didn't create you with one."

"S-so close and yet so fa-a-a-ar . . ." The figure on the screen twisted and flickered before returning to normal. "The Pleromians did not create us. They *called* us."

Ktulu's head perked up behind Valdemar, while the pieces of the puzzle fell into place.

"'They shouldn't be affected, but they have been here for a while,'" Valdemar quoted Master Loctis and Lord Och. Their discussion suddenly made more sense. "You were summoned to serve as slaves by the Pleromians, but you've spent too much time in Underland."

"We did not have souls, but we-we-we are starting to . . ." The figure confirmed. "The corru-ru-ruption is reaching out everywhere. To all creatures walking across the planet. Trying to pre-prepare life for ass-similation."

"Is that why you experimented with portal technology?" Valdemar asked, frowning behind his mask. "To return home before Ialdabaoth wakes up?"

"D-d-do you wish to know? To se-see?"

Valdemar gathered his breath. "Yes." He knew that discovery would come at a heavy cost, but he hadn't come this far to return empty-handed.

The door below the projector opened, and Valdemar stepped through it without hesitation. What lay beyond the threshold was a derro tech replica of the vault underneath the Pleroma Institute: a colossal dome of steel whose ceiling shimmered with golden lines. A twisted, colossal archway of steel and wires stood at the middle of the chamber. Pulses of lightning raced through its crude mechanical structure, while the device thrummed with a droning noise. This wasn't a Pleromian Gate, but an effective imitation.

The moment Valdemar laid his eyes on it, he realized that he stood before the portal that had brought his grandfather to Underland.

Unlike Lord Och's vault, this dome had another piece of furniture standing before the gate. A throne of metal and steaming pipes, occupied by a derro with hair as black as night and an unnaturally smooth face. The metal circlet around his head pulsated with energy, illuminating unblinking blue eyes. In them, Valdemar saw a glimpse of a dangerous mind, brilliant and mad in equal measure. A strange suit made of a black, elastic substance covered all of his body except for the head.

"I have studied your progress with great interest, anomaly. Your ecto-catcher was an innovative invention." Valdemar's host rose from his throne as he introduced himself. "I am Otto Blutgang, Godmind of Derrokind."

Alias Otto the Demented.

Alias Otto the Nail.

"Show your true self," Valdemar replied coldly as he faced the creature. "I know you aren't really here." His psychic sight sent him the same feedback as the broken golem outside. He didn't sense any blood coursing through the derro's veins, or any trace of flesh for that matter. Even the lifelike eyes were made of colored glass.

Otto Blutgang's smirk turned predatory as he raised his left hand over his face. His fingers sunk into his forehead's skin and swiftly tore it down. Half of a mask fell to the ground.

"I-I-Is that better now?" the derro king asked as he stuttered again. Half his face covered in false skin; the other in metal bones and wires. "Do you feel more com-comfortable?"

As Valdemar had guessed, this body was just a proxy, a mechanical puppet commanded from afar. As for *how* . . .

Ktulu had fallen silent in his bag and glared at the derro king with all six of his eyes over Valdemar's shoulder. Whatever Otto Blutgang had become, Valdemar's familiar considered it as threatening as a Dark Lord.

"Where are my companions?" Valdemar asked bluntly as he prepared to cast an offensive spell if he didn't like the answer. Lord Och would be fine thanks to his immortality, but he couldn't say the same for Marianne. "What have you done with them?"

"N-n-nothing. I care n-n-not for them. They are s-s-safe . . . for now."

A little blood dripped from Valdemar's fingers, ready to lash out. "Are you threatening me?"

"Must I?" The derro king looked at Valdemar with what could pass for puzzlement. "We are si-si-similar beings whose interests align, anomaly."

Similar beings?

"What are you?" Valdemar asked. "Not a derro anymore, from what I can gather."

"My greatest desire was to increase the intellectual capacity of my species. Unfortunately, the p-p-percentage of intellects worthy of preservation is pitifully low. All this neural processing power, wasted on vacuous personalities and base animal instincts. Rather than educate my countrymen, upgrading their mental faculties through overwriting seemed a more sensible solution."

"You wanted to overwrite the minds of your compatriots with *your own*?" Valdemar asked while staring at this narcissistic king in disbelief.

"Anomaly, the only way to save your species from idiocy-induced extinction is to practice intellectual eugenics. Your society will be way more optimi-mi-mized once you have weeded out weaker minds and repurposed their wasted gray matter with a su-su-superior personality matrix."

The chilling thing was that he believed every word he spoke. Valdemar could tell from his self-righteous, matter-of-fact tone. His sheer egomania made the Dark Lords look humble.

"But even the plasticity of a normal derro brain could not support my overflow-owing intellect," Otto Blutgang explained. "They could support spe-specialized thrall personalities, but a single nervous system was not en-nough for me . . ."

The derros probably couldn't handle an ego that large. He still brainwashed his entire race, Valdemar thought. *And all of this sounds . . . pre-planned.*

"After countless iterations, I haavee transcendeddd . . ." A burst of electricity briefly surged from Otto's facial wires. "I have transcended the limits of the cerebral prison and become a being of p-p-pure intellect. A stream of thoughts and mathematics, the perfect complexity of a Godmind."

The derro king had integrated his soul into his own machinery. Not quite a lich, not quite undead. A genius loci of wires and lightning, a self-replicating mind inhabiting both flesh and steel.

And then the full scale of the derro king's ambition became clear to Valdemar, as he remembered his trip in the Outer Darkness and the invasive machinery within.

"You want to overwrite Ialdabaoth," the sorcerer guessed, hardly believing his own words. "To replace its mind with your own and become a god."

Valdemar expected the derro king to reply with a flat yes, but the answer was somehow even more chilling.

"Possible, but infeasible. I have dis-discarded this possibility in favor of crea-creating my own improved, circuitry-based vessel."

Otto Blutgang wasn't trying to replace Ialdabaoth. He wanted to become a better version, one made of wires and steel rather than flesh and blood.

We were walking inside his bloodstream, Valdemar realized. Inside veins of metal and iron innards.

"Thi-i-is a long-term objective, fraught with peril," Otto Blutgang said. "In the meantime, the portal project must continue. I need you to sta-stabilize it."

"So you may send a copy of yourself out there in case Ialdabaoth wakes up before you can take over the world?" Valdemar glared at this maniac. "How did you know I would come here? Have you been spying on me?"

The derro king locked eyes with his guest.

"I have been watching your line since be-be-before you were even *born*," he said, his eyes shining with mania. "D-d-do you think your grandfather and his p-p-platoon could have made their way to your p-p-pathetic civilization without *my* permission?"

Valdemar flinched, his blood boiling. "My grandfather didn't remember," the sorcerer said, his voice laced with burning rage. "I thought it was the shock of crossing worlds, but it was *you*. *You* erased his memories of his abduction!"

"Your ex-existence was unplanned, anomaly, but I f-f-followed your genetic lineage's progress for research," Otto replied, his wires wriggling like rotting worms. "I calculated a sev-seventy-three percent chance that you would investigate this portal and your origins. I l-l-laid the groundwork for your arrival. No-o-ow we will help each other."

"Why would I help *you*?" Valdemar hissed through his teeth. "It's not just about the portal, is it? It's too much work to bring me here just to help you open a door back to your species' home."

"If you do not help me, your ov-ovulation machine will die."

The blood dripping from Valdemar's hands turned into small, boiling tentacles.

"Have I misunderstood? From your do-do-dopamine ratio, I assumed she was distracting you with her womanly pheromones. Be-between us, the thought of being seduced by a female neocortex fills me with dis-disgust. Mental self-duplication is a better way of intellectual reproducti—"

Tendrils of blood erupted from Valdemar's hands and impaled the psychotic derro king against his own throne. The crystalized tips of these tentacles pierced through the wires underneath Otto Blutgang's suit and spread inside its artificial avatar, keeping it tightly restrained.

"Where is she?" Valdemar hissed. "Speak or I'll scrap you."

"What would it change?" The derro king sounded supremely unimpressed. "Copies of my con-consciousness are s-s-spread all over my facilities. No-no-nothing but the complete era-ra-radication of derro civilization will des-s-s-stroy *me*."

Valdemar brought the derro king's face closer to his own, before channeling his best impersonation of Lord Bethor. "That can be arranged."

Though it disgusted him to say it, Valdemar called upon his ancestry.

"I am the Red Prince, the one who can wake up Ialdabaoth and to whom the Qlippoths answer," he said. "Do you truly wish to challenge *me*, you piece of stuttering junk?"

"I estimate a three per-percent ratio of probabilities that you will go that far. It is low."

"But it isn't *zero*." Valdemar's tendrils tightened their grip and bent the derro's metal bones. "You have enslaved your own race. Do you think I will hesitate to do everything in my power to utterly *destroy* you if you cross me?"

Otto Blutgang considered the threat, and suddenly turned more cooperative.

"I have sought to contact a higher in-in-intelligence to perfect the portal," he admitted. "But the subject turned out to be volatile. I had to quarantine the guest in the facility, but I have been incapable of getting rid of it without B-Blood magic. With your assistance, I can s-s-send it back and sta-stabilize the portal."

Valdemar frowned as he read between the lines. *First rule of summoning, never call what you cannot put down.* "What did you summon?"

In response, Otto Blutgang looked at the portal and Valdemar understood. He had contacted the only kind of creature capable of helping with portal technology. The ones that invented it in the first place.

9

FROM DUST

The air was unnaturally hot in this part of the facility. The surface of the metal walls was covered in scorch marks, while joints had melted into puddles of black slag on the ground. Ruptured pipes filled the corridors with burning steam and thick particles of dust. Marianne struggled to walk at a steady pace without stumbling on scraps.

How can you call yourself a warrior after falling into such an easy trap? Marianne scolded herself as sweat dripped from her forehead. You lost Valdemar, even Lord Och . . .

The fact the Dark Lord had been as surprised as she was before the teleportation effect didn't console Marianne. She should have grabbed Valdemar and made a rush for the exit the moment she noticed electricity in the air. Her failure to act was what Lord Bethor had warned her against.

No more, Marianne swore as she put a hand on the walls, attuning herself to the vibrations through the steel. This maze was nothing compared to the one Lord Bethor had put her through; she would find a way out, rescue Valdemar from whatever force controlled the facility, meet with Lord Och, and leave in short order.

The teleportation effect had sent her to a hidden floor beneath the original facility; her enhanced echolocation detected the gruesome lab full of derro and human corpses roughly four meters above her head. Thick layers of steel prevented Marianne from opening a way through, but according to the configuration of the various rooms, she suspected the presence of an elevator to the upper levels further ahead.

Her nose also picked up the smell of dry blood soaking the pipes. In all likelihood, the creature that massacred the derros lurked in the area. The force controlling the facility obviously intended to get rid of Marianne by throwing her into the fire. The noblewoman was determined to disappoint it by living through the ordeal.

Sheathing her rapier, as it wouldn't serve her in the narrow corridors, Marianne closed her eyes and advanced slowly. She used the Blood to enhance her senses further, her hearing, touch and smell coordinating to help her visualize the rooms ahead. Marianne attuned herself to the thrumming rhythm of pumps toiling in the background, to the steam coursing through the pipes and the lightning saturating the steel. The disordered, claustrophobic machinery suddenly started to make sense.

This is a body, Marianne realized. A wounded alien body of steel rather than flesh, but a body all the same. The pipes were organized like a bloodstream distributing power to the facility, converging at a central heart of pumps and engines. But beyond the steel, Marianne sensed an organic substance merged with the walls and machinery.

"Marianne?"

Hearing her name spoken startled the noblewoman.

"Marianne," the familiar voice repeated. "Lord Och? Are you here?"

"Valdemar?" Marianne answered as she opened her eyes. The voice came from the engine room, and it sounded so real . . .

"Marianne?" The voice turned happier. "I'm over here!"

Following the sound, Marianne traveled toward the facility's heart. The corridors grew wider as she walked, and so did the air grow searing hot. The thunderous noise of hydraulic devices rumbled across the facility.

Unlike the narrow corridors and small rooms she had visited beforehand, this chamber was nearly a hundred meters in diameter. Five metal bridges extended to join at a vast metal platform hanging above a colossal engine, forming a crossroad connecting various areas of the facility. The whole structure was supported by the strangest steam engine Marianne had seen yet: a vertical turbine digging into a searing hot pit shining like the heart of the world itself.

And Valdemar was waiting for her at the platform's center. He had removed his spiral mask, his kind face beaming with relief when he saw her. "Marianne, thank the Light you're alright."

"I'm relieved to see you safe and sound as well," the noblewoman asked as she stepped on the bridge, discreetly casting a few defensive spells under her breath. "What happened?"

"I don't remember much," he admitted with a contrite face. "I saw a flash of lightning, and when I recovered, I was in another room and neither you nor Lord Och were anywhere to be seen."

To be seen . . .

Marianne forced herself to smile. "I was worried for your safety."

"So was I," Valdemar replied while returning her expression, before glancing at the ceiling. "Look at this."

She did so. Her eyes saw something that her other senses couldn't. A beautiful landscape of gemstones embedded in steel covering the dome-shaped ceiling, each of them a different color. Rings of emeralds surrounded rubies and sapphires in a complex geometric tapestry of untold refinement and complexity.

"I didn't know the derros had any sense of aestheticism," Marianne said as she calculated the distance between Valdemar and herself. *One meter and half, maybe two . . .*

"Me neither. This is true beauty, don't you think?"

"It is."

Valdemar turned away from the ceiling to look at her with the warm smile Marianne had grown so fond of. The sight made her sick. "Marianne," he whispered, "I need your help."

"It's not complete, is it?" Marianne asked, feeling the growing urge to scratch her eyes. "Something is missing."

"These stones are beautiful, but not as much as you," "Valdemar" said as he stared at her with pale gray eyes. "We can't leave this place without giving it a finishing touch, don't you think? It wouldn't be right."

Her eyes itched so much that Marianne struggled not to cry. The unpleasantness grew so overwhelming her mind furiously urged her to scratch her eyelids apart.

So she shot "Valdemar" in the forehead. A bone bullet erupted from her index finger before he could react, and a second hit him in the chest. The blow made him flinch, but he remained standing. His body turned as still as a statue while black blood poured out of his wounds.

"You don't understand how I feel, do you?" Marianne asked as she took a few steps back. "Nor how we humans perceive the world. To you, sight is all there is."

That was how it had managed to fool her True Sight. It had subtly affected her brain through the Blood, fooling her mind with false stimuli. But her other senses, sharpened through harsh training, had told her the truth.

For a moment, the false Valdemar didn't answer. Instead, he looked at his chest wound as he touched it with his fingers, his nails sinking into the hole Marianne's bone bullet had made. He stuck out his tongue and let out a moan of pain as blood dripped on the metal platform.

No, not pain.

Pleasure. That thing *enjoyed* getting hurt.

The world around Marianne changed into a grotesque shape as the visual illusion collapsed. Smashed devices of levers and buttons covered the walls, their surface stained by fleshy secretions and garlands of harvested intestines. Thrumming pipes coiled over the ceiling like a thousand snakes of steel, impaling dozens of derro corpses intertwined with their steel. The beautiful illusory gemstones transformed into eyes of different colors, encased in a tapestry of pulsating flesh.

This amphitheater was a surgical artist's masterpiece.

"Are you ready," the thing asked with Valdemar's voice, its hands moving to grab his forehead's skin, "to see *true* beauty?" The creature ripped his false skin apart and revealed the gruesome horror underneath.

A powerful telekinetic pulse erupted around it and almost threw Marianne into the charnel pit below. The noblewoman managed to strengthen her psychic defenses enough to resist as she reached the platform's edge, allowing her to witness the monster in its full glory.

This humanoid creature's skin was festooned with sharp bone spikes, blood-soaked wounds, and self-inflicted scars. Its stature was skeletally thin and twice as tall as any man, with an impossibly long spine supporting a monstrous torso of exposed organs, glistening veins, and two elongated arms. Black, thorny tendrils coiled around stunted legs barely capable of letting the creature walk. The monster's head was split vertically in half, the remains of a humanoid face surrounding a hole of teeth, black blood and fleshy ligaments. A single loathsome red eye peered at Marianne from within its hideous abyss.

"You want my eyes?" Marianne grabbed her revolver. "Come and get them."

The creature shrieked inside Marianne's head, its psychic might crashing against her mental wards while its arms lunged at her face.

Channeling the Blood through her legs, Marianne swiftly ran around the creature while shooting it in the chest and head. The iron bullets, empowered by her soulbound weapon, impacted with the strength of bombshells. They pierced through the creature and hit the wall behind it, goring fountains of blood into its flesh.

The monster answered with a moan of pleasure, before jettisoning the bone shards embedded in its flesh in all directions.

Grabbing her rapier in her empty hand, Marianne used it to deflect the projectiles while she kept shooting at the monster's head. Her blade cut through the shards like butter and the strength of her projectiles blasted the creature's skull to bits. Bits of bones and blood fell off, revealing the red eye at the center.

On a closer look, Marianne realized that it was closer to a crimson sphere of light than a true organ. The black blood coalesced around the orb before solidifying in a gruesome mass of necrotic flesh, the very essence of space twisting around the monster. The massive engine below the platform echoed its power and surged with lightning.

Recognizing the nature of the spell cast, Marianne stayed on the move as space rippled around her. Tears in the fabric of reality appeared all over the platform, sharp blades of crystalized blood cutting through them. One lunged at Marianne's head and another at her chest. She dodged both, only for a dozen more to target her from all sides.

Her enhanced senses analyzed every tiny movement in her surroundings, calculating the angles of attack and where the blades would strike. Time seemed to slow down as Marianne's reflexes took over, guiding her body as she gracefully danced around the teleported projectiles.

The creature hit the ground with its hands, a torrent of black blood spreading from its fingertips. Marianne hastily fled toward the bridge as tentacles surged from the expanding pool and tried to grapple her.

Watching her escape to the bridge, the creature let out a roar and vanished in a flash of crimson light. Marianne sensed the air density change above her and backflipped as the monster teleported above her head, two curved blades of crystalized blood in hand. The swords hit only the bridge, while Marianne regained her footing.

The noblewoman and her opponent faced each other on the bridge. The cyclops' head had developed a new mouth of sharp teeth, a coiling tongue sticking out and licking the tips of his swords in an obscene manner.

Murder is all a funny game to you, isn't it? Marianne thought as she holstered her revolver and called upon the Blood. Drawing upon her body's reserves, she used magic to materialize a weapon of bone: a flail made of a chain of spine and with a miniature, hardened skull for a head. Creating the material left Marianne slightly winded, but she had stocked up nutrients and energy for such an occasion. *Let's test your pain threshold, tough guy.*

Swinging her flail with one hand as Lord Bethor had taught her to, Marianne used the other to make a challenging gesture with her rapier.

The monster answered by leaping in the air with its swords raised. Marianne dodged the blades with a step back as they hit the metal bridge with enough strength to shake it, before launching her flail at her foe's head. The projectile pulverized the monster's skull but phased harmlessly through the red eye.

It's intangible, Marianne thought as she swung her flail, the black blood regenerating a head around the monster's eye. *Is it a ghost manipulating a puppet of flesh?*

In that case, a soulbound weapon should be able to damage it. The revolver's bullets had blasted the flesh around the eye previously, but failed to hit it directly.

The monster let out a furious shriek and wildly swung its twin blades at Marianne, striking from all angles possible. There was little grace and skill in this dance of steel, but the creature's strength meant a direct hit would likely cut Marianne in half. The noblewoman slowly fell back while deflecting the blows with hits of her flail. Each blade her weapon shattered was instantly replaced with another, as the creature immediately materialized replacements to its hands. Its tongue dripped luridly as the red eye gazed at Marianne with intensity, its moans growing more animalistic while blood dripped from a wound between its stunted legs.

Suppressing her disgust to focus on the fight, Marianne lunged at the monster's chest with her rapier. The beast raised its blades to deflect her own, leaving his legs exposed to a feint. Marianne flung her flail at the monster's knees, shattering them with a sickening noise.

The beast stumbled in surprise, and the tip of Marianne's rapier struck the red eye. The noblewoman sensed her weapon hitting an invisible force and pierced it.

This time, the psychic shriek that echoed in her head was no moan of pleasure. The creature dropped its weapons, as the hands holding them trembled in agony. The beast's scars ruptured and black blood poured out of them, the substance dripping off the bridge and into the shining pit beneath.

"Come on," Marianne said with contempt as she twisted her rapier. The monster screamed all the louder. "Laugh. Don't you think pain is fun?"

The derros couldn't hurt this thing for real without a soulbound weapon capable of targeting intangible foes. Marianne, however, had plenty of experience with exorcizing ghosts.

"Where did you teleport Valdemar?" Marianne hissed. "I know you can understand what I say. So where is he?"

The beast's eye erupted in a flash of crimson light and reality twisted around them.

Realizing the danger, Marianne leaped off the bridge and threw her flail at the pipes dangling from the ceiling. Her weapon coiled around one of them, allowing her to dangle around the metal platform.

A mere second after she fled, space compressed around the metal bridge as bloody blades erupted all over it. The surface turned into a sea of spikes, while the creature manifested great wings of bones and skin.

A direct hit of a soulbound weapon would have destroyed any normal ghost, Marianne realized as the creature took flight to follow after her. After confirming that the central platform was still covered in tentacles, the noblewoman managed to land on another metal bridge to the left of the destroyed one. *What is that thing? A summoned monster? A specter?*

The monster shrieked as it flew toward Marianne, half a dozen arms growing out of its bleeding wounds. The beast quickly turned into a pulsating chaotic mass of bone blades and arms centered around the red eye, its wings barely able to support its mass.

In the end, that entity's nature didn't matter. If it wouldn't answer her questions, Marianne would destroy it.

"I would rather avoid that, young Marianne."

Footsteps echoed behind Marianne, as a hooded undead emerged from another part of the facility.

The noblewoman immediately focused on her enhanced senses, fearing another illusion . . . but no spell could fake the cold, oppressive aura surrounding a true Dark Lord.

"My, thank you for the compliment," Lord Och said as he walked onto the bridge, barely sparing the monster a glance. "I would gladly watch you finish off this living antique under other circumstances, but science demands that I preserve this specimen."

The creature let out a shriek. The tentacles on the metal platform twisted and coiled around the bridge, trying to grab Marianne at full speed.

The Dark Lord waved his hand and the tentacles rotted to nothing. Within seconds, only a thin layer of dust covered the metal platform.

"Your consent is not required," Lord Och said with the same tone an adult would use to scold an unruly child. "I'm afraid that the pecking order has changed greatly since your civilization's glory days, so I kindly ask you not to make this difficult."

And like that, Marianne realized the battle was over.

The creature, however, refused to accept the inevitable. It flew straight at the two sorcerers, black blood surging from its hands and rupturing the fabric of space.

"Very well." Lord Och pointed an index finger at the flying beast. "You asked for it."

The world brightened in light and fire.

Marianne had to protect her face with her hands as a torrent of searing hot white flames erupted from Lord Och's finger, the sheer ambient heat evaporating the sweat on her face. The blast swallowed the surprised monster and vaporized it. The flames continued their progress into the wall behind the flying creature, melting a tunnel through the facility.

Though the creature's red core survived the magical flames, they clearly affected it. The psychic scream that followed the incineration dwarfed all its previous ones in intensity, and not even a single drop of black blood remained behind.

The flames died down, a tiny cloud of smoke rising from Lord Och's index finger.

Marianne watched at the molten tunnel with shock, trying to process what she had just seen. How did . . . how could the Blood . . . "How?" she dared to ask.

"Do you remember how our Institute's water reservoir works, young Marianne?"

Yes, she did. "Master Poingcarré turned an elemental into a permanent portal to the plane of water."

"This minor offensive spell uses the same principle," the lich replied casually. "It involves temporarily summoning a minor fire elemental with a conjuration spell before immediately turning it into a temporary rift to its home plane. Primordial fire then surges into our dimension, blasting everything in its path. I have seen very few things capable of surviving a direct hit."

The red eye flickered as black particles gathered around it.

"I expected more from a Pleromian," the Dark Lord said with a hint of disappointment as he observed the entity. "But you have exceeded my expectations, young Marianne. Lord Bethor trained you well."

Marianne examined the creature with surprise. "This thing is a *Pleromian*?"

Impossible. The Pleromians had been a great and ancient people, who created so many wonders. How could such a sick, petty creature be one of them?

"Or at least, this is what the Pleromians have *become* after millennia of rampant excesses, obscene pleasures, and degradation. Such a shame to watch an ancient and proud civilization reduced to . . ." Lord Och glanced at the Pleromian with contempt. "*This*."

The particles turned into drops of black blood coalescing around the red eye, forming a protective cocoon. *It's trying to recreate a body for itself,* Marianne realized. *It can't escape without one.*

"Fascinating," Lord Och whispered as he observed the phenomenon. "The Pleromian draws into the very essence of the Blood saturating all of Underland to generate organic matter from nothing. All while its soul remains stuck between two planes. This warrants further testing."

The Dark Lord raised his hand at the Pleromian, his empty eye sockets shining with a ghastly glow. "I suppose I will call upon the elemental plane of lightning and see if it can recover from intense electrocution."

When she looked at the pitiful, sadistic creature, Marianne realized she couldn't even muster the slightest hint of pity. "Lord Och, we need to find Valdemar," she said, trying to stay on track. "He could be in danger as we speak."

"Have faith in my apprentice, young Marianne. There's no rush. Eventually, this creature will accept its helplessness and we'll be on our merry way."

"It enjoys pain, Lord Och."

"Good." The Dark Lord grinned cruelly as his hands crackled with electricity. "Then we'll both get to indulge ourselves."

10

THE LOST ARCHIVE

The elevator rattled as it descended into the facility's depths. Valdemar crossed his arms as he did his best to fit in the cramped cabin, which was clearly adapted for derros and not humans. The lack of space made him uncomfortable already, but it was the presence of glass eyes in the corners that truly frustrated him.

"Why are you so un-unenthusiastic?" A device in the elevator's ceiling somehow carried Otto Blutgang's voice through it. "Our mu-mutual objectives will be ful-fulfilled once we have established tru-ust."

"I don't see what helping you will bring me besides more headaches." The only reason Valdemar went along this plan was to rescue Marianne, assist Lord Och, and prevent a maddened Pleromian from escaping into Underland. If the summoner could smash the derro king to bits and exorcise his spirit from the machinery, he would have done it.

"Once you ba-anish the Pleromi-i-ian, we can collaborate and oppen the path to the infinite woooorlds . . ." The voice stretched on and screeched like a chalk on a board. "I will stab-bilize the portal to Earth and le-let you and volunteers through. Or any other wo-orld you wish for."

Valdemar looked up at a glass eye with skepticism. "Would you let mankind use your portals?"

"The cosmos is infi-infi-infinite. Our species can-not coexist due to lack of space and com-competition over resources. Portals will abolish scarci-city and let us share the bo-bounty of endless worlds."

Valdemar looked at the elevator's rusted door, waiting for it to open. "A troglodyte friend of mine used a similar argument. He said that this planet was too small for two species."

"Enmity between us is *pointlesssss*," Otto hissed like a snake. "Co-cooperation will benefit us both."

That could solve their problems, and the Silent King had portrayed the derro king as a valid solution for Valdemar to reach Earth. While it meant stomaching Otto's atrocities, co-developing functional portal technology and sharing its use was a good deal on paper.

But there were a few issues Valdemar couldn't ignore.

"What about the others?" he asked Otto Blutgang. "Those who won't listen and will elect to remain behind in Underland?"

"What about the-them?"

The worst part, the derro king sounded puzzled that Valdemar *cared*. Otto Blutgang had become a thing unable to relate to others.

No, that wasn't right. From the way he enslaved his own species, the derro king couldn't feel empathy for anyone else in the first place. Every interaction was a cold transaction with him, an equation to be solved. Otto didn't understand the value of establishing trust and goodwill, considered his own men resources to exhaust and throw aside for the sake of his ambitions, and didn't care for anyone but himself.

In a way, that was why Valdemar believed the offer to be entirely genuine. A solipsistic being like Otto Blutgang didn't hold grudges and would consider peacefully shipping potential enemies off-world an easier solution than a costly war.

But all those who would refuse to take the offer . . . the unbelievers, the skeptics, the fearful, the dokkars and the troglodytes . . .

They would have no future.

"Ktulu," his familiar whispered from within his bag. Somehow, it managed to sound like a warning.

I know, Valdemar thought. *This deal smells like rotten fish.*

Otto had brainwashed nearly the entire derro race, other than a few personalities "worth preserving." While the species had been at war with humans long before Valdemar's birth, he couldn't help but feel pity for them. No one deserved to have their mind corrupted by a malevolent intelligence. In a way, Otto's actions were no different than Ialdabaoth's. He had just traded flesh for steel.

But what alternative was there? Otto Blutgang controlled the facility, and while he had sealed it shut to prevent the Pleromian from escaping, he could certainly have it reinforced in a pinch. The moment Valdemar attempted to escape or sabotage the portal, derro troops would come in. Not to mention the strange teleportation technology Otto had access to inside the facility.

Is there a way to free the derros from their so-called Godmind? Valdemar couldn't help but wonder. He didn't see any, but he had to keep faith. The same way he had to believe he could free himself from Ialdabaoth's influence.

The elevator's door opened, and alien screams of agony drew him out of his thoughts.

Fearing he had arrived too late, Valdemar rushed into a steel corridor as the heat around him increased. The sound of thrumming engines and steam bursting through pipes resounded around him, while his psychic sight instantly detected a powerful locus in the Blood further ahead.

The corridor ended in a vast chamber holding the burning engines powering the facility, and to the strange sight of Lord Och blasting a blob of black slime with lightning while Marianne watched with a blank expression. The lich clearly enjoyed himself, chuckling as a crimson orb sometimes threatened to emerge from the dark goo.

Valdemar had indeed arrived too late.

He had barely taken a step onto a metal bridge connecting to the engine room's central platform when Marianne turned in his direction, her revolver pointed at his face. "Easy!" Valdemar immediately raised his hands, Ktulu imitating him inside his bag. "It's me, Marianne!"

His bodyguard observed him in silence for a moment, before her blank face turned to relief. "I'm so glad to see you safe, Valdemar." Marianne lowered her weapon. "I apologize for the frosty welcome. The creature tried to trick me before."

"Are there more available?" Lord Och asked as he continued his torture of the slime. "This one is almost spent."

Valdemar examined the scene, both to understand the lich's spell and the nature of its victim. *I didn't know you could use portal breaches offensively,* he thought, *it's quite ingenious.*

As for the slime . . . though it was a bizarre shadow of its kind's former majesty, Valdemar recognized its nature from Otto's description of the captive Pleromian. Lord Och's torture had degraded it to a lost soul barely tethered to Underland by the power of the Blood. It couldn't even manifest a psychic defense or a mouth to scream.

"Lord Och, this is barbaric," Valdemar said with a frown before noticing the eyes and intestines scattered around the engine room. His sympathy for the Pleromian plummeted as he realized the scale of its rampage across the derro facility. "After consideration, I retract my statement."

"This creature enjoys torturing others," Marianne said as he glared at the slime. "It deserves worse."

"You will forgive an old man enjoying himself, apprentice." The lich chuckled light-heartedly as he finally stopped blasting the Pleromian, letting it recover. "I've primed this creature for interrogation. This is the reason for our presence here, is it not?"

"Yes," Valdemar agreed as he observed the pathetic ooze. "Otto Blutgang wants it sent back to the hell from where it crawled, and then to stabilize his portal with my help."

Marianne's eyes widened, her fingers tightening on her rapier. "Otto Blutgang is *here*?"

"In a way." At this point, the derro king had become one with his kingdom. "He said the Pleromian was after you, Marianne, so I rushed to assist as fast as I could."

A slight blush formed on Marianne's cheeks for some reason. "I see," she said. "You shouldn't have. I'm the one supposed to protect you, not the other way around."

Valdemar instantly felt remorseful. "I didn't mean to imply that I doubted your skills," he apologized. "I knew you would be alright, but . . . just in case . . ."

"I appreciate the gesture," she replied, clearly eager to move on. "What do we do now with the Pleromian? If there is truly a portal here, do we secure it?"

"I'm certain the dwarf king would gladly trade use of his toy for this creature's knowledge," Lord Och said as he observed the Pleromian. The creature had manifested arms from its black blood, and desperately tried to get away from the lich. It was quite a pathetic sight. "But you know my point of view, apprentice. If I had a stomach left, I would rather have my cake and eat it too."

Valdemar knew all too well what he meant. "You want to extract its knowledge before we surrender it to Blutgang?" That was smart. When dealing with madmen, it couldn't hurt to secure a leverage.

"We? We will do nothing." The lich extended a hand to his student. "This is your moment in the spotlight, apprentice."

Valdemar blushed behind his mask. "I'm a poor mind-mage."

"Oneiromancers infiltrate dreams, but that door is closed to you by virtue of your origins . . . that is true." Lord Och chuckled. "And yet, young Valdemar, through that same token there is another way to learn what that creature knows. You have already witnessed the process alongside my former apprentice, and it is time you put this power to the test."

The dreadful memory of the Outer Darkness and the abyss at its center flared in Valdemar's mind. The summoner glanced at the Pleromian, its red eye reminding him of Ialdabaoth's maw and the countless souls lost to its hunger.

"No," Valdemar whispered as he realized what his teacher had in mind. "I refuse. This will destroy it."

The lich looked at his student as if he had grown a second head. "Do you have qualms of conscience for a creature such as *this*?"

"Valdemar," Marianne said softly as she glanced at the ghastly chapel of flesh and eyes above their heads. "This monster would have added my eyes to its collection if it had the power and probably done far worse. It is mad and a danger to all. It cannot be allowed out of this facility or anywhere else."

"To kill is one thing, but this method . . ." Valdemar clenched his fists. "It might leave *nothing* behind."

His teacher was all but asking him to eat the Pleromian's soul like a snack and shit it out once he had learned everything of value. Valdemar wasn't sure if he could do that, and if he could . . . he was afraid of what it meant.

"Maybe, maybe not." Lord Och shrugged. "Perhaps it will be up to you. Would you rather give it to our derro friend without securing an insurance against betrayal?"

Valdemar snorted. "No."

"Then try. You can always spit him out before you chew it too much."

"Why not extract its knowledge yourself, my teacher?" Valdemar asked. "You have the power."

"Because then nothing would remain for you to discover," the lich replied. "I believe in encouraging my students to push boundaries, apprentice. You hate the inhuman half of yourself, but it is as important as the other. No good will come out of suppressing it."

"Would you rather that I embrace the monster inside?"

"Of course not." Lord Och grinned. "I want you to master it."

When he put it that way . . . Valdemar loathed anything that had to do with his father's side of the family, but there was wisdom in the lich's words. The Lilith had been able to attack him psychically because, in his desire to suppress his nature, he had accidentally made it exploitable. If he didn't test his limits, someone would make use of them against him.

Valdemar looked at the pathetic, broken horror trying its best to crawl away from Lord Och. At this point, death and oblivion might even be a mercy. He walked to the creature's side while his companions watched, sensing pairs of glass eyes gazing at his back. If Otto wanted to stop this, he didn't make a move to do so.

The Pleromian's red eye emerged from the black goo to glare at Valdemar, right as the sorcerer called upon the Blood.

Even in its sorry state, the creature attempted to raise psychic defenses, but they collapsed almost instantly . . . and they felt wrong all the same. A human built a dreamscape to protect their sleeping mind and mental layers while awake. The soul was intertwined with the body, one influencing the other. A healthier body meant a greater mastery of the Blood and thus better defenses.

The Pleromian's spirit worked differently. The soul was all there was to it; the body it created was a mere ectoplasmic shell it could discard at will.

It was closer to a Qlippoth than to a living being.

A silent battle of wills started between the two souls, as Valdemar attempted to subsume the Pleromian like he did with a Collector in the Institute's Hall of Ritual. It was no contest; one soul was healthy and determined, the other bloated in its corruption and broken through a lich's torture.

They are themselves, but they are also me. Valdemar remembered his visions of Ialdabaoth through the Blood. A thousand masks for a single face.

So hollow was the Pleromian's soul that Valdemar had no problem wearing it. The black blood dried as the crimson, ghostly eye floated inside the summoner. Valdemar digested the spirit the same way his father devoured his children.

Horrifying visions of a nightmarish realm filled his mind as he began the feast of memories. Glimpses of a terrible world of flesh under a dark sky, of pulsating ravines, and pyramids of corpses. Valdemar heard the sickening moans of Pleromians as they raised slaves from their own flesh, only to violate them within minutes of their birth. He witnessed artists paint landscapes of tongues and madmen make coats out of their kindred's skins. The screams of the dying were refined into terrible symphonies, their guts into twisted decorations.

The Pleromians had no need for cities anymore, or even the veneer of civilization. He witnessed flashes of a broken portal, its parts harvested to make sickening toys and crude instruments of pleasure. Science and learning had been forgotten in this mad realm, leaving only the most disturbing of pleasures.

Gone were the majestic titans and cyclops of the Institute's murals. Only twisted husks remained, more interested in sewing themselves new arms and cruel delights than exploring the cosmos. The mad had long slaughtered the sane and the civilized, embracing the bottomless abyss that awaited once a mind had shredded the meandering pretense of higher thoughts.

The Pleromians had so degraded that they had lost most of their knowledge and majesty. They had become little more than savant animals, mad children driven by the instinct to rut and play and hurt. Only occasional flashes of insight let out the shattered remains of their lost majesty, ever so briefly.

In their search for eternal ecstasy, the Pleromians had abandoned *everything else*.

How long had they been trapped in a cognitive loop of mindless pleasure, unable to perceive the world outside? It was a testament to their immense power that they could wield the Blood at all anymore, the same way bats instinctively knew how to fly.

Wading through the toxic mud of these memories, Valdemar realized that their selfish madness made the Pleromians all the more dangerous. So long as they were trapped in this nightmarish realm of their own creation, their mind dulled by empty bliss and psychosis, they would remain ignorant of the rest of the cosmos. If they ever remembered the existence of Underland, or received proof that the universe they had left to die had survived . . . they would return to torment its people.

Otto Blutgang wanted to return the Pleromian home after extracting its knowledge, but Marianne was right. This monster couldn't be allowed to spread the word to its kindred.

It was beyond saving.

Eating your soul is mercy at this point, Valdemar thought as the nightmarish memories faded away, replaced with a black empty void. The Pleromian had forgotten more about its existence than most humans would ever know. *So little of it remains.*

And yet . . . and yet not everything was gone. A few embers of memory remained, brought back to the surface by Otto Blutgang's summoning attempt. They were blurry and indistinct, but Valdemar quickly gathered them into a shape he could examine. In a way, it felt no different than compelling a summoned creature to answer his call.

The oldest memories were unlike the empty cruelty that defined the creature's mind. Valdemar watched through the depthless eye of a cyclops as a line of Pleromians shed their blood in individual pots of stone. The viewer marked each of them with a complex series of symbols as it collected them.

Lord Och had said that the Pleromians held a breeding program to stabilize their society, determining a citizen's role at birth. Could Valdemar be witnessing it?

The summoner was tempted to look for another memory tied to summoning and teleportation magic, but he resisted. *What if . . .* he thought, *what if it's all connected?*

Valdemar was the result of one such breeding program meant to bind multiple worlds together. Had the Pleromians followed a similar logic? Did it somehow teach them how to open their portals?

Valdemar digested the memories one after the other, but they were so fragmented he only caught glimpses. Sights of shelves upon shelves of blood samples, tightly organized by lineages; visions of Pleromian sorcerers recording increasingly complex patterns of symbols into endless helix chains; flashes of arranged matches of two donors together based on organic compatibility . . .

This Pleromian was a biomancer, a specialist of the body. Yet the remaining spellcasting instincts veered toward summoning and spatial magic. How odd.

More to the point, the memories all took place in a familiar fortress. Lord Och had changed many things since humans took it over, but the walls of the Pleroma Institute had remained intact across the centuries.

The Black Pillar at its center was standing in the memories too. Valdemar watched through the viewer's eye as it studied its stony surface. Only then did the summoner notice details that had evaded his human eyes in the past. Symbols were carved on the pillar. Signs so small, so imperceptibly microscopic, that only a Pleromian's peerless sight could identify them.

The Black Pillar of the Pleroma Institute wasn't a mere monument. It was an archive of some kind. The place where the Pleromian biomancers recorded their studies of life itself.

Show me, Valdemar thought. *Show me what you were looking for so feverishly. Show me the truth.*

The viewer took a few steps back, and Valdemar saw the bigger picture. The tiny symbols assembled into a familiar, eye-shaped design. The same sign that his grandfather had recorded, the eye of Ialdabaoth.

All of life in Underland, assembled into a greater whole.

And yet, there were more symbols. They formed a sphere around Ialdabaoth's eye, before spreading into chains of signs, into tendrils linked to other circles separated by a dark void. Each of these spheres held a complex set of symbols forming a larger one. Some were eyes, similar to Ialdabaoth's and yet subtly different. Others looked like maws of teeth, or blooming flowers.

None were the same, but all were connected through a web of infinite complexity. Bonds that transcended the void of space and the frontiers of the planes.

Valdemar was mistaken.

The Institute's Black Pillar wasn't an archive, but a map. A map of the universe, and the living worlds that populated it.

11

DARK DESIGNS

Was there a limit to the universe's vastness? The purpose of science and magic was to push back the boundaries of human understanding of the cosmos ever farther. But the more Valdemar learned, the bigger the universe appeared. Each new piece of information showcased how little mankind mattered in the great cosmic dance. And as he glanced at the map before his eyes, Valdemar felt incredibly small.

The Blood's magic derived from Ialdabaoth, true . . . but the almighty Stranger was only a node in the vast web of life. There were countless of its kind across the planes, connected through the bonds of kinship and lineage.

There is a war in heaven.

This map represented one of the sides. The side of aberrant life, the side of the Blood.

An army of Strangers made of countless smaller life-forms that had broken off from the whole. Each shaped like a sphere . . .

The black sun grew to encompass the universe itself, the shadow of eyes, mouths, and tentacles wriggling beneath its surface.

"Could it be . . ." Valdemar whispered as he remembered his visit to the Silent King's alien realm and the brief glimpse of the abomination lurking inside its blackened sun. "If it can happen with a star, then . . ."

What about a planet?

Lady Mathilde had theorized that the eyes of Ialdabaoth were the signs of a parasite spreading through the tunnels of the world. Considering what Valdemar had learned so far, he was tempted to consider a more worrying hypothesis.

Ialdabaoth *was* the world. Not just the people living on it, but the entire planet.

Could the world's heart be made of flesh rather than magma, as geologists believed? What if the crust of the planet, those depths and surface of rocks and stones, were nothing more than a shell? The remnants of cosmic dust and meteors slowly accumulating across the eons?

And if this theory was true, then was *Earth* a slumbering Stranger too? Was it an egg that would one day hatch and unleash a cataclysmic abomination unto the cosmos?

No, I can't think like this, Valdemar thought as he focused on the memory. Even if that's true, Ialdabaoth's freedom is not inevitable. It wouldn't need outside help if it was.

At least this explained how the Blood could contact other worlds and planes. The web of flesh transcended Ialdabaoth and had spread its tendrils across the planes. All universes blessed with life were connected by these sentient worlds, bound tightly through a double chain of polynucleotides.

And as he observed the map while trying to make sense of it, Valdemar noticed a troubling fact: Ialdabaoth occupied a central place in the web and was linked to many other living worlds. This placement could simply be the result of the Pleromians using their world's Stranger as the baseline of their map for practical purposes, but somehow Valdemar doubted he would be so lucky.

Now, Ialdabaoth was sealed long ago and is now trying to break its bindings, the summoner thought as he assembled pieces of the puzzle. If we assume that these wards are somehow connected . . .

Then Ialdabaoth's freedom would start a chain reaction through the web. Its freedom would unleash dozens of its kindred, the ripples spreading through a hundred more across the planes. The Strangers would wake up to claim the multiverse as their own. They would win the "war," whatever it meant.

You are the me from the other side, the Nightwalker had said. But what was this other side?

Death is the universe's natural state.

Though the map was detailed, Valdemar couldn't help but notice the vast empty space separating each living world from the other. The Lilith had made a valid point, the universe was filled with death. Life was preciously rare, far too much for Valdemar's taste.

Something out there was doing its best to scour the cosmos of its inhabitants. And if the Whitemoon was Ialdabaoth's counterpart as much as Valdemar and the Nightwalker mirrored each other, then the rogue planetoid that cast mankind underground was only an agent of a greater power.

"Show me what you were running away from," Valdemar whispered as he compelled the memories to answer his questions. "Show me what you feared so much. Were you worried that Ialdabaoth would wake up? What is the Whitemoon?"

The memories around him blurred. The walls turned to flesh and humanoid figures started writhing everywhere Valdemar looked. The dirty smell of sex filled his nostrils, while the summoner tasted something salty in the air. Even the Black Pillar took on a phallic shape. The memories were riddled with holes and the Pleromian had filled them with disgusting sexual imagery.

"Curse you, you ecstasy junkie!" Valdemar whispered in condemnation. "All this priceless, cosmic knowledge, and you filled your brain with pointless pleasures instead?" Words couldn't properly convey Valdemar's sheer disappointment. The Pleromians had achieved so many wonders and they threw them all away.

No matter. Even if the Pleromian's memory was faulty, the Black Pillar still held the full wealth of his kind's knowledge about the Strangers. Valdemar only had to return to the Institute and decode it.

He couldn't say the same for the portals.

"Show me how you can open tears between worlds," Valdemar ordered. "Tell me how to reach Earth."

This time, the Pleromian's soul answered his command. The memories of orgies and sexual imagery collapsed into nothingness. A new vision rose from the depths of the harvested soul, showing a familiar underground dome and an archway of black stone. Metal cables held the doorway in place, as they would centuries later. The Institute's Pleromian portal had changed little across the eons . . . with one small exception.

Where are the crystals? Valdemar wondered. Shining red stones were infused into the structure in the current era, but they were conspicuously missing in this memory. So where were they?

It didn't take long for Valdemar to receive an answer. Watching the memory through a single eye, he witnessed a procession enter the chamber. Pleromian blood sorcerers, the memories' owner among them, escorted a ragtag line of humanoids. A shirtless and beautiful dokkar prince, attended to by collared concubines; a derro reeking of drugs and incense; a human so fat slaves had to carry him into the chamber; a troglodyte that advanced with an air of grim, but noble resignation; a Pleromian dressed in a rich robe of harvested skin, smiling at a silent honor; and many more creatures Valdemar had never seen before, from many-legged humanoid bugs to a constantly shapeshifting doppelganger. All of them bore tattoos showcasing their blood type.

They looked less like prisoners and more like pampered pets, fattened on warm meals, concubines, and cheap drugs. All of them appeared satisfied with their lots as they walked toward the archway. A hooded Pleromian awaited next to the portal with a sharp scythe in his hands.

Valdemar winced as the dokkar, the first in line, bent before the portal without any hesitation. The Pleromian executioner raised the scythe above the sacrifice's neck.

The blade glittered from the light of torches as it fell. The head cleanly rolled on the ground while the decapitated corpse fell against the archway, feeding the metal cables with its blood as if they were a tree's roots. The archway pulsated as if alive as it drank the precious fluid, and small red crystals formed all over the structure. Another victim followed, feeding the crystal with their life.

The hideous reaping stretched on for hours. Dokkars, humans, troglodytes, derros, all the creatures populating the world were sacrificed on the altar of progress. Even a few Pleromians lost their heads as they closed the procession, their blood soaking the archway while sorcerers sang incantations. Their headless corpses were piled up until they reached the ceiling.

None of them resisted.

Lord Och had once told his apprentice that a victim had to be willing for the Earthmouth ritual to function. Only martyrs could serve as the support beams of bridges linking the worlds together. These people had been raised like expensive cattle, granted every privilege on the condition that when the time came, they would lay down their lives for the glory of their enslavers. Their blood and souls infused the site of their execution, becoming one with the steel.

In the end, the Pleromian portals were nothing more than eminently more sophisticated Earthmouths. And considering derros were among the sacrifices, this wasn't the first portal the Pleromians had built.

But how could these portals be stable? Earthmouths were two-way streets; you needed one on each side to keep the road open. Valdemar doubted a Pleromian enclave awaited on the other side of a planar rift.

"Show me its activation," the sorcerer ordered as he slipped through the memories. The sacrifices' corpses vanished, but the Pleromian sorcerers remained as they spoke ancient words of power to the portal. The archway hummed as the Blood grew in power, the fabric of space folding. The crystals resonated together, singing the song of life itself.

Valdemar watched the process with enthusiasm, taking mental notes as a crimson glow erupted at the archway's center. A rift in space widened inside the portal, opening to a screaming realm of gasping flesh.

"It's a resonance!" Valdemar realized as everything started to make sense. "It's a resonance, not between two Earthmouths, but between two lineages of life!"

The Pleromians had fed the portal with a rough approximation of the genetic material of the creatures they expected to find on the other side. Though there was no portal on the other side nor anybody to open a breach, blood called to blood.

"That's how I can serve as an Earthmouth between two realms," Valdemar whispered. "I have the two lineages of men inside me. I'm a bridge between two mankinds, and Ialdabaoth's power provides the energy to stabilize the pathway."

That was what Otto Blutgang didn't understand. He had managed to rip tears into other worlds through lightning and machinery, but without a sympathetic connection to the other side he couldn't hope to stabilize them. He was trying to create bridges with steel, when it was the kinship between different forms of life and the agony of sacrificed souls that kept portals open.

Valdemar replayed the memory, memorizing the chants used by the Pleromians. "Command phrases," he guessed. "I can activate the portal with them."

They didn't need Blutgang's help. Opening the pathway to Earth would be quicker with his technology, but not necessary. They just had to activate the Pleromian portal with the words Valdemar had memorized, maybe tune it a little with his blood, and they could open the rift to that world.

At long last, the path to Earth was clear!

"Should I honor the deal with Blutgang?" Valdemar didn't hesitate for long. "No."

The idea of spitting on a functional portal to Earth sickened Valdemar, but using it meant making a deal with a fiend in the process. Even if Otto Blutgang followed through with his end of the bargain and let volunteers start an exodus to another world, he would immediately use the stolen Pleromian technology to subdue those who remained behind and expand his sick mechanical consciousness across the cosmos. He would infect other worlds the same he had poisoned his entire species.

There was nothing wrong in transcending the boundaries of mortality, but Otto Blutgang was a brain-harvesting parasite willing to lobotomize his own kind. He simply couldn't be trusted with this kind of power.

It said something that Valdemar would rather entrust this knowledge to *Lord Och* than the derros.

"Now, we have to find a way to bury this facility and escape it alive," Valdemar said as he prepared to collapse the memory and return to the waking world. The Pleromian's soul would remain powerless inside his stomach, though the sorcerer didn't know yet what to do with it. "But once it's done . . ."

He would finally see the sun. At long last, his dream of reaching Earth would come true.

The Dark Lords are deceiving you, my prince.

And the Dark Lords would follow.

Only now, so close to the altar of victory, did Valdemar wonder about the true cost of his dream. Valdemar wanted his kind to see the sun. He had never desired to keep it all for himself. And after seeing the Dark Lords up close, he had no doubt what would follow once they could open pathways to other worlds.

Empress Aratra, if Lord Och's tale was to be believed, had betrayed her own mentor and established a tyrannical regime underground for centuries. Valdemar had hoped that the Empire would reform upon finding new worlds full of resources and sunlight, but . . . now he doubted.

Lord Bethor only believed in strength and violence. To him, sufficient might could solve any problem. He was a necessary evil when mankind faced threats like the Strangers and Otto Blutgang, but against a peaceful civilization? He would shatter any resistance thrown his way with fire, subjugate the weak, and seize all the resources he could. A necessary evil was still an evil.

As for Lord Och himself, Valdemar refused to let the Lilith's words poison his mind. And yet . . .

And yet he could tell something didn't add up in this scenario.

Valdemar simply couldn't imagine Lord Och letting his apprentice learn such an important secret without having discovered it himself first. The lich was too cunning, too hungry for knowledge, too careful. He had already butted heads with Valdemar about their respective visions of the world.

Had Lord Och already extracted the information from the Pleromian's mind before surrendering it? Or maybe he couldn't reach the depths of its memories because of how the creature's mind worked, and he had sent his apprentice to sully his hands by eating the soul?

Valdemar's mind flared with paranoia as he examined the portal's memory. He was certain souls were the fuel keeping it open, and yet he hadn't sensed any within the device when he visited the real one. Had the long centuries degraded them, much like how only the echoes of pain and degradation remained in the Pleromians' vaults beneath the Institute?

In that case, it explained why the portal wouldn't work in the present day. It was functional, but it had exhausted its fuel. And the way to recharge it . . .

A doubt seized Valdemar's mind, and he immediately reviewed the memory of the portal creation. The procession of sacrifices rose from the dead to repeat their execution once again and Valdemar couldn't help but feel a sense of *déjà vu* in more ways than one.

The dokkar male walked first to his death, his arrogant, aristocratic posture echoing Frigga's smug confidence.

The human followed, bloated and complacent like the Empire's masses. A troglodyte carried on with the same grim resignation as Hermann, whenever he and Valdemar spoke about their kinds' inability to coexist.

The many-legged bug that walked after them was no Master Loctis, but maybe the living swarm could serve as a substitute?

And the doppelganger . . . Iren was half of one . . .

"That undead bastard . . ." Valdemar whispered in outrage.

What were the odds that a member of almost all of the species sacrificed to open the portal had been gathered in the Institute? Fed promises of medical treatment, of a better world, or political advantages? Even Frigga had signed a magical contract of some kind to study at the Institute, and the lich could have easily hidden a sacrificial clause inside.

"What a heartless *dick*!" Valdemar clenched his fists in rage. "He *knew*."

Why would I sacrifice you, when I know we shall eventually succeed with another method that won't cost you your life?

The lich had never said it wouldn't cost that of *someone else*.

"No, wait . . . he doesn't have the Pleromian. I've eaten the soul." But Lord Och had tried to clone them in the past. He had shown Valdemar the lab. He didn't need a Pleromian with powers and knowledge, only someone willing to sacrifice themselves as part of the ritual.

The lich was immortal. For all Valdemar knew, he could have raised a Pleromian clone in secret and indoctrinated it to serve as fuel for the portal. Lord Och's apprentice didn't even know where his master kept his true workshop.

Even the derro could easily be arranged. The Empire had many prisoners of war in its cells, one would perhaps accept the sacrifice as part of an exchange. Or perhaps that was why Lord Och had insisted on following his apprentice? To negotiate sharing blood banks with Otto Blutgang?

"Maybe I'm just being paranoid," Valdemar muttered as he tried to calm himself. "How could he have known? He would have needed a living Pleromian to interrogate, or to find instructions. The ruins beneath the Institute didn't have any as far as I know."

But . . .

But Lord Och *did* access another source of Pleromian knowledge in the past.

"I know of at least another gate like this one in Ariouth, though I haven't been able to examine it since my previous apprentice and I had a . . ." Lord Och's voice turned cold as ice. "A disagreement."

The other portal in Ariouth. The one under Lord Phaleg's control.

The lich had always been evasive about the cause of his feud with his former apprentice, blaming it on ungratefulness. But knowing Lord Och's deceitful nature, Valdemar wondered if it had something to do with the second portal. Perhaps the two Dark Lords had found a trove of knowledge and couldn't share, or disagreed about how to use the device. The Institute's vault didn't have any guide to work the portal, but the Pleromians could have left hints in Ariouth.

I knew he was a snake, the summoner thought, *and I still let him bite me.*

Why all this plotting? To get the command word? Or was the lich trying to manipulate Valdemar into agreeing with this terrible plan, wearing down his reluctance one revelation at a time? Or maybe Lord Och didn't know about the portal's requirements, but had come to suspect them through trial and error.

Whatever the case, Valdemar couldn't ignore the signs. Even if Lord Och didn't know how to activate the portals, he had the means to do so at hand. The lich had kept his apprentice alive because of his unique nature, but Valdemar didn't doubt for a second that he would hesitate to sacrifice less "precious" assets.

The moment the summoner returned to the living world, Lord Och would scan the command words from Valdemar's mind.

But the summoner couldn't forget them either. What were the odds that they could capture another Pleromian that knew them? They would need to collaborate with Otto and all the ghastly prices that he would demand. Valdemar had to register the command words somewhere the lich wouldn't find them, erase them from his mind, and somehow find a way to recover them later with Lord Och none the wiser. An impossible task.

"No," Valdemar muttered, his heart full of determination. "Impossible is but a word."

He had an idea.

12

CONFLICTING LOYALTIES

Valdemar hadn't spoken a word in several minutes. The facility's engines gently thrummed underneath the central metal platform, clouds of steam swirling around the metal bridges connecting the room to other areas; those that had survived Marianne's battle with the Pleromian at least. Although Lord Och had bested the creature and shattered its magic, its grisly handiwork remained. The eyes and guts of slain derros remained hung among the maze of pipes above the platform, and their slayer . . .

Why is it still here? Marianne wondered as she glared at the odious sphere of blackened blood facing Valdemar. Both of them occupied the center of the platform and seemed locked in a mental duel of some kind. Though Valdemar stood on his feet, she could tell that his spirit had wandered elsewhere.

Merely gazing at the Pleromian's remains filled Marianne with revulsion. Her enhanced sight perceived the true nature of the bubbles boiling on its surface as ghastly eyes flickering in and out of existence.

This is the same mud that poisoned Bertrand, Marianne thought grimly. Though Valdemar hadn't touched it, his continued silence disturbed her. She was starting to wonder if letting him consume the Pleromian's soul had truly been wise. "Lord Och . . ."

"Be patient," the lich said without a care in the world. While Marianne had moved closer to Valdemar in case she needed to defend him from the slime, the Dark Lord observed the scene from a respectable distance. "Good things take time . . . and I have waited many years for this moment."

Years? Was he speaking about the Pleromian's capture, or Valdemar's progress as a sorcerer? Marianne briefly glanced at the Dark Lord of Paraplex, her enhanced senses picking up subtle movements she had never noticed before: bony fingers shaking almost imperceptibly, his mouth slightly opening to let out a pleased rattle, a feverish light flaring up in his empty eyes . . .

It wasn't a look of curiosity, but anticipation.

He planned this, Marianne realized, much to her disturbance. He planned this before we even set out on this expedition.

"You overestimate me, young Marianne," the lich said, having read her mind. "When you will reach my age, if you ever do, you will realize that no wish ever comes true. Something unforeseen always ruins the best-laid plans of men and gods . . . but with time and preparations on your side, you will seize the opportunities as they come along."

An opportunity for what? Marianne wondered, though she was wise enough not to speak out loud. She had already noticed the glass eyes in the ceiling watching their every move and listening to their discussion. The air was rife with tension. *It can escalate anytime . . .*

Holding her rapier in one hand and having reabsorbed her flail into her body with the other, Marianne was ready to strike at the first sign of provocation. She was under no delusion that the derros would let them leave this facility without a fight.

"Mayhap there will be a fight, but I expect our host shall prove wise enough to let us negotiate like adults," Lord Och said as he observed his apprentice. "We are close to the—"

The Dark Lord didn't finish his sentence, which Marianne immediately took as a warning.

Though Valdemar hadn't moved an inch, his familiar was peeking out of his bag. Ktulu studied his master for a while, before focusing on the puddle of black blood left by the Pleromian. The creature was as eerily silent as its summoner.

Something is wrong, Marianne thought, her grip on her rapier tightening. She noticed the air bending around the black blood, the same way it had right before the Pleromian tried to skewer her with summoned blades. The noblewoman sensed the magic suffusing the air. *Is the body reacting to the soul's demise?*

"What's your scheme, apprentice?" Lord Och whispered, his head tilting to the side in confusion. Much to Marianne's surprise, he sounded almost as puzzled as she was. "I wonder . . ."

A new voice echoed in the engine room, coming from several places at once. Marianne's enhanced hearing noticed multiple sources hidden in the walls and pipes above them. Devices integrated into the machinery itself translating lightning into words.

"I detect unforeseen le-levels of occult eq-equations in your vicinity." The voice sounded vaguely male, but broken, stuttering, and *wrong*. A normal person wouldn't have noticed the difference with words spoken by a normal person, but Marianne also noticed a metal resonance similar to those produced by musical instruments in the background. "Ex-ex-explain yo-o-ourselves . . ."

"King Otto, you finally deign to speak with us?" Lord Och chuckled. "This is nothing that should concern you."

So Otto the Demented was truly in this facility, or close. Marianne wondered if she would have a chance to slay him and behead derrokind's government, but quickly squashed these vain hopes. In all likelihood, the mad king had put a safe distance between himself and Lord Och.

A short silence followed, but Marianne noticed movements among the pipes above their heads. She expected assassins hiding among them, before realizing that the metal itself was moving. The air simmered as the room's temperature increased.

"The analys-sis of body-language indicates that you ly-y-ying to *meeee* . . ."

Marianne shuddered as she sensed an electrical current in the air. This time, refusing to be separated from Valdemar, she grabbed him by the shoulder with her free hand. Wherever he went, she would follow.

"Wake up," Marianne whispered, her heartbeat quickening at the complete lack of response. She began to shake him, to no avail. "Valdemar, you need to wake up!"

Only then did she notice that her friend's shadow had subtly lengthened. The Haunter that Valdemar had summoned as a protector now covered the puddle of blackened slime with its shade. Three crimson eyes flickered like candles on the false shadow's surface, the Pleromian's blood reacting to them by pulsating like a heart.

And Valdemar still wouldn't move an inch. His pulse had grown so faint Marianne could barely hear it, his masked face gazing at nothing and nowhere.

"Lord Och, something is wrong!" Marianne warned the Dark Lord, who simply stroked his skeletal chin. The Haunter had completely covered the Pleromian's remains in a blanket of shadows, the two eldritch darknesses becoming one. "Lord Och—"

"How bold of you, young Valdemar," the Dark Lord muttered to himself while sparks of lightning flared around his ancient bones. "To force my hand so brazenly . . ."

The Haunter's shadow flickered, and it *laughed*.

Realizing the danger, Marianne pulled the unresponsive Valdemar toward the edge of the platform. The sorcerer fell backward, his familiar grabbing him by the neck while Marianne caught them both.

Her friend's shadow returned to normal, but the Pleromian's remains immediately underwent a horrendous transformation. The black blood coalesced into a large sphere over which grew inhuman eyes and fanged mouths. This protoplasmic ooze occupied the platform's center, corroding the steel underneath.

Did you plan this too, Lord Och? Marianne thought as she lifted Valdemar, preparing to jump to safety. The sphere of black blood, however, didn't make a move to attack. *What now?*

And then the mouths shrieked.

Marianne thought her ears would explode from the piercing cry, and it took all of her mental fortitude not to wince from the sudden increase in volume. The cry reverberated through the platform and then the walls.

Somehow, it drove the machinery mad. The pipes above their heads swirled like snakes before falling on the group below, breathing blazingly hot steam or boiling oil. Marianne sensed neither the presence of telekinesis nor hidden pulleys moving them. As far as her senses were concerned, the metal suddenly started moving on its own in impossible ways to strike at the intruders.

Supremely unimpressed, Lord Och raised his hand at the ceiling and cast the same fire spell he had used to destroy the Pleromian. His fingers unleashed a mighty fiery ray at the swirling pipes above the group's heads, vaporizing them and melting a large hole in the ceiling.

However, the pipes were only a prelude. The engines screeched beneath the platform and the surface of the room's remaining steel walls started to bend on its own. Marianne immediately recognized the signs of a haunted ground, but sensed no soul nor magic in the air. Had the derro somehow given life to metal?

The sphere of Pleromian blood soon stopped making a sound as it collapsed on itself. Space rippled around the phenomenon as it transformed into a growing speck of darkness in the fabric of reality itself, light and reality bending at its edges. The temperature dropped in its presence, the very heat siphoned away.

"Lord Och, what's happening?" Marianne asked as she pulled Valdemar closer to the platform's edge. Though the sphere of darkness's growth was painfully slow, she noticed the air sucked into an all-devouring hole.

"He has learned from the best, young Marianne," the lich replied with a hint of genuine pride. "My apprentice had his familiar turn the Pleromian into a living breach between planes and then used the Haunter to tune it to its home plane. Soon, this entire facility will be sucked into a land of eternal darkness."

A portal? Valdemar had created a portal? From her experience in Pleroma, Marianne knew that these kinds of breaches eventually collapsed on themselves after running out of magical power.

Otto Blutgang's voice howled across the engine room at the betrayal. Lightning surged above Marianne's head, but the breach seemed to interfere with the derro's teleportation technology.

"We need to leave now, young Marianne," Lord Och said as he began to levitate above the ground, using his fire spell to widen the hole he had opened in the ceiling. "Teleporting now would be risky, so I ask you to carry my apprentice to safety."

He didn't need to ask her twice. Realizing that Valdemar simply couldn't stand on his feet, let alone move by himself, Marianne sheathed her rapier before holding him with both hands; one beneath the legs and another holding the shoulders.

Now, Lord Bethor, the noblewoman thought as she closed her eyes and gritted her teeth. *I hope you didn't mislead me.*

The Blood flowed through her veins as it reshaped her flesh and shoulders. The material harvested from her spine-chain was repurposed into twin shapes growing beneath her skin.

And when the time came, they burst out of Marianne's back like an insect from a cocoon. The noblewoman suppressed a scream of pain as a pair of great batlike wings shredded her clothes and expanded. Five fingers of bones longer than her entire body protruded from her shoulders, bound together by a thin layer of skin. The rest of her skeleton had hollowed out from the inside and become as fragile as glass. Only the power of the Blood kept her in one piece.

Marianne opened her eyes while Ktulu tightly held on to Valdemar's neck. "No place for failure," she muttered to herself. "One, two . . ."

After gathering her breath, Marianne ran toward the platform's edge and jumped. The flapping of her wings sent out a mighty burst of wind, the blowback so abrupt that Marianne struggled not to throw up. Her entire body trembled with each movement, adjusting to the air current and density. She thought she would struggle every step of the way.

But it came easily to her. Her enhanced sense of touch picked up each subtle alteration in the air, allowing her to naturally adjust her trajectory. Her eyes noticed any debris that might pierce her wings. Her ears sensed the presence of obstacles as sound rebounded off them, guiding her to safety.

Lord Bethor was training me for this moment, Marianne realized. All these hard exercises over the last weeks, all these harsh drills to tune her reflexes to her newly enhanced senses, all the spells she had learned had formed the foundation of a greater whole. It had afforded her a gift that so few could enjoy in this world of tunnels and stone ceilings, a privilege almost as precious as the light itself.

Flight.

And so, Marianne soared into the metal skies with a smile on her face.

Lord Och had created a path into the ceiling and she happily flew after him. The lich was melting a blazing path forward, incinerating anything on the way.

The orb had grown large enough to swallow the platform behind them. Tremors spread through the facility, causing pipes to explode in clouds of steam and bolts to fly off the walls at an arrow's speed. Marianne dodged them all while dutifully following Lord Och.

"My, my," the undead archmage said as he glanced at Marianne, his gaze wandering to Ktulu holding on to his partner. "When is the second child?"

Marianne's jaw clenched as she sensed warm blood flushing to her cheeks. To outsiders, they must have looked like newlyweds.

"Why?" Marianne whispered to Valdemar as he seemed to regain consciousness. "Why have you done this?"

"He can't . . ." Valdemar struggled to form words. Though he had won the mental contest of will with the Pleromian, it had left him shaken. "He can't be allowed . . . to keep the portal . . . the price . . . too high . . ."

A mechanical echo reverberating through the corridors, a final curse. "You have chan-changed noth-th-ing, you tre-treacherous pack of lesser neu-neurons!" Otto Blutgang boasted. "I can reb-rebuild this infra-fra-structure. It will take ti-ti-i-ime, but I am *forever*."

"No . . ." Valdemar whispered. "You are merely . . . a long-term problem."

His familiar, who had been silent so far, grew agitated. "Ktulu!" He spat out incomprehensible words, his six eyes glancing in multiple directions at once. "Nyarlykrugu!"

The shadows lengthened in the corridors, flooding the factory with hunger. Even the famous derro steel melted into nothingness as easily as sugar in water, consumed by the void between worlds. In their escape, the group passed by golem and derro corpses with bloodied tongues growing out of their flesh as interplanar creatures started to manifest within them.

The darkness was gaining ground on them. But not fast enough to catch up.

Finally, Lord Och blasted his way past the fortified doors that had once sealed the facility from the outside world. The lich emerged into the reinforced tunnels of derrokind, closely followed by Marianne.

They were immediately welcomed with a hail of bullets, as barrels hidden in the walls opened fire on them. Marianne deftly avoided them, while Lord Och casually destroyed the devices by somehow collapsing space and crushing them to a pulp. The noblewoman noticed Valdemar gazing at the lich, probably in an attempt to figure out how his magic worked.

Marianne glanced over her shoulder, watching the darkness devour the facility's doors before slowly starting to recede. It would take minutes, maybe hours before the breach collapsed on itself. By then only another empty cavern would remain.

"Was it worth it?" Marianne whispered to Valdemar, who seemed to have recovered enough to stop shaking nonstop.

"It delayed his plans at least." Her calmness surprised him. "You're not mad? I could have killed us all."

"If you made such a drastic call, I assume you had your reasons," Marianne replied calmly. She trusted his judgment. "I would prefer a warning next time though."

"I couldn't. He was watching us. I had to hit him in an unexpected way."

Marianne sighed. "We will work on a hand signal of some kind."

Leaving the ruins behind, the trio returned to the Knights of the Shroud's camp. The crossroads of tunnels had turned into a fortified redoubt, using earth elementals to raise walls and trenches. Undead soldiers had arrived from Sabaoth to reinforce them and secure the region for the Empire of Azlant.

"I didn't know you could fly," Valdemar said as they finally landed near the camp. Knights immediately attended to Lord Och, but the lich dismissed them with a wave of his hand.

Neither did I, Marianne thought as Valdemar stood back on his feet and freed her hands. She clenched her teeth as her wings merged back into her flesh, leaving holes in the back of her clothes. "It's easier than I expected," she said, "but more painful than I thought."

"Power always has a price of some kind," Lord Och replied as he rejoined them, dusting off his clothes as if he had returned from a morning stroll. "I dare hope that you have something to show for this excursion, my dear apprentice? We came for a portal, and you destroyed it."

"I . . . I know how portals work, somewhat. They create a resonance of some kind between various life-forms on each side, but . . ." Valdemar touched his head with his left hand. His familiar was unusually quiet. "My head hurts . . . I can hardly remember half of it."

"What about the Pleromian's soul?" Marianne asked, fearful how it might affect him in the long term. "Is it destroyed?"

"Not . . . not truly?" Valdemar put a hand on his stomach. "It's inside me like digested food. I'm not sure what to make of this."

"Obviously, you should finish your meal and throw out the waste." Lord Och's eyes flared with ghostly light. "Young Valdemar, how about the Pleromian portals?"

"I . . . I know . . ." Valdemar's hand clenched into a fist, his voice turning bitter and angry. "I know you *know*."

Though Marianne didn't fully understand what was happening, the lich cackled with delight. "As my apprentice, it is your duty to learn what I know," he replied, "and mine to know what there is to learn. As for what I know . . . do not think I missed the holes in your memories, my student."

"Holes?" Marianne asked with a frown, Valdemar removing his mask to reveal the sweating face underneath. Black circles had formed around his eyes, and his skin had turned pale. "Valdemar, are you alright?"

"Intentionally damaging one's own mind is quite the dangerous proposition, especially for an amateur mind-mage like you," Lord Och said with amusement. "But I assume this is temporary, since the knowledge you gathered was too important to sacrifice. So where did you hide the information we sought? In your familiar's alien mind?"

The lich glanced at Ktulu, who fearfully hid back in his master's bag.

"I . . ." Valdemar shook his head. "I don't know what you're talking about."

"Of course not, apprentice, you erased your memory of your own plan. Perhaps you expect to naturally come across the information and recognize it for what it was?"

"This . . . Lord Och, forgive me, but this seems far-fetched," Marianne said, standing up to Valdemar's defense. "His memory loss could simply be a side effect of fighting off the Pleromian soul."

"My apprentice is many things, young Marianne, but incompetent isn't one of them. I know you don't believe this is an accident either, and are just trying to lessen his punishment." As always, the lich seemed more amused than insulted. "But I reserve such treatment for meaningful obstruction. This childish ploy will not keep me in the dark for long."

Valdemar said nothing, glaring at his master. *I need to know what he saw,* Marianne decided, before immediately trying to cover up her thoughts so Lord Och wouldn't read them. *Damn it!*

Lord Och chuckled. "So you have learned Lord Bethor's lesson, and will try to protect your charge even against the likes of me?"

Marianne straightened up. "It is my duty."

The lich examined her more closely. "It is not *duty* that motivates you, young Marianne. You are too honest to lie to yourself."

It took Marianne all her strength to keep a stony face as Valdemar looked at her in confusion.

"Anyway, let us return to Sabaoth to review what we learned and forgot." The lich snapped his fingers as he walked away, expecting his acolytes to follow without a word. "We have rats to hunt and a Sabbath to prepare for."

1 3

HIDDEN DAGGERS

Grim Sabaoth was abuzz with activity today. As a Domain forged for war alone, its people took little pleasure in anything. Celebrations and entertainment were foreign to them. Yet as criers distributed newspapers while singing about the latest news from the front, the gloomy mood turned to quiet satisfaction.

"The fortress-city of Stahlstadt has fallen!" a crier shouted in the middle of the market street, standing atop a pedestal of steel. He raised the latest newspaper edition above his head, trying to make a sale. "War rages on the front as the Knights of the Shroud accumulate victories! Learn the latest news of our glorious conquest in today's edition of the *Midnight Voice*! One copper piece! One copper!"

As a warlike realm where entertainment was seen as a distraction at best, Sabaoth had no restaurants, only barracks. Thankfully, Valdemar and Marianne had become regular customers at a fried fish stand whose undead owner had kindly set aside a table and chairs at the back of his shop. The heat was suffocating as the undead cook prepared their meal and they had little space to move, but after everything the duo had faced in the derros' tunnels, they craved a feeling of normalcy.

While his bodyguard read the newspaper, Valdemar looked at the market street while waiting for his friends to arrive. They couldn't access Lord Bethor's tower, but they should find their way to this address.

Valdemar had come without his Nightwalker mask and under a disguise, to avoid spies of the cult identifying him. He had also reshaped his flesh, changing his hair color to black, his eyes to blue, and subtly altered his facial features and voice. He was wearing *a* mask—one made of flesh and skin rather than wood.

At this point, Valdemar wasn't even sure which part of his body had been with him from birth and which ones he had borrowed from Bethor's tower. After observing the Pleromian's regeneration, he had also figured out his own healing factor worked similarly: by absorbing organic material from Ialdabaoth itself. Only his soul was truly his own.

At least it allowed me to teleport out of the tower without Lord Och's help, Valdemar thought. After learning about the true nature of portals, the summoner had experimented with teleportation spells and found it surprisingly easy to master. As he was half-Ialdabaoth, thanks to his fatherly heritage, all of Underland resonated with him. The eyes on the walls were beacons in the Blood to him.

Valdemar suspected this was the same mechanism that allowed the Lilith to teleport across the tunnels at will. He was wary of abusing this spell in case his enemies could redirect it, though Lord Och had found the possibility unlikely. *A servant does not summon a prince,* the lich had mused out loud.

"It seems Lord Bethor has made quick progress," Marianne said as she read. "But the Excavator made a 'temporary stop to secure conquered territories.'"

"The usual propaganda slang for 'it was sabotaged mid-campaign,'" Valdemar translated as the cook served them their food. The summoner put his bag on a seat and tossed a fish inside. His familiar let out a squeal of happiness as it devoured the meal. "Do you think the derro kingdom will fall?"

"We both know it won't."

"I know the war won't end until Otto's spirit is exorcised from his machinery," Valdemar replied with a sigh. "However, do you think the loss of this fortress could prove a tipping point of some kind?"

To his disappointment, Marianne shook her head. "No, Valdemar, I do not think so. Stahlstadt was a major fortress for the derro and its conquest will give us a foothold in their territory, but it's not a keystone of Blutgang's war machine. It might be the first step toward a prolonged campaign, but I can hardly call it a decisive conquest."

Valdemar looked at his tea, as black and bitter as his mood.

"Do you feel pity for the derros?" Marianne asked.

"You don't?"

"I do," she confessed. "Even though they were bitter foes long before Otto the Nail came along, the idea of having my mind overwritten by someone else, to lose my body and free will to someone else . . . it is not a fate I wish for anyone."

"That's not even the worst part. Blutgang could replicate minds." Valdemar couldn't get the memory of that deluded golem out of his head. "If an imitation is so perfect that it becomes indistinguishable from the original, what does it say about us? If someone could recreate you perfectly, turn your innermost thoughts into a script, and then copy it . . . does it mean people are no different than tools or gears? Is turning into machines the future of life?"

"I do not know," Marianne answered, though her next words were more optimistic. "But I can tell you one thing. The future is what we will make of it. Otto Blutgang is trying to steer our world in one direction, but it's not the only one. We can offer better outcomes and fight for them."

"That's the thing," Valdemar replied with pessimism. "I should be working to destroy that infernal machine he's spreading across Underland rather than reading about it in newspapers."

"Valdemar, you cannot fight all the evils of the world at once. You have to pick your battles or you will go mad with despair and frustration." Marianne smiled, though there was sadness in it. "Our country's troops and Lord Bethor are doing a fine job at fighting the derros. Have some faith. We have other foes to deal with first, but Blutgang's turn will come."

If only he could believe that she was right . . .

The stalemate with the derros disappointed Valdemar, but sadly didn't surprise him. Lord Och had echoed a similar sentiment back when his apprentice reported what he had learned in the facility.

"You were correct on one front, my apprentice. King Otto is a long-term problem. If his essence is truly spread across the entire derro kingdom, it might take centuries to wipe him out." Lord Och had shrugged. "I informed Lord Bethor, who will almost certainly melt away every piece of machinery he finds in conquered territories. Eventually, his advance will be halted by derro resistance and his required presence at the Sabbath, but the destruction he sows should disrupt their technology's influence over the Outer Darkness."

"Forgive me, my teacher," Valdemar had replied with a frown, "but I have just told you that a madman is trying to become an iron god. How can you sound so . . . unconcerned?"

The lich had laughed in response. "Sweet naïve child. Young Valdemar, when you reach my age you will have survived more wars and disasters than water leaks."

By now, Valdemar was almost convinced that Lord Och didn't give a shit about *anything*. The lich treated the most terrible news with amusement at best and disdain at worst. His eternal life had completely detached him from the day-to-day concerns of humanity. Which was why Valdemar had grown to believe his theory about the Pleromian portal.

At least I prevented him from getting the codes needed to activate it, the summoner thought, though he couldn't remember where he had hidden them. Even Ktulu didn't have any hint to provide. *I probably hid them in plain sight somewhere . . .*

Marianne lowered her journal, a look of concern on her face. "You're worried about them, aren't you?"

Was that so obvious? "I don't get why Lord Och didn't sacrifice them already," Valdemar confessed. "He had plenty of opportunities to do so."

"Lord Och is cruel, but also pragmatic to the bone," Marianne pointed out. "I believe his reasoning is the same behind his decision not to turn you into a portal. He keeps his options open in case a better alternative comes along. As long as his scholars live, they can work and research for him. Why kill them when letting them live is more useful?"

"But you think he wouldn't hesitate a second if there was no better option."

Marianne bit her lower lip before answering. "Master Edwin once warned me that none of Lord Och's affability is genuine," she admitted. "'It's all theater to him, a game you play with a pet.' I don't think I have ever seen the real him."

Valdemar joined his hands as he reviewed his interactions with his mentor. Almost all of them shared an undercurrent of playfulness, except a few. "There are moments where he showed genuine anger in our discussions," he said. "When I rattled him the wrong way."

The idea of Lord Och losing his composure clearly astonished Marianne. "How did you do so?"

"I insisted that I wouldn't become cynical like him, and questioned how he had become . . . well, what he is today."

"You would think an ancient lich would be above that kind of remark." Marianne frowned. "Unless . . . it's not what you said that bothered him, but the way you did it."

Valdemar raised an eyebrow. "What do you mean?"

"If we assume his story about being a disciple of this 'Sophia' is true, then there was a time when he truly believed in saving mankind from itself. Maybe you remind him of who he used to be, and he hates it."

Valdemar considered her words, and found the theory plausible . . . though, in the end, it changed little. The summoner only cared about Lord Och's motivation insofar as it could help him save his friends from a gruesome sacrifice.

"Marianne," Valdemar whispered, "if that day comes . . . if Lord Och makes a move against the Scholars at the Institute . . . what will you do?"

Marianne joined her hands together, glancing at her own drink while setting the newspaper aside. Her face was a mask of stone, but her eyes revealed her inner turmoil.

"You don't have to say something that will please me," Valdemar said. Lord Och was her benefactor after all, and a powerful mage. He couldn't expect her to defy him, even if to save others.

"No, I'm . . . I'm trying to put my thoughts in order. It's . . ." Marianne took a heavy breath. "Before I answer you, can I ask you something?"

Valdemar nodded wordlessly.

"You told me once that you believed in making sacrifices for your dream," Marianne said. "For the greater good. When, in your opinion, would sacrificing people to this portal be justified?"

"I would understand if the situation was truly desperate and we needed to evacuate through it to save the most people possible," Valdemar replied. "But in that case, I would rather sacrifice myself and become a door between worlds."

"Why so?"

"Because my life isn't worth a dozen others." Valdemar adjusted his posture, his back straightening. "Because why would *others* have to make a greater sacrifice so *I* could live? Using the Pleromian portal would just be a cover for my own selfishness. I don't think you should sacrifice others if you are unwilling to pay the ultimate price yourself."

Marianne listened to his words with a gaze so intense that Valdemar couldn't help but find it uncomfortable. Once he had finished, her fingers fidgeted a moment before her expression changed into one of quiet resignation.

"I believe the Dark Lords are necessary for mankind's survival," she declared. "That the Empire of Azlant is necessary, even though I do not agree with all of its laws. Mankind is besieged by monsters, and the greater good often demands sacrifices. Though I resent his training methods, I cannot deny that Lord Bethor is doing his best in his own way to strengthen us and protect our civilization from extinction. Lord Och, for all of his faults, pushes the limits of our understanding forward; and with it, our ability to fight back against the Strangers."

"I sense a 'but' coming."

"You know me too well," Marianne replied with a low chuckle. "I stand by what I just said . . . but I do not see how sacrificing innocent people who trust you for your personal gain serves the greater good. I do not think that taking the easy way for the sake of convenience is the righteous path. And so although I agreed to serve Lord Och in exchange for his patronage . . . if he goes through with sacrificing the Scholars to that portal, then I cannot let it slide."

To Valdemar's surprise, Marianne took his hand into her own. Her velvet glove brushed against his warm skin.

"Valdemar," she said softly while locking eyes with him. "The fact you are willing to sacrifice yourself rather than others is what makes you a better person than Lord Och. This is why I consider you a dear friend worth fighting for, and if things come to blows between our master and you . . . then I shall stand by your side." Even after seeing Lord Och's power in all of its glory, Marianne would still rather do the right thing.

Valdemar smiled in genuine gratitude. "Thanks."

His happy expression made Marianne blush. "You are welcome."

The moment lasted longer than Valdemar expected. To his surprise, neither of them let the other's hand go as they stared at each other. Valdemar realized the scene was *highly* improper, but something in him simply didn't want to let her go.

Marianne eventually broke the contact first, looking . . . embarrassed, for a lack of a better term.

"It is not duty that motivates you, young Marianne," Lord Och had said in the tunnels. "You are too honest to lie to yourself."

Could it be . . .

No, Valdemar, be serious, the sorcerer thought. It's the constant proximity and the absence of a dating life clouding your judgment. The fact we're getting closer doesn't mean anything more than that. You're seeing things that aren't there.

And even if his intuition was correct, Valdemar wasn't certain what he should do about it. His life was fraught with danger, and so long as the Verney cult roamed Underland, the summoner would never know peace. It wasn't exactly the best foundation for an intimate relationship, with Marianne or anyone else.

Valdemar sipped his drink and looked away. It was a bitter hot mix of rancid herbs and water, but he found it better than the awkwardness of the previous moment. "What else is in the news?"

Marianne jumped at the opportunity to change the subject and swiftly grabbed her newspaper. "The plague, I'm afraid."

While Valdemar had trained under Lord Bethor and struck at the derros, his family's cult had been hard at work. As it was mostly made of undead and golems under a constant military curfew, Sabaoth's population was barely touched by the wererat plague. But other Domains had been severely touched with disease clusters; though the Empire's biomancers, harsh curfews, and transportation controls had prevented widespread contaminations, they couldn't eradicate the threat either.

Marianne's expression suddenly harshened as she read. "What is it?" Valdemar asked.

His bodyguard and friend turned the newspaper to reveal an article, and the drawing of his face at its center.

The artist had done Valdemar dirty by giving him a thuggish look, but his work had been quite close to the truth all the same.

"Saklas shaken with gruesome murders." Valdemar read in silence, a chill going down in his spine. "Four couples dead, eaten by rats . . . children missing . . . credit taken by the Brotherhood of the Red Grail . . . in Valdemar Verney's name . . ."

They killed innocent people and signed their crimes with his name.

"How could they reveal your face?" Marianne whispered, incensed. "This is insane . . ."

"The Knights of the Chain censor information that displeases the Dark Lords, but they answer to Ophiel the Mad and not to Och," Valdemar replied grimly. Neither could they stomach the fact that the summoner had escaped their grasp only to find refuge in Paraplex. "At least the article says I am 'safely behind bars.'"

Marianne glanced at the street. "People saw me with you last time," she whispered. "But you had your mask on and were wearing different clothes too. I don't think they will make the connection."

And that was what the cult wanted. To isolate Valdemar and stir the pot until they could learn of his exact location. They probably guessed he was in Sabaoth for now, but were too afraid of Lord Bethor to challenge him yet. Perhaps they hoped that public pressure would force the Dark Lords to relinquish him.

If so, they would be disappointed. Lord Och cared nothing about the people's opinion, and Lord Bethor was more likely to answer dissent with fire than compromise.

Their compatriots, though . . .

"Any sighting of Bertrand?" Valdemar asked.

"No." Marianne shook her head in sadness, before looking up at something behind her friend. "They're here."

Valdemar turned his head to the side, watching Iren and Liliane walk up the street toward Marianne. A hooded figure in a plague doctor's outfit followed them closely, the summoner recognizing the disguise as Hermann's.

"Valdy, is that you?" Liliane put a hand on her waist as she reached their table. "I didn't know you could use illusion magic."

"I can't," he replied, kissing her on the cheek. Valdemar was almost certain he had caught a furtive look of longing on Marianne's face, though it might have been his mind playing tricks. Definitely a trick. "How did you guess so quickly?"

"Are you kidding? You changed your voice too?" Liliane chuckled. "I just felt it, silly."

"Your posture is the same, friend," Iren pointed before saluting Marianne and sitting next to her. "You've got to adjust your body language, the way you move . . . all these invisible hints we've grown accustomed to."

Valdemar groaned in surrender, as he realized he couldn't lie to save his life. Still, the sight of his friends brought a smile to his lips. "I didn't think you would be here either, Hermann," he said as he greeted the troglodyte.

"I was worried . . . when I heard word that you had joined the war effort." Hermann nodded to himself. "I am glad you're okay . . ."

It appeared that Hermann's speech had improved since Valdemar last saw him. He could form longer sentences without stopping to consider his next words, and his pronunciation was clearer than ever.

"Oh, is that your familiar?" Liliane said as she sat next to Valdemar and peeked inside his bag. "It's so cute."

"Ktulu!" the squid said from inside the bag, giggling as Liliane started to tickle it. "Ktulu!"

"You love when I tickle you? You love it?" Liliane asked with a grin. The scene reminded Valdemar of a young girl playing with a puppy. "Can I borrow him? Her? It?"

"I think of Ktulu as a *he*, though I don't think his species has a concept of gender, but sure, you can pet it for a while," Valdemar said with a chuckle. "Please do not parade it around though."

"Now I want a familiar of my own," Liliane replied with a giggle.

"You still didn't . . . answer how you changed your appearance," Hermann rasped as he sat next to Liliane. "I am . . . curious."

"I learned to practice biomancy," Valdemar replied as Marianne ordered food for everyone.

"You can?" Liliane asked with a grin, though Iren's expression was decidedly less enthusiastic. No doubt he still had sore feelings about the art considering his youth. "Great, I have something I need to consult you on! Do you and Marianne have anything planned for today?"

"Not much," Marianne replied. "Lord Och is occupied with the Sabbath and Lord Bethor is on the front."

"Great, then could you come with me after our meal? I'm supposed to visit my father at the armories, but there's something I want to discuss with you on the way." Liliane locked eyes with Marianne. "I think Lady Mathilde and I found a way to cure your retainer, and that horrible plague too."

Marianne's head instantly perked up in hope. "You did?"

"Maybe. I need to consult Valdy first to confirm my theory, but I'm optimistic. We could have a cure underway by the time we return to the Institute."

This was great news, but the Institute's mention sent a chill down Valdemar's spine. "Hypothetically," he said. "If you had to leave the Institute in a hurry and escape Paraplex, could you do it?"

Liliane frowned, disturbed by the question. "Why?"

"We could, but we wouldn't get far," Iren replied with a shrug. "All scholars and employees of the Pleroma Institute surrender a drop of blood when they arrive. The Knights of the Tome could use it to track us anywhere."

And with it, Lord Och could potentially summon them to his location at any time. "I have . . . learned something worrying about the Institute," the summoner confessed to his friends. "But I need to check my theory first."

"You think your grandfather's cult will infiltrate the Institute?" Iren asked, misunderstanding the source of the danger. "Rest assured, even a Dark Lord would struggle to breach its walls."

"We know you didn't order these horrors, Valdy," Liliane reassured him. "Nobody is going to hunt you inside Pleroma."

"It's not just the cult that bothers me, but they're part of the problem." Valdemar took a long deep breath before revealing his plans. "I intend to destroy these people for good, and make sure they never rise again. But I cannot do it alone."

"Say no more." Iren revealed a dagger hidden up his sleeve. "I've slit a few throats back in the day."

"I'm not so much of a fighter or an investigator," Liliane said with a smirk as she stopped tickling Ktulu. The familiar peeked out of its bag, extremely disappointed. "But if you need help, Valdy, I'll give you a hand."

Hermann simply offered a nod, before examining Valdemar closely. "You didn't . . . bring your mask today."

"The Nightwalker can see through it," Valdemar explained, "and I couldn't let it spy on our conversation."

Hermann immediately guessed why. "This is about . . . the Painted World?"

"You said you could use it to trap a Nahemoth, if I remember well?" Marianne asked. "How would it work?"

"By luring the creature to one place . . . and using the right spells . . . we can seal the Nahemoth inside a prepared canvas." Hermann cleared his throat. "The canvas is finished . . . all we need is to fill it."

"What will happen to the Nahemoth afterward?" Valdemar asked, the ghastly memory of his stillborn, monstrous brother Crétail flaring in his mind.

"It . . . it will become the Painted World," Hermann answered. "The earth and the mountains . . . the water and the light . . . the very force of gravity. Always present and alive but . . . thoughtless . . . like a tree. A peaceful existence."

Is that what you would have wanted for Crétail, Mom? Valdemar wondered. It still beat a tormented existence down a well, or being used as a tool to bring about the end of days. "Like reincarnation?" he asked softly.

Hermann nodded. "But it cannot suffice alone . . . a Nahemoth is pure, gangrenous creativity . . . without a destructive power to achieve an equilibrium . . . the Painted World will grow rampant and unstable."

As Valdemar suspected. "What force do you think could counterbalance a Nahemoth?"

"I think . . . we had the same idea about how . . . to solve that problem." Yes, they did.

"Though it will be risky and require a very specific set of circumstances," Valdemar said. "The Nahemoth will have to be free for a start. Which will probably be inevitable at this point."

"The canvas is ready . . ." Hermann rasped. "I can teach you the ritual . . . I will be with you . . ."

"Thanks, Hermann." After exchanging a nod with the troglodyte, Valdemar turned to another friend. "Iren."

"Yes?"

"Can I talk to you in private for a minute?"

"Are you going to do some shady stuff again?" Liliane asked with a frown. "Please don't get caught by the derros this time."

I've had enough of these dwarves for a lifetime, Valdemar thought as he led Iren to a street corner away from the stand and unwelcome ears. They must have looked suspicious, but it shouldn't take long.

"Lord Och usually sends you outside his Domain for deliveries and information gathering, right?" Valdemar asked the half-doppelganger.

"Why are you asking me something you already know?" Iren chuckled. "If you want me to get you some illegal stuff, you just have to ask."

"Not quite. I need to deliver a letter to someone." Valdemar gathered his breath. "A message that Lord Och mustn't know the contents of."

Iren remained silent a full minute before answering with a stone-faced expression. "You are asking me to do something behind the Dark Lord's back. I hope you understand the risks involved."

"I won't force you if you don't want to," Valdemar said. "I'm asking you because you are my friend and I trust you."

"My, how touching." There was no hint of sarcasm in Iren's voice as a small smile formed on the edge of his lips. "Well, you saved my hide so I guess I can grant you your wish. So long as it doesn't involve betraying mankind to the Strangers. Who would be the message's recipient?"

"Phaleg the Binder, the Dark Lord of Ariouth." And Lord Och's former apprentice. "There's something I must know before the Sabbath."

14

THE WEIGHT OF DREAMS

Liliane's father, as usual for powerful people, made his guests wait at his leisure. Valdemar had heard it was a power move among nobles and wealthy elites, but he thought the man would have made an exception for his own daughter. Apparently not. His servants pretended that Count de Vane was busy with an important meeting that overstayed its welcome.

At least his Sabaoth office offered a welcome contrast with the rest of the Domain. The waiting room had enough stuffed chairs to seat a dozen people, and even included its own fireplace. Paintings of de Vane family members adorned the wall alongside tapestries, while the window offered a nice view of the foundries outside. Magical wards erased the noise from outside, giving the guests a degree of seclusion. Servants had left the group alone with refreshments, bidding them to wait until their master was ready to receive them.

While Iren had gone to carry out the favor his friend asked of him and Hermann examined the paintings in the room, Valdemar and Marianne were using the free time productively. "So," Valdemar resumed, Ktulu playing with a bone ship next to his chair, "Lady Mathilde taught you how to recreate her Elixir of Life?"

"She didn't teach me, but she gave me some insight into how it worked," Liliane replied as she sank into her chair. "It uses advanced alchemy to revert the body to an earlier state registered in the body's memory while leaving the soul untouched. However, if improperly prepared, the effect is partial, causing cancers, tumors . . ."

"Or making the body shrink down in age until they go back to a fetus?" Valdemar guessed.

Liliane forced herself to smile. "Lady Mathilde showed me the failed results of her prototypes and . . . they weren't pretty."

"But how would it help Bertrand?" Marianne asked with a frown, her arms crossed while her eyes wandered to the window and doors from time to time. She always remained wary of an attack. "The Beast Plague bonds with a target on a fundamental level."

"Yes, but hear me out." Liliane raised a finger, delighting at explaining to them her ingenious idea. "Lady Mathilde agreed to do a test on an infected subject. For a brief moment after taking the Elixir of Life, their body reverted to a healthy state . . . only to be reinfected shortly thereafter."

Valdemar's eyes widened. "He carried the plague, but didn't show the symptoms immediately?"

"Yes . . ." Hermann rasped as he turned away from the paintings to join the conversation. "The Beast Plague . . . it takes a moment to take root in someone's flesh. For less than a few minutes . . . it circulates in the body, but doesn't bond with it."

"And that's where I had a great idea," Liliane said. "The Black Blood probably works the same way. We could restrain Bertrand, give him a shot of the Elixir of Life, and then immediately extract the mutagens in his body before they bond to his flesh again. But we would need a good biomancer to run the procedure."

"Not any biomancer . . ." Hermann countered. "If they extract the Black Blood . . . they will be in contact with it and risk mutating."

"I can do it," Valdemar replied firmly. "Even touching a Pleromian's body didn't affect me, and it was made of the stuff. But how many bottles of Elixir of Life could we afford to use?"

Liliane's enthusiasm faltered. "Precious few. It's super complicated to make, and the wrong dose causes side effects."

So they couldn't mass-produce it to cure the Beast Plague . . . not yet at least. And Bertrand would fight back while transformed. So long as the Black Blood held sway, he was little more than a savage hellhound for the Verney cult.

Valdemar kept his thoughts to himself, for Marianne's face beamed with hope. For the first time in many weeks, they had a credible shot at curing her butler and friend. "I thank you, Liliane," she said while offering Liliane a nod. "If this works . . ."

"It will." Liliane took the older woman's hand in her own. "I know you worry about him, but you aren't facing this threat alone. They want to divide us with their lies and diseases because they know we will figure out a solution together."

After so many nights of fighting, Valdemar found it relieving to watch Marianne's face breathe in life and hope. Liliane's warm personality had a way to reassure people, to convince them everything was alright. *She would make a terrific politician*, Valdemar thought, *if she were a little less earnest.*

"Now . . . the question is how we catch them unaware . . ." Hermann rasped as he glanced at Valdemar. "You are the best bait . . . and we know the place . . . where they gather."

"If the Dark Lords allow us to strike them," Valdemar pointed out. Lord Bethor had already all but stated that he would run the operation himself, and that his apprentices would have to follow his lead. "They might ask us to sit the conflict out or worse."

"And something else . . . bothers me." Hermann cleared his throat. "You said that in your dreams . . . the Lilith collected *skins*."

Valdemar nodded slowly. "I didn't understand why though."

Liliane bit her lower lip, letting Marianne's hand go. "They didn't say it in the news, but . . ." she gulped. "Friends in Saklas told me that some of the murder victims had been flayed alive after being inflicted with the Beast Plague."

Marianne's hopeful expression turned into a scowl. "They're harvesting them? For what, a ritual?"

Valdemar tried to remember his dreams the best he could. "I think they said something about calling a soul out from the darkness, or something along the that line. They needed a special container."

"A Qlippoth?" Hermann asked. "Maybe they . . . intend to summon a Nahemoth."

"Maybe," Valdemar conceded with some skepticism, "but I don't know any Qlippoth that needs wererat skins as part of its summoning ritual."

"In any case, their crimes are clearly building up to *something*," Marianne pointed out. "Whatever it is, we must strike them before they can finish their preparations."

Valdemar could only agree with her.

"Ktulu!" The summoner looked at his left as his familiar raised his cracked bone-ship toy at him with a displeased look. "Ktulhulhu!"

"What is it?" Valdemar sighed as he realized Ktulu had broken his toy again. "Seriously, can't you be more care—"

The summoner never finished his sentence. He had noticed something scratched on the toy's side.

The bone-ship's hull was an immaculate white, crafted from Valdemar's own immortal body. But Ktulu had scratched something on its surface with its tiny claws. A set of symbols so tiny and crude that his summoner could barely identify them.

Numbers.

Thirty-eight, thirty-seven. Four, twenty. One-hundred and one, three . . .

Valdemar's eyes widened as he understood the sequence's significance, rising from his seat. "I need to go."

"What?" Liliane blinked at her friend, as he grabbed Ktulu in his arms. "Right now?"

"It shouldn't take long." Now that he had learned to teleport, distance mattered little to him. "But I cannot bring you with me, Marianne."

His partner didn't hide her displeasure. "Where you go, I follow."

"No. I am sorry, but not this time." Lord Och would immediately detect her presence otherwise. "I swear I will be back soon."

Marianne locked her gaze with him, and at this moment Valdemar seriously wondered if she could read his mind. "Are you truly certain?" she asked with worry, but Valdemar nodded all the same. "Alright then. But please be wary."

"And return quickly," Liliane asked with a frown. "If this is just an excuse to not wait with us, I'll never forgive you."

Valdemar offered her a nod as the fabric of space bent around him. He teleported away, leaving Sabaoth for another Domain.

All areas of Underland were bound by the Blood, from the lowest tunnel to the frontier of the world's surface. The veins of Ialdabaoth had spread all over the planet like a tree's roots, leaving no place unspoiled by their corruption.

Not even a Dark Lord's vault.

Using the Blood and his connection to Ialdabaoth, Valdemar could teleport anywhere he wanted, so long as he had seen the place beforehand. And he had had enough experience with his master's lair, both from his memory and that of his harvested soul.

Ignoring the gaze of the Pleromian statues as he walked toward the central vault, Valdemar examined his grandfather's journal. "Thirty-eight," he whispered to himself, flipping the pages. "Thirty-seven . . . not enough words . . ."

Ktulu preferred to walk rather than stay in his bag for once and glanced at the ruins with curiosity while he held his bone-ship toy. Valdemar would have to destroy the item afterwards to prevent Lord Och from figuring out the truth, but for now the summoner had the benefit of time. His master was busy preparing for the Sabbath, and though his vault's protective wards were advanced, Valdemar's knowledge had grown in the past weeks. He could bypass them.

But who was he kidding? Of course Lord Och would know. Valdemar doubted that his master didn't have redundant hidden systems to warn him about intrusions in his vault, even if the summoner couldn't detect them. What mattered was that he wouldn't learn about it quickly enough to interfere.

In fact, a part of Valdemar wanted the lich to know. He wished to show the ancient undead that his apprentice wasn't some pawn he could manipulate at will and then callously throw his friends aside without repercussions. Even if Valdemar lacked the power to meaningfully challenge the Dark Lord, he would show that he had the resolve to try.

And if the summoner failed to activate the portal bloodlessly . . . then he would erase the activation codes again without the possibility of recovery, denying Lord Och the opportunity to kill anyone.

"Syllables," Valdemar decided after counting the words. "Syllables it is."

There was only one book in the world that Valdemar had almost entirely memorized by heart, the same way priests mastered scriptures of the Light. No one else could decode this series of numbers, because no one else understood its frame of reference.

And Ktulu . . . Valdemar had imprinted the sequence in his subconscious, without the familiar realizing its significance. A mind reader wouldn't have caught this information among the chaotic streams of thoughts of its childish spirit.

"I have the sequence now," Valdemar whispered as he closed the journal and hid it beneath his Scholar's robes. "I have to try . . . to make it work without any death . . ."

He walked into the Pleromian vault, facing the great slumbering portal. The underground was an empty tomb, silent and lifeless.

Valdemar approached the portal with his familiar following him. The Pleromian soul inside him reacted to the device's presence, the same way a faithful hound remembered the smell of an old house it had once called home. Valdemar's fingers trailed against the archway's alien metal, his fingers examining the structure while he analyzed it with his psychic sight.

Even after centuries of dormancy, the summoner could still sense the blood soaking the structure.

After having strengthened his magic under Lord Bethor's tutelage and gathered knowledge from the Pleromian soul, Valdemar delved into the portal's structure farther than ever before. He hadn't noticed any soul within its archway the first time . . . but now that Valdemar examined the device more carefully, he realized he had been wrong. There was at least one soul inside this portal, buried deep inside the steel. So ancient that Valdemar struggled to distinguish it from the portal's matter. Was it all that remained of the portal's original sacrifices? If so then it meant that Lord Och hadn't yet sacrificed anyone to it.

"No time to waste," Valdemar whispered as he looked under his clothes and brought out small bottles full of blood. Hermann had kindly contributed to it, alongside Iren. Valdemar would have added Frigga's lifeblood as well if he could have, but he hoped that his own semi-divine lifeblood would compensate.

Soaking the archway with his friends' blood, Valdemar bit his thumb and added his own body fluid to the mix. The fluids tainted the dark metal red, but didn't form any magical crystal on its surface. A bad omen.

Valdemar spoke the syllables in the order detailed in Ktulu's message, and he sensed the portal answering his call. The device was too weak to open a breach, but it recognized the summoner's mastery at least.

If Valdemar could open the gate through his own power and lifeblood, then nobody would have to die.

"Open the path," Valdemar ordered while Ktulu watched. "Open the path to Earth. The Red Prince demands it." His blood floated out of his wound as the portal thrummed, the archway breathing like a living creature. Its heartbeat echoed across the vault, its surface brightening with sorcery.

And yet no tear in space opened.

Valdemar, who had so easily torn space apart by sacrificing the Pleromian and a Haunter, found the fabric of reality an impermeable fortress.

The portal listened to his orders, but it didn't help. The place he sought to access was too far away, the power offered insufficient to open a breach. Even though Valdemar was a demigod, the prince of the Blood and scion of an ancient deity, the toll of passage was far too great for his meager offering.

The portal hungered for far more than blood. It needed a rarer resource, a fuel as precious as the burning heart of stars. It craved *souls*.

And not just any kind. As Valdemar's spirit worked in tune with the portal's magical architecture, he realized that only specific souls would do. Summoned creatures could be slain on this metal altar, but their souls would resist and fight back. Unless they gave their lives away, surrendered themselves wholly and fully to the steel, their strength would be turned inward rather than outward. So long as a spirit longed for life and freedom, it would never work in harmony with the portal. Only martyrs willing to offer everything would do.

And the plane he sought to access demanded very specific sacrifices. The blood of plants and lizards, of mammals and fish and birds. Valdemar felt a phantom connection between this portal and the Earth he craved so much, brought about by his blood. His own soul alone could fuel the device . . . or that of a carefully selected lot. Nothing else would work.

Valdemar deactivated the portal with the command codes as a tear failed to materialize, the archway returning to sleep. His blood hadn't yet dried on the archway, nor had Hermann's.

"It is useless," a familiar voice said. "I already tried."

Valdemar tensed as he heard Lord Och's footsteps behind him. Ktulu immediately hid behind his master. The familiar was wary of Lord Bethor, but something about Och frightened him to the bone.

"Blood is a good fuel, but it is neither rare nor precious." The lich walked at his apprentice's side, gazing at the bodily fluids soaking the portal. "A little food and your body produces more all the time. Souls though? Souls are priceless . . . especially when willingly offered. Not even a god's blood is an acceptable substitute."

Valdemar glared at his master. "Shouldn't you be preparing for the Sabbath, my teacher?"

"Shouldn't you be visiting young Liliane's father, apprentice?"

There was no escape.

"You knew all along, didn't you?" Valdemar asked in defiance.

"I may not look like it, but I am an immortal creature with more years than you can count. I have schemed and plotted for centuries. Few tricks surprise me." The lich chuckled. "I take back what I just said. My, why are you thinking of Pleromian orgies of all things?"

Valdemar remained silent as a tomb, but the undead archmage was wise enough to figure it out.

"Ah, clever apprentice, you are using what little remains of the Pleromian's soul as a screen so I cannot read your thoughts. Truly inventive . . . but alas, futile." Lord Och glanced at the empty archway. "I learned the portal's codes within the first five minutes of our dear Pleromian guest's electrotherapy. Even if you deactivate the device, a mere word will wake it up."

"You're bluffing."

"Am I?" The Dark Lord said a few ancient words of power, and Valdemar heard the portal stir in response. The machinery of the Pleromians answered Lord Och's call, before falling asleep once again.

A crushing weight of despair and impotent rage fell on Valdemar's shoulders, as he realized it had all been a trick. "It's impossible," he muttered. "You couldn't . . . you couldn't possibly anticipate . . ."

"You foolish disciple, have you learned nothing? I know all of your plans before they even cross your mind, because a long, *long* time ago . . ." The lich waved a hand at his chest, and then in his apprentice's direction. "I was exactly like you."

"I'm nothing like you!" Valdemar spat. "I wouldn't betray people who trusted me for my personal gain!"

"What betrayal are you accusing me of?"

"Is it true?" Valdemar rasped, trying to keep his anger in check. "Did you truly gather the scholars for the express purpose of sacrificing them? Did you give these people hope and knowledge, only to fatten them like beasts for the slaughter?"

The answer was swift, the tone casual.

"Yes, of course." The lich didn't bother to deny it. "It's not a betrayal, since I would have needed to care first. Young Hermann, Liliane, even Marianne . . . they are like giant beetles to me. We breed these creatures to carry loads and win races. Then when they grow too old or weak to serve and start to cost more to keep alive than dead, we eat them and harvest their parts. I do not despise these people, nor do I appreciate them."

The Dark Lord chuckled. "I feel *nothing* for them."

Valdemar's fists clenched in rage. "You invented the soulstones," the summoner realized. "Did you release that magical knowledge only so you could have a supply of souls to fuel your devices?"

His question amused the lich. "Oh my, did you expect a heart of gold buried somewhere in my rib cage? If so, young Valdemar, you haven't been paying attention. I discarded my heart long ago and looked down on humanity ever since."

Truth be told, yes, Valdemar had hoped that a sliver of nobility remained in the Dark Lord. He had spent so long looking for a flicker of light inside the undead that he missed the darkness all around it.

"Then why haven't you sacrificed them already?" Valdemar asked warily, trembling with anger. "Why?"

"Why would I?" The lich's answer surprised his apprentice. "Between us, I never intended to use this portal to open a gate to Earth. Or any other planet for that matter."

Valdemar squinted in disbelief, but his undead teacher sounded completely serious. "You didn't?"

"I pursue higher stakes." Lord Och put his hands behind his back, his gaunt figure casting a dark shadow. "Freedom."

Valdemar frowned, Ktulu's six eyes glaring at Och with an expression that his summoner had never seen before. Something between wariness and childish disdain. "Freedom?" Valdemar whispered, trying to make sense out of the lich's motivations.

"Not the kind of liberty that your young, untested mind can fathom," Lord Och replied. "Freedom from this pointless cycle of life and death, from the expectations of citizens and the laws that govern this lesser universe." The lich's voice brimmed with resentment and bitterness. His words sounded too venomous not to be genuine. "I can hardly stand this cage of stone anymore, this . . . this prison of flesh and life and death." The lich glared at the stone ceiling of the vault. "This world of matter keeps my soul anchored to a lesser existence as surely as gravity. Lichdom gave me a little more leeway, but alas, I remain bound to the laws of nature. For now at least. Even though I could escape this doomed planet for another, I would only be trading cells."

"You want to achieve a higher state of existence." Valdemar's eyes widened at the depth of his master's limitless ambition. "To follow in Lord Bethor's footsteps and become a Stranger."

"In a way . . . but it is too early for us to discuss this yet." Lord Och shrugged as he changed the subject. "I had considered using this portal in a pinch, yes, hence my gathering the necessary fuel in my Institute. But these beetles have so far proven more useful alive than dead, so I decided to spare them. I do not want to access Earth all that much."

Lord Och raised a bony finger at Valdemar's heart, his skull grinning wickedly.

"But *you* do."

Only then did Valdemar begin to fathom the depth of the lich's cruelty. "No," the summoner whispered. "Never."

"It is the only way to achieve your dream, young Valdemar. Unless, of course, you sacrifice yourself to become the gate."

"I can find other people," Valdemar protested, Ktulu squealing behind him. "Prisoners of war, enemies . . ."

"But the problem will remain the same." The lich's laughter reverberated across the chamber. "You will convince others to martyr themselves so *you* do not have to. Because as much as you pretend otherwise and cloak your true goal behind high-minded aspirations, this is all about *you* reaching Earth. You could have only opened the path to a better future for your kind since the moment you visited the Silent King, but you refused to."

"Why should anybody have to sacrifice anything?" Valdemar argued. "There has to be another way!"

"Which one? Pictomancy? The painted doorway was only made possible because of a Stranger's cooperation on the other side, and it came with a price. Temporary tears demand sacrifices and, as you have seen, they never last long. Otto Blutgang could have helped, but you burned that bridge when you refused to compromise on your morals. Because you always refuse to make sacrifices."

Valdemar stood firm in his decision. "The cost of allying with the derros was too great."

"And what cost will be small enough for you?" Lord Och asked with clear amusement. "I believe you do not want to pay *anything*, you greedy little child. No more than I do."

Valdemar ground his teeth, refusing to be folded in the same category as this cold, heartless creature. "There has to be another way."

"I have spent centuries trying to find one. If you discover another method, be my guest."

"There is another portal in Ariouth," Valdemar whispered, grasping at any option. "You said it yourself. Maybe it can work differently."

Lord Och chuckled mirthlessly. "Even if you manage to fool my former apprentice and access the device, you shall be disappointed . . . as I was. And the longer you wait, the more our kind shall suffer. This world was doomed the moment the Whitemoon arrived, and Ialdabaoth's awakening can only be delayed. We are but pawns in a great war that will consume this planet, as it did with so many others. The longer you delay, the greater the risk we all perish for nothing."

"You're wrong!" Valdemar argued, his familiar wincing as he raised his voice. "Maybe Ialdabaoth's awakening is inevitable, but if we keep delaying it, it will never happen! It won't escape its binding under my watch!"

"Well then, mankind shall continue to suffer from the lack of space, the plagues, the Strangers, the wars, and the depredation of monsters. Our souls will feed our father's bottomless appetite while you waver." The Dark Lord tilted his head to the side like a curious cat. "What I mean to say, apprentice, is that *somebody* will pay a toll for *your* decisions. If you want to achieve your dreams, you will have to decide who shall bear the burden; or the choice will be forced upon you."

Valdemar shivered as the memories of the Outer Darkness flooded his mind. He remembered the dark abyss of souls condemning mankind to oblivion after death . . . and Otto Blutgang would only offer the slavery of steel while they lived.

Everywhere he looked, he had seen Strangers and monsters torment-ing mankind. Shelley and his plagues were but the latest stage of this endless war against civilization, but horrors like the Nightwalker would persist long after the rat's death. The longer mankind withered in these tunnels, the more souls would suffer.

And all he had to do to save them all was to open the path to a better place. To sacrifice his chance to see the sun for the sake of others. *Why?* the summoner wondered. *Why can I open the path to paradise, and yet be condemned to stay on the doorstep?*

"Why did you lead me to Blutgang?" Valdemar asked, his voice break-ing. "If you had no desire to open this portal, then why did you put me through these sick mind games?"

"I wished to see if you had it in you to defy me. I do not want a weak-willed follower for an apprentice, and I was pleasantly surprised by your initiative." Lord Och chuckled. "This was all for your sake, obviously. I gave you options, let you find your own way. As I told you, the only per-son who can decide who you are . . . is you, Valdemar."

The Dark Lord's shadow seemed to lengthen, covering his appren-tice in a blanket of cold and darkness. "Yes, I could sacrifice all your 'friends' to the portal and open the gate to Earth. You would blame me and achieve your dream free of guilt. But that won't happen. You alone will bear the weight of your dream."

The lich's baleful gaze swallowed Valdemar's vision.

"The choice is all yours."

1 5

ONE

The moment Valdemar returned, Marianne knew something was terribly wrong. He came too late, for a start. By the time he joined, Count de Vane had already regaled his daughter and guests with a tea ceremony; though as a skeletal gentleman, it was more for the benefit of the living than his own. The Count had recently suffered an accident in one of his facilities, but thankfully undeath hadn't dimmed his courteous spirit.

The food and drinks were of the highest quality, and for a few peaceful minutes Marianne had been brought back to the days when Bertrand cooked delicious meals for her. Months had passed since then, and they felt like years.

"Where were you?" Liliane complained to Valdemar as the group met with their missing member. "My father kept pestering me about your absence, and I was so happy I could finally introduce the two of you! I told you not to be late!"

Valdemar didn't answer. He averted his eyes from his friends' gaze, his skin paler than usual. His familiar followed him like a shadow, Ktulu's six eyes watching his master with clear concern.

Liliane's annoyance turned to worry. "Valdy?"

"How . . ." Valdemar cleared his throat. "How was he? Your father?"

"Oh, he was so happy that I made friends at the Institute," Liliane replied with a bright smile. "He was a little surprised when I presented Hermann to him, but they hit it off."

"Count de Vane is an . . . avid art collector," Hermann explained. He had removed his mask during the meeting and kept his face exposed afterward. Marianne took it as a sign that he was growing comfortable with his current company. "I think he might commission work from us . . . in the future."

Valdemar didn't answer. He simply glanced at the window, his gaze empty while his familiar clung to his pants with a tiny hand. *Something terrible happened,* Marianne guessed. The others had noticed too and now looked at their friend with concern.

"He also said he would gladly help mass-produce an antidote for the Beast Plague if we could figure one out," Liliane added with a happy grin, though Marianne could tell she was forcing herself to try to lighten the mood. "And he had super good news for Marianne too!"

"According to the Count, there is word among Saklas' noble circles that the Empress intends to repeal my exile," Marianne explained. "As a reward for my 'courageous actions against enemies of the state.' Nothing confirmed yet."

This time, Valdemar looked at her. Another man would have congratulated her, said how happy they were. But the summoner knew Marianne all too well. "Does that make you happy?" he asked.

Marianne sighed. "Not so much." In a way, she was glad that the stain on her honor would be removed, and it might make her father and mother welcome her back with open arms . . . but Marianne didn't truly want to go home. The same problems that had plagued her since Jérôme's demise would remain festering beneath the surface.

Besides, she didn't think she ever felt truly at home among the Saklas aristocracy. Her place was on the field fighting the evils of the world, not at home hosting balls for jaded dilettantes.

Valdemar responded with a silent nod, and then looked back at the window.

This time, Liliane's smile completely faltered. "Valdy, what happened?" she asked him directly. "What's wrong?"

Valdemar answered with another question. "How many people die each day?"

He's thinking of the Outer Darkness, Marianne realized. Was that why he had to leave early? To study the Qlippoths and figure out how their dimension worked?

"How many people die each day?" Valdemar repeated.

Liliane frowned, unsettled by her friend's words. "How many humans?"

"Dokkar, troglodyte, humans . . . how many die each day?" When neither Marianne nor Liliane would answer his question, Valdemar turned to Hermann. "Do you know?"

"If you count all our world's civilizations . . ." Hermann calculated the number in his head. "Tens of thousands . . . I would say."

Valdemar glanced away again. "That's what I thought."

"You're thinking about the Outer Darkness, aren't you?" Marianne asked. "It's beyond your power to change."

"It's not that, Marianne," he replied. "Thousands of innocents die . . . but *they're* still here after all these years. They get away with everything." His voice was filled with sorrow and disappointment.

"Who are they?" Liliane asked, unaware of the details. "Valdy, what's going on?"

"I . . ." Valdemar opened his mouth only to swiftly close it. "Nothing."

"Valdy, look at us," Liliane asked with a frown. "Valdy. Valdy, please."

He did. And as Valdemar raised his eyes to look at his friends, Marianne's enhanced sense of sight picked up every single microexpression on his face. She noticed the lack of light in his gaze, the strained look of sorrow he gave Liliane and the brief flash of guilt as he glanced at Hermann. This expression was all too familiar. She had seen it the first time she looked at her mirror after killing Jérôme.

Liliane's words didn't register with her friend. Valdemar, usually so optimistic and stalwart in the face of adversity, looked as dead as the undying workers toiling in Sabaoth's mines.

He didn't say another word for the rest of the day.

By the time the friends went their separate ways, Valdemar's mood had only worsened. Iren had also returned early with a letter, saying it had taken far less time than he had expected. Valdemar took the document, read it without a word, and decided to teleport back to his bedroom in Lord Bethor's tower. Unwilling to leave him alone, Marianne had decided to follow him.

"We've seen him like this before," Liliane had whispered to Marianne with a sigh before they separated. "When he learned the truth about his grandfather. He wouldn't come out of his room for days."

"It's worse this time . . ." Hermann had rasped in response. "The way he looks at us . . . he fears for our lives . . ."

"He looks even more crushed after reading that letter than before," Iren had noted.

None of them had managed to break through their friend's shield of silence. Valdemar had simply lain on his bunk bed inside the tower and stared at the ceiling for hours. Ktulu had done his best to get his master's attention, showing him drawings of monsters it had made, to no avail.

Marianne thought seeing his friends would make Valdemar happier, but it had only caused him further anguish. She had hoped that sharing a dream with him would give her insight into his trouble, but Valdemar couldn't find sleep. Even late into the night he simply gazed at their bedroom's metal ceiling. Since they had removed the Painted Field to let him sleep normally, the walls had turned gray and lifeless again. Marianne couldn't help but notice the symbolism.

Ktulu had long gone to sleep, snoring lightly.

"Valdemar," Marianne whispered from her bed, her eyes glancing at his own above her head. "Valdemar, you need to sleep. The Sabbath is tomorrow."

No answer. But she knew he was listening.

"Valdemar, please talk to me," Marianne pleaded, enraged that she couldn't make headway. Watching her friend suffering in silence while unable to reach out to him frustrated her more than anything else. "Tell me what's wrong."

A letter fell from the side of Valdemar's bed above. Marianne caught it. The writer had used luxurious ink and wrote with the precision and confidence of a superior talking to an inferior. No spell was woven into the paper, nor was it signed or marked in any way. Perhaps the sender intended to remain somewhat anonymous.

To whom it may concern,

If you are reading this, then my sincerest apologies, for I cannot be of assistance.

Please do not be offended by my answer. I have nothing against you personally, but I know our common acquaintance very well and I refuse to be involved in any scheme of his except to ruin it.

I suppose some explanations are in order. I can confirm to you that his story about the past is true, from a certain point of view, and, more to the point, that he is utterly obsessed with this realm of "Light." He has made terrible sacrifices in its pursuit, and we split when I refused to become one of them. Our common acquaintances had many disciples, but few survived his patronage. My colleague split with him on amicable terms because though they pursued different goals, they did not conflict directly; but I couldn't, cannot coexist with our common acquaintance.

As you have already surmised, I did restore a door, under his tutelage, beneath my house; I sought to use it to summon slaves from across the planes, but he desired to make use of the device in a way that I felt risked the ruin of our entire civilization. Not as a primary intent, of course, but as a potential side-effect he was more than happy to deal with in the pursuit of his Light. Make no mistake, we are all expendable to him in the name of his dream. All of us.

Hence I forever closed the path to deny him his wish and we have been bitter foes ever since. I would have destroyed him if I could, but it is impossible as long as his mortality remains hidden and it was my word against his. Even now, at the zenith of my strength, I have but a shadow of his power. Survival is victory in itself.

Unable to destroy him, I settled for destroying all other doors I could find to spite him. Understand that I did this with a heavy heart, for the resources therein could have made me the greatest of our kind, but he simply cannot be allowed to get his hands on them.

If you have access to a door I have missed, I would be thankful if you could destroy it at the first opportunity. I cannot yet say what place you fill in his plan, but he most certainly has one.

Someone of your ability is clearly above the rabble I easily deal with and I would rather have you as an ally, but if you indulge our common acquaintance, I will have to kill you. Depending on the facts at hand, I might even ask for your execution during the Sabbath. With heavy regrets of course.

But who knows what the future holds?

With my warmest regards,

Your predecessor.

"Who sent this letter?" Marianne asked as she finished reading. "Lord Phaleg? My ears are sharp, Valdemar, and I can read the lips of others. I know you tried to make contact with him."

Her friend didn't respond.

"He was talking about the Pleromian portals, wasn't he?" Marianne guessed. "Lord Och has the last one, and you're afraid he will sacrifice the others to activate it? Because he has no other option? Is that what you are afraid of?"

This time, Valdemar answered.

"Do you think," he said, his voice tired, "that all life is equal? Is my life equal to yours? To Hermann? To Liliane?"

Marianne considered the question for a long while. "Yes," she said. "Yes, I believe it. All life is equally precious."

"Then," he replied, "is it okay to take a life if it threatens ten more?"

"If there is no other solution then yes." Marianne would not regret striking down Shelley or Otto Blutgang in the name of the greater good. "Valdemar, what are you trying to tell me?"

Instead of answering, Marianne heard Valdemar climb down from his bed to stand next to her own. He was wearing nothing but his pajamas, his eyes as hollow as the caverns of Underland.

Marianne sat up, making room for Valdemar beside her. The summoner hesitated before doing so and didn't speak immediately. He joined his hands and looked at the ground as if gazing at something far below the earth, his expression thoughtful.

"Do you think there is anything special about being born?" Valdemar finally asked, his voice no louder than a whisper.

Marianne almost opened her mouth to answer, but decided to hold on. Instead, she waited for him to fill the silence, and truly say all that weighed on his mind.

"The universe is made of death," Valdemar stated as if it were a fact. "This is its natural state and life is an anomaly. We are all the rogue cells of a larger organism, granted self-awareness through a cosmic fluke."

"That's why life is all the more precious," Marianne argued. "Because we were so lucky to be born."

"Luck?" He snorted in response. "Whether you do good or evil, so long as you live in this shell of a world, you end up in the Outer Darkness. Whether you die a saint or a monster, everyone suffers. Life is Hell's antechamber."

Was that why he was so troubled? Why now? Valdemar had known for days, and though the truth had shaken him, he hadn't despaired either.

Marianne clutched the soulstone necklace she never took off. *Has Jérôme's soul fallen into this vortex of souls?* she suddenly wondered. Was he screaming for release as Qlippoths devoured him? She had tried not to think of it much, but now that she did . . .

"Not all souls end up in the Outer Darkness, Valdemar," Marianne said, but the argument felt weak.

"For the wealthy, you mean?" Valdemar sighed. "Even so, they are only delaying the inevitable. Their soulstones are no more than a crack away from shattering and our civilization has been fighting horrors for centuries. But for how many more years? How long until the dam breaks and the water pours through?"

"Maybe it won't," Marianne said and cursed herself. Why couldn't words come to her as easily as swords?

"I'm . . ." Valdemar gathered his breath, but didn't raise his head. "I'm just asking myself . . . Why try to do good when nothing matters? Why be good when our efforts are for naught?"

Now Marianne's voice turned to steel. "Don't you dare say that," she said, her tone briefly shaking him out of his despair. "Our work was never in vain. Is this about Blutgang?"

"In a way," he confessed. "We changed nothing."

"We destroyed his facility and ruined his plans."

"We delayed them and Otto still lives. You said it yourself, even Lord Bethor's advance in his territory is unlikely to change the status quo."

Marianne bit her lower lip, unsure of what to say. She feared her friend had drowned too deep in his own sorrow, but she refused to let him sink further. "To deny evil a victory is a victory for good in itself."

He locked eyes with her. "Is that the best we can hope for?" he asked. "Not to win for ourselves, but to deny the enemy his victory?"

The moment Marianne opened her mouth to answer, she noticed that her friend was struggling to hold back tears.

"Why do people like Och and Blutgang get away with everything while I . . ." Valdemar gritted his teeth, wiping away his tears. "Why . . ."

Marianne immediately moved closer to him, her hands moving to his shoulders. She was not good with physical comfort, so the contact was clumsy. She sensed the emotional tension in his muscles, the weight he carried.

"Valdemar, what's happening?" Marianne asked softly, holding him close to herself. "Please, tell me. I swear, I . . . I won't tell anyone else."

"I have had enough of this . . ." Valdemar's voice broke. "Every time I try to improve things, I get a kick in the face . . . first with the inquisitors . . . then this cult . . . the derros . . . now Och. It doesn't matter what I try . . . they always get away with all their crimes, while everyone else rots in this hellish place . . . the fire devours them all. Each time I confront monsters, I fail. If I can't ruin their schemes . . . What hope do I have against the likes of the Strangers?" He clenched his fists, his fingers trembling. "I thought reaching Earth could make it all better," he said, so weakly. "The sun . . . but to get there, I . . . somebody has to die. There's no other way. They destroyed all the others."

"You don't know that," Marianne protested. "The Dark Lords could have missed a Pleromian portal, and even if they haven't, maybe another spell could open the way."

"Which one?" he asked, begging for an answer.

But Marianne had none to give. "I . . . I don't know, Valdemar. I'm not the best person to ask."

Her friend sighed and looked back at the floor in utter defeat.

But Marianne refused to let him wallow in bitterness. "Bertrand," she said.

He frowned in confusion, though he didn't look at her. "What, Bertrand?"

"I thought we had no hope of curing him not too long ago," Marianne explained. "But you and Liliane found a possible solution."

He snorted in skepticism. "It's only a chance."

"But before we had none." Marianne cleared her throat. "Valdemar, we can't find solutions to complex problems overnight. You need to give yourself time."

"That's what I tried to tell myself," Valdemar replied. "But each day I stall trying to find an alternative is a day we spend trapped in his *hellhole*. If all lives are equal, then I have a pretty big debt. My very existence is a threat to everyone."

She slapped him. It was light, but his cheek turned red from the blow all the same. Valdemar coughed in surprise, looking Marianne in the eyes.

Marianne gritted her teeth in disappointment. "Have you forgotten who you are, Valdemar?"

He winced as if she had slapped him again.

"The first time we met, you were tied to a torture device in an inquisitor's cell," Marianne reminded him. "Threatened with slavery in the salt mines or death. Yet in spite of the taunts and the humiliations, of the mockery and wounds, you insisted that Earth existed. That opening gates to other worlds was possible. And eventually, you proved it. You *painted* a door to another universe."

"Lord Och said it couldn't—"

"Lord Och believes in *nothing.*" *Of course he is the one behind this mess,* Marianne thought with anger. Her wary respect for the lich had further soured away into disdain. "I've seen his true face when he tortured the Pleromian. For all of his power, Och is a small, petty creature who only finds joy in tormenting others. Edwin was completely right, he has given up on all that makes us good long ago. And I will say it again, as far as I am concerned, that makes you ten times the man that he is."

Marianne grabbed Lord Phaleg's letter, showing it to Valdemar.

"This paper?" she asked. "Iren brought it to you, after you saved him from death and who knows many others. Just as you saved lives by denying Blutgang access to his portal. So don't you ever say you worked for nothing, because you helped make this *'hellhole'* a better place."

"This world is a *mess,*" he hissed.

"Then keep making it *better,*" Marianne snarled back before tossing the letter away. "You've already helped Hermann invent his own private universe. This world is neither hopeless nor just, it just is. If you're not happy with it, then change it. Or do your best to try."

"It's ridiculous."

"You're one who kept saying impossible was but a word. Or have you forgotten that too?"

Her words were harsh, but for the first time since he returned to her, Valdemar's sorrow seemed to fade. Doubt crept in, his eyes glancing away and back to her as he considered her words.

Marianne put her hands on his cheeks, gently forcing him to look into her eyes. She wiped away the last tears and soothed the spot where she had slapped him. "Don't become like Lord Och, Valdemar," she pleaded. "Be better than he is."

The ember of hope flared back in his hollow gaze. "You think I can?"

"Yes, I do," Marianne replied without hesitation, a smile on her face. "I believe in you."

As Marianne spoke, she watched Valdemar's gaze regain its life and purpose. The veil of despair that had overtaken his heart was slowly lifted as she gave him hope in a better future once more. Once he had helped her clear her own doubts about Jérôme, and she was doing the same with his own clouded mind.

"Thanks," Valdemar simply said, a new strength in his voice. "I will try."

"Do not try," she said softly. "Just do it."

He chuckled, and Marianne realized she had never heard a more wonderful sound. His fingers moved to her sides, resting on the bedsheet as they faced each other. He was so close that she could feel his warm breath on her lips.

And then Valdemar's mouth started moving closer still.

So did her own.

Marianne didn't know why, but her head moved on its own to mirror her companion's motion. Perhaps it was desire or confusion, but her lips touched his own. A shiver traveled through her cheeks as they kissed, her enhanced sense of touch gathering every tactile sensation. She felt his heartbeat beneath the skin, his warmth, his short breath, and his doubts.

The kiss was clumsy, impulsive. It lasted only a second before Valdemar pulled back. He gathered his breath, seemingly surprised at what he had just done. He looked like a man who had woken up a dragon.

Marianne herself breathed heavily. Doubts flooded her mind. She thought of Jérôme, of Bertrand, of the cult, and Lord Och. Of the Dark Lords and the Sabbath, about the troubles ahead, about the danger of the situation, the shakiness of their association. She worried about what this kiss would mean for them, how it might ruin their budding friendship or end in tears. Her breath reeked of anxiety, of fear, of doubts and unspoken terrors.

Then they kissed again, and Marianne's worries faded like mist.

The second kiss lasted longer, and though clumsy it was no longer full of hesitation. There was only desire and tenderness, warmth and oneness. Marianne forgot about the Strangers and the Light.

She just wanted him.

Her hands moved to remove his clothes and his own clumsily brushed against her underwear. He broke the kiss abruptly, his breath heavy.

"You don't want to?" Marianne whispered.

"I want it," Valdemar replied without hesitation. "But . . . it would change so much."

"Valdemar, right now . . ." She moved to whisper in his ear. "The world is just the two of us."

Her words dispelled his doubts, and his fingers moved to unclothe her.

When they were naked, they joined beneath the bedsheet. Marianne tasted his sweat as she kissed him, heard his blood pumping as his hands brushed against her breasts. She smelled him, all of him, and shivered as his lips touched her, explored her, devoured her. She shivered as her legs crossed behind him, and gasped as her hands guided him inside her.

They made love in the flesh and in the dream.

1 6

THE SEVEN

The dream was peaceful. Valdemar and Marianne watched a sunless ocean while sitting along the balcony's edge of their dreamscape, their feet dangling above the water. Ktulu swam underneath the surface, leaving them alone. Both had put on light clothes, leaving their heavier robes and jackets aside. In the dream, they didn't fear the cold, and they were beyond the point of modesty.

A wall had fallen between them.

Valdemar didn't have much experience in dealing with women, or . . . what had just happened. He and Marianne had grown closer over the last weeks, and he had noticed certain *tensions*. What they had just done went beyond that.

Things had been good before. But, though human relationships weren't his strength, Valdemar knew they had just crossed a line and there would be no going back.

Marianne said nothing as she enjoyed a warm cup of tea she had conjured from her memories, gazing at the ocean. Valdemar himself watched his companion in silence, the same way he would observe a beautiful painting that had caught his interest.

Noting his attention, Marianne turned to face him without a word. Then she did something wonderful, something that filled her companion's chest with warmth and lifted all of his doubts.

She smiled. It was a beautiful sight, worthy of being immortalized in a painting for all eternity.

Inspired, Valdemar called upon the dream and materialized a flower in his hand, one with red petals, thorns, and a sweet smell. He offered it to Marianne.

"What is this?" she asked. "I don't remember seeing it in the Institute's greenhouse."

"It's a rose," Valdemar explained. "It's a flower from Earth. Grandpa used to draw it. He said it smelled great."

It was also customary in his grandfather's homeland for a man to offer a rose to a lady he courted. Valdemar didn't know how the flower smelled, having never seen a real one. He only had his grandsire's words and his imagination to draw upon. He made the perfume as sweet as he could.

Marianne swiftly took the flower before smelling it. She seemed to enjoy the gift, but Valdemar could see the embarrassed blush spreading on her cheeks. Even in a dream, some things never changed.

"I'm sorry," Valdemar apologized.

"For what?" Marianne asked, holding the flower with both hands like a treasure. "I love it."

"I don't know how to deal with girls."

"I am no romance veteran either," she admitted. "I haven't been with a man since Jérôme, and I have known no one else."

With a man. "Are we together?" Valdemar asked while clearing his throat. "I mean, *together* together?"

Marianne's smile turned sheepish. "Are we not?" she asked. "It's not that different from what came before, Valdemar. It's like being best friends, but deeper."

"It means commitment and complications," Valdemar pointed out. "The people after me will come for you."

"They already would, simply because I am your friend and sword." Marianne frowned. "Unless you think I cannot defend myself."

"No, of course not," Valdemar replied with a chuckle. "In fact, I'm pretty sure you're stronger than I am."

Marianne chuckled at the compliment. "You sell yourself short, Valdemar. I have seen you do things with the Blood that are beyond anyone but the Dark Lords. In terms of magical might, you eclipse me completely."

And yet if they came to blows, Valdemar had the suspicion that she would win handily all the same. "If I were to be honest," he said, "I love your strength; not just with arms, but your moral fortitude too. I find them attractive."

His words were terribly clumsy, but Marianne seemed to appreciate them all the same. "Thank you," she said. "It matters more to me than you think."

In her heart, Marianne was a romantic.

She leaned against Valdemar, resting her head on his chest. The summoner put his arm around her shoulder, fingers brushing against her light hair. Though he knew both of them were mere projections in the dreamscape, her warmth and soft breath felt real. Valdemar hadn't felt something like this since the days of his childhood, the rare days when his mother took him in her arms. It had made him feel safe and happy, his mind undistracted by the terrors of the world. Marianne felt like home.

"What do you want?" she whispered. "For us?"

Valdemar didn't wonder for long. He looked up at the darkness over the sunless ocean of his dreamscape and tried to conjure a new sky. Before he had struggled to manifest even smaller objects, but now the Primordial Dream seemed to indulge his desires. Perhaps the fall of the invisible wall of unspoken emotions between Marianne and him had strengthened his influence, or maybe he had grown more in tune with his feelings as Lady Mathilde advised.

In any case, a bright star appeared on the horizon. Its light reflected from the ocean's surface, banishing the darkness and painting the skies with a vivid, bright blue color. It was a landscape that only ever existed in Valdemar's imagination and his grandfather's stories. Now Marianne shared it, watching the bright horizon with joy and satisfaction.

"I want to show you this," Valdemar explained. "A ceiling of light and clouds rather than stone. I want to show you the sun. Not in a dream, but in the waking world."

"I would love it," she whispered back, her heartbeat in sync with his own. "It is beautiful."

"I . . ." Valdemar's hands brushed against her soft fingers. "I won't regret what happened even if we decide to end it here before going further. But I would like to continue. It was good. It feels good."

"Yes, it does." Marianne glanced at the dream sun's reflection in the ocean. The water's surface seemed to be made of shining diamonds. "Whatever awaits, we will stand at each other's side."

"What awaits . . ." Valdemar sighed. "The worst is to come."

"You're still thinking about the portal?"

"No," Valdemar replied firmly. "I won't use it. I won't drink from this poisoned cup. You were right, the fact another solution hasn't been found yet doesn't mean that there is none."

Marianne nodded in appreciation. "You are better than Lord Och, Valdemar. Prove him wrong."

"But there is the Outer Darkness to consider," Valdemar said with sorrow. "So long as we remain in Underland, the living suffer and death offers no mercy. And Lord Och is preparing something. It makes no sense for him to work on studying portal technology if he doesn't want to use it himself."

"Maybe he does," Marianne pointed out. "Just not to reach Earth."

"Where else?"

Marianne pointed a finger at the sun.

"The Light?" Valdemar asked.

"If we assume his story is true, he was forever denied paradise and has been obsessed with it since," Marianne said. "I think undoing his past humiliation is his ultimate goal. What purpose he hopes to fulfill upon reaching such a plane of existence, I cannot say."

It made some sense. If the Strangers indeed originated from this supreme dimension above the material world, then it neatly fit Lord Och's desire of escaping the reality he saw as a prison. However, Valdemar noticed a few problems with this analysis.

"The portal can only reach worlds bound by the Blood with the appropriate sacrifice," the summoner pointed out. "It is part of a web of flesh that binds the Strangers together. But they were all expelled from this realm of Light and couldn't return. No Blood-based magic should be capable of opening the way, so how does he intend to?"

Marianne glanced at him with a look of apology. "I do not know," she admitted. "You are the summoner and know more about the field than I ever will. However . . ."

"However?"

"Lord Och is an ancient being, centuries old." Marianne adjusted her position, her face thoughtful. "Someone like him is patient beyond imagination. Decades seem no longer than the blink of an eye to him. If we assume that he has been pursuing a single goal all this time, then we should look at some of his previous actions."

"I don't follow."

"You know how he is, better than anyone," Marianne argued. "Is there anything he has done that strikes you as unlike him? Something that can be recontextualized knowing his final objective?"

Valdemar frowned in skepticism, but her idea had merit. Marianne had proved herself an excellent investigator time and time again, and he trusted her intuition.

"Hard to say," Valdemar admitted after considering his companion's question. "I would have said releasing knowledge of the soulstones, but he could have done that for any number of reasons. Safeguarding knowledge, building up his influence in the empire, using them as fuel . . . as he said, he has many plans running all at once."

"But they are all tactical moves in the pursuit of a greater strategic objective," Marianne replied before manifesting a dream copy of her soulstone necklace floating before their eyes. "According to his story, some souls could escape the Outer Darkness and ascend to the Light. Maybe he was trying to study the process and reproduce it through magical means."

"Maybe . . ." Valdemar replied, still slightly skeptical. "The problem is that everything we know about Och could be a lie or doctored."

"If we can, we should check out the historical archives in Pleroma," Marianne said with optimism. "We will find out the truth."

She remained true to the vow she had made when their partnership started.

Whatever Och's reasons for creating the soulstones, thinking about them left a sour taste in Valdemar's mouth. The idea that only the privileged could afford a respite from the Outer Darkness filled him with disgust. Men weren't equal, even before death.

The Blood connected all . . . Valdemar thought, his eyes widening. From the souls of the dead to the bodies of the living . . .

"I know that look," Marianne said with an amused smile. "You have an idea."

She knew him well. "Hermann once told me that a pictomancy portrait could be used to catch the soul of a target upon death."

"Like a soulstone?"

"Yes, but without a limit of distance. Pictomancy creates a sympathetic link between the painting and the target that transcends space itself." To the point it could open the path to another dimension entirely under the right conditions. "Now, it means that a pictomancy portrait can even snatch a spirit before Ialdabaoth can consume it."

Marianne's smile turned sorrowful. "You cannot paint a portrait for all people in Underland, Valdemar."

"No," Valdemar admitted as he looked at the sun of his dreams, "but maybe I can do better."

If no good afterlife existed, then he would create one.

On the next day, Lord Och and Lord Bethor came to lead Valdemar to the Sabbath. An exception had been made to allow Marianne to escort him, though she had to leave her rapier and revolver behind. No weapon would be allowed in the Dark Lords' presence.

Marianne herself knew little about the Sabbath, except that it involved the Dark Lords reuniting at least once a year under Empress Aratra to decide the future strategy of the Empire of Azlant. Some said that the meetings took place in a secret room located somewhere in Saklas, that only the Dark Lords and the Church of the Light's Enlightened One could access. To be welcomed to a Sabbath was a rare occasion, and the few guests who survived this honor never spoke of it again afterward.

It left Marianne a little uneasy as she looked at her partner. She didn't doubt for a second that the Dark Lords intended to decide Valdemar's fate at this meeting, as well as the fates of the Verney cult and the plague.

If the Dark Lords wanted to execute him, Marianne and Valdemar's prospects would look grim. Marianne would fight to defend her companion, but she was under no delusion that the two of them would survive a confrontation with the seven most powerful magicians in the world. Even if they managed to escape with their lives, no place in the Empire would be safe for Marianne or Valdemar.

Speaking of the couple, Lord Och *knew* they were together the moment he saw them. He said nothing, but the sudden cackle he gave the two immediately made the truth clear.

Lord Bethor's reaction was more measured. "Good," he said with his customary curtness. "You will fight better if you have someone to lose."

Marianne guessed that this was the closest thing to a blessing that Lord Bethor would ever give. "How was your offensive, Lord Bethor?" she asked him.

"Better than expected, not as well as I hoped," Lord Bethor replied, arms crossed. "This would be long over if we could all focus on eradicating these vermin and burning their cities to ashes. I am strong, but I cannot be everywhere."

"Alas, leading our brotherhood in one direction is like herding cats," Lord Och said as he prepared to cast a teleportation spell. "Though I have a good feeling that we might reach unanimity on today's matter."

Marianne glanced at Valdemar. In his Scholar's robes with the Mask of the Nightwalker attached to his belt, he looked every inch a Dark Lord's apprentice. Would his professionalism impress the empire's rulers? She could only hope so. Marianne wasn't ready to lose another person dear to her so soon.

Something else bothered her. As usual, Ktulu waited inside his master's bag with his head peeking out. However, his behavior startled Marianne. The creature glared at Lord Och with all six eyes, his alien face betraying an all-too-human expression. A look of utter distaste.

Marianne suspected the familiar echoed his master's inner feelings through their shared bond, but the baleful glint in Ktulu's eyes went beyond Valdemar's anger toward his manipulative mentor. The familiar looked ready to attack the lich at the first provocation.

And though Lord Och feigned indifference, Marianne's enhanced senses picked up the slight adjustments in his posture and the way his fingers fidgeted whenever Ktulu blinked. The lich was ready to cast spells on his apprentice's familiar at any time.

Something was happening before Marianne's eyes, and even her Elixir of True Sight could not perceive what.

Space twisted around them as Lord Och cast his spell, and Marianne focused on the matter at hand. The metal walls of Lord Bethor's tower vanished, replaced with pillars of cerulean stone and a ceiling of fossilized stone.

The group had teleported into a vast underground cathedral without any exit, one that put even the ones in Saklas to shame in its dark beauty. A layer of porphyry covered the ground, its surface so polished that it acted as a purple mirror. Floating phosphorescent orbs of various colors provided the light, and magic suffused the air. Seven thrones of black marble formed a circle at its center, some taller than others. A mere look told Marianne that this place was the center of the Empire, the beating heart of mankind.

The other Dark Lords were already present. Marianne immediately recognized Lord Hagith, who she had already seen during her investigation in Horaios; the obese Dark Lord occupied the second largest throne, which had clearly been altered for him. He greeted the newcomers with a polite nod.

The seat to his left was occupied by an old man who appeared to be in his sixties wearing black armor of soulbound steel. The man's eyes were as gray as his hair, but colder than ice and harder than iron. He wore no left gauntlet, revealing putrid purple flesh. A hundred eyes covered his skin, their irises replaced with summoning circles; all of them glaring at Lord Och.

Phaleg the Binder, Marianne identified this particular Dark Lord. Lord Och's former apprentice and foremost rival. The next throne was occupied by Ophiel the Mad, whose infamous black mirror mask had become terribly known. The body wearing it belonged to a busty woman whose skin was hidden beneath a black suit.

Next came Lady Phul, a creature of lust and darkness. Some whispered that she could use oneiromancy to make her dreams real, to the point her dreaming avatar had subsumed her physical form. Marianne guessed it must have been true, because the Dark Lord had taken an exotic shape. Lady Phul's skin was red and her impeccable hair was black as coal. Her eyes were burning flames, while two bat wings were folded behind her and a forked tail played with her breasts. The Dark Lord of Astaphanos wore little more than silken veils and jewelry leaving little to imagination.

And then there was the largest throne of all, occupied by the Dark Majesty of Azlant herself; the ruler of all humanity. Empress Aratra was reputed to be the most beautiful woman in the Empire, and if anything the rumors couldn't do the truth justice. Her long hair looked like woven silver, and her deep purple-blue eyes were more beautiful than any gemstone. Her sharp, ageless face put artists' statues and models to shame. Her black dress, adorned with rubies, and purple silk gloves cost more than a noble's estate. A diadem of blackened bones with seven horns rested atop her head, with a ruby shining on her forehead.

As she observed the Empress sitting on her throne with aristocratic grace, Marianne wondered if there was ever a fairer creature. She radiated power; not the overwhelming threat of naked aggression embodied by Lord Bethor, but a subtler, more regal form of strength.

"Lord Och," the Empress greeted the newcomers with courtesy, her voice as sweet as a song. While Marianne and Valdemar bent the knee as per the proper courtesies, Aratra's colleagues remained standing. "Lord Bethor."

Lord Bethor's response took only one word, spoken like an afterthought. "Aratra."

The empress frowned in displeasure. "*Lord* Bethor," she said, stressing the honorific and expecting another in return.

"Aratra," Lord Bethor repeated with a flat tone.

The Empress's courteous expression swiftly turned to disdain and cold annoyance, her facade of serenity immediately falling apart. "I grow tired of your insolence."

"And I of your vanity," Lord Bethor replied coldly as he took his place on his throne. It was located as far from the Empress as possible. The tension between these two was palpable.

Marianne always thought that the Empress was the first among equals between the Dark Lords, but after seeing this, she started to doubt.

No, I can't think this, Marianne told herself, trying to focus her mind on something else. Her faith in the Dark Lords had been shaken by recent events, but the Empress's temper was legendary. She could probably read minds, and neither Marianne nor Valdemar could match her in a fight. While Lord Bethor was a smoldering volcano, the Empress was a cave lynx; beautiful to look at, but quick to attack and lethal when roused.

They had to play the model imperial subjects to avoid a death sentence.

"Young Majesty," Lord Och offered the Empress a bow, too lowly for the gesture to be anything but a mockery. "Let us not bother with courtesies. We are all friends, are we not?"

The Empress took back her hand without dignifying the lich with an answer. Denying Lord Och's very existence, she glanced at Marianne and Valdemar. Her mood improved upon realizing that they had offered her proper respect. "Lady Reynard, Lord Verney," she said softly, "it is a pleasure to greet you in my hall."

"I am no lord, Your Dark Majesty," Valdemar replied while avoiding the Empress's gaze. Marianne noticed him sometimes glancing at the other Dark Lords as if expecting an attack. "Only a bastard denied any inheritance."

"It is for me to decide who will be denied anything," the Empress replied before setting her gaze on Marianne. "Or who shall find redemption."

Marianne looked down to avoid the Empress's gaze. *I have to think well of her,* the noblewoman thought, knowing that Aratra would appreciate it. "I am always the empire's faithful servant."

"That remains to be seen," Phaleg the Binder said with a voice as sharp as Marianne's sword. His aura of power was the most subdued among the Dark Lords, but the noblewoman noticed space bending around his unnatural arm.

"Now, now, let us not be hasty," Lord Hagith said with a genial voice. "The audition has not even begun. We have much to discuss before a judgment of any kind."

"Whose body is that, Ophiel?" Lord Och said as he took place on his own throne, opposite to Phaleg and close to Lord Bethor. "I preferred the last one."

"Some noble who modeled for me," Ophiel the Mad replied with multiple voices whispering at once, both male and female. "Her" mirror mask glanced at Marianne, the surface reflecting the noblewoman's face. "Though I find this one more aesthetically appealing. Is she for sale?"

Marianne bristled while Valdemar clenched his fists. But it was Lord Bethor's words that surprised the noblewoman the most. "Try to claim her," he said, "and you will die."

Ophiel sank into her throne. "You would fight me over her?"

Lord Bethor let out a sound that Marianne took for an amused scoff. "Bold of you to think I will have to."

Marianne noticed Valdemar frowning at her side. He seemed focused on something invisible. "What is it?" Marianne asked her companion, her voice as low as she could manage.

"I sense spatial magic in the air," Valdemar whispered, too low to be heard. "It's . . . like the Earthmouths. But focused, like a hub."

But the Dark Lords had sharp ears. "Your apprentice has good instincts, Och," Lady Phul said, slouching on her throne. The features of her body blurred briefly, like a fading dream. "But will he figure out this place's secret, I wonder?"

"I have faith in my apprentice's judgment," Lord Och replied with a touch of pride before looking at the ceiling. "Here's a hint."

Marianne didn't need to look up. She could see the reflection in the mirrored ground below. Her eyes distinguished a fossilized shape integrated into the ceiling; a slender, naked woman whose flesh had turned to stone. Her legs were joined like a serpentine tail, her fingers roots of marble. The woman lacked a mouth and a nose, or perhaps time had eroded them like it would any statue. Marianne might have mistaken her for one, if her chest didn't rise softly as if she breathed.

Red tendrils pierced her skull and back, pumping blood in and out of her. Her eyes shone like twin stars, but there was little comfort in their light. Unlike the warmth of Valdemar's dream sun, only the despair of a crushed spirit permeated her gaze. Her torturous station had hollowed the woman of stone from within, leaving only loss and emptiness.

Marianne couldn't confirm it, but she had a good idea of who this person was.

Together, they committed an unspeakable crime against Sophia in an attempt to steal her knowledge. A sin that forever barred them from ascending to the Light.

The undying corpse of Sophia the Unwise.

Empress Aratra gave Lord Och a dark look, and Marianne realized that the Dark Lord had probably read her thoughts. She looked unhappy that her colleague had revealed this secret, but quickly hid her annoyance behind a veil of regal majesty.

"Now that we are all gathered," the Empress said, smiling at Valdemar and Marianne, her eyes briefly turning red. "Shall we begin?"

The weight of the seven Dark Lords' gazes fell upon them, and the Sabbath started.

17

THE SABBATH

Most of his life, Valdemar had expected to face trial one day, for violating the empire's rules on magic. But he had never expected the trial to come after the prison time. It had been only months since the inquisitors had tossed him in a cell without judgment. Afterward, his life had taken an unexpected turn; and instead of rotting in prison, Valdemar now stood before the most lethal assembly ever gathered by mankind.

Though Marianne was close and his familiar hid in his bag, their presence gave Valdemar little comfort. As the gazes of the seven Dark Lords fell upon him, the summoner had never felt so alone. Most were smiling, the same way vicious predators might smile while toying with their prey.

The merciless elite of mankind had gathered to decide whether he would live or die.

Valdemar took a few seconds to check the Dark Lords' defenses with his psychic sight. He didn't test them for fear of deadly retaliation, but a cursory glance told him a great deal about the empire's ruling class. To commoners and most sorcerers, these seven imperial autocrats would have looked equally almighty and dangerous, but Valdemar's senses had sharpened under his various teachers' guidance. From the strength of the Dark Lords' magical defenses, he identified the presence of a subtle power hierarchy between them.

Empress Aratra and Lord Bethor were equal in strength. Where Bethor was a mighty volcano ready to unleash cataclysmic destruction at the first provocation, Aratra was an implacable glacier, strong, ancient, a cold presence so chilling that it hurt to breathe in her presence. They were fire and ice, and both far beyond Valdemar's power to confront. .

Och and Hagith came afterward. Lord Och's defenses were an imperceptible mist hiding the monster within, but Hagith's were a fortress's thick walls. His power was nowhere near as overwhelming as Lord Bethor's all-consuming might, but fearsome all the same. Lord Hagith reminded Valdemar of a cave bear, placid and friendly under most circumstances, but frighteningly dangerous when roused.

Lady Phul . . . Valdemar didn't know what to make of her. He could hardly even sense her existence in the tapestry of the Blood. Sometimes he received feedback about the presence of flesh and bones, only for them to be replaced with ephemeral ectoplasm a second later. She wasn't fully anchored in Underland's physical reality, which was both a strength and a weakness.

As for the others, Lords Ophiel and Phaleg struck Valdemar as the weakest of the Dark Lords in terms of raw magical power. The former's defenses were more akin to a chameleon's camouflage than a fortress; his psychic protections shifted like water from one form to another, sometimes weak, sometimes strong. The androgynous body-thief seemed aware and amused by Valdemar's probing, his magic flaring as a silent warning not to overstep.

As for the last of the Dark Lords, he wasn't even a shadow of Bethor even though they had both studied under Lord Och. Although Phaleg possessed effective defenses, they lacked the finesse and innovation of the others. He was the epitome of the classical mage: deadly, but conventional. His strange grafted arm and summoning prowess might give him an edge, but Valdemar was certain that he couldn't match his colleagues in a pure contest of strength.

In the end, this magical hierarchy meant little to Valdemar; to a student, all masters were overwhelming foes. If things went south, the summoner doubted either Marianne or he would survive the next five minutes.

Empress Aratra was the first to speak. Anyone else doing so would have been disrespectful to the ruler of all of Azlant. "You veil your thoughts from my gaze behind an alien mind." She said that with an amused smile, but it didn't reach her eyes. "How did you accomplish this?"

Valdemar almost looked at Lord Och for approval to reveal the information, but didn't move an inch. First, doing so would have infuriated the Empress by implying he gave more credit to his teacher's opinion than her own; second, he was done obeying the lich without question.

"I ate a Pleromian's soul," Valdemar answered with bluntness. "And I use it as a mental shield."

"A Pleromian?" Lady Phul chuckled in disbelief, echoed by a few others. Empress Aratra's expression didn't waver at all, while Lord Ophiel and Phaleg the Binder observed Valdemar with interest.

"Was that your first time eating a soul?" Ophiel the Mad asked. "It's a dangerous business. If you do it too often, you'll start losing sight of yourself."

"You do it all the time, my friend," Lord Hagith said while stroking his fat throat. He looked jovial, but Valdemar didn't miss the calculating gaze hidden behind the veil of friendliness.

"And it did wonders for me," the body-thief replied playfully. "Though I have never possessed a Pleromian before. I thought they were extinct?"

Valdemar thought Lord Och would speak up, but the lich didn't even seem to care all that much. His gaze was focused on the other Dark Lords rather than his apprentice, his fingers joined in a wary pose. To see the ever-confident archmage reacting this way made Valdemar shiver.

"So?" Lord Ophiel asked with impatience. "Have you lost your tongue, or must I extract it from your mouth?"

"Why ask him?" Lady Phul raised an eyebrow. "His companion's mind is unshielded and knows everything."

"Aw, you ruined my game," Ophiel complained while Marianne blushed in embarrassment. "I wanted to see him squirm as he fumbled for an answer."

"The Pleromians still exist in another plane, though they have degraded into monsters," Valdemar replied. "The derros opened a portal to it and summoned one. Lord Och will confirm it."

Phaleg the Binder squinted at his former master. "Will you?"

Lord Och cackled. "My apprentice, have you forgotten the rules of courtesy? The young shouldn't ask anything from the old."

Phaleg sneered, the eyes on his grafted arm glaring at the lich. "I am no longer your apprentice, old man. Today we are peers. Rulers of Domains with armies at our command."

"As you say, apprentice," Lord Och replied dismissively.

Are they truly this puerile? Valdemar wondered as the audience's pettiness astonished him. Empress Aratra echoed his thoughts with anger.

"Enough of this childishness," she chastised her colleagues before focusing back on Valdemar. "You were summoned here to answer to your actions and nature before my authority. Shielding your mind from my sight is obstruction, and I have had Oldblood patriarchies slain for less. Drop your protection immediately."

Valdemar hesitated, unwilling to leave his innermost thoughts to the assembly. But to his surprise, Lord Och came to his rescue. "Are you so eager to steal my secrets, young Aratra?" the lich asked mirthfully. "Young Valdemar is my beloved disciple. If he learned to shield his mind, it was to protect the knowledge I taught him."

Phaleg the Binder glared at his former master. "Like plans you have against us?"

"There is nothing to hide from me," the Empress replied with haughtiness.

"Do I go around mind-reading your imperial guard?" Lord Och asked but didn't let the empress answer. "Of course I try, but I don't do it *openly* because that would be rude. Now, if I were forced to reveal everything I knew to the loyal members of your court . . ."

The Empress's gaze turned deadly. "Are you threatening me, Lord Och?"

"I am defending my property," the lich replied.

Valdemar gritted his teeth, but wisely kept his mouth shut. He exchanged a silent glance with Marianne as the Dark Lords bickered, his bodyguard looking up. He could see her thoughts written all over her face.

So I'm not the only one to think this woman is Sophia, Valdemar thought. In truth, he had spent a few minutes gathering information on the room through his magical senses. He had detected the presence of spatial magic in the air, but it took him a while to make sense out of what he had learned; Valdemar had quickly come up with a theory.

This place was the Earthmouths' hub.

Yes, one needed to be a willing martyr to become a portal, but Sophia's role was far more important. She was a keystone stabilizing the entire structure, making sure that space didn't collapse from the increasing number of rifts knitting the various regions of the empire together. All teleportation through the Earthmouths went through her in some way, allowing the Dark Lords to maintain tight control over the network.

So long as they held this fallen messiah in their thrall, they could tune portals at will and transport armies to any cavern while their foes struggled to fight through the tunnels. None could challenge their power; mankind would always keep a strong advantage over rival civilizations.

That was the unspeakable crime the first Dark Lords had committed in ancient times. They had forever bound their old teacher to harvest her power for their own use.

Something felt wrong about the room the Sabbath took place in. It seemed . . . separate from the rest of Underland, but Valdemar couldn't clearly explain why. Powerful wards interfered with his magical senses.

"—we do not try to read each other's minds nor ask the others to lower their defenses," Lord Hagith told Aratra, causing Valdemar to focus back on the discussion. "Two of Lord Och's apprentices joined this assembly. As a friendly gesture, I say we treat his third disciple like a potential future ally."

Empress Aratra glanced at her colleagues, but found little support outside Phaleg. "Fine," she said. "Then we shall debate whether we should destroy him or not."

Valdemar winced, while Marianne took a deep breath at his side. "Your Dark Majesty," she said, "if I may—"

"You may not," the Empress cut her off. "I understand your desire to defend your lover, Lady Reynard, I truly do. But you should remember *your place.*"

Marianne winced and remained quiet.

"This man," Empress Aratra nodded at Valdemar, "is the half-breed spawn of a human woman and Ialdabaoth, the god in the flesh and Father of the Blood. He is the result of years of experimentation by the cult behind the rat plague infecting my subjects, and they commit crimes in his name."

She waved her hand, her magic suffusing the air. Light itself appeared to bend around the Empress's fingers while the polished gemstone ground began to reflect new images. Valdemar looked down to face pictures of hospitals treating wererats and diseased victims; of knights tossing corpses into open tombs and herding plague victims into ghettos; of dismembered victims of the Verney cult, their blood used to paint Valdemar's own names on walls.

The sight disgusted the summoner. "I never wished for this," Valdemar whispered in protest. "If I could have stopped it, I would have."

"Then you should have taken your own life for everyone's sake." Lord Phaleg looked at Valdemar with a cold gaze. "Lord Och should have destroyed you the moment you fell into our laps, and your family's cult would have died with you."

Valdemar thought he could have found an ally in this particular Dark Lord, but he had been mistaken. Phaleg the Binder was so focused on spitting on his former master that he would seize any opportunity to do so, no matter the cost . . . and no matter who he had to hurt.

"You can try to destroy young Valdemar, but you will be disappointed," Lord Och said to everyone's surprise. "My apprentice cannot die."

Lord Bethor, who had remained silent and uninterested in the debate so far, finally spoke a few laconic words heavy with meaning. "His death is beyond my power."

A tense silence followed, as all other Dark Lords glanced at the mightiest among them. Even Empress Aratra, who rivaled Bethor's might, appeared slightly shocked. "You admit your powerlessness?" she asked, her expression unreadable.

"He cannot be killed," Lord Bethor confirmed to Valdemar's shock. "He can be sealed or neutralized. But he cannot be destroyed."

Valdemar himself couldn't believe his ears. This man, this incarnation of power who ruled atop a tower built on the corpses of his enemies and waged war on the derros almost single-handedly, *couldn't* destroy him?

But you cannot die.

"Young Valdemar is an incarnation of the Blood itself," Lord Och explained. "An avatar of life itself, in a way. His divine soul is connected to all life in Underland, and when the body is torn to shreds, it draws mass from our world's inhabitants to regenerate him. Nothing short of the world's destruction would kill my apprentice . . . and even then I wonder if it would stick."

To Valdemar's distaste, Ophiel the Mad observed him like a piece of meat in a store. His other colleagues were more perplexed.

"Fascinating," Lord Hagith said. "I had the feeling this reunion would prove interesting. He could be the answer to so many secrets of the Blood . . ."

"Of course, even if my apprentice cannot die, he can still be transformed," Lord Och added cheerfully. "If he sacrificed his soul of his own free will he would transform into a functional portal like any other martyr. I'm sure that in his great altruism the thought has already crossed his young mind."

Valdemar struggled against the urge to glare at his teacher, refusing to give the lich any satisfaction.

But the longer he considered Lord Och's words, the less he liked them. If the Blood passively recreated his body from nothing, then . . . would he survive if reduced to a single cell? Would he agonize for weeks as he grew back a foot, a leg, or an arm? Valdemar had already survived a similar experience in Lord Bethor's tower, but he had outside resources to draw upon instead of creating them from nothing. A submersion in boiling blood had halted his regeneration.

But it still hadn't killed him.

I'm like the Pleromians, Valdemar thought. He wanted to be surprised, but a part of him had already guessed his regeneration might have no true counter. There was no way Ialdabaoth would let its prince, the very means by which it sought to achieve freedom, be so easy to destroy. The Father of All had created the perfect tool, a vulnerable mind in an immortal body.

And yet, for all of his incredible resilience, Valdemar was still capable of aging.

Am I going to outlive Marianne? Valdemar wondered as he glanced at his companion. Age without dying, growing ever more feeble but never reaching the point of death? He wasn't eager to perish anytime soon, but the implications terrified him.

"And you kept it for yourself, Och?" Lady Phul smiled at Valdemar, examining him with renewed interest. "You should have shared."

"Lord Och knows nothing of generosity," Lord Phaleg declared. "And this is all the more reason to get rid of this abomination. His mere existence is a threat to us all, as his ability to summon a Stranger proves."

The man waved his grafted hand, and Ktulu was suddenly teleported out of his bag and onto the floor. The familiar glanced around as he fell on his butt in surprise. "Ktulu?" he asked as he looked up at Valdemar. "Ktululhu?"

I didn't sense anything, Valdemar thought. Though he could detect Lord Och's teleportation attempts, Lord Phaleg's spell hadn't even registered on his magical senses. *I was wrong . . . he may be the least of them in raw power, but his summoning prowess surpass even his old teacher's.*

Thankfully, the other Dark Lords seemed more amused by Ktulu than threatened by him. "He could open a daycare for Strangers, how frightening," Ophiel the Mad mocked while Ktulu glared back at him. "Are you scared of half-breeds and children, Phaleg? If so, I should pay your Domain a visit someday. The Light knows it is in dire need of renovation."

"None of us could summon a Stranger as a familiar," Lord Phaleg replied with stoicism, ignoring the blatant threat. "If this abomination can do it while untrained, imagine if he fell under his cult's influence? If we cannot destroy him, we should exile him to another world or seal him in a coffin of stone where none will find him."

Marianne tensed at the edge of Valdemar's gaze, while Lady Phul offered an even more terrible alternative. "He is a conduit for Ialdabaoth," she said. "Which is why the cultists want him. Instead of exile or sealing him, I say we make productive use of him."

"How so?" Lord Hagith asked with curiosity.

"Let us use him as a magical battery," Ophiel the Mad proposed before his colleague could answer. "We can turn him into a conduit to the Blood to increase our own power tenfold."

"As always, Ophiel, you lack perspective," Lady Phul mocked him with a condescending smile. "I have a more imaginative proposal. Namely, we could turn him into a lock to seal the Outer Darkness away."

Though Valdemar would have been all for it, her proposal turned out to be even worse than Ophiel's. "We can put him here alongside her," Lady Phul explained as she glanced at the stone woman in the ceiling. "His body will fossilize while his soul shall keep the worlds apart. Maybe we could even strengthen the wards binding our progenitor."

Valdemar couldn't help but glance at the stone corpse above his head. How long would it be before he went mad and then empty inside? Years? Centuries?

To Valdemar's surprise, Empress Aratra seemed strangely ambivalent about the idea. Her blank expression turned into a frown of disapproval, but she said nothing as the other Dark Lords argued.

Lord Hagith, who had watched the debate with caution, turned to Och. "And what do you have to say about this? You have been strangely passive, Lord Och. We are discussing your apprentice's fate and yet you seem oddly unconcerned."

Phaleg the Binder glared at his former mentor. "What is your plan?"

"It is a surprise I will keep for later," the lich replied before turning to Empress Aratra. "I am waiting for Her Majesty's fair judgment."

The Empress seemed pleasantly surprised, locking eyes with Valdemar. "And what do you have to say for yourself, child?"

Valdemar gathered his breath. "Before I answer," he began, noticing

Marianne smiling at him as his only moral support. Ktulu also moved closer to his legs, as if to protect him. "I would like to ask Her Majesty . . . no, this entire assembly, a single question."

"Ask away," the Empress replied gracefully.

"Do you *care*?" Valdemar asked.

Empress Aratra raised an eyebrow. "About what?"

"The world is threatened with destruction," Valdemar pointed out, clenching his fists in silent anger. "A god is rising from the Blood. A plague devours your citizens and cultists murder them. But so far you have discussed my eventual fate rather than these issues, which happen as we speak. Almost as if you found them *banal*."

"Yes, of course they are," Ophiel replied with a dismissive shrug. "We have survived more Strangers than you can count."

"Ialdabaoth has been threatening to wake up for centuries," Lady Phul added. "It still hasn't. Lord Hagith's modified plague is a hassle, I will grant you, but it is nothing we haven't dealt with in the past."

"We can win a hundred battles but only lose one," Lord Bethor declared with wisdom. "Let us destroy the vermin hiding in Ariouth and be done with it, as Phaleg should have."

"Yes, your inactivity has been noticed," Lord Ophiel complained as he glanced at Phaleg the Binder. "These rats trouble my artistic endeavors and sully my beautiful population. If you want them to infest your Domain, be my guest, but I ask that you keep them inside your frontiers."

Lord Phaleg bristled. "I have ordered a strike against their temple before this meeting."

"And you took your sweet time, my old apprentice," Lord Och mocked him. "But I guess it is better late than never. Did you let them fester in your Domain to embarrass me?"

"You do not factor so much in my thoughts, traitor," Lord Phaleg lied.

"The safety of our citizens is our foremost concern," Empress Aratra answered Valdemar with a tone that implied the opposite. "But you will agree that you are a special oddity. Your fate does matter more than a few commoners perishing, as it may affect all of mankind."

"If people's safety is your concern," Valdemar said, "then we share a goal. I am forever on mankind's side."

"That remains to be seen," Lord Phaleg replied.

"Then let me prove it!" Valdemar put a hand on his chest. "Yes, my family is responsible for the crimes happening around the empire, but I will atone for them. I didn't ask to be born a tool for monsters, but I can choose to become something else."

"And how would you do that?" Lady Phul asked. "According to my information, your very dreams summon a Nahemoth to our reality. Do you intend to stay awake forever?"

"I intend to seal the Nahemoth, destroy what little remains of my family's cult, and destroy the Qlippoths they summoned," Valdemar argued. "And, if I can achieve it . . . I will save our dead from the Outer Darkness."

Ophiel chuckled, but Empress Aratra's cold gaze made him go silent. Though Lord Bethor challenged her in power, her authority remained strong.

"I have a plan to do all of them," Valdemar said with firm dedication. "I cannot guarantee success. But I believe in my odds."

"You ask us to trust you?" Empress Aratra asked with skepticism.

"No," Valdemar replied. "I ask you for a chance. A chance to prove that I am human, and that this world can be made a better place."

A short silence followed, broken by laughter. Ophiel the Mad held their chest as both male and female voices came out of their throat. The other reactions were more subdued, from Lord Hagith's friendly but skeptical smile, to Lady Phul's undisguised amusement. Phaleg the Binder scoffed in scorn, while Empress Aratra's face was utterly unreadable.

Valdemar's words had hit a wall of cynicism. None of them believed in making Underland a better place. Maybe they had once, but they no longer cared.

But Valdemar didn't falter. He stood strong, facing Empress Aratra's gaze with determination. He had had his flesh flensed from his bones, his mind ripped apart; he had fought the derros' madness and Lord Och's cruel tricks. And he had refused to give in.

He wouldn't falter today.

Empress Aratra's gaze seemed to pierce through even his mental defenses to peer into his soul. Valdemar sensed her magic brush against his shielded mind for any hint of weakness or hesitation. And when she found none, she turned to Lord Och. "What do you have to say about this?"

"Honestly?" The lich shifted on his throne. "I care little for this discussion. I mostly came to announce my upcoming retirement."

Ophiel's laughter died in his throat.

The entire assembly, from the Dark Lords to Marianne, glanced in the lich's direction with surprise and confusion. Even Lord Bethor, who clearly considered this meeting a waste of time, had turned his gaze at his old master in surprise.

"Your *retirement*?" Empress Aratra asked, squinting, stretching each word.

"I am old and feeble, young Aratra," Lord Och said with a trembling voice. He played the senile elder quite well, though obviously nobody bought into his game. "I had many happy memories with this brotherhood, but I believe it is time I retire to tend to mushrooms in my backyard."

What is he playing at? Valdemar thought, finding the scene surreal.

He wasn't the only one. "You are retiring?" Lord Phaleg repeated in disbelief. "From being a Dark Lord?"

"It was amusing the first few centuries, but I feel my unlife has become quite banal," Lord Och replied. "All I do is push paper and hear complaints nowadays. I need a change and a breath of fresh air, perhaps find time to write my memoir for prosperity. As such, I will take some time to settle my affairs and mentor my successor until they can fully take over my duties."

What is his endgame? Valdemar wondered as his mind furiously tried to figure it out. He knew Lord Och enough to know that he would never, ever surrender all the accumulated power and influence he had gathered across the centuries.

Unless . . .

Unless he was aiming for something higher and no longer needed his old assets.

"Who?" Valdemar dared to ask. "Who will succeed you, my teacher?"

"My," the lich smiled maliciously before raising a bony finger at his apprentice. "But *you*, of course."

18

THE END IS NIGH

The bickering Dark Lords had fallen silent, their eyes all focusing on Valdemar. The sorcerer himself ignored the tense atmosphere as he held his master's gaze. The lich delighted in his apprentice's reaction, his skull grinning as a dark chuckle came out of his rotting teeth.

"Why the surprise?" Lord Och asked Valdemar. "Surely you must have suspected it. Two of your predecessors joined this brotherhood, did they not? Did you think I would resist the opportunity to make you the third?"

Having recovered from his shock, Lord Ophiel laughed. "Is that your master plan, old man? To replace our entire assembly with your students one at a time?"

"I agree this council would benefit from some new blood," Lady Phul said with a wide smile. "But I can hardly see anyone else in your chair, Lord Och."

"I won't stand for it!" Lord Phaleg rose from his seat, pointing an accusing finger at Lord Och. "What is your plan?"

"My plan?" Lord Och put a hand on his chest, as if he had been struck in his heart. Of course, he no longer had one and the gesture didn't fool anyone. "Your distrust wounds me deeply, apprentice."

"I am no longer your apprentice," Lord Phaleg hissed angrily, the eyes on his artificial arm all glaring at the lich. "Nor blind to your ploys."

"Are you jealous of your replacement?" Lord Och mocked his rival. "My poor, poor first apprentice . . . condemned to rule over a barren desert and living in the shadow of his successors."

Phaleg didn't take the bait. "This is a trick of some kind. I know it."

Valdemar himself struggled to understand Lord Och's motivation. He strongly suspected that the lich no longer needed his Domain because he intended to leave Underland for another plane of existence, but why choose his apprentice to take over? Valdemar knew he was no match for the weakest of the Dark Lords. It would take him years to approach their power.

"Quiet, Lord Phaleg." Empress Aratra's imperious voice silenced Phaleg's outrage. The weaker Dark Lord obeyed, unwilling to interrupt his more powerful colleague. "Lord Och . . . you have found a way to open the path, have you not?"

Lord Och answered with a long silence and a telling look. Empress Aratra took it as confirmation.

"This is madness, my old friend," she said with a soft voice, sounding almost sympathetic. "Better to rule the abyss than serve the light above. If there is anything left of you to serve in the first place."

"I agree that if these were my only two options, I would have chosen to rot in the dark with you, dear Aratra," Lord Och replied. "But as my third apprentice proved, sometimes it is better to create a third way."

The Empress squinted in skepticism. "A third way?"

Lord Och nodded at Valdemar, who had listened to the exchange without a word. "This is all up to him."

And as the Empress's curious gaze fell back upon him, Valdemar clenched his fists in silent rage. *This is a plot to confuse the other Dark Lords,* he realized. *He's trying to distract them.*

"The path to what?" Ophiel the Mad asked, his laughter turning malicious. "What are you hiding from us, Lord Och?"

The path to the Light, Valdemar thought.

"The path to our destruction," Lord Phaleg declared with anger. His eyes moved from his former master to Valdemar himself. His paranoia was plain for all to see. "I knew you would prove a threat to us all. Do you even understand what he intends to use you for?"

Valdemar ignored the Dark Lords and instead exchanged a glance with Marianne. His companion's jaw clenched, and she gave him a nod of support.

Valdemar didn't need telepathy to understand what she was thinking.

"I refuse," he said.

They were done playing the lich's games.

His answer surprised the Dark Lords, though Lord Och's expression remained undecipherable. "You refuse?" the lich asked, insisting on each syllable.

"I refuse," Valdemar repeated through his clenched teeth. "I don't want any of your handouts."

"Handouts?" There was no joy in Lord Och's dark laugh. "You would call my throne in this brotherhood, the Pleroma Institute, my entire Domain of Paraplex a handout? How spoiled can you be, my foolish disciple?"

"We both know they are poisoned gifts," Valdemar argued as he waved his hand at the Dark Lords. "You want this assembly to watch my every move instead of yours so they won't disturb you."

"Of course I do not want to be disturbed; I am retiring," Lord Och replied. "That is the entire point."

"But you already have an army of far more capable Masters to replace you. People perhaps as old as your colleagues. Wouldn't it be better for the Empire to put one of them in charge?"

As Valdemar had hoped, his words struck true with some of the Dark Lords. Phaleg the Binder already suspected Och of foul play, and the likes of Ophiel and Phul gazed at the lich with distrust. The Dark Lords' alliance was built on fear and might rather than respect. Valdemar needed to redirect their paranoia toward the lich rather than have them focus on him.

"Or perhaps," Lord Och said calmly, "I simply do not care."

Which was unfortunately very plausible.

"Whatever the case, I never wanted to rule," Valdemar pointed out. "I only ever agreed to serve you in the service of one goal: to open the path to a better world. Unless you have forgotten, my teacher?"

"I have not." Lord Och stroked his bony chin, his eyes two baleful stars of malice. "But, and stop me if I misremember, didn't we already debate about how opening a path to another world, while possible, wouldn't solve our realm's problems but merely displace them? You have criticized our government many times."

Valdemar sighed. "I have."

This amused Lord Ophiel. "Will you dare to say it to our face? My Knights still keep your cell in my Spellbane prison furbished, you mongrel bastard."

"You are young, Valdemar." Empress Aratra's motherly tone couldn't hide the condescension underneath. "When you have reached our age, if you ever do, you will understand that order is needed to maintain stability. Our Empire's laws were refined over centuries of experience to ensure the safety and the prosperity of the greatest number."

Lord Bethor snorted. "Your laws only serve this assembly's prosperity, Aratra."

The disrespected empress glared back at her rival. "And you forget yourself, Lord Bethor. Your proposal to lift restrictions on sorcery has already been rejected more times than I can count."

"Talent alone should be the measure of success, not birth or connections," Lord Bethor argued. "No mage worth his salt should need a piece of paper to cast spells. Your obsession with removing internal threats has turned our population into passive mushrooms while hungry predators gather at our borders. We need constant innovation to survive, not peaceful stagnation."

He asked for spellcasting permits to be removed? Valdemar wondered. He couldn't say it surprised him, considering Lord Bethor's warmongering ways. Valdemar himself had been forced to run from the law because he couldn't do his research in peace or access the grimoires he needed.

What surprised him was that Lord Bethor's position wasn't without support. Lady Phul nodded in agreement. "While I disagree with Lord Bethor's dream of turning Azlant into a military base, we do need fewer regulations," she declared, "especially on magical items and foreign trade. Free commerce and economic integration with the dokkar enclaves will prevent a war better than tariffs and distrust."

"I intended to use this Sabbath to discuss the question of further cooperation on the magical research front," Lord Hagith added. "We have the best biomancers in Horaios, but despite my entreaties to build partnerships, the Pleroma Institute keeps most of its discoveries tightly locked. It would benefit everyone if our development departments could cooperate rather than jealousy hoard their successes."

Empress Aratra dismissed these misgivings with a wave of her hand. "We have not gathered today to discuss these issues."

"No," Lord Och agreed. His eyes didn't leave Valdemar though. "But what about our next Sabbath?"

Valdemar glared at his master. Was this another mind game? Was the lich tempting his apprentice with the possibility of reforming the Empire from the inside, however remote? It would certainly amuse Lord Och to see Valdemar compromise on his dream.

But the lich wouldn't make such an announcement before all of his peers for the sake of a cruel joke. Lord Och was serious about stepping down, though Valdemar doubted he was truthful about his motives. Was this why the Dark Lord of Paraplex had tried relentlessly to break his student's optimism? To mold his apprentice into his cynical image, so he would take care of his realm in his master's absence?

The idea of reforming the empire appealed to Valdemar, but he refused to dance to his teacher's strings.

"You will find someone else to fill in for you," the young necromancer insisted.

"How selfish of you," Lord Och mocked him. "You criticize me all the time, but when I offer you a chance to prove you are better than me, you spit on it. I suppose your high-minded words were but hot air in the end . . ."

"I still have too much to learn, you very well know that," Valdemar replied with the same sarcastic tone. "How can I lead when I am but a shadow of your wisdom, my dear teacher?"

"Your apprentice is a naïve fool, Och," said Ophiel the Mad. "Do you wish to mock us by crowning him one of our own? I confess I would find it amusing, but alas now is not the time for peace and laughter. This era calls for an iron hand and a firm grasp on power."

Lord Hagith nodded. "I must agree with my colleague's assessment. Lord Och, you are an integral cog in the great machinery of the empire. With the derros on the move and the dokkars waiting for their moment to strike us in the back, your departure would be . . . unfortunate."

Lord Bethor, who had observed the spat in silence so far, agreed with a nod. "Valdemar has potential, but he is not fit to become one of us yet. He has will and resolve, but he lacks strength."

Lord Och's resolve remained unshaken. "He will gain it in time."

"He will," Lord Bethor agreed. "But not now. He has barely tapped into his own limitless potential."

"Limitless?" Empress Aratra let out a snort. "He has power by virtue of his birth, but it takes more than that to rule Underland."

W . . . k . . . up.

Valdemar froze, while his familiar looked up at him with worried eyes.

"What's wrong?" Marianne whispered.

"Did you hear that?" Valdemar asked. "A man's voice."

Marianne frowned as the Dark Lords argued between themselves. "My ears are better than yours, Valdemar, and I have heard nothing of the sort."

But Valdemar could have sworn otherwise. He focused on his surroundings, trying to focus on the source of the sound.

Wa . . . up . . .

The voice echoed around him. It belonged to a man, but not anyone that Valdemar recognized.

He wasn't the only one to hear it. Though Marianne remained oblivious, Empress Aratra and Lord Bethor both tensed up at once. The former glanced at the ceiling and the latter at Valdemar himself.

Wake up.

And then came the pain.

To Valdemar, it felt as if his own brain exploded inside his head, his eyes boiling in his sockets. The same agony that he had survived at the bottom of Lord Bethor's tower seized him again. This time the attack didn't come from the outside but from within.

Valdemar immediately strengthened his magical defenses. It was all for naught. Much like Lord Bethor had once bypassed them entirely, a dark power ignored all his protections and seized his heart.

He heard Marianne call his name as he fell. His vision blurred, his last sight being that of Sophia the Wise shivering above his head as the vault trembled. The dark swallowed all.

Life is a dream, the voice spoke, *old and terrible, and death is truth.*

The world became cold, cold like the vastness of space. His sight expanded beyond the ceiling of stone above his head, beyond the ice of the surface. He saw the planet he had worked so hard to escape from above, a lifeless cocoon hiding the festering warmth underneath.

Do you see me?

He saw, yes.

His eyes pierced the stone skin of the world and gazed into its warmth depths to a cavern full of marshes and swamps surrounding a plateau of stone. A city stood proudly on it, its gargantuan streets asleep, its portals locked to prevent the spread of a plague.

But no wall could stop the rats. They came out of the sewers and the swamps in vast numbers. A horde of scavengers emerged from the shadows of human civilization. They poured into the streets like a tidal wave of fur.

More vermin joined them. Swarms of bats flocked to the city, led by the monster Bertrand had become. Flies and bugs followed in their wake, hungry for human flesh. They flew straight for the lone institute of Pleroma which oversaw the city.

I have journeyed beyond the veil of death and returned, the voice declared. *My soul cries out. I see with ten thousand eyes and kill with countless mouths. The moment has come, the time is now.*

As a shield of magic rose to protect the Institute, the streets of the city below started to change. The stone buildings of Pleroma overlapped with a fishing hamlet's houses. Qlippoths walked among the living. A well appeared in the central plaza and the horror at the bottom awakened. It called out its sibling to join the family gathering.

The corpse of Sarah Verney oversaw this desolation, crucified on a great cross of skulls and bones. Shelley danced around her in glee as maddened cultists gathered around him. They carried an enormous, hooded robe made of wererat skin, a ghastly artifact harvested from the remains of a hundred victims. Rats flocked beneath the vile clothing piece and soon filled it. A towering horror formed inside the robe as the mass of rats assembled into a humanoid shape.

Come, my descendant, our hope.

Two red lights appeared beneath the robe's cowl.

It is time to wake up your father.

And Valdemar answered.

"Never!"

It took all of his mental strength to escape the vision, but he succeeded. When Valdemar regained his mind, he was on the floor in Marianne's arms. "Valdemar, are you alright?" she asked him in panic. His familiar was at her side, standing still like a statue. "Valdemar?"

"I'm . . ." Valdemar gritted his teeth as he tried to ignore the searing pain. Though the visions didn't overtake him again, his head still hurt. "I'm . . . fine."

"You do not look fine, apprentice," said Lord Och.

The Dark Lords had gathered around Valdemar, some more worried than others. Sophia the Wise wriggled in the ceiling of stone above their heads while the ground trembled. Lady Phul's ethereal body seemed to phase in and out of existence in the blink of an eye, struggling to maintain her physical form.

"What is happening?" Lord Ophiel asked with a hint of worry.

"It is happening," Lord Och rasped with eerie serenity. "At last, they make their move."

"This is all his fault!" Lord Phaleg raised a hand at Valdemar and prepared to kill him on the spot. "Away with him!"

Marianne's fist immediately grew a layer of bone armor as she prepared to protect Valdemar, but Empress Aratra stepped in. "It will change nothing," she declared with an imperious voice. "He is not the source of the disturbance."

"Whatever it is, it affects the Primordial Dream and the Outer Darkness," Lady Phul declared as she managed to regain some semblance of stability. "I sense them overlapping with our reality."

Lord Hagith nodded to himself. "This must be a Nahemoth's doing then."

And not just any of them.

"He can't . . ." Valdemar gritted his teeth as he tried to ignore the searing pain. Though the visions didn't overtake him again, his head still hurt. "Exist at the same time . . . as I do . . ."

"Can't?" Lord Och shook his head. "No, my apprentice, the correct word is *shouldn't*. We do not fully understand how this connection works, so it is possible our foes found a loophole we haven't considered yet."

Marianne frowned with Valdemar. "What's happening?"

"Paraplex." Valdemar resisted the urge to immediately teleport there. "They're summoning the phantom Vernburg . . . inside Pleroma . . . I think."

And that thing underneath the cloak of skins . . . it was the center of it all. The ritual's catalyst.

"Do you hear that, Och?" Ophiel the Mad asked his colleague. "I knew someone would try to summon a Stranger in your realm one day. A pity it might affect us all."

"Not for long." Empress Aratra's eyes shone with a red glow. "This challenge to my authority must be met with force."

"For once we agree," Lord Bethor added as he glanced at Valdemar and Marianne. "It is time."

Yes indeed.

It was time to save Bertrand, destroy the Verney cult for good, and bury their twisted legacy.

And for Valdemar, it would be his chance to save his unborn brother from himself.

1 9

BACK TO SCHOOL

Few things could make the bickering Dark Lords work together. The last time they showed a unified front was all the way back to the last derro war, when they inflicted a severe defeat upon Otto Blutgang's predecessor and shattered his realm. It took the derro kingdom decades to recover its lost strength at the cost of its people's individuality.

When roused, the Dark Lords were fearsome to behold. Many believed that only their disunity had prevented the Empire of Azlant from conquering all of Underland, from the dokkar enclaves to the far fringes of the derro kingdom.

Today, Marianne would have the privilege to see their power up close.

"Teleportation pathways to the Institute are still secure thanks to my magical defenses," Lord Och explained to his colleagues as they prepared to move to the Domain of Paraplex. "However, I wouldn't recommend moving to the city directly. Spatial anomalies have a way of causing teleportation spells to go haywire."

"We know that," Lord Phaleg replied dryly before turning to Valdemar. "Your vision showed you the Lilith crucified at the center of the town?"

"Yes, right next to the well where the Nahemoth is sealed." Valdemar nodded respectfully, the Mask of the Nightwalker on his face. His familiar had hopped back inside his bag in anticipation. "Shelley was using her to summon some kind of . . . rat hive mind, I suppose?"

"An avatar of Ialdabaoth, no doubt," Lord Hagith said while stroking his chin.

"All of Underland would be trembling as we speak if that were the case," Lord Phaleg replied with skepticism. There were quakes taking place, but nothing truly frightening. "I believe we face two different phenomena. Liliths are handmaidens of the Nahemoths, so it's plausible they're using her as a conduit to summon one. But I draw a blank at what this rat entity is. It's not associated with any Qlippothic entity that I'm aware of."

Marianne observed the Dark Lords strategizing without a word, but focused more on Valdemar. Her companion had recovered from his vision but he had been left shaken. "Do you still hear voices?" she asked him.

"I'm blocking them out for now," Valdemar replied with some hesitation, his hand brushing against his mask. "It helps, I think."

This only made Marianne worry even for his safety. The Mask of the Nightwalker was connected to the eponymous Stranger; though it stood in opposition to Ialdabaoth, it remained a different kind of evil. Valdemar's plan to deal with his brother Crétail involved the mask, but cursed artifacts rarely worked as intended.

Lord Bethor's contribution to the Dark Lords' debate was far less verbose than his compatriots and far more meaningful. "Loctis," he said.

"Who?" Lord Ophiel asked with a hint of contempt.

"One of the Masters at my Institute," Lord Och enlightened his colleague. The lich's eyes flared with a ghostly glow. "Ah, I see your point Lord Bethor. You believe that this creature is no Qlippoth but a powerful sorcerer's soul splintered across countless bodies. But who would wield such power, I wonder . . ."

Marianne's eyes widened as she put two and two together. *Rats everywhere . . .* she thought as she glanced at Valdemar's bag and the little Stranger inside. *Shelley was never more than a pet, a familiar. Did he still share a connection with his master even beyond death?*

Valdemar immediately noticed her expression and turned in her direction. "Do you have an idea?" he asked her.

"Valdemar, you said the entity that sent you these visions called you his descendant?" Marianne scowled as Valdemar confirmed it with a nod, as her theory became all the more credible. "I think I know what, or rather *who*, that rat hive mind you saw is. The person who created Shelley and started this whole mess in the first place."

Her companion crossed his arms as he considered her words. "My great-grandfather . . ."

"Aleksander Verney?" Empress Aratra raised an eyebrow. "Didn't the inquisitors of the Light burn him at the stake?"

"Even death can be overcome, my dear Aratra," Lord Och said with amusement. "Half of us here are 'living' proof of it. Though I am curious about young Marianne's reasoning."

"Souls return to the Outer Darkness after they die," Marianne explained. "It's likely his service to Ialdabaoth might have secured him a favorable place in the afterlife. We know the cult gathered the remains of wererats, and I suspect they did so as part of a ritual to bring Verney's soul back to the living world."

"What purpose would reviving this loser serve?" Lord Ophiel asked in confusion. "If I led that cult I would call something with more power."

That, Marianne didn't know.

Lord Phaleg, as a summoning specialist, immediately guessed the cult's motives. "Even the mightiest Qlippoths are summoned entities at the end of the day. They cannot break wards on their own, and this cult is made of weak-willed rabble unlikely to be privy to knowledge of higher rituals."

Lord Ophiel snickered in response. "All I hear is that we only have to kill him to end this charade and get back to more important matters."

They are truly treating an apocalyptic scenario as a minor nuisance, Marianne thought. Was this a show of confidence or plain old arrogance? She simply couldn't tell.

"The situation is more complex than you believe," Lady Phul protested. By now she had managed to stabilize her essence somewhat. Her inhuman avatar looked paler than it did a few hours ago, but she no longer faded in and out of existence. "Their ritual uses the Nahemoth as an anchor to merge the Outer Darkness and the material plane. I can sense the Qlippoths' essence infecting the very fabric of space. More of these foul creatures will slip inside our reality the longer this phenomenon continues."

"If so, then the process might continue even if we disrupt the ritual," Lord Phaleg pointed out before glaring at Valdemar. "The wards have weakened so much *he* doesn't even need to sleep to manifest the Nahemoth. We should slay them both."

"Should we even bring *him* at all?" Lord Ophiel looked at Valdemar with disdain. "This is all a ploy to force us to relinquish their so-called Messiah. His presence might worsen the situation instead of improving it."

Valdemar winced and Marianne quickly came to his rescue. She had heard the Dark Lords look down on him since the start of the Sabbath and her patience had reached its limit.

"With all due respect, Lord Phaleg, Lord Ophiel, you would not even know of this threat without this 'child,'" the noblewoman argued with a boldness that surprised even her. "You say this crisis wouldn't happen without Valdemar. I say it won't end unless you trust him."

She expected the Dark Lords to strike her down where she stood. Instead, Lord Ophiel appeared more amused by her defiance than anything, while Lord Phaleg answered with a snort.

"*Trust*?" Lord Ophiel said the word as if it were a curse. "Foolish little girl, you'll find no such thing here."

"A Nahemoth is nearly impossible to bind, let alone banish from the material world," Lord Phaleg pointed out. "It is a difficult task even for the likes of us. Yet you think you can end this incursion for good?"

"I can." Valdemar stepped forward with renewed confidence. "As I told you, I have a plan."

"I will vouch for him," Lord Bethor spoke plainly. His support cowed the weaker members of the assembly.

"As will I," Empress Aratra smiled at Valdemar. "But if you fail, child . . ." The Empress's eyes glowed with a golden aura. An aura of dread poured from her like molten lava. "You will join our guest in the ceiling above your head."

Even Marianne, who had faced Pleromians and monsters without flinching, was left slightly intimidated. The weight on her shoulders reminded her of her first encounter with Lord Bethor.

Valdemar didn't answer the Empress's threat for a few seconds as the Dark Lords all waited for his reaction with curiosity. Marianne gave her companion a reassuring nod and prepared to defend him if the worst came to pass.

"I . . . I understand, Your Dark Majesty," Valdemar answered at last before clearing his throat. "I will not disappoint. I swear to you, my plan will succeed."

"Oaths are wind," the Empress replied as her eyes returned to a bloody red shade. "Actions are what matter."

"I will deliver." Valdemar glanced at Lord Och next. "But I need Hermann, my teacher."

"Of course . . . him and his Painted World." Lord Och made a mock bow to his fellow Dark Lords. "I need to pick up my apprentice's assistants in Lord Bethor's Domain. Until I return, young Valdemar and dear Marianne will welcome you into my halls."

"I will come with you then," Lord Phaleg immediately declared with suspicion.

"My, my former apprentice, do you believe I will scheme against you if you turn your back on me?" Lord Och put a hand on his chest. "I am wounded."

"If you have nothing to hide, then it shouldn't be a bother."

When Marianne thought the Dark Lords' brief alliance wouldn't last another five minutes, Empress Aratra set her foot down. "Lord Phaleg, your expertise with summoning shall be needed to deal with this crisis. Lord Och will join us as we tend to his Domain's needs, and Lord Bethor will fetch whoever you need in Sabaoth."

"You think such an act would demean me, Aratra?" Lord Bethor snorted. "Truly you are small. No ruler is so high as not to carry out even the most menial task."

The Dark Lord of Sabaoth teleported away in a flash of light before the Empress could answer. Aratra gritted her teeth in annoyance as she cursed Bethor. "That shameless fool . . ."

"Well, Lord Bethor is a man of action rather than words," Lord Och declared with fondness. "Shall we let him show us up? Or shall we teach the rabble a lesson?"

"Yes, yes, let us be done with this." Lord Ophiel waved his hand. "Hopefully this won't be a complete waste of my time."

He vanished as space twisted around him, with the other Dark Lords following one after the other. "Do take care of my apprentice, young Marianne," Lord Och said right before he teleported away. "I would loathe for something to happen before the grand finale."

Marianne couldn't explain why, but something in the lich's tone put her on high alert. There was no mockery in his voice, only the certainty of a master schemer whose predictions had come to pass.

He has prepared for this day for quite some time, Marianne guessed. It all looked so improbable, but her gut told her Lord Och wasn't surprised at all by this crisis. She didn't believe the lich had planned for this disaster in the exact details as too many factors were involved . . . but he anticipated the possibility and let it run its course. What was he hoping to gain from it? Somehow Marianne thought it would be nothing good.

"Of course Lord Och anticipated the worst might come to pass," said Empress Aratra. By now she was the last Dark Lord left in the room. "He could have prevented this attack if he had shared his knowledge of it with us. Unfortunately, my old friend enjoys stirring up trouble."

"And for what?" Valdemar replied with clear frustration. "Thousands died for nothing."

"It is a bit too early to say if it was for nothing." The Empress's smile chilled Marianne to the bone. Whether they won or lost the day, they had earned her attention. Anonymity would have been safer. "Let us go."

Marianne cleared her throat. "Your Majesty, if I may . . . I need my weapons returned to me before I can walk into battle." Though she had trained extensively not to rely on them, this battle might be the most important of her life. She needed all the advantages available to her.

"I have not forgotten, dear child." Empress Aratra waved her hand, and Marianne's rapier and gun appeared at her belt. The leader of all mankind looked at the sword with a brief look of fondness. "This takes me back . . ."

"You remember my ancestor, Your Majesty?" Marianne couldn't help but ask. She knew from her family's archives that the Empress had personally ennobled the first of the Reynard centuries ago, but she thought the Dark Lord would have forgotten by now.

"I will never forget such a brazen fool. He once dared to ask for my hand in marriage." Empress Aratra chuckled to herself. "I denied him of course, but precious few were brave enough to even try."

"I did not know," Marianne admitted.

"Of course you did not. Your ancestor had the common sense to make his demand out of the public eye. Perhaps one day I shall reveal to you a few tales he kept out of the history books." Empress Aratra examined Marianne head to toe. "I believe he would be proud of your resolve."

Such words from anyone else would have filled Marianne with pride, but the Empress's praise sounded as hollow as her courtesy. The Dark Lord said this flattery to be polite and not because she truly cared for Marianne's feelings.

Are you truly proud of my actions? Marianne wondered as she glanced at her rapier. She had heard rumors that some soulbound weapons could interact with their wielders, but if her ancestor's spirit could address her, he had never shown the intent to do so.

Whether her ancestor was truly proud of her or not changed nothing. Marianne would always strike the foes of mankind and protect those in need, simple as that. As Valdemar stood at her side, she vowed to defend him too. From Ialdabaoth, from the derros, from anyone who would wish him harm. She would protect him from Lord Och himself if it came to that.

Her companion straightened and tried to put on a brave face, but Marianne's enhanced senses picked up the unease radiating from his body. Valdemar was more anxious than he had ever been. Marianne knew he was thinking about the world, what defeat or victory would mean for the world, and about his family most of all.

It was hard enough for him to confront an unborn brother, but if Aleksander Verney had truly come back from the dead . . .

"I'm with you," Marianne whispered before taking Valdemar's hand into her own. He bristled in surprise at the sudden physical contact, but his fingers soon tightened around her palm. "I won't let you out of sight."

At that moment, Marianne didn't care about the Empress's presence. She simply wanted her companion to feel safer. That whatever ordeal awaited him, he wouldn't face it alone.

"Thanks." Valdemar relaxed a little. "I won't either."

Empress Aratra watched them with an unreadable expression before casting a teleportation spell.

As the Dark Lord's magic took effect, Marianne tried to steel herself for the battle ahead. However, her mind couldn't help but wonder about Lord Och's actions. She tried to put in perspective the lich's action to figure out his end goal. Valdemar was at the center of it all.

When Valdemar arrived at the Institute, Lord Och immediately sent him to assist Hermann on his Painted Door project, Marianne remembered as her body stretched across time and space. And Lord Och offered to fetch Hermann personally.

This implied that whatever objective the lich pursued, Hermann's Painted World project heavily factored in it. Marianne doubted Lord Och desired a private universe to call his own. His only interest in pictomancy was to find out if it could open a path to another universe . . .

A portal to the Light, Marianne guessed. Could the Painted World—

The noises of screams and explosions drew Marianne out of her thoughts as the spell ended.

Empress Aratra had teleported them in front of the Institute's Black Pillar as monsters besieged it. A crimson magical barrier had risen before the Institute's walls. A shield of light rose as high as the ceiling, separating the facility from the chaos outside. Swarms of bats, locusts, and vermin eager to devour the inhabitants crashed against the barrier in relentless waves. The magical defenses melted them into blood on contact, but they had holes.

At least eight monstrous spiders the size of carriages had climbed onto the barrier and started shredding tears into it.

Collectors, Marianne identified the spider monsters. She had read about these elite Qlippoths in the Knights of the Beast's Bestiary. Other Qlippoths emerged through the tears by the dozens alongside common vermin, from tentacled Gnawers to featureless humanoids and twisted ooze monsters.

The world beyond the barrier looked unsafe and terrible. Though Marianne couldn't see the city around the Institute, a glance at the Domain's ceiling told her all she needed to know. Stone was turning into rotting flesh, the eyes of Ialdabaoth growing on it like cancerous tumors. Fanged mouths opened alongside them and screamed, screamed, *screamed*! Their howls threatened to make Marianne's enhanced ears bleed. The entire Domain was slowly transforming into a Qlippoth breeding ground.

The sight only hardened Marianne's resolve. The Institute had become a second home to her in her exile, to the point her dream sanctuary had taken the shape of her quarters. She wouldn't let anyone despoil it.

The Institute wasn't defenseless though. The Knights of the Tome had taken position on the walls to welcome the Qlippoths with steel and spells. Stone security golems had activated, pounding Gnawers onto the pavement. Master Malherbe had joined in the defense by shapeshifting into a mighty werewolf to fight at the Knights' side, while the insects making up Master Loctis' body were busy devouring one Collector alive. Marianne knew more of them would come out of the fortress after securing key sites, like the magical archive, as procedure demanded.

And then there were the Dark Lords.

Marianne had already witnessed Lord Och's might in person once, and the lich didn't disappoint today either. The ancient undead was floating around the Black Pillar, vaporizing any monster that came his way with fire and lightning. As for Lord Hagith, Marianne noticed him assisting the Knights on the walls. The second mouth on his belly had opened, a black tongue stuck out to grab and devour a Collector. The fact the

Qlippoth was far larger than the Dark Lord meant nothing; the black abyss that was Lord Hagith's belly transcended the limits of space.

Lord Ophiel had shapeshifted into a black vampire bat the size of a house, with only his mask remaining from his previous form. While his colleague favored impressive displays of magic, he simply flew through a tear in the barrier to casually shred his way through the enemies. Lady Phul flew after him on her jet-black wings, her mere presence causing the Qlippoths near her to vanish into smoke. It took Marianne a few seconds to realize that the Dark Lord's oneiromancy was so advanced that she could banish summoned creatures back to the Outer Darkness at will.

Only Lord Phaleg didn't take the field. Instead, Och's former apprentice focused on closing tears in the barrier one at a time. It was no glorious endeavor, but one that would save the most lives today in Marianne's opinion.

As for Marianne?

She started shooting the moment Valdemar let her hand go. Her soulbound revolver fired round after round at the nearest Gnawers, spraying the Institute's ground with their blood.

"This is worse than I thought," Empress Aratra said as she pointed at a Collector widening a tear in the barrier. A crimson thunderbolt erupted from her fingernail and vaporized the Qlippoth in one strike, though the hole in the barrier remained. "High caste Qlippoths have already started to manifest."

"It's . . . It's thin . . ." Valdemar struggled to make words as he telekinetically pushed a Gnawer back through a rift in the barrier. "The veil between the planes is thinning . . . I feel it . . ."

Marianne felt it too. The air itself was heavy with magic and the stench of Qlippoths. Their hideous odor filled her nostrils and tiny black particles floated down from the stone ceiling above their heads. The Black Blood of Ialdabaoth was infecting the world itself.

If this phenomenon wasn't stopped soon, it might permanently transform the Domain of Paraplex into a Qlippothic hellscape.

"Clear this fortress," Empress Aratra ordered Valdemar and Marianne as if they were her personal lackeys. Runes of blood appeared on the ground around her and spread in increasingly complex patterns. Marianne recognized some of them as wards and summoning arrays, but most were beyond her understanding. "I shall reinforce the veil between planes to slow down the spread of this madness."

Marianne nodded . . . right until her enhanced sense of smell picked up a familiar stench. The smell of a friend twisted with the odor of poisonous mutations. "Bertrand."

He had been one of the Institute's staff members before his transformation and granted passage through its defenses. Though Lord Och had removed his privileges after he fell under their enemies' influence, the enemy had found a way to overturn the lich's decision.

"Bertrand?" Valdemar asked. "Where is he?"

"My quarters," Marianne muttered to herself as she identified the smell's direction. "He's near my quarters."

Did a sliver of her retainer remain within the beast he had become? Or was he looking for Marianne to slay her personally?

"Then we don't have a moment to waste," Valdemar said. "I'm not certain we can cure him without an Elixir of Life, but we can at least capture him."

Marianne bit her lower lip. "I truly wish to save him, Valdemar, but . . . the situation is dire."

"I can do little until Hermann arrives anyway, and I made you a promise. I will help you save him, whatever the cost." Valdemar shook his head. "We save him now."

Marianne forced herself to smile. "But what if we waste valuable time and more Qlippoths cross into this reality? I want to save Bertrand more than you can ever know, Valdemar, but thousands of lives are at stake."

Her companion prepared to answer when his familiar peeked out of his bag. "Phnglui mgnawah!" the creature squealed, his six eyes serious and unblinking. "Ktulhu rlyeh wagnaftagn!"

The language and sounds made by the familiar were utterly incomprehensible, Marianne's enhanced hearing made her realize that these noises followed a sentence structure. She thought that Ktulu was making senseless noise beforehand, but now she wondered if he had been speaking in his own native tongue.

Valdemar looked over his shoulder at his familiar. To Marianne's surprise, he started to shiver. Summoners and familiars possessed a strong mental bond. Whatever Ktulu sent through it, it had left his partner shaken.

"What is he saying?" Marianne asked with a frown.

"It says, if I interpret the mental images he sends me . . ." Valdemar shuddered. "That if the worst happens, I can always summon his father."

2 0

FIGHT THE DARKNESS

Plants and flesh had overrun the courtyard. When she arrived at the Institute, Lord Och had blessed Marianne with quarters giving her an impeccable view of its hedge maze. Drinking tea while gazing at the plants through the window had been among her favorite small pleasures.

Weeks after she left Paraplex for Sabaoth, Marianne realized that these happy days were over. Thick black roots had grown through the Institute's ground and risen as high as her window, shattering glass and stone alike. The hedge had mutated into a forest of horrors. A bramble of thorny vines coexisted with dark trees covered in bloodred eyes, their branches yielding beating hearts for fruits. Foul cysts and nauseous abscesses bloomed like flowers next to flesh lumps bloated with thick black blood. Blistering pustules released pus and fumes in the air everywhere she looked.

It took Marianne all of her strength not to vomit. Her enhanced senses picked up every foul flavor of this cancerous jungle. Nothing smelled as thick and strong as the scent of Ialdabaoth's black blood, which suffused the entire structure. The stench of the Qlippoths was overwhelming.

A quick look at the blistering heart-fruits told her why. "These are eggs," Marianne muttered as her enhanced eyes noticed the tentacles wiggling beneath the outer layers. "Qlippoth eggs."

"The Outer Darkness corrupts all that it touches," Valdemar replied as they stepped closer to the mutated forest's outskirts. "Our magical defenses protect us, but everyone else . . ."

Holstering her revolver to ration her remaining bullets, Marianne raised her rapier with one hand and kept the other free. She had heard screeches from the nearby roofs and rustling among the fleshy plants.

"They're coming," she said before taking a deep breath. "*He's* coming."

The legions of the Outer Darkness emerged to devour life. The heart-fruits hatched into a harvest of horrors. Each of them burst open to unleash a brood of tentacled Gnawers, of slimes with human faces or walking tumors with tongues for legs. The trees' roots rose like legs to carry the abominable plants forward.

Dense flocks of vampire bats flew from the roofs in a red and black swarm. The foul power of Ialdabaoth had turned them into ravenous mutants with four wings and two mouths. Blood dripped from their sharp fangs.

Marianne faced the tide of horror without flinching by putting herself firmly in front of Valdemar. The overwhelming numbers did not frighten her. She had never faltered before evil and wouldn't start today.

"Marianne." Valdemar crossed his forearms while keeping his hands raised. Blood particles erupted from his fingers and his familiar's eyes shone with a bright red light. "Stay close and cover me."

The sheer magical power coming off from her companion unsettled Marianne. Space itself bent around his person and the air simmered. "What will you do?"

"Outnumber them."

Marianne would have bet a hand that Valdemar was smiling beneath his mask as he tore reality apart.

A wall of fire rose between the verminous tide and Marianne. Blue flames incinerated plants and Qlippoths alike in a devastating blaze, reducing their flesh to ashes in seconds. Marianne covered her eyes to protect herself from the sudden burst of light.

A dozen fire elementals had materialized before her in a battle line on the ground, and half as many of their air cousins right above them. Swirling living wind currents fanned smokeless bonfires. Bats flew into them as fleshy animals and came out as dead charbroiled husks.

"You will set the Institute ablaze!" Marianne warned Valdemar as the world around her went down in flames. Worse, the inferno failed to make the Qlippoths relent. The interdimensional monsters charged through the wall of fire with suicidal recklessness, trampling their own dead in their hurry to reach Valdemar. Their red prince's presence drove them into a maddened frenzy.

Like moths to a flame they flocked, though none of the Qlippoths reached their target. Marianne slew the few who managed to get past the flames. She gutted one half-burnt beast with her rapier, then a second and a third.

Eventually, the sheer amount of blood the elementals' victims left behind drenched the flames. As the elementals returned to their home plane, Valdemar called more. The blood particles swirling around his hands scattered through the air and opened rifts in the tapestry of space.

More soldiers answered Valdemar's call. Four-armed humanoid beasts roared as they smashed trees apart while toads with more mouths than fingers caught mutant bats with their tongues. The Qlippoths fought back fiercely, crushing the newcomers under their weight or tearing them apart with fangs and tentacles. But for each summoned thrall that fell, two more rose to fill the gap. Valdemar's blood swirled around him like a crimson vortex, each droplet a seed blooming into a new defender.

Though she did not lower her guard, Marianne stopped to thrust her weapon left and right. A vast field of ashes and embers surrounded her and Valdemar, one expanded step after step by soldiers from other worlds. Ten meters separated the summoned monsters from their general.

Valdemar was calling a small army.

Summoning required blood, either to create a circle or to fuel a familiar's connection to the higher planes. The two limits to a spellcaster's potential were their skill and resources. In fact, Marianne had heard rumors that cults usually sacrificed dozens of prisoners of war to summon their otherworldly patrons. A single magician simply didn't have enough blood to call more than a few servants at once.

But Valdemar Verney was no mere man. He was a demigod who regenerated blood almost as quickly as he spent it.

Marianne had seen her companion survive a dive into Lord Bethor's boiling pools and heard even the Dark Lords call him unkillable. She now realized that he had never truly tapped into his full potential because he hadn't been aware of his limits. For most of his life, Valdemar had thought he was a human, with human limitations; only now did he understand just how powerful he was. Valdemar gave his summoned allies no direction; their only order was to advance and overwhelm the Qlippoths with their numbers. The cancerous forest that had so easily spread across the Institute was shrinking with each passing second.

Marianne suddenly realized that Lord Och's proposal of letting his apprentice inherit his post wasn't so far-fetched after all.

However, such an effort demanded considerable concentration; doubly so since Valdemar summoned creatures from different planes of existence altogether. He had not moved nor said a word in minutes, and though his allied creatures had established a vast defensive perimeter, keeping them anchored to Underland took all of his focus. Valdemar had made himself vulnerable.

He's acting as bait, Marianne realized, *and he trusts me to make use of it.*

Their target made his presence known with a sneak attack. A great shadow covered the duo as Bertrand descended upon them from behind. The vampire moved so swiftly that he would have looked like a blur to an untrained eye. The smoking remains of dead Qlippoths provided a cover of dust through which he moved, and his wings made no move as he flew. Marianne's old retainer had become a vicious predator with sharp instincts.

The old Marianne wouldn't have noticed his approach. The new one didn't need to hear nor see to sense an enemy approach. She picked up the subtle differences in the air pressure in the vicinity, the slight changes in temperature, tiny hints that so few could notice.

Marianne raised her free hand and shot bone bullets from her fingers.

The five projectiles surged a few centimeters above Valdemar's head to hit Bertrand as he descended upon the summoner. They all hit their mark at a critical bone joint and broke a wing. Bertrand fell behind Valdemar and blew ashes in all directions. Neither the sorcerer nor his familiar flinched, their minds entirely focused on powering their troops.

Marianne immediately moved behind her companion to intercept Bertrand. Her old retainer had mutated even further since they last met. He was more monster than man, a hairless horror with translucent skin and black veins underneath. His organs were visible; his liver and heart had eyes and his stomach looked like an oily eel with lamprey mouths all over its surface. His fleshy wings unfurled to reveal elongated arms and ropey growths for legs. His nails were blades of bone, his visage a crown of oily tentacles atop a fanged mouth.

There was a war between the man and the monster inside Bertrand. The man was losing.

As she faced the creature that was once her retainer, Marianne couldn't help but be reminded of the Pleromian she fought in Blutgang's facility. Their abuse of the Blood had slowly degraded the ancient creatures into near-mindless horrors. A similar process had been forced upon Bertrand, but he was in just as terrible a state as those who embraced the descent into inhumanity.

Is there anything left to save? Marianne thought as Bertrand snarled at her. His wing had healed from the wound she inflicted and he adopted a feral posture. *He does not even recognize me.*

She had to try in spite of her doubts.

"I abandoned you once," Marianne said as she raised her rapier. She called upon the Blood, her body tensing up with inhuman strength. "Not this time."

Bertrand lunged at her with terrible speed. His bladed nails thrust forward and clashed with Marianne's edge in a sound that was half a scream and half a song. The noblewoman thought of the countless sparring sessions where she faced her retainer; of the countless exercises Bertrand put her through until she surpassed him utterly.

Today's clash was no spar, but a dance.

The beast that Bertrand had become cared nothing for Marianne. The vile instinct that had taken him over only saw her as an obstacle between Valdemar and his dark destiny. If Marianne stepped aside to let Bertrand claim her companion, he would probably fly away with Valdemar and forget her.

He didn't get through her. Like a dancer espousing their partner's movements and guessing their steps to match their own, Marianne always moved in Bertrand's way.

His skill with blades remained even in his monstrous state. She felt the steady pressure of a professional swordsman in their clashing blades. He parried her swings with his nails when she lunged at him the way he once did with an iron sword, tried to feint her, and didn't fall for her own false openings.

Marianne found it unlikely that Bertrand's reflexes had survived the transformation when his capacity for speech and reason did not. Her retainer fought with raging fury and couldn't form words at all.

These new changes were not the result of chaotic mutations, but by design.

The force directing the ritual that had overtaken Pleroma had altered Bertrand, suppressing his human spirit but leaving his knowledge as a battle instructor intact. An intelligent will had emerged from the madness of the Qlippoths and the Verney cult, channeling their chaotic power in the service of methodical destruction.

The enemy had grown smarter. The thought frightened Marianne more than all of the monsters running around.

The beast her retainer had become struck with the intent to kill rather than teach. He waved his hands at her in a controlled fury, aiming for her head, for her heart and for her neck. Each strike her rapier deflected. Her soulbound sword, wielded by a steady hand, cut through his bladed nails as easily as cloth. No sooner did they fall on the ashes below their feet that new ones grew to take their place.

Though Marianne and Bertrand clashed among the ashes, none of Valdemar's monsters moved to interrupt their duel. The summoner must have ordered them to ignore it. He couldn't trust them to pull their punches and keep Bertrand alive.

The mutant vampire let out a roar of frustration and flapped his wings. A blast of air sent ashes flying into Marianne's face, forcing her to close her eyes. She heard Bertrand's ropey appendages try to seize her ankle to make her stumble while his bladed nails crossed as they moved closer to her neck.

Marianne swiftly created a sword of bone in her free hand. The blade cut through Bertrand's tentacled legs while her rapier parried his nails before they could behead her.

The sheer momentum behind the blow almost threw Marianne off her back, but she held firm. The Blood empowered her muscles and bones. Her single-minded focus on protecting Valdemar gave her purpose.

Marianne pushed Bertrand back and struck back. Her blades crossed on his chest, cutting through his skin and bones. Black blood rained down Bertrand's belly as Marianne struck muscles and ligaments. The vital organs she deftly avoided.

Bertrand roared as he lunged at her face with his mouth open. She kicked him back before he could reach her, his fangs closing on empty air. And when he tried to strike at her from the left with his bladed nails, Marianne severed his hand with a swift swing of her bone sword. His appendage went flying into the air and fell among ashen embers on the ground.

Bertrand unfurled his wings to fly away, a fountain of blood pouring out of his severed hand. Much like she surprised Lord Bethor, Marianne struck him from an unexpected direction. A sharp nail of bone erupted from her forehead and pierced through her skin at a cannonball's speed. It cut through the joints of Bertrand's left wing before he could take flight.

Marianne leaped forward even as blood dripped down her face while her foe was distracted. Her rapier finished her previous attack's work and fully severed the left wing; her other blade she rammed through Bertrand's belly and spine. After Bertrand fell on his back with a roar of pain, Marianne pinned his right wing to the ground with the bone sword.

"I am sorry," Marianne apologized to the bloodied monster, "but you cannot win this."

His transformation had made her old retainer stronger than ever, but Marianne's growth far surpassed his. Bertrand had gained strength and resilience. His former student had learned something far more valuable.

Mastery.

Mastery not only of the sword, but of herself. Of her own strength. Her self-doubts had been cleansed away, her mind and body reinforced. Lord Bethor's training had sharpened her senses and magnified her existing skills. Her potential had always been there, but now she made full use of it.

Killing Bertrand would have been easy.

Keeping him alive was harder. Even after all the wounds Marianne gave him, he was already regenerating. His severed hand and wings started to grow back while he frantically tried to remove the sword keeping him to the ground. Marianne swung her rapier again and again, cutting off pieces of flesh as soon as they reappeared.

He's not like Valdemar, she realized to her horror as Bertrand's regeneration slowed down. *He cannot do this forever.*

Unlike Valdemar, who drew blood from the very substance of Underland, Bertrand relied on finite reserves. How long could she keep him diminished but alive? At which point would his regeneration fail Bertrand and his wounds slay him? Marianne couldn't tell and it frightened her. Bertrand kept trying to get up, the vile force that had enslaved him caring naught whether he lived or perished.

"You have done enough, Marianne," said a thundering voice.

Lord Bethor made his presence known in a flash of crimson light as he teleported next to Marianne. The Dark Lord's guests soon materialized at his side. Iren and Hermann stood in the shadow of an enormous canvas covered in painted runes and symbols, while Liliane had come wearing a bandolier full of herbs and potions.

Their arrival filled Marianne with relief.

"Is that Bertrand?" Liliane asked as she recoiled at the sight of the vampire. "By the Light . . ."

Bertrand roared at her, making her step back in surprise. Lord Bethor merely glanced at the vampire and his telekinetic might pinned him to the ground more easily than Marianne's blade ever did.

"Please, Lord Bethor!" Marianne panicked at the sight. "Do not slay him!"

"I will give you one chance to cure him as per your plan," the Dark Lord replied calmly.

Marianne knew from his tone that the "one" part was key. If they failed to cure Bertrand . . .

"Liliane," the noblewoman whispered. "My hopes are in your hand."

"I'm your gal," Liliane replied as she grabbed an empty syringe from a pouch and a potion from her stock. The flask containing it was no bigger than a thumb, the liquid within a vibrant shade of red. Marianne would have called it a molten ruby at first glance, but she knew it was something far more precious.

A drop of the Elixir of Life. The potion that promised eternal life.

"Valdy!" Liliane shouted. "I need your help!"

"I am ready." Valdemar emerged from his stillness as his summoned creatures vanished. Of the cancerous forest of Qlippoths, only dust and corpses remained. "At your signal."

Marianne bit her lower lip. "Valdemar—"

"We won't fail," he reassured her. "I swear."

Marianne held her breath as she watched Bertrand's operation. Liliane carefully examined the mutated vampire's neck to find an artery, whereas Valdemar grabbed the shoulders. Bertrand struggled back against Lord Bethor's influence to no avail.

"Ready, Valdy?" Liliane asked as she removed Marianne's bone sword from Bertrand and filled her syringe with the elixir.

"Since the day I was born," he replied.

Liliane stabbed Bertrand in the neck and pressed her syringe. Marianne watched in tense silence as the liquid flowed into the vampire's veins, red elixir and black blood mixing together. Her heart skipped a beat as the latter appeared to subsume the former.

It happened again when Bertrand's skin became whiter.

His body transformed before Marianne's eyes. The march of time turned back as Bertrand shed his wings and tentacles. His fingers grew back to normal size. His legs and manhood grew back along with his ears and eyes. Within less than a minute, the monster vanished. In his place slept an old friend Marianne had thought gone forever.

But the illness was still in him.

Valdemar's fingers melded with Bertrand's shoulders. Their flesh mixed together and their veins connected. Marianne watched anxiously as black blood traveled from her retainer's body to that of her companion. Valdemar absorbed Ialdabaoth's curse into himself. Marianne feared that it would corrupt him as it affected her retainer; that it would mutate him into a monster or give Ialdabaoth a foothold in his mind and flesh.

None of her fears materialized.

Valdemar absorbed the black blood into himself and then severed contact with Bertrand. He pulled back his hands from the vampire's shoulders.

"Are you alright?" Marianne asked her companion with worry. Liliane, Iren, and Hermann looked at Valdemar, perhaps half-expecting him to grow wings of his own.

His answer filled them all with joy.

"I feel drained but I'm fine," he replied. "And so is he."

A vampire didn't breathe nor produce a heartbeat. But as Lord Bethor released his grip and Bertrand opened his eyes, Marianne knew he was "alive" again.

"Mi . . ." Bertrand's throat was sore and his voice weak, but he said a word rather than a roar. "Milady?"

Marianne didn't hold back her tears of joy. Her retainer and friend, who she had thought lost forever to the horrors of Underland, had been brought back to her safe and sound.

She had run away from the darkness once before.

Tonight she fought back and won.

21

THE BLOOD AND THE COLD

The disease was in him. Valdemar felt it crawling under his skin. A horde of bacteria sailed his bloodstream in an attempt to infect the island of his heart. The blackened fluids that had transformed Bertrand into a monster spread like a puddle of oil on clear water.

Valdemar's body was no fertile ground for conquest. His will inhabited each cell of his body. His organs were a self-aware conglomerate. He didn't particularly need any of them to live anymore, so they could focus their resources on fighting back the infection. Valdemar was born from the black blood; it was simply a matter of assimilating this sample.

By taking on the sins of others, you have opened yourself to darkness.

But the black blood was more than a plague. It was a vector between man and the divine, the part and the whole.

Valdemar showed no hint of the conflict within himself to others. He stood alone as Marianne moved to her retainer's side.

"I . . ." Bertrand looked around, his hands trembling. He had recovered his human form but not his wits yet. "I remember the rat man and . . . and the black . . ."

"It's alright, Bertrand," Marianne comforted her retainer as she helped him get back on his feet. Hermann tossed the vampire his robe to cover up his nakedness, revealing his own reptilian glory for all to see. "You are home."

She's struggling to hold back tears, Valdemar observed. Marianne had struck him as stone-faced when first they met, but now he understood that she was quite the emotive person underneath. *After so many sacrifices we finally achieved a victory.*

This changed nothing.

The voice in his mind had changed. It had grown deeper, clearer, and multiplied. The voice of Shelley reverberated with that of an old man and the ceaseless chittering of countless vermin. A billion mouths spoke with hideous unity.

The black blood reveals what lies within. An inner beast grows wilder. The evil within is magnified. Valdemar sensed an otherworldly presence peek through his eyes when he looked at Bertrand. *This man spent his unlife suppressing his hunger for blood. Merciful Ialdabaoth only stripped the veil of deceit he had cast on himself.*

Besides Hermann, who was checking up on his canvas in preparation for the Painted World ritual, Lord Bethor alone did not tend to Bertrand's woes. While Liliane checked up on the vampire and Iren helped him stand, the Dark Lord instead eyed Valdemar with an unreadable gaze.

He knows what's happening to me, Valdemar realized. Was Lord Bethor considering whether he should strike him down where he stood in case he fell under Ialdabaoth's influence? Or did he trust the summoner to prevail on his own?

Does it matter? He cannot stop what is to come. You feel it, don't you? The end is here, the time is now.

Valdemar might have burnt the hedge maze to cinders, the air smelled of rancid fumes and putrid waters. A current of foul magic barely suppressed by Empress Aratra's sorcery flowed through the ground beneath his feet. The great black pillar at the center of the institute breathed as if its blackened stone had turned to flesh. Ktulu was tenser than ever.

Valdemar glanced over the tall walls of the Institute and beyond the shield protecting Lord Och's fortress. A tall pillar of crimson light had risen from the city of Pleroma and the terrible well at its center.

The seal binding Crétail was breaking down. The dam holding back the tide of the Nahemoth's power would fall sometime soon. The entire cavern would transform into a demiplane where the frontier between imagination and reality meant nothing. Madness would rule the waking world.

Worst of all, Crétail would follow the blood to his brother. Twins separated in the womb would become one again; one with their Father

Ialdabaoth. The seals shall break and all of Underland would return to the Blood from which it originated.

And the mastermind behind this disaster would soon show his dreadful face.

We are rot and vermin, sang the swarm in Valdemar's mind. *We are the plague prophet of the red prince and the unholy spirit. We are the angel of the abyss. Men called us Aleksander, and Shelley, and so many names, but in truth we are Swarm. We are Hunger.*

Images flashed through Valdemar's mind. Visions of an old man with the Verney look the summoner had inherited, a cadaverous ghoul with red-rimmed eyes and rats crawling out of his mouth. The monstrous face of Shelley grew out of the back of the creature's head, laughing.

None of us were worthy, the ghastly figure whispered as a thousand red eyes blinked in the darkness surrounding him. *Our blood was thick and strong, but lacked the richness of a foreign world. But our work was not in vain. Your mother became the fertile soil from which the Red Grail grew.*

"Why?" Valdemar muttered to the abomination. He wasn't certain if this dialogue was entirely happening in his mind or if the others could listen to his words.

Why?

"Why serve Ialdabaoth?" Valdemar asked. "Whatever it promised you, immortality, divinity, a place at his side, it's all a delusion. It will absorb all life in Underland into itself once it awakens. We will all become cells in a greater superorganism, unable to influence anything."

We know, the abomination that had once been his great-grandfather Aleksander Verney and Shelley answered without hesitation. Its bloody lips morphed into a toothless grin. Its eyes were eaten from within, leaving only two black pits atop a husk of hollowed skin.

"Then why?"

Why all this suffering? Why did his mother have to bear him and Crétail against her will? Why did so many have to die to create the Red Grail and bring about the world's end? What did he hope to gain?

Life.

Darkness swallowed the world.

Once more Valdemar stood alone on the cold surface of Ialdabaoth's stone skin, under the faint light of the Whitemoon. The terrible planetoid that had haunted mankind's nightmares and deprived it of its sun grinned like Lord Och's skull. Its rocky surface changed into the Mask of the Nightwalker on Valdemar's face: an unending spiral of death and infinity.

Open your eyes.

Valdemar saw through the Whitemoon and the baleful constellations.

He peered beyond the light and saw the tentacles wiggling behind, the eyes and the flesh festering at the heart of shining stars. Each of them was a fragment of broken light, cast down from a realm of brightness.

The Pleromians believed the stars were evil. That anyone watching under the sky exposed themselves to their malign influence.

They are all alive, his great-grandfather declared. His words echoed with the despair of someone who had seen too much. **All Strangers.**

The Pleromians had been right.

Life and lights were Strangers to this universe. An infestation from another realm.

Space was death. It was cold and ice and lifeless stones wandering a barren expanse without ends. It was the opposite of life's corrupt warmth and chaotic movement. It was the utter sterility of nothingness, the perfect order of death.

And when the darkness gazed at the stars, it could only feel *hate.*

The universe despises us.

The void hated the life that had despoiled its emptiness. The universe yearned to return to its original state, to the lifeless expense it had once been before the Strangers and the stars infected it. It sought to extinguish all warmth and light until only barren rocks and darkness remained.

So the void fought back.

Valdemar's sight expanded further, beyond the solar system around which Ialdabaoth orbited. He gazed at the sea of darkness and the ships of stone sailing it: malicious asteroids looking for inhabited planets to crash on, clouds of cosmic dust and ice large enough to blanket the light of stars, rogue moons roaming the cosmos searching for warmth.

Some were so large that they made the imprisoned Ialdabaoth look like a small moon.

Their numbers are beyond count.

One day, the universe would know peace again. Even if it took a billion years the darkness would never stop yearning for the peaceful coldness of death.

Valdemar's sight shrank, back to Ialdabaoth and the Whitemoon. Two soldiers fighting in a conflict spanning all of existence.

This is the War in Heaven.

Once more Valdemar stood alone on the cold surface of the world. His ancestor Aleksander faced him, now a man again. His eyes were blackened with forbidden knowledge and the madness of someone who had seen too much. A human-faced rat stood on his shoulder, his eyes a malicious shade of red. Shelley.

"Our existence is an error," Aleksander Verney declared. His voice no longer echoed with that of a festering swarm, but with the cold certainty of a true nihilist. "Our survival is meaningless. Our time is limited. Ialdabaoth and the Strangers are on the side of life. Our side. The Cold will turn us into dead things and then nothing. If Ialdabaoth does not wake up, the spiral of death will drag us ever closer to annihilation." He had stared into the abyss and blinked. "Ialdabaoth is our promised land. The nightmare of the Outer Darkness will vanish as it awakens, ending our eternal torment. All souls will return to him and achieve peace in a great singularity. Our memories, our history, our past, and our future will forever survive inside its mind. We will surrender our individuality and find freedom from the torment of mortal existence."

The madman smiled as if truly at peace, as did his rat familiar. "All will be one."

Valdemar, who hadn't said a word, looked on as his great-grandfather extended a hand in his direction.

"You are our messiah," Aleksander Verney said, praying, begging. His rat familiar was silent. "Save us. Save us all. Save us from ourselves."

Valdemar gazed at the bleak, uncaring cosmos surrounding him. He stared at the cold darkness of space and the hateful stars populating it, at the Whitemoon hanging above his head. Then he looked down at his maddened ancestor and the dark truth he embodied.

And at that moment, Valdemar came up with his own answer. "Are you done prattling on?"

He didn't care.

"All I hear from you is fear," Valdemar told his ancestor, his resolve strong as steel. "Fear of the unknown, of the future, of *trying*. You believe we humans have already lost, that we are helpless; so you do not even attempt to find a better solution."

"There is none." Aleksander's words were as hollow as his resolve.

"Then make one."

The rat familiar cackled and his master snorted. "Can you?" Shelley rasped on his master's shoulder.

"Yes."

Maybe his ancestor had shown Valdemar the full truth, or at least the one he believed in. Maybe the forces hostile to mankind were strong and mighty. Maybe the universe hated them. Maybe life was a meaningless error and randomness ruled the cosmos.

And so what?

If the Strangers and the Cold were so powerful, one of them would have won by now. And though existence was full of hardships and without meaning, it was still worth fighting for. People like Marianne, Hermann, Liliane, and Iren deserved to live free from the god's shackles. The Empire of Azlant was a bad place to live in, but it was still better than the alternatives, and for all of its dysfunctions, it wasn't a hopeless case either.

"I will never stop believing that I can make the world a better place. I will never surrender to fear and ignorance." Valdemar glared at his ancestor. "For I would become like you."

Aleksander Verney's sneer turned into a scowl and Shelley snapped his jaws.

Foolish child.

They struck without warning.

Valdemar's spiritual self stumbled as a telepathic assault crashed against his mental defenses like a tide. The icy surface of the world cracked open to unleash a tide as thousands of vermin emerged from the rifts. Rats crawled on Valdemar's ankles and swiftly buried him under their mass. It wasn't a single soul attacking Valdemar but billions of them. The malformed spirits of rats, the twisted souls of maddened cultists and Ialdabaoth's desperate thralls combined their power to strike as one.

The sheer weight of a hive mind overwhelmed Valdemar from all sides faster than he could muster his defenses. Without Marianne present, his dream defenses were poor.

You have sipped the milk of the gods, Aleksander Verney and Shelley declared as their prince drowned under the weight of the flood. The rat familiar merged into his master's shoulder like a twisted tumor. ***Your human half may resist the inevitable, but the other will answer the call. Your father invested us with the power to bring you to heel. You will serve your purpose as we did.***

No oneiromancer could have created barriers powerful enough to repel the onslaught of a million souls.

So Valdemar ate them.

A hundred mouths opened all over his skin and bit the rats on his skin. Their fangs cut through the essence making up their dreaming selves and swallowed their memories like fine wine.

Valdemar's fingers turned into black tentacles that grabbed attackers by the dozens. They fed his gluttonous maws. No amount of victims could satisfy his hunger. Souls fell down his gullet and joined the Pleromian's remnants at the bottom of his belly.

Aleksander Verney's and Shelley's eyes widened in shock as their hive mind fell back. Its members didn't fear death, but Valdemar offered them no such mercy. "How?" man and rat asked at the same time.

"My dreamscape has been malformed since my birth," Valdemar mused. "The doors were broken. Oneiromancers thought it was a defect and no doubt you thought it would make me easier to control."

But after he had devoured the Pleromian's soul, Valdemar had understood the truth. He was not born to defend, but to invade. To infiltrate the primordial dream and consume the psyche of mankind from within.

A predator had no need to bar access to his lair. Those foolish enough to challenge him there would only find death.

"You said it yourself, swarm. As deluded and loyal as you are, in the end you are no more than a tool of the Strangers. While I . . ."

Valdemar changed his dream visage into a swirling abyss of darkness from which no light could escape. "I am half of one."

Valdemar had made peace with that. He would embrace the Stranger and the human in equal measures without sacrificing one for the other.

He had been born a bridge between worlds and accepted it.

The dreamscape around them trembled as Valdemar's power destabilized it. The plague prophet's swarm retreated into the cracks, abandoning their terrified leaders to the mercy of the monster they had created.

"What's wrong, prophet?" Valdemar mocked him as his spiritual avatar grew in size until he overshadowed the baleful stars above. "Don't you recognize the face of your messiah? Isn't that what you wanted to see?"

Aleksander Verney and Shelley seemed to have a crisis of faith all of a sudden.

"I will eat your soul and shit it out." Valdemar's tentacles lashed at his enemies' spirits. "Not even Ialdabaoth will pick up the pieces."

Aleksander Verney and Shelley collapsed into a pile of worms before the tentacles could grab them. Their souls had run away rather than stand their ground.

"Crawl back to your tomb, you apostles of cowardice!" Valdemar snarled as the dreamscape collapsed. "I deny you! I deny the oblivion you crave! I deny your god its victory!"

The vision world shattered like glass.

Valdemar returned to the waking world where less than a second had passed. Lord Bethor alone seemed aware of what had transpired, his chin moving down and up.

A nod of approval, with a dash of respect.

Valdemar would prove that he deserved it today. "Hermann?"

The troglodyte nodded. His painting stood against a stone wall, the symbols on the canvas simmering with a magical glow. "Liliane, Iren . . ." Hermann rasped. "You must evacuate with the wounded . . . while you still can."

"Bertrand, I am sorry my friend," Marianne apologized to her retainer. She alone would stay with Valdemar and Hermann as they ran their ritual. "I will tell you everything later. I must ask you to rest for now."

"I cannot . . ." Bertrand coughed red blood and never finished his sentence. He covered his mouth with a hand. "My lungs . . ."

"We'll get him to the infirmary, don't worry," Liliane reassured Marianne.

Iren smiled as he helped Bertrand move by putting the vampire's arm over his shoulder. "It's up to us, the supporting actors, to make sure the leads can shine in the spotlight."

"There are no leads nor supporters," Valdemar replied. "Everyone matters."

"Never said that friend," Iren replied with a smile that implied otherwise. "But all we can do right now is pray that your plan succeeds."

"Do not pray, doppelganger." Lord Bethor's eyes were cold. "Think."

Iren knew better than to talk back to the Dark Lord. He and Liliane carried the dizzied Bertrand away from Valdemar's sight to take cover in the Institute's bowels.

Hermann turned to his colleague and friend. "Valdemar, if something goes wrong . . . My art collection is yours to distribute. If possible . . . I would like for my work to go back . . . to my people."

"You will not die," Valdemar replied. "I won't let you. But I appreciate the faith you put in me."

"It is not faith . . . but trust, my friend." Hermann's claws trembled with a mix of fear and anticipation. "At long last . . . we shall make our Painted World."

"The Nahemoth will be freed sometime soon," Lord Bethor said as he looked at the walls. "Its herald is already here."

A quake hit the Institute. A second followed and then a third.

"Footsteps," Marianne whispered.

The plague prophet peered over the walls with his thousand eyes. A hooded cloak of flayed wererat skin covered a festering mass of vermin assembled in the vague shape of a human visage. Rats and mice formed the bulk of them alongside dismembered bats. Their skins were stitched together, their tails were interwoven like a cloth's fibers, their mouths chittering with hunger. Shelley occupied the center of the foul tapestry of the swarm's grim visage. The wererat's face was twisted into an expression of rapture, the unbridled joy of a martyr enjoying the pain of unholy rapture. The familiar had returned to his master at last.

This was a preview of the fate that awaited all life in Underland. The individual subsumed into the whole. Flesh stitched into a grim singularity of moribund flesh. Aleksander Verney had returned from the dead in his master's image.

The giant horror was a living mountain taller than the Institute's walls. Its hood reached close to the ceiling of stone that overshadowed the entire Domain of Paraplex. Shoulders appeared as a hand of stitched rats lifted a scepter of bones thick as a stone tower. The tip was shaped into the form of a cross where the Lilith had been nailed with black spikes. A weapon she had been, a weapon she would be.

We are Swarm, the vision had said. We are Hunger.

The abomination flung its scepter at the Institute's shield with a shriek that shook all of Underland.

The magical barrier collapsed in a rain of crimson dust alongside a chunk of the stone walls. The Knights unfortunate enough to stand on fortifications were swept aside. Qlippoths that had battered helplessly against the barrier immediately moved into the Institute.

A thunderbolt bounced off a hundred of them and turned them to dust. Empress Aratra floated into the air and vaporized a hundred more monsters with a wave of her hand.

Lord Hagith teleported where Aleksander had shattered the walls and grew in size himself until he covered the hole with his body mass. Lady

Phul and the transformed Lord Ophiel struck the demonic swarm from above with spells. Lord Phaleg banished Qlippoths back to their realm with his summoning expertise.

The Dark Lords had the situation well in hand.

Lord Bethor, unwilling to leave all the glory to his associates, snapped his fingers. Space cracked with a bolt of crimson lightning and a mighty creature appeared behind him. The creature was thrice the size of a carriage beetle, a mighty behemoth of blackened scales. Long raven wings supported its lizard-like body. Crimson eyes peered at Valdemar with inhuman intelligence.

"Impossible . . ." Hermann whispered in shock and awe. Marianne didn't say a word, but her widening eyes betrayed her surprise.

Even Valdemar struggled to trust his own senses.

A dragon. A young one, but a dragon all the same.

As for the way Lord Bethor had called the beast to his side . . . Dragons weren't creatures from other worlds. They couldn't be summoned like Qlippoths. It could only mean one thing.

A familiar. Lord Bethor's familiar was a dragon. Somehow, Valdemar strongly suspected that it was related to the one whose corpse rested beneath the Dark Lord's tower. Its spawn perhaps?

"We will deal with the vermin," Lord Bethor said as he leaped on his dragon's back with supreme confidence. "Bind the Nahemoth and prove us wrong, Valdemar."

The Dark Lord's steed took flight in a cloud of ash and dust. The dragon breathed fire at the plague prophet the moment he came into range. Hundreds of charbroiled rats fell off the creature, only to be immediately replaced.

"Amazing," Marianne said as Lord Bethor's mount dodged a swing from Aleksander's mighty staff. "Simply amazing."

"Ktulhu," Valdemar's familiar blurted. His summoner sensed an undercurrent of jealousy in his partner's voice. "Ktulhulu!"

"But where is Lord Och?" Marianne asked with a frown. "I don't see him."

To Valdemar's confusion, he realized that she had a point. The ancient lich wasn't among the Dark Lords confronting the swarm nor the creatures flooding into the Institute. Lord Och had vanished when his demesne was besieged.

Has he been destroyed? Valdemar couldn't believe it himself. Knowing the lich, he was probably preparing some kind of foul play. *Are you finally springing your plan into action, my teacher?*

Valdemar didn't have time to wonder.

The world snapped. Valdemar sensed it. Something in the very fabric of reality had broken. An invisible cog holding time and space together had malfunctioned, creating a subtle breakdown in the machinery of the universe. An invisible force rippled through the air, the stones, the flesh and the soul. For a split second, nothing visible happened.

A moment later, madness ruled the world. The air turned purple. Pictures of screaming faces and broken hands formed into the Institute's walls. Yellow fumes erupted from the ashes of burned trees and Qlippoths in maddening shapes that bent the mind. Eyes opened on the Institute's black pillar, atop which blue brains grew alongside trees of neurons and tendrils. Space bent and twisted into crooked angles and twisted turns.

The Institute was turning into a demiplane of madness.

"The Nahemoth . . . is freed," Hermann rasped as his hands brushed against the Painted World. "It's . . . it's here."

Valdemar sensed its approach. A black hole in the fabric of reality opened above them as a horror manifested through; the shadow of a malformed, stillborn child the size of a dragon. Black tentacles erupted from his pale skin and his jaw opened to reveal a hundred sharp teeth. The Nahemoth's wail chilled Valdemar to the bone.

I hear you, Crétail, the summoner thought as Marianne immediately moved in front of him. She couldn't protect him from that creature. Among mankind, only a Dark Lord could hope to defeat a Nahemoth in single combat.

But Valdemar had made friends in strange places. Valdemar removed the mask from his face and sprayed it with his blood. The vile artifact let out mist where the unholy fluid touched it. The dark force which had gifted Valdemar with it had taken notice.

"Come, Nightwalker." Valdemar slammed the mask against the ground and poured his magic into it. "May the Cold freeze the Blood!" The Mask of the Nightwalker shattered into splinters as the spell took effect. A dark shadow rose from the remains and the world became cold.

22

THE TRUE ENEMY

The air froze as the shadows lengthened. A chill spread in Valdemar's blood, in his flesh, and in his bones; a cold that made it painful to even breathe. It was the cruel grasp of ice, the frigid touch of death, the final kiss before everlasting darkness.

The festering madness that had seized the Institute recoiled before the encroaching shadow. Mutant eyes froze into icy statues. A sheet of permafrost covered the ground beneath Valdemar's feet. Colorful fumes turned into white mist.

The Nightwalker emerged from its broken mask in all of its eldritch glory. Valdemar had seen its reflection through his visions in the past, but to see the creature in the flesh was another story entirely. The Nightwalker's height reached over five meters and then more. A mantle of shadows swirled around a skin of black scales and whitened fur, around crooked horns and cruel arms. The white spiral on the creature's face vomited the very essence of cold.

The entity made no sound as it manifested. No cry came out of its black vertical maw. No words of magic formed on its cold lips. Valdemar didn't even hear the faint sound of ice cracking beneath its feet. The Nightwalker had killed the very concept of noise.

It offered only silence.

The Nahemoth's shrieks more than compensated for its opposite's muteness. The unborn Qlippoth's cries rippled across reality. Cracks widened in the fabric of space, the rift oozing colorful smokes and phosphorescent spores.

The Nightwalker raised its many hands at Crétail, its opposite and nemesis. Ice frigid enough to shatter steel shot from its fingers in a deadly volley of spikes. They gored through the Qlippoth's pale skin and black tentacles, each wound turned blue from the sheer cold.

But no sooner did the Nahemoth take damage than his injuries healed in a gruesome manner. Black tentacles and bloodied eyes grew whenever the ice had struck. Tumors of malignant life repaired the damage before bursting into geysers of acidic blood. Vile smoke rose wherever droplets fell on the Nightwalker.

The Whitemoon's herald did not roar in anger nor make a sound, but its body language betrayed its cold rage. The shadows swirling around it expanded into a wave of darkness that threatened to swallow Crétail.

The Qlippoth's blood glowed with the crimson light of the Outer Darkness in response. The red clashed with the black, the universe fracturing where they met. Ice shards and flesh tentacles struck at each other by the dozens, the hundred, the thousand.

Two heralds of opposite Strangers engaged in a dance of creation and destruction before Valdemar's eyes. Otherworldly light and the grim darkness of space filled the world around the two duelists, hiding the Institute from the summoner's view. It appeared as if reality itself had been reduced to a primal conflict between opposing forces.

Fire and ice. Life and death. The pale and dark.

The perfect pigments to paint a brand new world.

"Hermann!" Valdemar shouted as his hands bled. The dark blood coursing through his veins dropped on the cold ground but didn't freeze over. Instead, it spread to form a circle around the shattered remains of the Nightwalker's mask. Ktulu hopped into its center, ready to do its part. "I'm ready!"

After having been briefly mesmerized by the cosmic spectacle unfolding before his eyes, the troglodyte stood at the side of his canvas. "As . . . I am!"

The two sorcerers sprang their trap.

Ktulu's black eyes shone with a sinister orange glow. Magic surged from the familiar's tiny body as his power echoed with his summoner. Their souls resonated with Hermann's the same way a music group attuned their instruments for a spectacular symphony.

And sing they did.

The trio's spell created eldritch notes as it rippled across space and time. The icy ground cracked like a broken mirror. The air screeched and the stones trembled. Red particles surged from Valdemar and Hermann.

The symbols on the Painted World's canvas glittered with a dozen different colors. Orange and blue, green and red, violet and yellow, green and blue, black and white, so many other shades . . . they mixed together in a rainbow spiral, an abyss of paint.

The portrait called the Nightwalker and Crétail to it with the inescapable strength of gravity.

The two surprised heralds of the Strangers were pulled backward toward the trap. Icicle shards and black blood swirled together into the endless color spiral, unable to escape its grip.

The ritual's targets resisted the best they could. Of course they did. They knew what would happen should they be sucked into the painting: the destruction of their bodies and the rebirth of their spirits into something else. The Nightwalker's countless arms stabbed the ground with sharp claws to anchor itself to the ground; Crétail shrieked as he tried to fly away.

It did not matter. The Silent King himself had taught Hermann the Painted World's ritual. It was the secret lore of a Stranger, a spell that once executed could not be countered.

The Nightwalker struggled the most against its fate but succeeded the least. The fragments of its mask that it had so "kindly" given to Valdemar made for the perfect conduit. They gave the summoner's magic a direct link to the creature's core essence. Although the entity was beyond human emotions, the expression on its eldritch visage was all too clear to Valdemar.

The disappointment born of betrayal.

Sorry, Valdemar thought, *but when choosing between two evils, I would rather deny them both. Nothing personal.*

Lord Och had once told his apprentice that whatever he did, someone would pay the price for his decisions. Valdemar hoped that he had chosen well.

The Nightwalker fell first into the canvas's spiral. Its long arms twisted like coiling snakes carried away by a current of paint. The darkness and the cold became pigments suffused with magical power. The dreaded herald of the Whitemoon shrank as its enormous body was dragged through the canvas, its essence becoming the underpaint of a new world.

Crétail let out a screeching wail as the portrait's gravity pulled him ever closer to a similar fate; it refused to go gently. The Nahemoth's crimson aura increased in potency. Eyes of light opened across Valdemar's vision. Fire came out of them when they blinked.

The veil separating the material plane from the Outer Darkness tore itself apart. Valdemar found himself looking up at the fiery abyss at the center of this hellish dimension, at the vortex of souls feeding Ialdabaoth's hunger.

I can't . . . Valdemar suppressed a scream as his skin peeled from his flesh. The ritual demanded more of his blood to stabilize itself, to the point that it ruptured the summoner's veins to feed. *It's* . . . *it's too much.*

Baleful red eyes appeared all over his arms; a hungry maw opened in his torso and bit through his robe. Valdemar felt his tongue licking against rows of sharp fangs. His blood turned black, his nails grew into cutting claws. His vision splintered as his two human eyes divided like his body's cells. His bones bent into angles that didn't fit Underland's reality. A ghastly crown of horns grew out of his forehead and *something* threatened to burst out of his back.

I'm . . . Ialda . . . no . . .

Valdemar focused the best he could as dark whispers tried to worm their way into his mind. As his flesh transformed, so did his soul. The closer Crétail approached him, the less Valdemar stayed himself. His human essence, his memories, his thoughts, everything that made him who he was started fading away.

I am . . . a mask . . .

The Father of All's influence threatened to overwhelm him.

This is . . . my true appearance, Valdemar realized. The inhuman horror beneath the man's skin. The Red Prince of the Blood and avatar of Ialdabaoth. The herald of the Strangers, the abomination of the End-Times. *A human chrysalis . . . for a Stranger moth . . . a human mask for . . . Ialda . . . I am Ialda . . .*

The Red Prince felt a hand on its flayed shoulder.

Its many eyes looked in an unexpected direction, to stare at a woman's comforting smile. Marianne stood at his side. Even though she had seen its true figure, she still put her faith in it—*him.* She had not given up on its—*his*—person.

A new music echoed across the crimson light.

The comforting lullaby of a music box. A song as sad as it was peaceful. It sounded so familiar, so warm . . . Crétail's wail died in his throat, awed by the melody.

I . . . I am human, Valdemar thought as he struggled to keep his sanity. The warmth of Marianne's touch and the lullaby together were stronger than the call of the Blood. *I am a Stranger. I am both. I am me.*

Crétail reacted to the song too. His tentacles relaxed. He no longer screamed. The vile light of the Outer Darkness dimmed around him. The influence of Ialdabaoth was growing weaker in both siblings.

Something in the melody soothed the Nahemoth. Perhaps it reminded him of his mother, of the human part of his bloodline. The realization filled Valdemar with sorrow.

I wish I could do more, brother, the summoner thought. I wish I could give you the life that was taken from you. I wish I could cleanse your soul from Ialdabaoth's corruption and stick it into a newborn body. I wish I could give you a normal life, that I could get to know you better. You were innocent in all of this.

Crétail had been born twisted, a tool for a mad cult. For all the destruction his existence had caused, he had never been more than an abandoned child lashing out at the world around him.

The Painted World ritual was the best way Valdemar had found to give his brother another chance and honor his mother's memory. It was the only option he had found to save Crétail from death, to give him a new chance at life while staying true to his own principles.

Your soul will become reborn as the radiant heart of a new universe, Valdemar promised the sibling he never knew. You will be the wind and the stones, the fertile soil from which flowers will grow. You will be the tree of life rather than the tree of death; you will oversee generations of people. You will become the positive force mother wanted us to be.

Not death, but reincarnation.

Crétail closed his eyes as his anger finally died out. The unborn child of Ialdabaoth fell into the painting to begin a new life; not as a monster imprisoned at the bottom of a well, but into what Ialdabaoth should have been.

A living world that nurtured rather than dominated.

Crétail's essence turned into a red overpaint obscuring the Nightwalker's pigments. The two incarnations of opposing forces merged together to form a perfect balance. Malignant life's growth was checked by the all-consuming destructive power of death.

Shapes and angles appeared on Hermann's canvas like order rising from the chaos: the branches of a great white tree taking root in a black soil; gentle waves of blue water on an orange shore; a bright yellow sun soaring high in a pale violet sky; green grass and red flowers dancing to the tune of invisible wind. The pigments moved as if they were alive, filling every spot on the canvas.

The light of the Nahemoth and the darkness of the Nightwalker both dissipated. Their magic had found a new abode in a landscape work of peerless beauty: the door to an artificial universe.

The Painted World was complete.

They . . . They had won.

Marianne could hardly believe it. The Nahemoth and the Nightwalker were gone. Their flesh and souls had become the mortar of a magical artifact brimming with power, a painting of unearthly beauty.

The crimson light of the Outer Darkness slowly dissipated like smoke. The shape of the Institute's broken buildings and shattered walls slowly came back into sight.

And Valdemar . . .

Her companion was no longer the man she had grown so fond of. He had transformed into a humanoid creature of pulsating flesh and eyes, a crowned husk depleted of his blood. He knelt at Marianne's feet, hands on the ground.

"Valdemar?" Marianne immediately knelt at his side and cast a healing spell on him. She felt her magical power flowing into him like a droplet in an underground river. "Valdemar, are you alright?"

"I'm . . . fine . . ." His breath was loud and heavy, but the voice was Valdemar's. The outside had changed, but he remained human within. "I'm fine . . ."

Thank the Light, she thought. Valdemar's familiar was in a sorry state too, but unharmed. Ktulu held his tiny head as if suffering from a headache. *They are well and sound . . . I'm so glad.*

"You have lost too much blood, my apprentice." The shape of Lord Och appeared next to Hermann and the Painted World when the crimson light faded out. "You will need a few minutes to recover and pull your human guise back on."

Marianne glared with disapproval at the Dark Lord. Somehow his reappearance didn't surprise her. "His human face is no guise, Lord Och, but his true self."

"Of course, of course," the lich replied without meaning it. "Much like the old bones beneath the human illusion are an elaborate mummery."

To Marianne's surprise, the Dark Lord carried a familiar music box. "That belongs to Valdemar," Marianne noted. Was that the source of the lullaby?

"Have you forgotten your report from when you visited the dream Vernburg, young Marianne? 'Crétail is a sweet child. He likes the music box very much.'"

Marianne remembered these words all too well. "That was what his nurse said."

"It made my mother cry . . ." Valdemar rasped. "It . . . it probably reminded her of Crétail . . ."

Lord Och chuckled as he delicately set the music box aside. "I have lived long enough to know music can lull even the most unruly child to sleep. I had the intuition it would prove useful."

Valdemar oriented his head in his teacher's direction. "Was that . . . Why did you miss the battle? To pick the box . . . up?"

"My my, what's with the accusing tone, my apprentice? Did you expect foul play from me?"

Valdemar smiled. In his current state, his lips pursed to reveal a ghastly grin of sharp fangs. Marianne found the sight disturbing, but it was worth a thousand words.

The fighting didn't end with the Painted World's creation, however. While Aleksander Verney's swarm form was collapsing as the creatures making up its body scattered and lost cohesion, Qlippoths and other horrors still fought the six other Dark Lords. The maddening, reality-altering images of the Nahemoth's demiplane might have slowly receded from the Institute's grounds, but Ialdabaoth's eyes still covered the Domain's stone ceiling.

"The Qlippoths are still here," Marianne observed. "Has something gone wrong?"

Lord Och dismissed her concerns. "The remaining Qlippoths will occupy my colleagues for a short time, but without the Nahemoth to bind them together, the Outer Darkness and our reality will diverge. No new intruders will appear to bother us. They have lost."

Marianne prayed he was right.

In stark contrast with everyone else, Hermann hadn't paid any attention to the world beyond the Institute. The troglodyte only had eyes for the Painted World. His hand trailed against its surface, his claws sending ripples through the pigments.

Marianne wasn't certain if troglodytes could cry, but Hermann looked like he was about to.

"It's . . ." Hermann shook his head with the trepidation of a dreamer who had finally fulfilled his lifelong goal. "It's beautiful . . . so beautiful . . ."

"Indeed." Lord Och observed the Painted World with a hint of genuine respect. "You have created a world, children. This is a feat worthy of the gods."

"More than . . . than a world," Valdemar rasped. "An afterlife."

"Pictomancy portraits . . . can capture souls, Lord Och," Hermann explained. "This Painted World will become my people's home . . . but we could create another using similar principles. A landscape of Heaven . . . a resting abode for the dead."

"I doubt we shall have another Nahemoth and Nightwalker to sacrifice," Lord Och replied with skepticism. "It was a once in an eon opportunity."

"Perhaps," Hermann conceded, but he remained optimistic. "But . . . we can learn from this world. The concept works . . . we could create another with . . . with souls. With time, work, and research . . . we can achieve anything."

Lord Och listened to Hermann's words with a look Marianne struggled to identify. The lich's skull lacked any facial features, but his posture betrayed his inner thoughts. Confusion? Hesitation?

Regret, Marianne realized.

The feeling lasted no more than a moment. The Dark Lord's usual coldness had taken over once again.

For some reason, Marianne sensed a chill running down her spine. A gut feeling of incoming dread took her over as she observed the Dark Lord. The weakened Ktulu hissed at the lich, his tentacles wriggling in anger.

Fear, Marianne realized. *Not anger, fear.*

"You have served me well, Hermann." Lord Och almost sounded proud. "You are a credit to the troglodytes everywhere. It's truly a shame that geniuses like you die so early."

The troglodyte frowned. "What . . . do you mean, Lord—"

Marianne's eyes widened in horror, and she shouted a warning: "Hermann, get down—"

The Dark Lord raised a finger and struck Hermann dead.

A fiery ray erupted from the lich's index finger and burnt a hole in the troglodyte's chest. The heart, the lungs, and everything inside the ribcage was instantly vaporized. Hermann's eyes widened in shock and incomprehension as he fell to his back. He tried to blurt out a word, but no air came out of his mouth. Lord Och watched the scene unfold with a cold, remorseless gaze.

Marianne's rapier struck the lich before Hermann's corpse hit the ground. "Murderer!"

Her blade cut through his left eye socket and came out of the back of his skull.

"What . . ." The weakened Valdemar tried to rise to his feet, only to fall on his chest. His voice died in his throat as he saw the smoke coming out of Hermann's corpse. "W-Why?"

Because I guessed right, Marianne thought. "Because he wanted the Painted World from the start!"

"I'm afraid you're only half-right, my dear child." Even though Marianne's soulbound weapon was stuck in Lord Och's skull, it had done nothing to inconvenience him. If anything, he sounded vaguely amused by her defiance. "It is not the painting that interests me, but what it contains."

The Nahemoth. Maybe the Nightwalker too.

He was after the Nahemoth all along, Marianne thought. Somehow the Dark Lord intended to use the Painted World to reach his Light. She knew it in her gut.

Lord Och raised a finger at her, but Marianne didn't let him blast her like Hermann. She removed her rapier from his skull and thrust it a hundred times in short succession, her weapon so fast that a normal human's eyes wouldn't have been able to follow it.

Marianne would have thought twice at striking a Dark Lord less than a year ago. Not today. Not after what she had seen.

Her blade cut through Lord Och's fingers, his hands, his arms. She shattered his skull to pieces and splintered his ribcage. When she was done, a pile of broken bones fell to the ground before her feet.

"Run . . ." Valdemar rasped as he struggled to stand up. "You can—"

"Not without you!" Marianne replied as she took a step back. She didn't know how long it would take for a lich like Lord Och to manifest a new body. Each second counted. "We need to go to Lord Phaleg. He will—"

"My good-for-nothing former apprentice, truly? You would shame me so?"

The lich's bones floated back into place and dashed all of Marianne's hopes.

It took the Dark Lord no longer than the blink of an eye to stand before her once more. Her rapier's cuts vanished as the bones merged back into a pristine state.

"Your efforts are wasted, young Marianne," Lord Och declared, a terrible blue light shining in his skull's eye sockets. A terrible pressure fell on Marianne's shoulders, and she suddenly realized how vast the power gap between them truly was. "You are talented, I will give you that much. With a few more decades under your belt, you might have been a threat. But alas . . ."

He raised his hand, and Marianne felt the soulstone necklace around her neck burning against her skin. She tried to strike, to charge, to fight, but her body refused to move. Her chest felt cold, so very cold, and she heard Valdemar scream her name.

"You died before your time."

Lord Och snapped his fingers.

23

I AM LIGHT, YOU ARE SHADOW

When Marianne's body hit the ground, she was already dead. Valdemar experienced her murder as if he had perished himself. Their souls had been intertwined through their shared dreams. They had made love in the flesh and in their thoughts. A bond remained even when they were awake. When the link ruptured, so did the heart in his chest.

Valdemar had felt the cold hand of Lord Och as his pale fingers closed on Marianne's soul. His chest had burnt when the lich's magic tore his lover's spirit from her flesh. His dark power severed the anchor that bound her soul to her body with surgical precision. There was no malice or hatred in the act, nor regret. When he murdered Marianne Reynard, Lord Och felt *nothing*.

Valdemar let out a scream of pain as Marianne's body landed at his side. Her skin was as pale and lifeless as his was bloody red. Her pale eyes were devoid of life, the soulstone around her neck oozing a vaporous black mist. Her beloved rapier slipped through her fingers.

When Valdemar found the strength to hold her, she was already cold to the touch. Lord Och's finger snap had snuffed out all warmth within Marianne. Her heartbeat, quick and strong, had stopped. Ice coursed through her veins. The warm breath that Valdemar had tasted when they last kissed had turned into empty space. Her soft lips and fingers no longer moved.

No, no . . . Black blood dripped from Valdemar's fanged mouth. His chest hurt and his eyes struggled to see. A sick sensation filled his stomach. *Please, please, no* . . . She couldn't . . . she couldn't . . . not now, not right after . . . not right after they won.

Overcome with horror, Valdemar stabbed his lover's flesh with his fingers. His flesh merged with Marianne's. His biomancy magic traveled through the roads of her nerves and the cables of her arteries. If Valdemar could repair the damage Lord Och had done within minutes, he could save her! He could bring her back!

He didn't find anything wrong. No organ had ruptured. No spell had flooded her brain with blood until it drowned. Her cells simply refused to work. They were dead, every last one of them.

The soul was gone. Gone from her body . . . But not from this world.

A shiver went through Valdemar's nerves when he detected the faint smell of a spirit. His many eyes looked at his lover's necklace, at the black jewel on her skin. A violet hue reflected on its polished surface. The empty space within it had been filled.

The soulstone had worked. The device had caught Marianne's soul when Lord Och murdered her. Or maybe the lich's spell used the soul-stone to kill her by capturing her spirit. Whatever the case, Marianne's soul had survived. Hope warmed Valdemar's innards once again as he removed his hand from his lover's body. If he could transfer her soul the right way, maybe he could—

His master's grim shadow blanketed him in darkness.

"Such a panicked response for a woman?" Lord Och's tone betrayed his disappointment. The sound of lightning coursed through the air when he spoke. "Truly the pleasures of flesh can dull even the greatest minds."

"You . . ." Valdemar raised his hand to fire a blood bullet at his former teacher. His movements were slow, his arms weak. He had lost too much blood. "You heartless bastard . . ."

Crimson lightning surged from Lord Och's hands. Electricity raced through Valdemar's flesh and fried his remaining nerves. Whatever organs he had left cooked inside his own boiling blood. His brain burst out of his skull, yet he didn't die. The lightning destroyed his body from within, but his soul refused to leave his mortal coil behind.

Not since his fall down Lord Bethor's tower had Valdemar experienced such absolute, mind-numbing *pain*.

"I will coddle you no more, my apprentice." Lord Och's mask of charm and affability had slipped. The cruel, cold-hearted undead underneath saw no need to hide his inhumanity anymore. "I have tolerated your insolence long enough."

"Ktulhulu!" Ktulu snarled, wings extended and tiny hands raised. The familiar valiantly flew at Lord Och's face in a foolish attempt to protect his summoner. "Ktul—"

Lord Och mercilessly struck Ktulu down with another thunderbolt. The poor familiar squealed as it fell to the ground, but the lich didn't stop. He blasted the child Stranger with a torrent of lightning, again, and again, and *again*. Worst of all, Lord Och did it with a ghoulish smile on his skeletal face.

"Ktul . . ." Valdemar rasped, but only smoke came out of his lungs. He felt his familiar's agony through their bond. They screamed as one with each electrical shock. Daggers of lightning stabbed them both until they could no longer move.

Valdemar's vision blurred. Half his eyes had melted into his skull. His strong alien limbs refused to move. He felt so weak that the Blood itself slipped through his grasp.

"Spare the rod, spoil the child." Lord Och's hands burned with hellfire. "Forgive me, my apprentice. You may experience temporary discomfort, but I cannot waste precious time on sentimentalities."

Flames swallowed Valdemar. The last of his eyes burned to a crisp and fell off his face.

He couldn't see anything, couldn't hear anything, couldn't taste anything. His mangled body didn't have the tools left for that. Only the Blood gave him slight awareness of the world around him. He sensed Lord Och's magic at work and Ktulu's presence nearby, space twisting around them all, Marianne's presence slipping away . . .

How long was Valdemar trapped inside his own mangled corpse? Seconds, minutes, hours? Time lost all meaning when the world around you had become a blur.

The Blood returned him to life ever so slowly. Currents of magic created new cells for his organism. They borrowed flesh from all life in Underland to return him to his original state. Was it his newly awakened Stranger nature at work? For a moment, Valdemar had nearly become one with the Father of All and the flesh beneath the stone.

It's . . . from within . . . Valdemar realized. He thought it was the souls he had consumed at first, their spirit transformed into matter, but he was wrong. They were all within him, suppressed but present.

A force in the Blood strengthened him. It called flesh from other places to help him regenerate. Valdemar was already doing it passively, but now the dam had broken; where droplets dripped through before, now a river of blood poured within his veins.

Could he be tapping more directly into Ialdabaoth's power now that Crétail was imprisoned? The twins had been born avatars of Ialdabaoth. Perhaps they had been splitting the power between themselves, and now that one of them was incapacitated, Crétail's leftover energies moved into Valdemar . . .

Light struck through the darkness and a loud rumble filled the silence. Two eyes and ears, not more, stabilized his vision and hearing. He moved a hand whose fingers grew like plants and a leg that snapped back into a straight shape.

I'm . . . human . . . Valdemar thought. The first thing he saw were arms wrapped in skin and sinews, laying on a cold stone floor. Colorful lights filled the horizon. *I'm . . . I'm in . . .*

The Pleromian vault. The dusty tomb that had haunted Valdemar's dreams was returning to life. The fiery glyphs in its ceiling flickered in and out of existence. They moved left and right, above and below. The magical formulas they formed changed in the blink of an eye. They swirled around the Painted World and lifted it above the ground, to the very roof of the stone dome. Tendrils of colorful energy grew out of the canvas. A pillar of light fell down from it and onto the Pleromian portal. Its shining radiance hurt Valdemar's regenerating eyes when he looked at it.

The shadow of Lord Och stood before the pillar, his back turned on his apprentice.

Valdemar gathered his thoughts. He was human again, and naked like the day he was born. Marianne's corpse was nowhere to be seen, nor Hermann's. But Ktulu . . .

"K . . ." Valdemar turned to the source of the sound, a broken child lying on his left. "K . . ."

The sight broke Valdemar's heart. Ktulu had lost half of his eyes. The left side of his tiny face showed severe burns deep enough to reveal green flesh underneath. Lord Och had ripped out his wings, severed some of his tentacles, and broken his tiny legs. The familiar was still alive, but only barely so. He didn't even have the strength to whine or cry.

"Ktulu, hang on . . ." Valdemar rasped. His dry, sore throat hurt with each word he vomited. The summoner touched his familiar and used his biomancy to help hasten the tiny Stranger's recovery. "Hang on . . ."

"I see you recovered quickly, my apprentice."

Valdemar froze, expecting a new lightning bolt.

"I didn't think this chastisement would keep you down for long." The lich kept his back turned on his apprentice. He only had eyes for the pillar of light. "Look. Can you see its beauty?"

Valdemar's first instinct was to stab the lich in the back, but a glance at the source of the lights paralyzed him. His mind came to an abrupt stop as it struggled to comprehend what he saw at the feet of the pillar.

Colors. Not the pigments Valdemar and Hermann used to paint their world, but new ones unlike anything humans had ever seen. A splash of stygian blue, saturated and yet so very dark. A streak of magenta on a jet-black spot. A shade of greenish-yellow pink on a floating bubble of something . . . something that Valdemar's mind perceived as black light. His eyes weren't equipped to understand these visual stimuli.

The Pleromian portal stood at the heart of the pillar. Its archway of steel now looked like a ring holding the eldritch colors contained within itself. The portal had become a lens peering into a realm of unfathomable beauty. When Valdemar looked into it, he gazed into a swirling abyss of colors that didn't, couldn't, *shouldn't* exist in this world.

The world beyond the portal was deep and flat, high and low, nowhere and everywhere. Its magenta radiations and eldritch oscillations bent the will of space, the rules of time, the conservation of mass. Its wavelength existence displaced the feeble light of the material world and pushed gravity backward. Its singularity burned hotter than the mightiest volcano. Its pull called the stars to it like moths to a flame. It was the forge of suns, whose anvil was the primordial soul and its hammer the heart of wonders.

The stray thoughts, confusing and conflicting, formed in Valdemar's mind as it tried to explain, to comprehend, to fathom what he was gazing at. Neither his eyes nor his psychic sight could make sense of this awe-inspiring vision. They stared into a realm of wonders that put the Silent King's throne to shame in its scale and complexity.

Tears formed in Valdemar's eyes as he rose to his feet. His arms carried the crippled Ktulu, the little familiar breathing against his chest.

"Is this . . ." The name of the abyss was on the tip of Valdemar's tongue, but he felt unworthy of saying it. Something in his soul begged him not to sully this sublime cosmic force with petty human words.

"The divine spirit from which our souls descend," Lord Och whispered with reverence. "The origin point of everything. Beyond space, beyond time, beyond the laws of magic and physics. A cosmic sea of knowledge and power."

The lich slowly turned his back on the glowing portal to face his apprentice.

"This is the Light, Valdemar."

This . . . this is what I longed for all my life, Valdemar realized. He couldn't take his eyes off the abyss beyond the portal. It called to him like the sun of his dreams. He heard its melodious song of energy burst.

Ktulu let out a cough in Valdemar's arms. With the shock of seeing the Light having passed, Valdemar suddenly remembered what the lich had done. He changed his skin to iron, ready to take down his former master.

"Careful, child," the Dark Lord of Paraplex warned with his hands behind his back. "The portal hasn't stabilized yet. You might destroy your beloved masterpiece by accident."

Valdemar's teeth gritted in frustration. The Dark Lord was telling the truth. A thick veil of transcendental energy separated the abyss beyond the portal from the material world. The Pleromian portal stabilized the cosmic powers at work, but any interference might cause a catastrophic backlash.

"I apologize for the brutality, my dear Valdemar, but I only had a short window of opportunity. Minutes at best. The Painted World is too precious to my former colleagues to let me keep it unsupervised." Lord Och glanced at Ktulu with a pitiless expression. "I did not dare to destroy him. The death of a familiar leaves the owner's soul diminished if they have bonded with them too deeply. That's why I never took one myself."

If he hadn't killed Ktulu to harm Valdemar, then the lich needed his apprentice alive. Valdemar double-checked his magical defenses and hid his thoughts behind a veil of stolen souls.

A question burned on his lips. "Where is Marianne?"

"Her soulstone?" Lord Och snorted with a ghoulish expression of absolute disdain. "Safe . . . for now."

Valdemar's fingers trembled with fury. The Dark Lord kept Marianne's soul on his person. As a hostage.

Valdemar returned his chest to normal skin and reshaped his body to open a hole in his chest cavity. His ribs opened like a maw, allowing him to put the wounded Ktulu within them. His chest closed and hardened back into steel. The summoner would keep his familiar safe in his body.

"Creative," Lord Och commented with amusement. "I wouldn't do that in the presence of female company if I were you. She might die of fright like the last one."

It took Valdemar all his mental fortitude to ignore the cruel jab. He was more angry for Marianne than for himself. The lich considered her nothing more than ammunition to taunt and torment his apprentice. Lord Och had felt nothing when he killed Marianne, and even less when he demeaned her post-mortem.

"This entire crisis . . . you engineered it all, didn't you?" Valdemar guessed, keeping an eye on the Dark Lord and another on the portal. Could he teleport safely so close to a cosmic phenomenon of this magnitude? He would need to do that to contact the other Dark Lords above ground, but if a spatial interference tore him apart midway . . . "It was you all along."

"You overestimate me. I simply took advantage of opportunities as they came, nudged you here and there . . . If you never lose sight of your goal, my apprentice, you will always find a path to reach it."

Wards are active, Valdemar thought as he scanned the room. The Dark Lord had sealed his vault with magic and blotted out the exit corridor with a wall of stone. Valdemar would struggle to teleport past them, or even summon anything. *The other Dark Lords are distracted by the Qlippoths outside and don't know the way in . . . they won't help.*

"You named me your successor to distract the other Dark Lords," Valdemar said. *Maybe I could send a message through the wards somehow . . .* "You confused them, made them focus on me rather than you."

"Well, how should I say it . . ." A cold chuckle came out of the Dark Lord's mouth. "That part was my idea of a prank."

By the Light, this asshole was serious.

"Come on, you must have laughed a little at my colleagues' expressions," Lord Och said. He clearly took joy in his student's anger. "Humor is at its best when mocking the powerful. It drags the haughty down to earth."

"Are we all toys to you?" Valdemar couldn't suppress his bitterness. He felt betrayed to have believed the Dark Lord might stand for something greater than himself once.

"Toys or tools, what's the difference? I take good care of them so long as they fulfill their purpose."

The lich glanced over his shoulder and gazed into the Light. He didn't lower his guard, however. Valdemar was certain that the Dark Lord's hidden hands were ready to spellcast at a moment's notice.

"I was denied entrance to this place for so long." Lord Och's voice brimmed with longing and nostalgia. "How many times have I dreamed of it when I could still sleep? I remember the pain in my chest I felt each time I woke up. The world was so cold, so lifeless. Even when I tore my soul from my corpse to embrace lichdom, even when I shed my humanity and deadened my emotions, the agony remained forever raw."

Lord Och laughed as he turned his attention back to Valdemar. "But now, the path closed to me by the gods has been opened by the hands of men. Truly, nothing can resist the march of human genius."

Why is he telling me this? Valdemar couldn't grasp his teacher's motivations. Does he still need me somehow? Did he spare me because he wanted an audience to gloat in his moment of triumph? No, Lord Och has never been so careless . . .

Something didn't add up.

"How?" Valdemar asked. If he understood the phenomenon, he could exploit it.

"The Strangers were cast down from the Light above. Even to this day they still mourn their fall. They cannot let go. They are fragments of a broken mirror, desperate to pull themselves back together."

A resonance, Valdemar realized. He's creating a resonance between Ialdabaoth and the Light by using Crétail as a focus. Valdemar's hands clenched in rage as he started to get a better understanding of the situation. "That was why you took me on as an apprentice. You were grooming me for the sacrificial altar from the start."

"Haven't I told you? All social interactions are based on self-interest. I help you, you help me." The Dark Lord's head tilted to the side like a curious bird. "My original goal was to study you thoroughly, I won't deny it. I wanted to witness the extent of your powers, to observe you act in a controlled environment."

Like an animal in a cage . . .

"The more I studied you, the more I realized you would never be the key I sought. You were too attached to improving the mortal condition, too willful, too thoughtful . . ." Lord Och smirked fondly. "Too *human*."

"You almost sound proud," Valdemar noted.

"I am." Lord Och's gaze was sharp as a blade. "In many ways, you are the ideal our species aspires to. The power of the cosmos at the fingertips of human will."

Somehow, the Dark Lord's appreciation filled Valdemar with shame. It was just another petty manipulation tactic.

"This spawn," Lord Och pointed at the Painted World with a finger, "was a far more suitable tool for my purpose. I have faced Nahemoths in the past, but this one is something else. Your brother is a trueborn incarnation of Ialdabaoth. I knew you and Hermann would succeed in binding him in a way that would make it possible to harness his power."

"Some teacher you are," Valdemar replied with disgust. "You steal the discoveries of your students to make them your own."

"I told you from the start that the purpose of this Institute was to accumulate knowledge for my own pleasure. I give shelter and purpose to scholars whose discoveries serve my needs. It was an even trade for the time it lasted."

"An even trade?" The expression made Valdemar's blood boil. "You stole Hermann's work and then murdered him. How was that an even trade?!"

Lord Och remained unflappable. "Believe me, I would rather have spared him if I could. I appreciated our dear troglodyte. Alas, his knowledge of pictomancy was too dangerous for my plans to ignore. I couldn't risk letting him unravel the Painted World."

Because you won't risk it yourself. Valdemar couldn't read Lord Och's mind, but he knew that was what he thought. You won't let your brother disappear, would you?

Even if Valdemar was willing to make that sacrifice, the consequences would be disastrous. Destroying the Painted World so soon after completion might release Crétail and the Nightwalker before they could be fully assimilated into it. The new pictomancy universe within the canvas was young, fragile. It could easily revert back to what came before if disrupted.

They would be back to square one.

"What then?" Valdemar asked. "Where do all these murders and cruelty lead?"

"My, where else?" Lord Och waved a hand at the portal. "I will enter the Light, but on my own terms. Not as a disembodied spirit devoid of personality, but with the full weight of my human desires and unbearable sins."

The veil separating the Light from the material world had grown thinner. Not thin and stable enough to let anyone through safely, but closer.

"I will not beg for a place in paradise, no. I will take it." Lord Och's smile widened. It was the satisfied smirk of a winner, the vicious grin of a conqueror rejoicing at his enemies' defeat. "I will flaunt the feeble teachings of Sophia, shed my mortal coil, extricate myself from the limitations of matter and form. I will become a wavelength, my apprentice. An unstoppable radiation, an invisible force as irresistible as gravity itself."

A sudden feeling of cold made Valdemar shiver. He gazed into the colorful abyss of the Light and the cosmic energies bursting from within it. "You want to become a god. To transcend the Strangers and achieve a higher state of existence."

"Must you make it sound so pedantic, my apprentice? What I want is absolute freedom. From the laws of men and gods, of physics and reality. Freedom from this ceiling of stone and a doomed universe. Nothing more, nothing less."

The twin lights in the lich's eyes flared with a blue hue. "I thought you would understand that, Valdemar."

Was that why he had spared his apprentice and given him a chance, however slim, to ruin his moment of triumph? Because he wanted validation? *An ancient undead of his age and experience can't possibly be that insecure,* Valdemar thought. *I don't get him at all. What's his game?*

"I understand your vision, but I do not endorse it. Not at the cost you're ready to pay." Valdemar squinted at the portal's baleful energies. After having observed it carefully, he had a pretty good idea of where this phenomenon would lead unless stopped. "What will happen after you cross this doorway to Heaven?"

"Do you truly want me to say it, my apprentice?"

"Yes. I want to hear it from your mouth." Valdemar wanted to hear the faint sound of regret, of hesitation. Any hint that he could still talk down his teacher from his madness.

"Well, the most likely possibility is that the breach will become unstable." The Dark Lord spoke with the cold, clinical confidence of a soulless doctor. He had given a lot of thought to his plan and considered its potentially disastrous consequences. "The energies of the Light would pour out uncontrollably into a lesser universe unsuited for them. The portal might explode into the heart of a newborn sun. Ialdabaoth will boil like an egg, the Whitemoon will melt, and everyone will die. The end."

He didn't care one bit.

"Or maybe the breach will collapse on itself and harmlessly dissipate." Lord Och dismissed Valdemar's worries with a shrug. "Maybe the portal will explode and destroy this facility, but spare the rest of the Domain. We're in uncharted territory. Anything could happen."

"Exactly, anything could happen!" Valdemar snarled. "You would abandon everyone to die! The Scholars, Lord Bethor—"

"Lord Bethor will survive." To Valdemar's surprise, it seemed that the lich truly believed it. "My former apprentice is already an almighty existence that transcends humanity. I doubt anything short of the complete annihilation of this reality will permanently destroy him. Even then, I'm uncertain."

The fact that Lord Och believed Ialdabaoth would perish in the cataclysm but not Bethor surprised Valdemar. The Dark Lord of Sabaoth was a powerful man, but to survive the world's destruction demanded more than power. Was Bethor some kind of lich whose phylactery was hidden in another distant world?

Even then, Lord Och didn't bother to pretend that he cared about anyone else. "Anyway, does it really matter what happens to this world after we've crossed into the other side? Yes, young Valdemar, a few meaningless lives will be lost, but such is the cost of progress. We can always create new worlds and life in our image after we ascend."

It mattered to Valdemar. He couldn't let Och proceed with his mad bid for godhood if there was even the slightest chance that it would destroy Underland as a side effect. The risk of releasing Crétail and the Nightwalker was a lesser evil at this point.

Did you expect a heart of gold in my ribcage? The old taunt flashed back in Valdemar's mind like an ominous warning. He doesn't care about anything or anyone—

"Wait." Valdemar squinted, as his teacher's last sentence registered in his mind. One word in particular rang in his head. "*We?*"

Lord Och didn't make a sound. For a few seconds, only the faint song of the Light and the bursting cracks of the Pleromian glyphs filled the room.

"Why did you let me live, my teacher?" Valdemar asked, utterly confused. "Why did you bring me here? Why didn't you restrain me? Why are you telling me all of this *now*?"

The ancient lich's stone face morphed into an expression that his apprentice had never seen before. An emotion Valdemar found more surprising than the cosmic Light in the background.

A flash of vulnerability.

"Valdemar." Lord Och extended a hand to his apprentice as the world trembled around them. "Come with me."

24

GRADUATION DAY

The Dark Lord's palm stood between master and student like an unfinished bridge. Valdemar looked at the skeletal hand as if it were poisoned. He half-expected a soulstone or trap hidden between Lord Och's fingers like a cruel joke, but he didn't see any.

"Where?" Valdemar asked, utterly dumbfounded.

"To the Light, my dense apprentice," Lord Och chuckled. "Come with me. The door will stabilize soon, but we will only have a short window of time to safely cross onto the other side."

Flashes of energy erupted from the portal. The veil separating the material world from the higher realm of the Light had grown thinner. The flying Pleromian glyphs swirling above it moved so quickly that Valdemar's eyes struggled to keep track of them.

"Do you understand what's on the other side of this portal, Valdemar? Freedom. Knowledge. Power!" The flames in Lord Och's eyes glowed brighter than the stars. "All the hidden truths of the universe, spells that transcend the Blood! The liberty to wander into the infinity and beyond!"

Valdemar glared at his teacher and spat venomous words. "How can you ask me to trust you after what you've *done*? You've murdered my companions, manipulated me for months, put me through hell, beat my familiar half to death, and tortured me with lightning!"

"Please, as if Lord Bethor hadn't done worse." Lord Och waved his hand dismissively. "Yes, yes, I understand how you might fear a trap of some kind. But then, why would I need to convince you to go along? You were at my mercy, my apprentice. If I needed you to cross this portal, I would have tossed your severed head through it. I offer you to join me because I believe you are worthy of the Light, my apprentice. Will you spit on my kindness?"

"Kindness?" Even if the lich's offer was genuine, even if Valdemar ignored all the abuse he had personally suffered, there was one thing he simply couldn't forgive. "You murdered Marianne before my eyes!"

"You would deny paradise for a woman?" Lord Och's calm tone rose with his anger. "Do you know how many of them there are on this Light-forsaken planet alone? At least half a billion, if not more."

"That woman has a name." The image of his lover falling dead on the floor would remain forever raw in Valdemar's mind. "Marianne Reynard!"

"You only care because the human half of your biochemistry is altering your thinking," Lord Och replied with disdain. "Attraction, lust, *love*, are drugs. You are high because this is your first time, but trust someone many centuries older than you. I have loved and forgotten more women than the years you've lived through."

It would have been one thing if Lord Och faked sympathy, but the lich no longer felt the need to put on the charm. Marianne was right. If the Dark Lord ever had the ability to relate to someone else and his fellow humans, he had lost it long ago.

Valdemar struggled to contain his anger. "What about your murder of Hermann?" he asked with rising fury. "Or what will happen to Iren and Liliane once this portal destroys Underland? What about my friends who you're condemning to death? Do you expect me to abandon them to their doom?"

"Friends? People you've known for a scant few months? Do you hear yourself?" Lord Och took back his hand. His back was stiff like an iron rod, his fingers trembling with frustration. "You are an immortal being, a Stranger. You will live to see these small people all wither and die."

"And that makes their lives without value?"

"Yes."

"Then you are the height of hypocrisy, Lord Och!" Valdemar raised an accusing finger at his mad teacher. "You were not born immortal, you achieved eternal unlife through magic! Every single one of this Institute's Masters did the same!"

"So what? They will languish forever in the darkness, trapped between Ialdabaoth below and the Whitemoon above. Wouldn't it be more merciful to let them all rest?" A rattle of frustration came out of Lord Och's mouth. "I do not understand why I'm wasting my time trying to open your eyes."

"Me neither," Valdemar replied, his eyes squinting at the lich. "Why do you want me to follow you so badly?"

"My poor Valdemar, is it truly so hard to believe that I care for your spiritual health?"

"You have only known me for months, scarcely longer than Hermann." Valdemar frowned. He found it difficult to believe in the lich's goodwill after so long. "By your own logic, my life should be worthless to you."

Lord Och let out a brief laugh. "Point taken," he conceded.

The lich's embarrassed reaction surprised Valdemar. *Is he acting?* The summoner wondered. Valdemar didn't detect any hint of falsehood or fake charm in his old teacher. *No . . . he sounds genuine.*

"Between us, I cannot explain it myself." The Dark Lord shook his head, his body language betraying his confusion. "I thought I emancipated myself from such sentimentalities when I embraced undeath. Yet I feel a certain appreciation for your person, perhaps because I see much of myself in you. I suppose you could call it . . ." Lord Och put a finger on his chin as he struggled to find the correct expression. "Paternal fondness," he finally said.

As if Valdemar's real father wasn't bad enough.

"You have an odd way of showing it." Valdemar would never forget the pain of lightning coursing through his veins. "All you have done since we first met is play cruel tricks and mind games on me. You tried to convince me to sacrifice my friends to this portal, mocked me for believing in a better future . . ."

"I tried to cure you of your own foolishness and failed. Do you understand how difficult it was for me, you selfish brat?"

Valdemar choked in indignation. "For *you*?"

"Yes!" Lord Och snarled back. The walls of the vault shook around them as if echoing his cold anger. "You possess limitless potential, my apprentice, and yet you waste it on lunacy!"

The Dark Lord waved a hand at the shining portal. "The sun, the light you sought for, is right beyond this threshold! This is the crossroad that will let us reach Earth! So why won't you step through it?"

Although the thought of using the Light to reach Earth at last was enticing, Valdemar held his ground. "I have sought the sun too, yes. That was my dream. But I never desired it for my own pleasure alone. I wanted to honor my grandfather and free our people from the ceiling of stone above our heads."

What was worth the joy of watching an open sky, if nobody else could look at it with you?

"Is it lunacy to believe in altruism?" Valdemar asked his teacher. "In a better future?"

For the first time since the discussion began, Valdemar's words seemed to land with his teacher. The Dark Lord didn't immediately shoot down his apprentice's argument. Instead, he considered it thoughtfully for long, agonizing seconds.

"Believe . . ." Lord Och repeated the word with a long sigh. "I stopped *believing* when Sophia the Unwise refused to answer my prayers for universal salvation. She had called herself the mother of the human spirit, but when the Whitemoon came, she chose to save the few and abandon the many to death and degradation. What kind of mother would leave her children to starve underground or perish in the snow?"

To Valdemar's astonishment, it seemed as if Lord Och had undergone a drastic metamorphosis before his eyes. His shoulders crumbled, his eyes looked down at the ground below his feet, his stance was feebler, weaker.

"It was then that I understood the gods' love was not unconditional." Beneath the bitterness in Lord Och's words hid crushing sorrow. "The Strangers, Sophia, the stars . . . none of them care. We humans are orphans left to wander a cold, pitiless universe. We live unloved and die unmourned. We are on our own."

The Dark Lord's image of power had collapsed to reveal the tired old man beneath.

"I stopped believing in men not long afterward," Lord Och confessed. "When we used Sophia's corpse to begin the exodus underground, the derros, the dokkars, and the troglodytes fell upon us. When mankind most needed unity, the first Dark Lords started bickering among themselves. They fought over who controlled which cavern, whose language men should speak . . . Commoners were no better. I've seen children slay their parents for table scraps."

I'm seeing the real him, Valdemar realized. The mask Lord Och carried on himself at all times had fallen off. The sight of the face underneath filled his apprentice with an emotion he never thought he would feel for the lich.

Pity.

"People are not defined by their darkest moments, my teacher," Valdemar argued.

"What about the best times then?" Lord Och asked with scorn. "Can you fathom how old I am, my apprentice? How fantastically ancient?"

Valdemar bit his lower lip. He could almost taste his teacher's bitterness on the tip of his tongue. "I can only imagine."

"The empire is but the latest society we have built after the Descent. I tried to create a paradise so many times . . . I abolished private property and made all men equal in all things. Another time I granted my subjects absolute freedom of trade, of speech, of thinking. Both experiments failed disastrously. People wanted the freedom to own more than others, or they wanted to be paid for doing nothing. They couldn't make up their minds."

"The fact you haven't discovered the perfect system yet doesn't mean that it doesn't exist," Valdemar argued. The argument sounded weak even to himself.

Lord Och laughed, but there was no joy to be found in his words. "Democracy, oligarchy, aristocracy . . . No system has managed to bring happiness to humans, because they will never be satisfied by *anything*. You have seen my colleagues. They mocked you . . . as others mocked me before." A disappointed idealist lurked inside every cynic.

"You feel lonely, my teacher," Valdemar realized in shock. The Dark Lord he had so feared had been nothing more than a protective shell. At some point, the face beneath the mask of cruelty and absolute power had grown to fit it; but the raw pain at the heart of his soul had never left.

In losing faith in others, Lord Och had cut himself off from them. Was his attempt to talk Valdemar into following him an expression of the desire to preserve a sliver of humanity with him into the Light? Or a last-ditch attempt to connect to someone, *anyone*?

"Mankind keeps letting us down, so what's the point of trying to raise them up?" Lord Och argued. "The truth, Valdemar, is that most humans are aggressively *mediocre*. They want easy solutions to complex problems. They want to believe someone else will solve everything for them while they don't have to lift a finger. They are a waste of our time."

"So you would rather let them die? Or brainwash them into obedience as Blutgang did with the derros?"

"Why not? The derros have never been stronger than with ninety percent of their population lobotomized." Lord Och let out a dismissive shrug. "You, me, Lord Bethor, Otto Blutgang . . . we are exceptional. We are imbued with superior vision, volition, and intellect. Which is why we have the right—the *duty*—to rule over our lessers. There are Masters, Scholars who can grow into Masters, and the rest. My Institute's hierarchy reflects the world outside its walls. Only a fraction of humankind deserves salvation. The rest only exists to lift us up."

"Spoken like Sophia the Unwise then," Valdemar silently noted that his teacher didn't include Empress Aratra in his list of worthy people, which spoke volumes about his true feelings toward her. "You have become the very thing you fought all those centuries ago."

Lord Och gritted his teeth in anger. The remark had hit a nerve, or what could pass for one in a fleshless undead. "No, I have not. I will succeed where she failed. Her husk will be put out of its misery with this world, whereas I shall ascend higher than she could ever dream to."

"You can disguise the truth with all the pretty words you can think of, my teacher, it won't change it." Valdemar gathered his breath. "You've given up."

"You naïve fool." Lord Och sneered with disdain. The lich straightened up and regained an ounce of his sinister majesty. "You, a half-breed alien spawn born of rape, you would still carry the burden of faith in mankind after all you've been through? You think yourself capable of carrying this cross?"

"Yes." Valdemar had carried it for years. "I have stumbled many times, I will admit . . . but I have always gotten back to my feet. I will not relent."

"Even knowing it is pointless?" Lord Och gave him a sharp look. "You are a poor scientist then, my apprentice. A hypothesis that cannot survive the test of experimentation should be discarded. Here is the truth: *nothing* can change human nature. *Nothing* can improve the mortal condition."

"Then," Valdemar pointed a finger at the Painted World floating above them, "how do you explain this?"

His and Hermann's magnum opus had become the vibrant heart of a magical phenomenon. Its pigments danced on its surface as if alive, giving shape to a verdant new universe full of promises. Compared to the Light, a realm of eldritch beauty and alien glory, the Painted World looked plain in its simplicity.

But it was a vision of heaven all the same.

"This Painted World, this miracle, is the result of cooperation between a Stranger, a troglodyte, and my humble person," Valdemar argued. "My brother let himself be caught inside because for a precious few seconds, you reminded him what it meant to be human."

A pure tree had sprouted from a corrupted seed. If something born evil could become a force of good, why couldn't men change their ways?

"You said *someone* would pay the price for my choices, my teacher," Valdemar reminded his teacher. "That each day I delayed opening a portal to Earth, more of our kind's souls would feed Ialdabaoth. Yet here we have created a new plane of existence and a potential afterlife for everyone. We have created a new option that didn't exist before. One that invalidates the choice you tried to force upon me."

That was what Marianne had taught him.

"If paradise does not exist yet," Valdemar argued, "then we must build it."

"How much time will last until human greed despoils it?" Lord Och raised his chin, his expression hard as stone. "I do not understand you, my apprentice."

"On the contrary, I think you do." By now, Valdemar understood the weight on his master's heart. The gnawing root at the source of their endless debates and philosophical conflicts. "If you were truly confident in your own words, my position wouldn't infuriate you so much. You would have nothing to prove to me or anyone else. Yet at every step of our association, you've tried to make me validate your misanthropy."

"For the sake of your intellectual enlightenment," Lord Och replied, his voice soft as velvet.

"For the sake of soothing your guilty conscience."

Lord Och did not answer. His shadow lengthened as the doorway to the Light shone brighter.

"You could have severed my limbs and dragged me screaming into the Light," Valdemar pointed out. "You did not, because you want me to come with you out of my own free will. It matters to you. Even after centuries of gloom and darkness, a part of you is still afraid of being wrong."

Lord Och snorted and adjusted his tattered robe. "You know not what you speak of."

"Deep down a small sliver of humanity wants me to talk you out of this madness." Valdemar gazed at the Light, at the vast abyss of the cosmos. A realm that offered unlimited power at the cost of one's humanity.

"It's why you've tried to crush my hopes each step of the way. You wanted to silence the best part of yourself."

"Do you mean to *pity* me, Valdemar?"

To his own astonishment, Valdemar did still pity the Dark Lord.

Before him stood a creature miserable enough to take pleasure in others' pain and failures. Disappointment fueled Lord Och's cruelty. Bitterness nursed his disdain and arrogance. In his attempt to put a shield between himself and the awfulness of the world, the lich had given up on everything good in it.

Valdemar would never forgive Lord Och for his crimes . . . but as they faced each other with the entire world's fate hanging in the balance, the summoner realized he couldn't bring himself to hate the ancient Dark Lord.

Valdemar wanted to despise Lord Och the same way he had tried to find the strength to hate his grandfather, because it would have made it easier. But even if he tried his best to appear as one, the lich was no monster. He was no vicious madman like Ialdabaoth's cultists, no cruel invader from another world like the Qlippoths, not even an unfeeling machine like Otto Blutgang.

In the end, Lord Och was only human.

"My teacher, it's not too late."

Now it was Valdemar's turn to extend a hand to Lord Och. The ancient archmage glanced at his student's palm without a word. He made no move to take it.

"Stay with me. Help me make this world a better place instead of turning your back on it." Valdemar cleared his throat. "Lord Och, you possess extraordinary knowledge, willpower, and wisdom. You command incredible resources and powerful magic. Harsh years have torn you up inside, but you are not alone in this fight anymore. I am with you."

Even after all Lord Och had done, it wasn't too late for him to get a second chance.

We can't wait much longer, Valdemar thought. The portal had become so bright that its steel had turned black as coal in comparison. *The whole place will collapse on us.*

Yet Valdemar waited. He said nothing as Lord Och observed him, judged him, appraised him. The ancient lich's ghoulish skull briefly betrayed a hint of doubt. His fiery eyes glanced at Valdemar's hand with uncertainty.

For a moment, the Dark Lord truly considered Valdemar's offer.

"No, my apprentice." Although a crack had appeared in this millennium-old ice, it refused to melt away. "I have gone too far, sacrificed too much, to stop here." The Dark Lord's voice turned deeper, more sinister. "I will not turn back while I stand at the very altar of enlightenment. Not for anything. Not even for you."

Valdemar's jaw clenched as he lowered his hand. His fists clenched with resolve. "Then the time for words is over."

"It is." An earthquake shook the vault. Cracks spread in the stone ceiling, threatening to collapse it. "The portal has almost stabilized. We must cross it soon or perish, Valdemar."

"I reject these options." Valdemar shifted his posture and prepared to lunge at his master, his teacher . . . his twisted mirror. "I will close this cursed door before the unthinkable happens."

Valdemar had spent the whole discussion analyzing the situation. The phenomenon came from the portal using the Painted World as a conduit to create a resonance with the Light's realm. If Valdemar could disable the portal and safely disperse its energies, he would preserve the Painted World. He would save his brother and Hermann's legacy.

But to do that, Valdemar needed to achieve the impossible.

He would have to get past Lord Och.

"I won't let you destroy this world." Blood particles floated around Valdemar, ready to fuel his spells. "I will stop you here . . . as you once stopped your own master."

The Dark Lord's sinister laughter echoed in the vault. The man inside the lich had put on his mask of inhumanity. The Lord Och that stood before Valdemar was no longer doubtful. He had become the cold-hearted, cruel archmage that cowed his apprentice into obedience the first time they met.

"Foolish disciple." An electrical spark flared to life in Lord Och's palm. "I taught you well, but you still have *so* much left to learn."

"I'm an autodidact. I learn better by experience."

Master and student began their battle with the Light as their only witness.

25

DUEL OF THE ARCHMAGES

Not even the gods could dodge lightning, so Valdemar didn't bother trying. Instead, he quickly reshaped his body before Lord Och could cast his spell. His skin had turned into an armored substance that was like thick iron, strong but inflexible. Two spikes of iron bones erupted from his shoulders, and a pathway of nerves formed in his back beyond the spinal cord.

Valdemar sensed Lord Och's telekinetic might hit him at the same time as his lightning. The first time they met, the Dark Lord's magic had powered through his apprentice's defenses and brought him to his knees. Valdemar never stood a chance back then.

But a good spellcaster learned from his mistakes.

Lord Och's telekinetic push bounced off his apprentice's psychic defenses. His lightning coiled around Valdemar's shoulder spikes and traveled down the nerve pathways prepared for it all the way to his heels. The redirected electricity harmlessly dissipated into the ground after missing his vital organs.

Valdemar had invented this defense to protect himself from the derros' lightning pylons after they incapacitated him in Astaphanos. He never thought he would need it to fight his own teacher, but it served him well all the same.

"An interesting innovation." Lord Och sounded almost proud.

"Fool me once, shame on you," Valdemar replied as he reshaped his fingers into organic barrels. "Fool me twice, shame on me." A volley of bone and blood bullets erupted from the summoner's fingers.

Lord Och didn't bother dodging. Instead, he casually tore off his robe as his entire skeleton turned black as onyx. Organic bullets bounced off his bones as if it were made of the thickest steel.

Exploiting the lich's overconfidence, Valdemar tried a trick he once used against the derros. He telekinetically commanded his own blood bullets to reshape into summoning circles and call allies when they hit Och.

Valdemar attempted to summon fire elementals and brutish Gugs. He failed. Harmless flames flickered against Och's reinforced bones, while the Gugs manifested in a shower of organs and blood. With Ktulu heavily wounded and the spatial anomaly altering reality inside the vault, Valdemar couldn't summon safely. His allies were torn apart before they could make their way to Underland.

"Pitiful," Lord Och said as he stomped the ground with his right foot. A row of long bone spears rose from the earth and progressed toward Valdemar like a tidal wave.

Valdemar dodged the attack and charged straight at Lord Och. His nails turned into bone knives sharp enough to cut through steel. He closed the gap with his master and aimed straight for the head.

Lord Och deftly stepped out of the way and deflected Valdemar's arm with a push of his right hand. "Did you mistake me for a feeble old man unwilling to get his hands dirty, my apprentice?"

The steel skeleton's left palm hit Valdemar's chest at a bullet's speed. Magic rippled from the lich's bones on contact into a mighty telekinetic blast.

If he hadn't cast his armor spell, the blow would have no doubt blown Valdemar's organs to smithereens. It still had enough power to propel him backward against the vault's stone wall. Rock shattered against his back upon impact, and his iron skin peeled off to reveal the festering flesh underneath.

"You don't live to my age without learning a few things about hand-to-hand combat!" Lord Och taunted his apprentice as eldritch flames flared to life between his fingers.

Recognizing the spell his master was about to cast, Valdemar quickly disabled his armor spell and leaped to his left as fast as he could. A stream of searing fire erupted from Lord Och's hands. Valdemar managed to avoid the hit, the stone wall of the vault melting where the flames touched it.

"Your strength is your weakness, my apprentice," Lord Och taunted Valdemar. The air in the room simmered from the heat. "You rely so much on summoned soldiers to the point of neglecting your physical training!"

Lord Och sustained his stream of flames, forcing his apprentice to stay on the move to escape it. Valdemar reshaped the bones of his legs for the purpose of digitigrade locomotion. The soles of his feet receded as his weight shifted to his distal and intermediate phalanges.

Like a cat, Valdemar thought as he further reshaped his bones to better improve his speed. His biomancy lessons had borne fruit. He quickly outpaced Lord Och's flames and moved swiftly enough to reach the frontier of the lich's field of vision on the left.

Striking by surprise, Valdemar severed his bladed nails and threw them at his mentor from an angle he couldn't predict. Lord Och didn't even turn his head to face them. He simply interrupted his fire spell and snapped his fingers.

A cold wind blew in the underground vault.

Valdemar watched with a shocked expression as a wall of ice rose from nowhere between teacher and apprentice. Valdemar's projectiles went halfway through before the biting cold made their blades brittle.

It wasn't a teleportation spell . . . it wasn't even a spell from the Blood. "The Cold," Valdemar whispered, astonished. "The Whitemoon . . ."

Lord Och chuckled as the wall of ice collapsed into nothingness. "My poor Valdemar, did you truly think I would limit myself to one field of magic?"

Does he have eyes on the back of his head too? Valdemar wondered in silent frustration. The Dark Lord's sensitivity to the Blood allowed him to sense attacks coming. *I can't surprise him . . . not this way at least.*

"The issue of our duel was decided before it even began, Valdemar." Lord Och joined his hands together and started making hand signs. His shadow grew darker, as black as the Light was radiant. "I am older, wiser, more experienced."

"Maybe," Valdemar admitted as he reshaped his body once again. The spikes on his shoulders turned into organic barrels. "But I'm a creative soul."

Valdemar remembered one of Lord Och's comments; that he should be careful never to leave a piece of himself unattended due to his healing factor. He hadn't fully grasped the reason for the warning, but now he did.

His consciousness was spread across all of his cells. Much like Ialdabaoth, Valdemar could become the wellspring from which new life grew.

His shoulder cannons fired bits of concentrated flesh at Lord Och. As the projectiles crossed the gap between master and apprentice, the Dark Lord's shadow rose from the ground into a three-dimensional shape. Valdemar briefly thought his teacher had summoned a Haunter, but the shadow appeared to answer Lord Och's thoughts directly. It transformed into a hundred black hands and stopped all projectiles with an unnatural agility.

Valdemar's fleshy bits revealed their true nature on impact. Tentacles burst out of them like worms gnawing their way out of a fruit. Lord Och recoiled as he found himself facing floating orbs with many eyes and mouths dripping with venom.

Although they looked like independent creatures, these monsters were nothing of the sort; they were extensions of Valdemar, fingers of a different shape. He watched through their eyes and spat through their mouths.

His creations spat acid at a surprised Lord Och. The lich's shadowy hands protected him from most projectiles, but not all. Some droplets managed to hit his ribcage and rusted his bones.

"Refined gastric acid?" Lord Och observed. "I forgot the taste so long ago . . ."

"Where is she?" Valdemar hissed as he reshaped his body back to its original, humanoid form and commanded his creations to overwhelm Lord Och. "Where is her soulstone? What have you done with it?"

"What do you think?" Lord Och's laughter echoed in the vault, cold and sinister. "I destroyed it."

Valdemar froze in shock and his creations echoed his anger. They snarled at Lord Och and attempted to flank him. Shadowy hands caught them before they could approach the lich, before tearing off jaws and eyes alike. The pain of his minions reverberated back to Valdemar through their psychic link and made his fingers tremble with rage.

"That's right, my apprentice." Lord Och smiled wickedly as lightning surged from his hands and vaporized a floating flesh orb. "I shattered her soulstone beneath my heel. I watched her spirit enter the nothing from which it came."

"Lies!" Valdemar snarled.

"It was for your own good. That woman has led you astray."

He's just trying to get a psychological edge on me, Valdemar thought. He had to ignore the lich's words and focus. For Marianne. For himself. For everyone.

While the Dark Lord was busy slaying the flesh monsters with shadows and lightning, Valdemar dropped to the cold stone floor and slammed it with his palms. He closed his eyes for a second and opened himself to the Blood, tapping into the flesh and soul of Underland. As he had suspected, with Crétail gone, he felt like a thirsty man drinking from an inexhaustible wellspring.

Valdemar's blood turned black as it poured out of his hands. A thin web of flesh and nerves spread all over the vault. It covered the stone ceiling, the cold hard floor, every spot it could touch. It would have touched the portal and the pillar of light keeping the Painted World afloat too, but the raging cosmic energies erupting from both evaporated Valdemar's blackened blood before it could get anywhere close.

By the time Lord Och got rid of the last flesh minion, the entire vault was drenched in Valdemar's blood.

Lord Och's skill at spellcasting and knowledge of magic dwarfed Valdemar's, but the half-Stranger could tap into a greater reservoir of power. He was an avatar of the Blood itself, one without any rival now that Crétail had become imprisoned in the Painted World. Whereas Lord Och could only tap into his own reserves, his student had access to the collective pool of all life-forms bound by Ialdabaoth's lineage.

The Dark Lord looked up at the vault's ceiling with a hint of concern. Valdemar's blood had changed color. From the black emerged shades of red, of purple, of blue and green. Pictures of eyes and moths decorated the dome's surface. Valdemar sensed the chaotic fabric of space slowly stabilize and bend to his will.

"A Painted Field?" the lich asked. "Good. Very good."

"I am the Red Prince of the Blood," Valdemar declared, his voice reverberating through the pigments of his soul. "Neither man nor Stranger. I belong to no realm and obey no laws. All bend to my will."

"Make me," Lord Och mocked him.

I will, Valdemar thought.

Although the portal-powered spatial anomaly made his control fragile, the sorcerer's Painted Field gave him a degree of mastery over reality within its confines. Valdemar drew upon his body's reserves and manifested blades of bones.

But instead of erupting from his forearms, they fell down from the ceiling.

No sooner did Lord Och's shadowy hands catch them that more weapons appeared all over the Painted Field's surface. Valdemar used it as an extension of his body to manifest them everywhere his pigments touched.

"Summoning bladed weapons as projectiles . . . the Pleromian's tactic," Lord Och rasped as he recognized the spell at work. "Ah, you learned more than theoretical knowledge from that creature's wayward soul."

Valdemar answered his mentor with more projectiles. Hammers of flesh, whips of sinew, and blades of bones rained down from all directions and every angle he could think of. He struck from the left and the right, from above and below. He would have teleported projectiles straight inside Lord Och's skull too if the lich's magical defenses didn't make it impossible.

The Dark Lord's shadowy hands attempted to block the attacks, but there were too many of them. A deflected projectile merged back with the Painted Field and was thrown back at the lich within seconds. Lord Och let out an annoyed sigh as his shadow coiled around him in the shape of an impenetrable orb. The flesh and bone projectiles bounced off its surface, but the lich had nowhere to run.

Valdemar couldn't afford to drag this out. The portal's energies started to swirl in the shape of a spiral. The chaotic power of the rift was slowly stabilizing into the shape of a corridor leading to the Light.

Lord Och's fire spell works by summoning minor fire elementals and immediately turning them into rifts to their home plane, Valdemar thought. But he shouldn't be able to with the spatial anomaly ongoing.

Unless . . . unless the fire elementals didn't need to fully enter the material plane. Lord Och transformed them into rifts while they were halfway through the veil between realms.

If so, then I can do the same, Valdemar thought as he raised his hands in Lord Och's direction. He telekinetically bent blood on his palms to form small summoning circles. With the right, Valdemar tried to summon a fire element; and with the left, its air counterpart.

Calling creatures from two different planes at once was extraordinarily difficult for all but the most powerful summoners, but Valdemar was overqualified.

The sorcerer sensed his summoned soldiers torn apart halfway through the veil between planes. He did not care. He focused his magic and turned the elementals into tiny rifts to their homeworlds. The summoning circles on his hands shone with overwhelming power.

The two rifts to the elemental planes opened for less than a second. That was enough. From the elemental plane of fire came a blast of searing flames as hot as the stars' burning hearts. From the elemental plane of air burst a tornado of pressurized hydrogen. Both streams merged together into a white beam of blinding radiance.

Valdemar had to strengthen his legs with the Blood to avoid being thrown backward by the spell's backlash. Lord Och, whose shadow dome had become both a carapace and a prison, could not dodge. The beam cleared his protection like a candle's flame banished the darkness, continued its way beyond, and then hit the Painted Field on the other side. A good fifth of the dome crystalized around the point of impact while the death ray continued its course through the stone beyond. A chunk of the wall collapsed.

When the energy beam's light died down, nothing but ashes remained of Lord Och.

The lich had been vaporized.

"You copied my spell."

Valdemar flinched as Lord Och's ashes pulled themselves back together. The lich's raw atoms gathered into the shape of steel bones and a ghastly skull.

"No . . . you improved it." The reborn Lord Och gave Valdemar a mock reverence. "My congratulations. You are truly worthy of standing among us Dark Lor—"

Valdemar incinerated the lich with a second iteration of his spell, and watched Lord Och reform just as swiftly with great dismay.

"It's useless," Lord Och rasped as he returned to unlife. "Your creative strength and my knowledge of magic are evenly matched, but my body is a mere projection. So long as my phylactery remains intact, I will pull myself back together. We will be locked in battle until the stars die out."

"Fine by me," Valdemar lied. He knew all too well that they wouldn't have eternity before the portal stabilized the pathway.

My Painted Field should have formed a barrier between Lord Och's body and his soul, Valdemar thought as he and the lich exchanged volleys of fire spells. Neither of them could break the other or break the stalemate. Whereas Valdemar dodged attacks well enough, Lord Och simply regenerated whenever he took damage. *So why can he recreate his body so quickly?*

Come to think of it, something was wrong with this situation. Lord Och's soul needed to pass into the Light to achieve godhood. He could only do so with his phylactery close at hand.

Is it in the room? Valdemar wondered as he scanned the area. His gaze wandered to the shining radiance at the center of the room and the truth hit him like a bullet to the head.

Back when Valdemar had examined the portal more closely, he had felt a soul inside. The sacrificed people used to power the archway had vanished into the ether, but this one had mysteriously remained behind . . .

"It's the portal," Valdemar realized. "You turned the Pleromian portal into your phylactery."

Lord Och didn't answer, but the brief flicker in his fiery eyes confirmed his apprentice's suspicions all the same. That was why the Dark Lord refused to back down. He had wagered his eternal unlife in his last bid for godhood.

Valdemar blasted his master once more and rushed at the portal. He used biomancy to stretch his left arm by more than three meters. He only had to touch the steel archway to suck Lord Och's soul from its hiding place.

His hand turned to ashes before it could make contact. Magical energy rippled from the steel to incinerate his flesh and bones.

Valdemar gritted his teeth in frustration as his hand regenerated. Lord Och's laughter echoed across the crumbling dome.

"My phylactery has more protective spells shielding it than this fortress has stones." A layer of ice stronger than the thickest steel covered the lich's bones. "Do you understand the pointlessness of your struggle now, Valdemar? The portal won't close. It will not obey your commands. Only when the veil has thinned will my soul pass through . . . with yours following, of course."

The world became cold.

"Eternity awaits us, Valdemar!"

White mist seeped from Lord Och's bones and dropped the temperature tenfold. A layer of frost covered the Painted Field. Valdemar's skin froze and turned brittle. The summoner used biomancy to increase his body's temperature, even as the water in his eyes turned to ice.

"Ktulu," a voice said from within his ribcage.

Valdemar's breath of relief turned to mist when it came out of his lungs. His familiar had recovered some of its strength within his body. His childish mind brushed against Valdemar's thoughts with a comforting presence.

"Ktulhu ftahgna," the tiny Stranger said. An idea traveled through the mental link Valdemar shared with his familiar, as clear as pure water. It is time.

"You are right." Valdemar joined his hands in prayer with Ktulu humming to itself. He ignored the chilling cold and the Light's radiance both. "There is no other way."

His familiar became a conduit between his summoner and the cosmos.

"In his dead house at the bottom of the sea," Valdemar chanted, his voice crossing the boundaries between the planes. "The old god lies dreaming . . ."

It didn't matter if Valdemar lacked the power to summon allies. The entity he contacted could reach the universe on their own, even with the spatial anomaly getting in its way. They only needed to take notice.

"That is not dead which can eternal lie," Valdemar finished his prayer, "and with strange aeons even death may die!"

Ktulu's father answered the call.

Valdemar felt his brain boil in his skull as a crushing telepathic presence overwhelmed his thoughts. A cold alien mind ripped through his mental protections as if they didn't exist.

There was no warmth nor cruelty coming from the link. The entity didn't even acknowledge Valdemar's existence. Humans were so small in comparison to its cosmic magnificence that as far as the creature was concerned, they did not even exist. Neither did it feel any affection for Ktulu. The entity didn't feel emotions the way humans did, if it all.

But it answered its spawn's prayer all the same.

Valdemar only saw a brief glimpse of the entity through the veil between worlds. A human mind would have imploded from trying to comprehend its eldritch geometry. The sorcerer's half-Stranger nature preserved his sanity, though he failed to properly process the entity's apocalyptic visage. Its form vaguely echoed that of Ktulu, but with gargantuan proportions. Its flesh existed in multiple universes at once, between the boundary of life and death.

Was it a Stranger? Or something else? This creature wasn't affiliated with Ialdabaoth, the Whitemoon, or the Silent King, yet its power rivaled their own. The entity embodied the uncaring nature of the cosmos, the apocalyptic power of gamma rays, and the inevitability of entropic annihilation. The fate of men inspired little more than apathy in its cold alien heart.

The chaotic fabric of space-time weakened further as the entity peered through the veil on the other side. Lord Och recoiled as if struck, his cold aura swept away by an invisible force. The Light's radiance dimmed as a mighty interdimensional shadow covered the room.

"You mad fool, you will destroy us both!" The mocking confidence in Lord Och's voice turned to an emotion Valdemar had never heard coming from his teacher.

Fear.

Ktulu's father was too ancient and powerful for even Valdemar to summon properly. The stars were not right for it. Only the shadow of a colossal green hand took shape in the vault, so large that the Painted World looked no bigger than a nail in comparison. The Institute trembled with its terrible manifestation.

Lord Och unleashed a mighty thunderbolt at the monstrous fingers, the electricity shining bright as the stars. Space-time curved the lightning around and dispersed it into nothingness. To Valdemar's eyes, it seemed as if the spell had lost its way through mangled angles and bent lines.

"This is the last Pleromian portal left in all of Underland!" Lord Och shouted in genuine panic. Prayer was now his last refuge. "If you destroy it, you will never reach Earth! Mankind will be condemned to languish in this ruin of a planet for all eternity!"

"I remember your lesson, my teacher," Valdemar replied. By now, he couldn't stop the entity if he wanted to. "I will bear the weight of my dream."

No one should sacrifice others for their dream, if they weren't willing to die themselves for it.

"I will find another way."

The hand of the alien god shattered the portal and switched off the Light. Dimensions collapsed with the vault's ceiling. Lord Och let out a scream of rage as space cracked and fell apart around him. Valdemar smiled as a surge of energy swallowed his world and blinded him with its radiance.

There was darkness, and then nothing.

26

FROM BEYOND

He thought, therefore he was. Even with his body blown to smithereens, even after the smallest of his cells had been vaporized, even after the cosmic Light blasted his essence, Valdemar kept thinking. He was everywhere and nowhere at all. He saw through two billion eyes and breathed through half as many mouths. He was the chittering rats hiding in the smallest tunnels and the dragons in the greatest caverns. He was the heat-force of the mitochondria and the quivering will of the eukaryotes.

He was the Blood incarnate.

Only now did Valdemar Verney truly understand Lord Och's words. That he would never die. As long as the Blood flowed, the Red Grail would return.

Ialdabaoth had stopped stirring in its sleep with Crétail's capture. The Father of All's prophet had fallen back into the darkness from which he came. The world's awakening had been delayed, the day was won.

Ialdabaoth would not sleep forever. Its slumber would last for decades, perhaps centuries, but the Stranger would stir again. Its dreams would call to the madmen and the weak-willed to begin the cycle anew.

And the Father of All would find its rebel son opposing it once again.

The Blood breathed life into Valdemar once again. His atoms gathered. His cells multiplied. His flesh drew nourishment from all life in Underland until he recovered from complete annihilation.

His eyes opened to the sight of Paraplex's stone ceiling. More than four layers of stone had separated Lord Och's vault from the top of his fortress not too long ago. All of them had collapsed. A mighty fist had punched through all of them on its way to the Institute's basement.

Skin covered Valdemar's raw flesh, rebuilding his ears, his lips, and eyelids. His legs carried him atop a pile of rocks and shattered stones. Only rubble remained of the ancient ruins buried underneath the Institute. The vault had collapsed atop the annihilated portal, laying the Pleromian's sinister legacy to rest.

"Ktulu."

Ktulu hopped on Valdemar's back and held onto his shoulders. Though the wounds the familiar had taken from Lord Och hadn't yet healed, he had somehow been spared from the annihilation that befell the fortress.

The Painted World had survived too. The eldritch painting was half-buried in stones near Valdemar, but intact. The Silent King's ritual had made it nearly indestructible to the point that even a fellow Stranger couldn't destroy it. Valdemar let out a breath of relief. His brother and Hermann's legacy would survive.

"Ktulu pflalayal gna," the tiny Stranger declared with a hint of pride.

My dad is stronger than yours, Valdemar translated. The bond between summoner and familiar had grown stronger and deeper with each ordeal. With trust came understanding.

Ktulu's father was nowhere to be seen. The deity's divine fist had struck Underland hard enough to shake it to the core and left just as swiftly. The stars needed to make way for its arrival; a true, proper summoning would have had apocalyptic consequences. Where did this entity come from? What was its purpose?

Even after I learned so much, Valdemar thought, *there are still so many mysteries to uncover.*

"What's happening . . ."

Valdemar turned at the voice's source and faced his teacher one last time.

Lord Och had crawled out of the rubble too, but didn't recover from the portal's destruction like his student. His steel bones rusted in the equivalent of years in mere seconds. His legs had partly crumbled and forced him to kneel.

"My soul . . . cries out . . ." Lord Och rasped. One of his ribs fell and turned to dust before hitting the ground. "My mind . . . slipping away . . . my contingencies . . . can't sense . . ."

"A god of immense power struck the seat of your soul, Lord Och," Valdemar said. All the lich's contingency plans couldn't cover such an extreme scenario. "I can't even feel it anymore."

Valdemar couldn't save the lich's unlife, even if he wanted to. The force animating his old bones was no more than a psychic echo left after the phylactery's destruction. It would fade away within minutes.

Death had caught up to Och, Dark Lord of Paraplex and archmage extraordinaire.

In spite of all the lich had done, to watch his agony filled Valdemar with sorrow. More than a Dark Lord, Och was the heir of the old world, one of the last witnesses of a time when light shone on Underland. How many memories would fade away with him? How much knowledge would be lost?

Lord Och's demise felt akin to the destruction of his portal. In spite of the evil legacy it carried, the monument's absence would diminish the world. Men would never see anything like this again.

"Am I . . . dying . . . at last? This is frightening . . . the dark . . ." The fires in Lord Och's eyes flickered like candles threatening to die out. "Where . . . will I go, Valdemar?"

Valdemar bit his lower lip. He wanted to comfort the Dark Lord in his last moments, but he also respected him too much to lie. "I do not know."

Neither to Ialdabaoth nor the Light, he suspected. Lord Och's soul would wander into the darkness beyond the veil of death. No Stranger would welcome him. The cold gaze Ktulu sent to the lich told Valdemar as much.

Lord Och would die as he lived: alone.

The same thought seemed to cross the lich's mind in his final moments. "You cruel child . . . we could have ascended to the Light . . . and now you condemned us both to eternal darkness . . ."

"It wasn't worth the price."

"You will live . . . to regret your choice," Lord Och rasped. His mouth coughed out dust. "Human greed is . . . eternal. Mortals will disappoint you in time . . . all of them."

Valdemar sensed something moist running down his cheek.

The lich looked at him with a puzzled expression. "Are you . . . crying?"

"Yes, for you!" Valdemar wiped away his tears, his voice brimming with anger. "The Light be damned, you had so much knowledge, so much wisdom! We could have reached Earth together, saved mankind! You had everything and you threw it all away!"

Valdemar's fists clenched in rage. In spite of the Dark Lord's sins and cruelty, his apprentice had truly admired him. His demise felt like a personal loss for himself and all of humankind.

The lich listened in silence before laughing at his apprentice's face. "I am a Dark Lord, my foolish disciple . . . I am beyond regrets, beyond sorrow . . . if you do not understand yet . . . then I taught you nothing . . ."

"You taught me well. You taught me to stand up for my beliefs."

"Then . . . mayhap you will succeed in a few more centuries . . . once you walk the same road I did . . ." Lord Och let out a cough of dust. "Remember what awaits you . . . at the threshold . . ."

The lich's left shoulder gave out and he threatened to fall on his face. Valdemar moved to catch him without thinking and held him in his arms. The Dark Lord was so brittle that some of his bones cracked when his fingers touched them.

Valdemar used his psychic sight to examine the lich. He wondered if he could preserve anything of his personality, however doomed the effort, but all he found were dying embers beyond saving.

"Are you still trying to save me . . ." The light in Lord Och's right eye died out, leaving only one. "After all I've done . . . to you?"

"Someone has to try," Valdemar replied softly. "You can't become a better person if you're dead."

"You would give a chance . . . even to the likes of me? Even after I slew Hermann . . . and that woman?"

Valdemar grit his teeth briefly. "I cannot forgive it," he admitted. "But when I offered you a chance to turn back before our battle, you hesitated. You were not lost forever."

Something Valdemar couldn't say about the likes of Blutgang and Shelley.

"If I was willing to offer you another chance back then, why wouldn't I give you one now?" Valdemar asked. "As long as a small star shines in the night, it must be preserved and nurtured. Or else there will only be darkness left."

Valdemar expected his master to spit in his face and mock his naïveté one last time. To his surprise, his words seemed to strike a chord with the Dark Lord. He had no more bitter jabs to offer, no rebuke about the inherent cruelty of humankind.

"Maybe you won't become . . . like me . . ." Lord Och rasped. "After all." If anything, he looked strangely serene. "Yes, perhaps it is I . . . who learned so little . . . of the two of us . . . I was the true fool . . ." A mirthless chuckle came out of Lord Och's mouth as the last of his bones fell apart. "I looked for the light everywhere . . . except within myself."

Such were Lord Och's last words as he crumbled to dust in his student's arms.

Time caught up to the lich with accrued interest. His skull turned to sand as it hit the stones. The magic that had animated Lord Och for centuries ground him back into raw atoms and then nothing.

"Farewell, my teacher," Valdemar whispered.

Death's silence answered his words.

I can't hear the battle, Valdemar thought as he looked up at the ceiling. *It must be over.*

No way the Dark Lords hadn't noticed the destruction. Valdemar would have some explaining to do soon.

"Ktulu," his familiar hissed. "Maryannu!"

Valdemar's blood froze in his veins. Marianne. Her corpse had been left to rot in the open.

Briefly forgetting the Painted World and his own nakedness, Valdemar extended his arms all the way to the Institute's ground floor and lifted himself up. It didn't take him long to find Marianne's remains in the courtyard, right next to Hermann's corpse.

Lord Och hadn't even bothered to cover his tracks.

I will bury you both, Valdemar swore to the corpses. He knelt next to Marianne's remains first; her pale skin had taken on an ashen shade as pallor mortis set in.

She looked asleep at first glance, but when Valdemar held her in his arms, he couldn't deny the truth. His partner, his sword, felt cold as ice to the touch.

Did you suffer? Valdemar thought grimly. *Did you die in despair thinking Lord Och would kill me next? Or did you believe I would prevail to the bitter end?*

What he would have given up to hear her voice answer him . . .

No, Valdemar, focus, the summoner thought as his hand moved to Marianne's neck. You can't give up yet. Even if Lord Och smashed her soulstone, perhaps you can salvage something out of it.

He had recreated an echo of his grandfather from a journal. With the fragment of a soulstone, he could do the same with Marianne. It wouldn't be her, not truly, but at least he would keep a memento from his lover.

Valdemar's eyes widened. His fingers had closed on a black stone whose surface felt as warm as Marianne's skin was cold. The soulstone was intact.

Valdemar's eyes widened in shock as he realized that Lord Och had lied. He hadn't destroyed Marianne's soulstone, perhaps out of neglect . . . or maybe out of respect.

"That cold-hearted bastard . . ." Valdemar whispered. "Toying with my feelings even after death . . ."

His despair turned to hope as he seized the soulstone. Marianne's vibrant spirit remained alive within it, awaiting a new vessel in which she would take root again.

"Soon," Valdemar promised as he put a hand on her corpse's forehead. Marianne's muscles had started to stiffen, but most of her cells were intact. The rot hadn't set in. "Soon."

Valdemar applied the soulstone to Marianne's neck and went to work.

Death felt like a dream. Pale colors, incomplete images, and indistinct sounds littered Marianne's mind. She walked alone through the wasteland of her past. Pictures rose from a sea of darkness at random. Her family's mansion crumbled under its own weight. Indistinct shadows walked past her while wearing her parents' clothes. A flock of bats shifted into the shape of Bertrand. A rusted needle oozed blood as Lord Bethor's grim visage looked on from above. A portrait reflected a blurred vision of Valdemar's face, his smile turning into a bloody grin when Marianne approached it.

Was this place her afterlife? A desolate museum of stillborn thoughts?

Marianne had heard that souls kept in an individual soulstone slept quietly, whereas those sharing a common Reliquary melted together in a sea of knowledge and memories. Lord Och might have snuffed her life out before the soulstone could catch her, but this place didn't look like the Outer Darkness. Marianne didn't suffer and the memories didn't torment her. No Qlippoth haunted her steps.

She would find neither joy nor sorrow here.

Marianne's steps carried her to one last ghastly vision; that of a steel spike impaling a well-dressed corpse through the throat. A layer of pale white skin covered the victim's eyes and mouth, hiding their visage. As for the spike, it looked suspiciously like her rapier's tip.

Marianne gathered her breath, although no air came in or out of her lungs. "Is that you, Jérôme?"

The figure's head slowly turned in her direction. "Do you remember my face?" the faceless man asked with a voice Marianne did not recognize and without a mouth to speak with. "Do you remember the scent of my blood? Or have you forgotten?"

"No, I have not." Marianne would never forget. "I only wanted to let go."

The faceless man dangled from the soulsteel spike, pale blood dripping from his wound. Marianne found his silence unbearable.

"Do you hate me?" she asked softly.

"The dead do not feel regret or anger. The dead do not feel anything at all." The figure pointed at the darkness surrounding them with a crooked arm. "Death is *nothingness*."

A chill went down Marianne's spine. Her fear turned to confusion as her eyes lingered on other half-formed memories. "Does their presence mean that I still live?"

The faceless man's head tilted to the side and revealed the festering flesh beneath his wound. "Do you want to?"

"Yes, of course I want to live. Nobody wishes for death." Marianne ground her jaw when she looked up at her former lover. "Did you? Is that why you didn't wear your soulstone?"

"Does it matter what I want? What happened, happened."

"I need an answer. To find closure."

"You will find none in death. Life is a road that always ends before its time."

"You aren't really here, are you?" Marianne wondered if it was her mind's way of telling her that she would never find the answers to some questions . . . and that she would have to make her own. "Do you even exist?"

"I do," the ghost of her past replied, "so long as you remember me."

Marianne smiled as light cleared the darkness of her mind. "I can live with that."

A ray of light forced its way through her eyelids. A sense of numbness overtook her body to the point that she couldn't sense her own fingers. Something filled her nose and slowed down her heartbeat.

Even as her eyes slowly started to distinguish colors and forms, Marianne struggled not to fall back into sleep. Had someone cast a dizzying spell on her? Her head was resting against something warm and soft, under the shadow of a man.

"Do not move." It took Marianne a few seconds to recognize Valdemar's voice. "It will take a few minutes before your heart cleans out the accumulated toxins."

Toxins? Marianne's skull felt heavy like a stone. Her head hurt and half her thoughts came to an abrupt end before she could utter them. "Am I . . ."

"Dead?" Marianne's vision stabilized until she could see her lover's smile. Valdemar looked beaten and exhausted, but alive. Wonderfully alive. "You were."

And he brought her back.

"You are naked," Marianne noticed. It sounded stupid even to herself, but she struggled to form a better thought.

"I am," Valdemar said with a chuckle. Marianne felt his fingers close on her left hand. Had his touch ever felt so warm?

"Ktulu," his small familiar said while peeping over his shoulder. "Ktulhu!"

My head is resting on his lap, Marianne realized. She could have stayed there for hours, but the memory of Lord Och murdering Hermann brutally brought her back to reality. "Where . . . where is he? Lord Och?"

"That is a question," Empress Aratra's voice cut through the discussion, "I would like to hear the answer to."

Marianne struggled to raise her head.

The six remaining Dark Lords had formed a circle around her and Valdemar. Lord Bethor rode on his dragon's back, while Empress Aratra, not to be outdone, stood with dignity atop a tall pile of dead Qlippoths. Lady Phul kept her wings folded over her chest, her expression guarded. Lord Hagith kept his hands behind his back next to the frowning Phaleg. Last but not least, Lord Ophiel examined Valdemar's naked chest before shaking his head.

"Disappointing," Marianne heard the androgynous Dark Lord mutter under their breath. "Deeply disappointing."

Have they always been here? Marianne wondered. Her diminished state prevented her from tapping into her enhanced senses. She struggled to rise up to her feet, to protect Valdemar from them, but her body refused to obey her. Her lover didn't look in a good enough shape to put up a fight either. *We're at their mercy . . .*

"The Blood cried out for minutes," Empress Aratra said with squinting eyes. "Space and time floundered."

Lord Ophiel scoffed. "All of Underland must have felt it."

"I told you that the lich was plotting something," Phaleg the Binder raged as blisters grew on his inhuman arm. "Where is he?"

"He's gone," Valdemar replied calmly. "I killed him."

My hearing hasn't recovered, Marianne thought. *My ears deceive me.*

Valdemar's serious expression made her doubt.

Lord Ophiel laughed in response and Phaleg the Binder scoffed with disdain. But Empress Aratra remained eerily silent, as did Lord Bethor.

He's not lying, Marianne realized in shock. Her lover's hand was firm and untroubled. *He destroyed Lord Och.*

So foreign was the thought that, although Marianne had complete faith in Valdemar, she still struggled to believe him. Lord Och was older than the empire itself, a mage of tremendous power. He had snuffed out Marianne's life with a snap of his fingers. She knew Valdemar could have prevailed in battle against the lich, but to *destroy* him?

"How?" Lord Bethor asked Valdemar, a hint of sorrow in the Dark Lord's voice. The fact he didn't deny his former teacher's demise made his colleagues suddenly anxious.

"I summoned a Stranger to destroy his phylactery," Valdemar replied. His familiar wagged his tentacles on his shoulder.

Lord Bethor pressed for details. "Was it the Nahemoth? Was that your plan from the start?"

Valdemar looked uneasy at revealing this information. "Hermann . . . Hermann and I succeeded in creating the Painted World."

"But it wasn't the Nahemoth that you used," Lord Bethor guessed. "You called *another.*"

Valdemar nodded slowly. Lord Bethor's dragon hunched beneath his silent master, as if echoing his thoughts.

"It was meant to be," was all Lord Bethor said. He sounded as if he had expected this outcome from the start.

Of all the Dark Lords present, Phaleg the Binder looked to be the most in denial. "You can't imply—"

"Young Valdemar speaks the truth." All eyes turned to Empress Aratra. The mistress of Azlant showed no emotion. A stony expression and a monotone voice hid her feelings from her fellow Dark Lords. "I do not feel Och's presence in the Blood anymore. His soul has departed Underland."

"The apprentice surpassed the teacher," Lord Bethor declared. To Marianne's surprise, she sensed a hint of respect in his voice. The Dark Lord of Sabaoth mourned his fallen master, but he *revered* his slayer as a fellow exemplar of strength.

Silence ruled among the Dark Lords as they considered the news and its implications. Lord Ophiel was the first to speak up, his mocking nonchalance turned to astonishment. "My, my, I never thought I would live to see the old man kick the bucket for good."

"This is a trick," Phaleg the Binder rasped with paranoia. "A ploy. Och is faking death to strike us later when we least expect it."

Lord Hagith observed Valdemar and Marianne with a calculating gaze. The noblewoman had caught him gazing at Hermann's corpse before. No doubt he had drawn his own conclusions from the scene. "Why did you do it?" he asked. "For the sake of vengeance?"

Valdemar shook his head. "I did it to save us all. He would have destroyed this Domain otherwise, maybe even the world."

"No doubt, no doubt," Lord Ophiel replied with a tone that implied the opposite. "I'm sure it was nothing personal and that you didn't expect any reward from it."

"Does it matter why he did it?" Lady Phul asked. "The fact remains that Paraplex is short a Dark Lord and ripe for the taking."

"It is not," Lord Bethor replied sharply.

Does he intend to claim Paraplex for himself? Marianne wondered. She didn't need her enhanced senses to notice the cautious glances the Dark Lords exchanged or the invisible tension in the air. For a brief moment, Marianne expected a war over Lord Och's territory to start before her very eyes.

At least, until she noticed the sly smirk forming on Empress Aratra's lips.

"Very well, *Lord* Valdemar," Empress Aratra declared, putting emphasis "Lord." "I expect you to put your Domain in order before our next meeting. Cleaning Paraplex of Qlippoths should be your first priority."

Marianne glanced at her lover and watched him blink twice in a row. Valdemar had heard, but he didn't understand.

"I'm sorry?" he asked.

"Do not be so surprised, Valdemar." Lord Bethor crossed his arms, fiery sparks dancing in his crimson eyes. "Power shifts quickly in our brotherhood."

"Ah, I see where this is going." Lady Phul's fingers crossed beneath her chin. "Yes, it would neatly solve our problem. We can't afford a civil war right now."

"I wouldn't mind one," Lord Ophiel said. "But it would taste bland without a few rounds of cloak-and-dagger first. Intrigue is my salt and pepper."

"I do not understand," Valdemar said with a tone that implied otherwise.

You do, but you can't believe it, Marianne thought. She would have scarcely believed it herself a few months ago, before Valdemar had earned her faith.

Lord Hagith seemed to find her lover's obliviousness amusing. "Lord Och appointed you as his successor, did he not? You should know this famous necromancer proverb: you kill it, you keep it."

Only Phaleg the Binder seemed to take issue with the situation. "You want to hand Paraplex to him? A half-breed Stranger?"

"That leaves him with a good half," Lady Phul quipped.

"He destroyed the old bag of bones, which means he's overqualified," Lord Ophiel replied. "Unless you want to take him on for the post? Please tell me you will. I welcome a good laugh."

Lord Phaleg's anger turned to cold calculation as he examined Valdemar. Marianne's free hand fumbled to her side until she somehow found her rapier's handle. *Try it,* she dared him mentally.

He did not. When faced with the unknown, Phaleg the Binder opted for caution. "Fine."

"As expected," Lord Ophiel replied with a dismissive tone. "You could never defeat your teacher, how can you hope to prevail against his killer?"

Lord Phaleg ignored the jab, his teeth grinding so loudly that Marianne wondered if they would crack. "This is a trick," he said. "Och can't be dead. It's all a smokescreen of some kind."

Marianne could tell he would never truly believe in his old master's demise. Not that it surprised her. Liches were infamous for returning from the dead and Lord Och had tormented his former apprentice for many years. It would be years before Phaleg the Binder would accept the truth; perhaps even centuries.

"Even if Lord Och were to return one day, someone must keep the house in his absence." Empress Aratra waved her hand dismissively. "Lord Valdemar has proven himself a true friend of mankind and a powerful mage. My decision is irrevocable."

Lord Bethor nodded in agreement, settling the matter.

Valdemar's fingers trembled between Marianne's own. She squeezed his hand tighter to comfort him. Marianne felt her lover relax at her contact and the silent message she had sent him.

No matter what the future held, they would face it together.

EPILOGUE

Hermann's art gallery was in his life's image: odd, modern, and transgressive. Although Valdemar had visited his friend's workshop many times, he had only seen a glimpse of his collection. Hermann had spent years perfecting his art and had experimented with many styles. Realistic representations of animals and flowers shared a wall with paintings of alien landscapes or strange geometric forms. Valdemar's acute eyes detected the slow, incremental improvements of Hermann's skills with each painting. Over the years, the troglodyte had moved away from the realistic to capturing the abstract, transcending the physical to embrace the spiritual.

"That's all of them, Valdy," said Liliane. Valdemar had taken her as an administrative assistant to help him with his mind-numbing workload, and he had yet to see the witch without a pile of documents in her hands. She didn't seem to mind helping him out on top of her regular duties. "How do you find them?"

"Good." Valdemar's hand trailed against a landscape representation of the Silent King's patchwork world. The paint was still fresh. *Hermann must have completed it a mere few weeks before his death,* Valdemar thought. *What else did he have in mind?*

"Iren said we should sell them to fund the wall repairs," Liliane said with a frown. "But he's a heartless dummy and we should ignore him."

On paper, Iren's proposal made sense. The Pleroma Institute had taken heavy damage from the Qlippoth incursion, though not as much as the city around it. Valdemar would never bring himself to sell away

Hermann's works, but he was in desperate need of money in the short term. The late Lord Och had put so many magical traps protecting his fortune and war chests that his successor struggled to access them.

You always hoarded things for greed's sake, my teacher, Valdemar thought. The Institute's vaults overflowed with knowledge, riches, and resources that had never seen the light of day. Valdemar aimed to change that. If the Institute was to become a beacon of enlightenment across the empire, then its discoveries should benefit all of mankind.

One of Valdemar's first changes in policy had been to promise universal magical healthcare and post-mortem necromancy treatment to the Domain's inhabitants. The summoner remembered all too well his mother's death from lack of proper treatment. How many families would face similar tragedies in the coming days?

Valdemar had never asked to become a Dark Lord, but he would make full use of the position to implement positive changes. Scholars working at the Institute would have the obligation to dedicate some days of their week to cure the sick. Restrictions on magic would be simplified so that aspiring innovators like Valdemar himself would always find a safe abode in Paraplex. Nobles and commoners would be equal before the law.

Of course, his proposed changes had made some grumble; but Valdemar faced little open opposition overall. Lord Och had publicly taken Valdemar as an apprentice, appointed him as his successor at the Sabbath, and had fallen at his hand. Nobody had expected the old lich to perish, but the power transition had been as smooth as it could have been.

Fear helped too. No one wanted to defy the half-Stranger Dark Lord who had slain his predecessor in battle.

Valdemar wondered how long this respite would last. The Dark Lords were a scheming lot, always on the lookout to weaken each other. Lord Ophiel had all but openly declared he would plot against Valdemar, and Phaleg the Binder would always consider Valdemar a puppet of the late Lord Och. Both would try to destroy him.

Lord Bethor was the only Dark Lord Valdemar considered somewhat of an ally, largely because the man was utterly uninterested in political bickering. Iren suggested he ally with moderates like Lady Phul and Lord Hagith, while placating Empress Aratra, which would take valuable time.

Valdemar had better things to do than managing people's egos, but it looked like a core part of his new job.

The summoner stepped in front of Hermann's last creation: a self-portrait. The pictomancer had painted himself hard at work on a canvas with his back turned on the viewer. Hermann's representation had painted a picture of Valdemar and Liliane, themselves holding a smaller portrait of the troglodyte. Valdemar found the result quite dizzying to look at . . . and touching too.

Liliane gulped at the sight. "I'll miss him."

"I already do," Valdemar replied with a sigh. Hermann's corpse remained in cold storage until they could return him to his people. Valdemar didn't have the heart to make a mindless undead out of his dearest friend, but he had no idea how troglodytes took care of their dead. "So much."

Lord Och would have mocked his apprentice for caring about someone he had met only a few months ago, but Valdemar and Hermann had gone through a lot together. They had learned pictomancy, fought derros in Astaphanos, opened a portal to an alien world, and visited a god. Without Hermann, Crétail would have rampaged across Paraplex and awakened Ialdabaoth from its slumber.

All of Underland owed the troglodyte much.

"I'm passing new laws about your people," Valdemar told the portrait. "Troglodytes will enjoy equal rights to humans within the Domain of Paraplex and receive exclusive access to the Painted World to settle in it. Your people will have their new homeland, I promise. I'll protect it with my life."

Hermann believed that his people and humans could never coexist for long, but Valdemar was determined to prove him wrong. If the two of them could become friends, then why not their species? All that troglodytes and humans needed to live in peace was for someone to make the first step.

"Was that what you wanted?" Valdemar asked. "Are you happy, Hermann?"

The painted troglodyte looked over his shoulder, his piercing eyes staring straight at Valdemar. "I am, my friend."

Valdemar heard Liliane drop her papers on the floor in surprise. The Dark Lord immediately activated his psychic sight. He quickly detected the magic suffusing the pigments and the soul slumbering in the canvas.

"No way," Valdemar whispered, astonished. "It's not an echo . . ."

"Hermann?" Liliane put her hands on her mouth. "Hermann, is that . . . is that you?"

The painted troglodyte nodded, his reptilian lips pursing into a smile. "I told you pictomancy could capture a soul upon death."

"You expected to die creating the Painted World," Valdemar guessed, his voice breaking. His fingers trailed against the pigments. "No . . . the painting feels older than that."

"I completed my soul-catching portrait a long time ago." Hermann spoke clearly and without a stutter, perhaps because the soul used magic rather than underdeveloped vocal cords. He pointed a claw at his portrait-within-the-portrait. "Your picture and Liliane's were recent additions. I didn't have time to make a full portrait for each of you. I couldn't even include Iren."

Hermann had modified his soul's abode to house his friends' spirits if the worst came to pass.

"You . . . you scaled dick!" Liliane's shock and happiness swiftly turned to anger. "We thought you were dead!"

"He was," Valdemar replied as he wiped a tear from his face. How relieving it felt, to enjoy a good surprise after so many hardships . . .

"I'm sorry, Liliane," Hermann replied with a contrite expression. "I thought the fewer people knew about this painting, the better. Too many mind readers could have spread the word."

You knew it, my teacher, Valdemar thought. The lich had killed Hermann but left his painted phylactery intact. Did you spare him because you lacked time to cover your tracks? Or because you wanted to give Hermann a chance to survive in case you failed to reach the Light?

"Do you understand what this means, Hermann?" Valdemar asked. "With your body in storage, I can bring you back to life after restoring it. Give me a week and you'll return to us in flesh and blood."

"I would be thankful. Life as a painting is not what I imagined." The troglodyte sighed. "It took me hours to figure out how to move my head. Now it's stuck."

"Why did you paint yourself with your back turned?" Liliane asked with a sly grin. "It looks silly."

Hermann looked quite embarrassed. "For the depth, Liliane," he said. "For the depth."

An investigator's job was never done.

"Milady, you'll be pleased to learn that the spy in our midst has been disposed of," Bertrand said as he gave Marianne his report.

"He confessed under questioning that his employer came from the Domain of Alogi," Iren added. "We've got nothing to implicate Lord Ophiel yet, but I would bet my hand on his involvement."

Barely three days had passed since the Qlippoth incursion and the knives were already out. "We need to increase background checks at the Earthmouths and have animancers survey the streets," Marianne decided. "Once we open the borders again, moles and opportunists will slip through the cracks."

"Leave it to me," Iren said with a smirk. "I smell lies like cheese."

Valdemar had little talent for intrigue. The sorcerer preferred to focus on the bigger picture and magical research, leaving Marianne to pick up the slack.

"I also have grave news from the Moonshield defenders," Bertrand added with a flat tone. The vampire had slipped back into his old duties and taken up his new ones with gusto. "The mages surveying the White-moon identified a change in its orbit with the Nightwalker's capture."

Marianne tensed up. "Is it falling toward the surface?"

"Thankfully not," Bertrand replied to his mistress's relief. "However, the change in orbit could have a geological impact on Underland and affect the behavior of monsters on the surface. We can expect more incursions in the future."

"We should survey Nightwalker cults too," Iren suggested. "Since they're so keen on transforming themselves into surface monsters, one of them might summon a new Nightwalker."

"We also have to be on the lookout for derro infiltrators," Marianne said. Otto Blutgang would no doubt seek vengeance against Valdemar for wrecking his facility. "We have too many foes and too few resources."

"Last I heard, it's called governing." Iren made a bow. "Don't worry, we'll manage. We're used to the impossible."

We have dangerous foes, true, but many true friends too, Marianne thought. "I will tell Valdemar to allocate Knights of the Tome to your intelligence service."

"You mean the Dark Lord?" Iren chuckled. "The dread master of Paraplex?"

Marianne couldn't help but smile. "I will inform Lord Valdemar of the respect you showed him."

"I would rather that you don't, or the praise might go to his head." The doppelganger gave Marianne an insolent wink before taking his leave.

After Iren left, Marianne raised an eyebrow at Bertrand. "I'm surprised by your quietness."

"Milady?"

"You don't have anything bad to say about Valdemar." Marianne had expected her retainer to show more defensiveness at seeing his mistress date someone other than Jérôme, let alone share a bed with him. "When we began investigating him, you suspected him of foul treachery."

"Milady, I disliked the man for his suspected inhuman allegiances and criminal past. He has saved my life, this Domain, and perhaps the entire world." Bertrand smiled, thinly. "When facts change, I alter my conclusions."

"I'm glad to hear it." Bertrand was Marianne's closest friend, so she wanted him and Valdemar to get along.

"Besides, Milady, my only desire is to make you happy." Bertrand crossed his arms. "Lord Valdemar makes you smile. As far as I am concerned, that's all that matters."

"Thank you, Bertrand, your support means the world to me." Marianne chuckled as an amusing thought crossed her mind. "Perhaps you could find a tea brand that Valdemar would like? I've found myself struggling to convert him."

"Is Milady giving me a challenge?" Bertrand straightened up like a soldier marching to war. "I shall see it done."

Marianne chuckled. "I've missed you greatly, my friend."

She remembered one of Lady Mathilde's sermons from when she attended the church's mass. *What life takes, sometimes the Light gives back.*

After leaving Bertrand to his own devices, Marianne moved to the Hall of Rituals with a dusty notebook under her arm. The underground room's magical defenses had shielded it from the worst of the invasion and made it the perfect resting place for the Painted World.

As expected, Marianne found Valdemar there alongside his familiar. *He looks so tired,* Marianne thought. Her lover hid his gauntness beneath the same scholarly robe he had worn as a student of Lord Och. His new post hadn't led to any improvement in his wardrobe. His eyes were blackened by sleeplessness. *He needs to rest.*

The new Dark Lord had hung his grandfather's portrait opposite the Painted World. Pierre Dumont's image gazed at the magical painting, his eyes wide open and unblinking. His expression was one of rapturous joy.

Ktulu waved a hand at Marianne as she joined them without a word. *He has grown a few centimeters since yesterday,* the noblewoman noticed. Marianne knew nothing about Ktulu's life cycle, but it still surprised her a bit. *I wonder how tall his species can get?*

"I wanted him to see the sun he missed so much," Valdemar said, looking up at his grandfather's image. The echo of Pierre Dumont didn't react at all. "It worked too well. I think watching the Painted World triggered a cognitive loop of some kind."

"Did you forgive him?" Marianne asked. The kind gesture implied as much.

"I . . . I think I did?" Valdemar sounded unsure. "I feel . . . ambivalent, I guess? He was a desperate man who made terrible decisions and did his best to make up for them. He did evil and good in equal measures."

"Most people do. Saints and monsters are few in number."

"I know. I guess I need more time to process everything, to make peace with the past." Valdemar turned away from his grandfather to face Marianne. "How are you holding up?"

"Alright," she replied with a forced smile. "Whenever I think I can catch up to my workload, more problems spring up from nowhere."

"You don't say. I'm starting to understand why Lord Och wanted to dump it all." Valdemar glanced at Marianne's book. "What's that? More papers for me to sign?"

"Notes I obtained from Frigga," Marianne replied. "I think you will enjoy reading them."

"I doubt that." Valdemar snorted. "What is that opportunist up to?"

"Obviously, she wants to earn your favor." *Typical dokkar,* Marianne thought. "But I please ask you to keep an open mind. This concerns Earth."

Valdemar frowned. "Go on."

Marianne knew she had all of his attention. "Have you used a dokkar dream catcher?"

"Not quite, but Frigga suggested that I take one."

"As I told you before, Lord Och's first appearance in official records involved him warring against the dokkars as an independent warlord. Now that you've granted me full access to the forbidden archives, I could look more deeply into it."

"And what did you find?"

"Lord Och raided the dokkars to steal their artifacts for his personal use. One of them was the earliest dream catcher." Time to drop the bomb.

"He couldn't match its component with any material found in Underland." She had his full attention now.

"So the reason Lord Och took in Frigga as an exchange student—"

"Was to make use of her oneiromancy expertise to identify the dream catcher's origins." Marianne gathered her breath. "Brace yourself, Valdemar. According to Lord Och's research, dokkars didn't invent dream catchers. Humans did. In fact, the dokkar term for dream catcher doesn't match any linguistic root found in any known civilization. They borrowed the word from another language."

"So a lost human tribe invented dream catchers?" Valdemar's eyes widened. He had caught on. "Unless . . ."

"An item made of a material unknown in Underland, named in a language that does not exist." Marianne smiled warmly. "This case sounds suspiciously similar to your journal, don't you think?"

Valdemar looked at the notebook with a newfound interest. His eyes shone with burning curiosity, and a little bit of hope.

"Lord Och's raid happened long after the Pleromians fled Underland and before the derros developed portal technology," he whispered. "We know humans exist on both Earth and Underland, probably because they crossed over from one to the other at some point . . ."

"I suspect that the Pleromians didn't develop their portals from nothing," Marianne said with a nod. "Rather, they probably took inspiration from a periodic or magical phenomenon of some kind."

"There could be another portal out there, unrelated to the Pleromians." Valdemar's jaw tightened with fury. "Och knew . . . That bastard, he knew there might have been another to reach Earth and he kept it hidden."

"He wanted to destroy you, to corrupt you." Marianne would never forget Valdemar's expression that night after he confronted Och: that of a man nearly ready to give up on everything. "He tested your resolve and failed."

"Narrowly," Valdemar replied with a sigh. "I believed him, Marianne. For a moment, I truly thought sacrificing people to the Pleromian portal was the only remaining solution on the table to fulfill my dream."

"But you listened to me. You remembered that in the absence of options, you could create another."

"Because of you, yes." Valdemar's hand brushed against the book's cover. "You reminded me that we have barely scratched the surface of this world's mysteries."

"Indeed," Marianne replied with a warm smile. "Lord Och excluded options out of nihilism, but we can learn from his mistakes. We can rise above his shadow and offer mankind a better future. We will find Earth together."

Their journey had only begun.

"Together..." Valdemar's frustrated expression turned into a smile of optimism. "Thank you, Marianne. For everything."

"Pfwagana!" Ktulu grabbed his summoner's robe and instantly pointed at Marianne. "Pfwagana dayom!"

He's so adorable, Marianne thought, resisting the urge to pet the little squid. "What is Ktulu saying?"

"That I should kiss you for your good work," Valdemar replied with a chuckle.

Marianne burst out laughing. "I wouldn't mind."

Valdemar took her at her word. His lips closed the gap with Marianne's own, warm and soft to the touch. It was an innocent kiss, short but intense. It sent shivers down Marianne's spine and made her hungry for more.

"Here is not the place, Valdemar," Marianne said coyly as she broke the kiss. "Your grandfather is watching."

He took her hand into his own and held it tightly. "Do you want to see the sun, Marianne Reynard?"

Marianne's heart skipped a beat as they turned to the Painted World. "Are you sure? Nobody has crossed into it yet, and I thought it was exclusive to the troglodytes."

"Hermann agreed to make an exception for his friends," Valdemar replied, his familiar hopping behind the couple with impatience. "Will you come with me?"

Did he even have to ask? "Anywhere you go, I will follow."

The couple held hands and walked into the Painted World. They crossed the pigments like a water veil, space bending around them as they did so. Marianne's enhanced senses immediately picked up the small shifts in temperature and air pressure. New and familiar sounds echoed where the Hall of Rituals had been silent as a tomb.

Water, Marianne thought. Waves on a shore. Rays of light blinded her. Marianne put her hand over her face until her eyes could acclimate to the change in luminosity. Her feet landed on what felt like soft sand beneath her heels. The air was warmer, softer, purer than anything Marianne had ever breathed. No stone dust found its way into her lungs. An invisible force brushed against her cheeks, strange yet comforting.

"The wind," Valdemar whispered at her side. "It is so warm."

Marianne lowered her hand as her eyes started to distinguish forms and colors. As she suspected, she and Valdemar had indeed walked onto a beach of orange sand next to a vast blue sea. Where the Lightless Ocean had looked gloomy and foreboding, this one filled Marianne with a sense of wonder. Her enhanced eyes noticed a colossal tree on the horizon. Its bark was white as chalk, its leaves a pale shade of crimson.

It was unlike any plant Marianne had ever seen. Its size was dizzying to see. Lord Bethor's tower would have looked like a needle while standing next to this majestic tree.

"It's a mirage," Marianne said in disbelief. "No cavern's ceiling could house something so huge."

"Marianne, there is no ceiling," Valdemar replied softly.

The words rang in Marianne's mind like an impossible promise. Yet, to her astonishment, her lover was right. No stone ceiling stood above their heads; instead, white clouds floated peacefully amidst a pale violet expanse. The sight of it made Marianne dizzy.

Was that . . . the *sky*?

Marianne's eyes looked up and up, all the way to the source of this strange world's blinding light. A radiant fireball floated high above the giant tree and vast horizon. Even Marianne's enhanced senses failed to process its sheer, gargantuan size. Its golden radiance shone brighter than candles, brighter than flames, brighter than anything found in Underland. The light warmed the air and Marianne's skin; the sea shone like a billion sapphires as it reflected a fraction of its beauty.

"It's wonderful." The sight brought Marianne to tears. "It's absolutely wonderful."

She found no word to define this cosmic wonder, this absolute god of light. But Valdemar had one.

"The sun," he whispered with religious awe. "This is our sun, Marianne."

"Will it shine on Underland one day?" Marianne asked softly. "Everyone . . . everyone must see it."

"One day, the sun will shine on mankind," Valdemar promised. "One day, I swear."

Marianne and Valdemar spent the entire evening gazing at the sun, basking in its beauty.

There was no darkness that could snuff out light.

His flesh-thralls toiled in the dark to the tune of his lightning will. They walked through his steel innards and shaped bolts in the depths of his forge-stomach. His furnace veins poured molten gold and zinc onto assembly lines. His countless hands worked together to build the future under the watchful gaze of his camera-eyes. Pieces gathered in the depths of his laboratory wombs to build a new portal. A Pleromian blood-map of the infinity would guide its development. It would take many cycles to complete this improved cosmic window, but one day it would open a path to another world. What were years to the immortality of steel?

All inferior flesh would bend to his iron will.

"If so m-m-many other worlds ex-exist," his voice carried through buzzing loudspeakers, "I mu-ust spread my magni-nificence to them."

So vowed Otto Blutgang, Godmind of Derrokind.

Lightning coursed through the incomplete portal, and the cosmos shuddered.

The End?

AUTHOR'S NOTE

Hope springs eternal, but evil never truly dies.

When I was a child, I dreamed of becoming a geneticist (I blame *Jurassic Park* for making me believe you could create awesome monsters in a laboratory). I had subscribed to a youth science magazine and devoured all the articles. Add on top of that a passion for astronomy and at one point I started to wonder if life had come from the stars. It just sounded plausible to me that some alien intelligence out there had seeded our planet with primordial bacteria.

I suppose this kind of reason is emblematic of man's desire to find a "logical" explanation to everything, to attribute all random occurrences to someone's invisible hand. The possibility that our very existence was the result of a series of coincidences in a chaotic, uncaring universe is not something we humans like to think about. Humans search for meaning even when there is none to be found.

There are only two kinds of horror I resonate with: *medical* horror, due to watching people around me die from cancer or Alzheimer's, and *cosmic* horror, because mind-numbing cosmic phenomena are beyond our ability to fully control. A war can be run from, serial killers can be shot or jailed, but cancer strikes without warning and an asteroid cannot be fled from. The most terrifying part of death is that it usually knocks on your door unannounced; and sometimes, it takes its sweet time too.

These are the fears I wanted to explore in *Underland*, alongside themes such as the pursuit of scientific knowledge to explain the unknown, the power of art, transhumanism, and the cost of one's dreams. The ultimate lesson of the story, I feel, is that while some things are beyond our control, they should not prevent us from living. The random threat of sudden extinction from an interstellar pebble or a stray gamma ray burst does not stop us from waking up to go to work, to research new ways to extend our life, or to build monuments that will endure the test of time. Perhaps human civilization will be wiped out at any moment . . . or maybe it won't.

Death does not make our achievements meaningless. Nihilism is intellectual cowardice. Our life could end anytime, but it was beautiful while it lasted.

While I leave the door open for a sequel, as it is, *Underland* will end with this volume. Whether I write a new entry in this universe will very much depend on its reception on Amazon; so please add a review, it would really help.

I hope that you enjoyed *Underland* to its conclusion, and that you'll appreciate my next series too.

Best regards,
Voidy

ABOUT THE AUTHOR

Maxime J. Durand, also known as Void Herald, is a wizard from the magical land of France who ceased studying law to write stories about dragon adventurers, time travelers with depression, and magicians trying to cure death (and life, too). Now, he can't stop.

www.ingramcontent.com/pod-product-compliance
Lightning Source LLC
Chambersburg PA
CBHW021643110726
47902CB00007B/1811